Redeemer!

Megan—

Redeemer!

Thank you so
much for your
patience & support

C.E. MURPHY

a Miz Kit production

REDEEMER

ISBN-13: 978-1-61317-142-4

Copyright © by 2018 by C.E. Murphy

Editor: Mary-Theresa Hussey / goodstorieswelltold.com
Copy Editor: Richard Shealy / sffcopyediting.com
Cover Design: Tara O'Shea / fringe-element.net
Cover Artist: Lindsey Look / lindseylook.com
Book Design: The Barbarienne's Den

For Harry Turtledove
who for some inexplicable reason liked my tweet :)

(also because WW2 alternate histories are totally his domain)

ONE

The punch clock bit holes in Rosie's time card with a satisfying *ka-chunk*. Another week's work done and another thirty-one dollars, forty-seven cents to tuck into the bank. Another Friday night to spend a little, maybe dinner at Big Bob's Diner to celebrate the work week ending. Rosie's stomach rumbled, notification of a good appetite after a day's work. But if it was just a burger and shake, and not a movie afterward, that only made sense. Men were coming back from the European theater. *Theater*, as if they'd been out for an evening's entertainment instead of being sent away for months and years to fight and die for their countries. Anyways, they were coming back and that meant they'd need work. *That* meant Rosie wouldn't be a riveter anymore, so she skipped the movies and saved a few more pennies toward the future. Toward college and an education so she could hang on to her hard-earned independence, the way she'd promised herself she would.

Somebody jostled her from behind. "Hey, Rosie, c'mon, either punch in for overtime or get out of the way! I got a letter from my Donny last night, he's coming home in a month, so I only got four Fridays left till I'm somebody's girl again. I gotta make the most of 'em!"

A wolf-whistle and raucous laughter punctuated by applause split the air. Rosie shifted away from the punch clock and waved her time card in the air. "Another day, another dollar—"

"—now let's go and make 'em holler!" A dozen women shouted back at her as they all clocked out at once, the hulking black clock's minute hand clicking loudly over the bite of its chunky teeth. Then a mass of girls headed down the echoing hall, their voices bouncing off steel walls and shaking the bare bulbs that dangled to provide light. Rosie swept along with them, elbowing back when she got elbowed, smiling, helping tug gray coveralls off slim shoulders. Men wore their slacks and button-downs beneath those coveralls, but the girls were a rush of dungarees and nipped plaid shirts by the time they reached the break room they'd converted into a changing area.

Household mirrors lined its walls. Rows of metal clothes racks, welded by women who'd just learned the skill, bore dresses and high-heeled shoes looped over wooden hangers. The room was crowded already, women pouring in from all over the factory. Big girls, little girls, girls younger than Rosie's twenty-two years, and older women, mothers and grandmothers, in their thirties and forties and even fifties. Rosie loved them, especially the older women. She'd been working since the war began, and it was all she knew. To start work in a factory at forty-five, take a job after being a mother and living through the Great War, to have that initiative and willingness to change: Rosie wanted to be like them someday. Bold and beautiful, because the riveters—whatever their actual job—all seemed beautiful to Rosie.

"Rosie, what is it, you've got lead in your pants today? Scoot!" Someone from the punch clock line nudged her out of the way and fell into a gossiping group as Rosie stepped aside. "I, for one, can't wait until the boys get home. I mean, look at my fingernails. Is that worth thirty dollars a week? No, I don't think it is. And my hair. I had to cut it, even pin curls take too long. All I want to do is marry some handsome soldier, have some babies and never work again." The rest of her litany was muffled as she squirmed into a dress, but others took up the conversation, part-complaining and part-happy.

"Seems like half the plant's already quit. I've been on double shifts all week."

"I turned down Carol Ann's shift last night. Did you know her husband is back? She just up and left three days ago."

"And before that it was Ruby!"

"I'm still here!" a woman protested, and the first girl laughed.

"No, the other Ruby. The machinist. She left last week, and I didn't even know she was married. Funny the things we know about each other and the things we don't. I mean, I know you stuff your bra with tissues, Ethel—"

"I do not!" Outrage broke above the rest of the babble, then shifted into false dignity: "I stuff it with cotton batting."

More laughter swept the aisles. Rosie slipped between racks, searching for her own dress. It suddenly popped out from a rack like it'd taken on a life of its own, green pinstripes folded in on themselves so it looked tiny. Rosie took it, then ducked to look through the remaining outfits on the bar to find her roommate smiling at her. "Irene. Thank goodness. I thought maybe my clothes had come to life." She toed her work shoes off and shrugged her coveralls off before slipping the dress on.

Irene's smile widened before the dresses fell back into place as she began pulling her own dress on. Her voice carried over the top of the rack, bright and tangy with a Brooklyn accent. "Did you hear Carol Ann's husband is back? She quit Tuesday. And I just heard Jean-Marie's gone too, as of last night. I tell you what, Rosie, if I was any of them I wouldn't have gone running home to my husband, not if that sheik they've hired was my new supe. Have you seen him? His name's Johnny," Irene went on without waiting for an answer. "Back from Europe since March, he got his hip shot up and has a limp. But he's swell, Ro, you should see him. All pale and convalescent, with haunting dark eyes. Working the night shift. They say it's so he doesn't have to face so many people at once, but I think it's because the girls are friendlier at night. Even Carol Ann was stuck on him, and her married, it turns out! Shame, shame, Mrs McKay!"

Rosie flattened her hands against her stomach, smoothing faint wrinkles from the fabric, then frowned over the clothes rack at Irene. "Carol Ann McKay?"

"Sure, honey. Do you know any other Carol Anns working here?"

"No, but Carol Ann McKay isn't married."

Irene pushed the racked dresses apart again, peering through them at Rosie. "Are you sure? Say, you look swell, Ro. The green really suits you. Is Rich home? He'll be a happy man to see his girl looking so good."

A cold pang ran through Rosie's belly, cutting off any hint of hunger.

She felt like the girl whose Donny was coming home soon: glad he got to come home safe but like it meant she only had a little time left as a free woman. "Not yet, no, he isn't. And you know how things are there. Anyways, yes, I'm sure Carol Ann's not married. I've known her since I was twelve. McKay's her maiden name."

"*I* know how things are there," Irene muttered. "But does Rich?" She stepped through the racks, pulling her shoes on as she came, and spun a quick circle to send her skirt flaring. "Do I look swanky, hon?"

Rosie glanced up, then looked again, a smile blossoming. Irene wore green too: a full-skirted swing dress in silk rayon with white accents. "You're beautiful. Got a hot date tonight?"

"I hope so. I'm going to the USO homecoming. Planning to meet me an officer."

Dismay creased Rosie's forehead. "Not you too, 'Rene."

Irene shrugged and spun again, making both her skirt and her hair flare. She had real beauty, not just strong and confident from working with machines and doing a man's job all day. Her auburn hair couldn't be gotten from a salon, though a lot of girls tried, and her fair skin didn't have a freckle on it. "What else am I going to do? The men will need the jobs."

"Go to Hollywood," Rosie said, only half-kidding. "Be in the pictures."

Irene rolled her eyes. "The things you say, hon. But the USO's closer and a sure thing. Won't you come along? It'll be fun. Might as well enjoy it before Rich gets home, right?"

Rosie pursed her lips and glanced at her own cotton shirt-dress. "I'm not dressed for it. And I've been sweating all day."

"We've all been sweating," Irene argued. "You look pretty as a picture, and we can stop at home on the way for a spit bath. Come on, say yes."

"Oh, all right. Just so I can watch the officers fight over you." Rosie tucked her coveralls under her arm, glad that Friday meant she could scrub them and let them dry over the weekend. "Are you ready?" They joined the flow of girls heading outside, bits of gossip passing over them and Rosie adding her piece as their heels clacked against concrete floors. "Did you say Jean-Marie quit too? That's strange. I saw her yesterday, she didn't say anything about leaving."

"Maybe her fella came home last night."

"No, she doesn't have one. Jean-Marie has never gone with anybody. It's just her and Ruby all the time, thick as thieves, ever since high school. I know for a fact three boys asked Ruby to prom and she went with Jean anyways because Jean didn't have a date."

Irene rolled her eyes again, though she smiled. "You just know everyone, don't you, hon? Small-town girl."

"Detroit's not that small."

"It is compared to New York!"

Rosie laughed. "What isn't, compared to New York? Anyways, you're the one who came out here to work."

"Well, sure, hon, I was seventeen and Mama told me to marry Danny O'Brien or get out. She had it all set up, but he was bad news, Rosie, he really was. I knew a couple of the girls he went steady with. Nobody walks into doors that often, you know? So I got on the train and came out here where I knew I'd get work. Mama still hasn't forgiven me."

"See? You know the girls you grew up with, I know the ones I did, that's all. Maybe everywhere's a small town. Wait." Rosie scanned the women around them, looking for the one who'd spread the other piece of gossip she'd heard. "Someone said Ruby quit too, machinist-Ruby, that they didn't know she was married either. But that's Jean-Marie's Ruby. They both quit?"

"Sure, I guess so. Why, is that so strange?"

"No, I just thought they . . . " That they were like her. Wanting to work. Liking the job, the independence, being new women for a new era. But she'd thought Irene felt that way too, and it looked like she'd gotten that wrong too. "Look, Rene, I think I'm going to stop by Jean and Ruby's place and see what the story is. I'll meet you at the USO later."

"Sure you won't." Irene lifted her hand to shield her eyes as they stepped outside into late-afternoon sunlight reflecting hard off the factory's walls. Heat rose in shimmering waves off the asphalt, and all the girls heading for town faltered. Irene gasped and fanned herself. "Gosh, and I thought it was hot in the factory. We're both going to need to wash up before we go to the USO, and I know you, Rosie Ransom. If I let you go see Jean and Ruby alone you'll never get to the dance. So we'll go there and then home for a sponge bath and then to the party. Jeez but it's hot! I'm catching the tram and hang the expense. If I walk my dress will melt right off."

"That'll get you an officer for sure." Rosie laughed and skipped out of reach as Irene threatened her with a fist, but neither tried harder than that in the muggy air. "The tram will be stifling too, Rene. And it'll smell worse than we do."

"Faster, though. Besides, doesn't it go right by Jean's place?"

"Is there anywhere the tram *doesn't* go straight by?" Rosie asked dryly, but Irene waved her off.

"Well, that's one of the things I think is swell about Detroit, honey, there's hardly even a side street you have to walk down, you can always take the tram. We'll kill two birds with one stone, stop by Ruby and Jean's and wash up there too. Maybe they'll want to go out with us. I'm getting ice cream at the diner, never mind what it'll do to my figure. It's too hot to care!" Irene rattled on cheerfully as they made their way onto the wooden trolley with dozens of others. Mostly young women excited for their evening out, but their exuberance made the quieter ones, the older women, that much more noticeable to Rosie. It would be so much harder to work a long day at the plant only to go home and feed, bathe and entertain children for the few hours before bedtime. If she and Rich had gotten married before he shipped out, she might have had a four-year-old to go home to herself.

"Lucky for a million reasons," she said under her breath, and Irene gave her a sharp look.

"You're thinking about Rich again? Don't lie, I know you are. You get a certain look, hon. You can't dump him, Ro, you're what he's coming home for. Besides, you won't be able to keep on at the factory. What will you do if you don't get married? Be a secretary? You'd be bored. At least babies keep you fit."

Rosie flexed her arms instinctively, feeling the hemmed sleeves tighten around muscle. Irene had remained petite, but lifting a riveting gun, leaning in for a punch of steel, had all left a mark on Rosie's physique. She'd lost weight, too, her middle whittling as her shoulders got broader, and the boxy fashions with their tucked waists gave her an appealing figure. She'd been a bit soft, coming out of high school. Rich hadn't minded. Neither had Rosie, not until she got strong. The idea of going back—and babies wouldn't keep her as fit as riveting did—made her nose wrinkle. "Well, I wasn't going to write him a Dear John letter, was I? I just want to get to know him again, Rene. It's been years. I've changed. I'm sure he's changed. What if we haven't changed the same ways?"

Irene sighed loudly enough to be heard over the general clamor and elbowed Rosie's ribs. "You should be glad you've got a man, Ro. At least you won't be out there with the rest of us, trying to find one. It'll be easier for you."

Easier. As if giving up her independence could be considered a relief. But so many of the girls she knew thought that way, sometimes it made Rosie wonder if she was wrong to want more, to want an education and employment of her own even after the war. She sure hadn't told much of anybody about her dreams, not knowing the looks and the comments she'd get, even from Irene. Maybe it would be easier and more comfortable to be a wife and mother instead of a steelworker and wage-earner, but she just couldn't see it. "If it works out. Anyways, you'll like him, Rene, you really will, so don't let that officer you're going to catch take you too far away. Come on, now. The next stop is Jean's house."

They pushed through packed-in girls to the front of the tram, waved a good-bye to friends, and together staggered into the shade of Jean's tree-lined street. "Maybe Jean didn't quit," Irene wheezed. "Maybe it was just too hot to come to work today. Jeez! I wish I had a tub of ice to sleep in!"

"It'll be cooled off some by the time you get to sleep anyways." They hugged the shade as best they could, grateful to turn down Jean's short driveway a few minutes later. Jean's car sat there, a big 1941 Oldsmobile she'd paid a whopping $545 for. Its green paint gleamed even though most everything else seemed to have a thin coat of dust, and the heavy steel body gave off heat waves of its own. The windows were both rolled down, safe enough with the dry spell, and probably keeping Jean from roasting like a chicken the moment she sat in the car. Rosie envied her the big beast of a vehicle, but not quite enough to have bought one of her own. Rich would want a car when he got home, but having two would be silly when only one of them would be going to work. And that would be five hundred dollars she hadn't saved, five hundred dollars that wasn't money all of her own. That money would pay for a whole year of college. Too much, no matter how tempting the Oldsmobile, or even cheaper vehicles, might be.

"Come on, you silly goose." Irene climbed the steps to the front door, knocking vigorously while Rosie lingered over the car. Jean owned the house, too, like she owned the car, more independent than even Rosie. Jean's father held the deed, of course, because Jean could never get a mortgage herself, not without a husband, but the white-painted siding and yellow trim and everything within belonged to Jean. Rosie envied that, too, and wondered what Rich would think if he came home to a girl who'd bought a house of her own.

No point in worrying about it just now. Rosie hurried up to the porch as Irene called, "Come on, Jean, we're cooking out here! Invite us in for some lemonade!" Irene tried the knob, found it unlocked, and pushed the door open to stick her head in and shout, "Jean? Ruby? It's Irene and Rosie! We're going to the USO, you should come with us, it'll be swell! Jeez, where are those girls?"

"Maybe if they quit they went off for a weekend holiday to celebrate." Rosie cast a dubious glance at the car, then at the open door. "Only Ruby doesn't have a car for them to take, and they left the door unlocked . . . " She edged inside, meeting a breeze from a fan hidden behind the door. Sagging with relief, she came all the way in to a smart living room, furniture and carpets so new they had no signs of wear. "Whew, it's cooler in here, at least. Jean? Jean-Marie? Ruby?"

"I'm right here." Jean-Marie came into the living room with unsteady steps. Rosie let out a breath of relief, and Irene, just behind Rosie, launched into a good-natured scold. "Gosh, Jean, didn't you hear us shouting? We were getting worried! Sorry to barge in and all, but the door was open and—"

She kept going, but a similar scold caught in Rosie's throat as she took in Jean's red-rimmed brown eyes and faint white streaks on her cheeks. She had always been big and strong, even before the factory jobs came along, but she looked thinner now, and not in a good way. Like the life had gone out of her. Like the soul had gone away. Her healthy summer tan had sallowed, and her nose, like her eyes, shone red. "Hey," Rosie said underneath Irene's chiding, "hey, hey, hey, Jean, Jean, Jeannie, what's wrong?"

"Ruby," Jean said, and tears came. Not deep sobs, but restrained, reserved silver sliding down her face, the only breach in a facade of calm. "Ruby is dead."

TWO

Irene made lemonade after a while, and Rosie sat on the couch with Jean-Marie, keeping quiet as the other girl's grip crushed her fingers. "She didn't quit," Jean said for the dozenth time. "She didn't come home Monday, but I knew she was working a double shift into Tuesday so she could go out and see her Nan Wednesday and Thursday, she had a mid-week weekend, you know that awful shift. So I didn't worry because I wasn't going to see her until yesterday. But last night, her Nan called me, and Ruby's Nan is way older than telephones, she doesn't trust them, she thinks someone's listening in. And they are, of course, party lines always have people listening in, but she called anyway because Ruby hadn't gotten there."

"Ruby was supposed to visit on Tuesday and her Nan waited to call until Thursday? Why did she wait so long?" Rosie wondered.

Jean gave a tight, watery smile. "She thought Ruby maybe just forgot and she doesn't like using the phone except on Sundays because she thinks fewer people listen in then, so she kept putting it off. But then it got to be Thursday evening and she hadn't heard from Ruby so she called. She said she knew girls would be girls and that Ruby had probably forgotten or was working, but she wanted to be sure, and that's when I knew she hadn't come home. It's that new supervisor," she snarled, reserve suddenly giving way to rage. "He did something to her, I know it. She was fixated on him."

"Aw, honey." Irene came out with the lemonade, set it on the coffee table, and crouched to take Jean's hands. "Girls go and fall in love all the time. Doesn't mean something's happened to her. Maybe they're having a fling, she's staying with him?"

"Not Ruby." Jean cast Rosie a desperate glance. "Tell her, Rose. Ruby never fancied any of the boys at school. We're, we're pals, her and me. There's nobody else."

"Could just be he's the one, honey," Irene began, but Rosie shook her head uncomfortably.

"Ruby's pretty, Rene. I mean, pretty like you, Hollywood pretty, not just home-town pretty like me or Jean. Boys were after her all the time and she never went with any of them. All us girls were jealous, we wished we had a girlfriend like Ruby and Jean, together through thick and thin. Ruby leaving would be like splitting up peanut butter and jelly. I can't imagine it. They'd be married if one of them was a boy." Rosie winked and Jean's cheeks turned red under the tear stains. "Well, you would be!"

"Aren't we lucky we don't have to bother with all that," Jean whispered, but her eyes flooded again and she wiped them dry. "Rosie, it's not like Ruby, it isn't. Something's happened to her. I know it. I feel it. I called the cops, even her parents called them, but the police wouldn't listen, they think it's like Irene says, that she ran off with some sheik. She's a grown-up woman, they said, she'll be fine. But she's not, I know she's not, Ro."

"Why do you think it has something to do with the new supe? Johnny, you said his name was?" Rosie shot a look at Irene, who nodded.

So did Jean, bitterly. "Private First Class John Goode. He's all right, if you like the consumptive look. He works the midnight swing shift and half the girls are out of their heads over him. It was like he'd mesmerized Ruby, Ro. She kept talking about him, she even made us sit at a different table at lunch so she could look at him. But then when we'd get off shift she could barely even remember what he looked like, never mind being hot and bothered over him. Carol Ann was like that too, and she's gone too. Something's not right, Rosie. It's not right."

"Did you talk to the boss?"

Jean sneered, such an ugly expression that Rosie wished she hadn't asked. She hadn't really needed to, anyways. The plant supervisors were men, and most of the girls knew their concerns would be chalked up to women being unable to handle doing a man's job. Worse, if the complaint was about one of the supes themselves. A girl concerned about a newly returned war hero's effects on her friends would be laughed out of her job.

"I'm sure Ruby's okay," Rosie said with less conviction than she wanted. "Tell you what, sweetie, I'll go back to the factory tonight and talk to some of the other girls under Goode's supervision. Maybe one of them saw Ruby, or maybe I can find out what he's doing to make them all like him so much."

"He's a handsome man just back from the war, Ro," Irene said. "That's all he needs to do."

Jean and Rosie both shook their heads, though Jean let Rosie do the talking. "No, not if Ruby and Carol Ann were mad for him. Ruby never cared very much about boys and Carol Ann's a prude. She wouldn't admit she had ants in her pants if Gary Cooper put them there himself. I'll just go talk to a few girls. It won't take long."

"But the USO!"

"Take Jean-Marie," Rosie said firmly. "No, don't argue, Jeannie. You need something to take your mind off Ruby, and Irene needs someone to make sure she doesn't get married before morning. I promise I'll be there before midnight."

"It's only six o'clock now!"

"Then I have lots of time." Rosie squeezed Jean's hand, then stood up and made a shooing motion at her and Irene. "Go, get burgers and milkshakes and have a good time."

"You'd better drink this lemonade first," Irene muttered, and Rosie did, gratefully, before she left to catch another tram. Even with a breeze flowing through the open windows, the heat stuck and clung worse than ever after Jean's fan-cooled living room. A worm of regret squirmed in Rosie's chest. Odds were she'd volunteered to go back to the sweltering factory instead of out for an evening of fun for no good reason. Especially if Goode worked the night shift, eleven at night to eight in the morning. He wouldn't be there for hours yet.

But him not being around yet might make mid-shift girls, the three-to-midnight crew, more willing to gossip, and if she could learn *anything* that would make Jean feel better, that was worth it. Besides, at least she could get a look at the PFC before going to the dance, maybe even talk to him. Maybe she *would* find something, something to find Ruby or something to make even the cops take notice if Ruby couldn't be found. The dance would still be there later, after all, and Jean could have fun if she knew Ruby was okay.

She donned coveralls when she got back to the factory, and slid heavy boots over her feet to clump along the concrete halls in. Clocking in would be too much, but at least she could look the part. No one would question another girl hurrying from one station to another.

Hardly anyone, anyways: a couple girls caught sight of her and called her name teasingly. Rosie waved them off with a laugh. "I couldn't stay away. Decided I needed that extra dollar in the bank!" Which wasn't so far from true, though she had other things to worry about just then. She picked up a riveting gun and slipped into place on the line, half-acknowledging the curious women around her. "Taking over for Ruby. What happened to her, anyways?"

"Got married."

"Got bored."

"Got sick."

"Got out," said someone beneath the more usual answers. Rosie ducked to get a look at her, a girl she didn't know. Slim and almost pretty, more a face they'd call interesting or handsome, she met Rosie's eyes, then glanced away. She was pale, unhealthy pale, like she'd forgotten the sun even existed. Rosie nodded and changed the subject, grousing about the gun's weight, about her own weight, about tight-fitting shoes and an utter lack of a romantic life. Others picked up on the cheerful complaints, muttering about sweat and steel and veering the discussion into territory that made even the least modest of them blush. Rosie's own ears burned, but she laughed too, and wouldn't commit either way when the girls next to her wanted to know if she'd gone all the way with her boyfriend before he left for war.

She had, as a matter of fact, and had dated a couple of other boys seriously since, too. Rich didn't know about that, but Rosie reckoned what he didn't know wouldn't hurt him any. Three years was a long time, and if boys could sow some oats, she figured she could too. She was a little proud of that.

Rosie Ransom, liberated woman with a job and a sex life and a future of her own, if only she could figure out how to build it. Hardly anybody she knew went to college, especially women. She wanted to do something bigger than herself, like learn to design the planes she'd been building for years now, or—or, well, she didn't know, not yet. Something that used her brain and her body, because she loved the weight of the riveting gun, loved the kickback and even the bruises it sometimes left. Her mother understood, at least some. Her mother had been a suffragist, working for something bigger than *her*self. Even so, Rosie hadn't told even Mom that she wanted to go to college, for fear she'd be told not to be silly, that education wasn't for women and she should accept things the way they were.

But then, if the suffragists had done that, women wouldn't have the vote, never mind the chance, no matter what the reason, to work in a man's job like this one. The scent of hot metal and blue flame, the squeak of steel sheets and the relentless thud of rivets driving home would always be a part of Rosie's memories now. They might take the job away, but they'd never take the knowledge that she could do it, and if she could do this, she could by gum do anything.

Somehow it sounded more certain in her head than it felt in her heart. Rosie set aside her riveting gun to help balance a stack of metal sheets being lifted across the floor, then took up the slack on a line of welders, idly asking about Ruby every time she shifted into a new group of workers. No one had seen her, and as the shift got later, fewer girls wanted to chat. Fingers, hands, arms could get crushed in the machines if somebody got careless, and mid-shift started out tired already. Rosie fell into the pattern of work too, focused entirely on the bang and thump of machinery.

"Why were you asking about Ruby?" The pale girl stopped at Rosie's elbow, startling her. She turned her welding torch's flame off and stepped back from the job, flipping her face guard up and rubbing an arm across her forehead to wipe sweat away.

"She hasn't been home since last Monday, is all. Her roommate's worried. Have you seen her?"

"No." There was no conviction in the girl's whisper.

"You said 'got out'," Rosie said. "Why'd you say that?"

The girl's gaze shifted like she expected trouble from any side. "I can't tell you here or now. He's coming on shift. In the locker rooms later, where for sure he can't hear."

"Already?" Rosie glanced for a clock she wouldn't be able to see. The factory had a few, always obscured by pieces of machinery or vast steel girders. Time went faster when they couldn't see it passing, and whistles told them when to take a break. Eleven o'clock meant she wouldn't make it to the USO at all. Irene hadn't believed she would anyways, but Rosie had thought she might. She hoped the girls were having fun, and hoped even more that she'd have good news to bring Jean. "Well, that means the last break is coming up. We can talk then?"

The pale girl nodded and hurried away, leaving Rosie looking down a line of shifting bodies, each doing their part to support the war effort for just a while longer. The European war was over. Japan couldn't hold out much longer, not against America's determination, Rosie just knew it. Almost knew it for sure, at least. She rekindled the torch flame again, but the supe—PFC Goode, it had to be—crossed the head of the aisle and caught Rosie's eye.

She shouldn't be able to tell from the distance that his eyes were brown, not just shadowed. She shouldn't be able to see circles under his eyes, either, or the gaunt line of cheekbones under bare light bulbs. His hair was almost black and tidy, but not a soldier's crew cut. Not the parted wave that lots of men were wearing, either, but somewhere in between, a military cut growing out. He wore slacks and a shirt, but they did nothing to hide a thin frame that reminded Rosie of the pre-serum Steve Rogers. He looked like he couldn't have passed the physical to be a soldier, never mind have gone to war and come back alive.

Consumptive, Jean had said. Handsome if you liked that sort, but a chill ran down Rosie's spine as he broke gazes with her and moved on. She didn't see his appeal at all, and if *she* didn't, it seemed impossible that Ruby had.

A few minutes later the lunch whistle blasted. Women up and down the line put tools down, patted the section of airplane they were working on—for good luck, everyone agreed—and became gregarious again. Rosie trailed behind the bulk of them, veering off toward the changing rooms when she got the chance. The pale girl would be waiting, if she hadn't chickened out.

She hadn't. She waited among the clothes racks, hiding her slim form between slimmer pickings for dresses. The late shift came in already wearing dungarees and shirts, with no expectation of dolling up to face the morning, and the racks showed it. Still, the girl chose to hide. Rosie's heart went out to her. Rather than make her more uncomfortable by exposing her, she idled near the end of the racks and murmured, "I'm here, if you want to talk."

"You gotta get out of here." The girl's intensity drove her from her hiding spot. Color was high in her cheeks, making her prettier than she'd been on the plant floor. "Honest, miss, just go before he notices you. You're just what he likes. All the girls who are disappearing have dark hair and light eyes like you do. At first it was some of the Negroes, some who could almost pass. Girls with soft black hair and those funny gray-green eyes a lot of them have? But there were only two or three even working in the factory and once they were gone it started being the white girls." She picked up speed as she talked, until the last words were a blurt. "I feel terrible, I didn't even see the pattern until the white girls started going missing, I guess I'm gonna go to hell for that, but maybe God'll take a little time off my sentence if I get you out of here safe. You gotta go, miss, you really do."

"He already saw me." Rosie knew the confession was a mistake before it left her lips, but couldn't stop herself. The girl's shoulders slumped like all the air had been squeezed away. Rosie came up to her carefully, offering a hand. "What's your name, honey? Oh, sweetheart, your hands are like ice. If the supe's got you so scared, why are you still here?"

"Pearl. I'm Pearl, and where else am I gonna go? I'm not his kind." She gestured at her light brown hair. "I've got no husband, not even a boyfriend, and this job is my only way out. I can't quit, don't you see?"

"I understand." Under different circumstances, Rosie would have commiserated with the girl—with Pearl—and might still, later. But now she squeezed Pearl's hand and tried to sound encouraging. "Tell me about them going missing, okay? You're sure it's missing, not girls quitting to get married?"

"Some, sure, but some of everybody quits. Redheads, blondes, brunettes, Negroes, everybody. And they talk about it before, they're excited that their fellas are coming home, or that they've met somebody and are giving up work for the easy life. Carol Ann and Ruby and some of the others, they never said a word except for to the supe, and had stars in their eyes when they were doing it. And then they were gone, just gone, between one day and the next."

A whistle blasted, drowning Pearl out. They both turned to the break room clock, which said lunch hour was nowhere near over. The intercom crackled as the whistle gave way to the blare of an alarm. Pearl paled. "Something's happened. That's how they blow the system when someone's gotten hurt or killed on the line. It happened once before while I was here."

"Maggie Byrnes." Rosie nodded. It had been the only really bad accident in all the time Rosie had worked for the factory, but it had been enough to scare everyone, even those who hadn't been there. A lot of girls had quit after Maggie's death, but more had come to replace them, their need greater than their fear. The rest of them had gotten more cautious, and almost two years later the caution still lingered.

Pearl tugged Rosie's hand. "We'd better go. You can get out of here and be safe. Don't come back, miss." They hurried from the break room, other women leaving the lunch room well ahead of them. The whistle and alarm roared again, making both Rosie and Pearl jump. Both sounds faded away, leaving the lingering thin edge of a scream behind.

Rosie stopped, resisting Pearl's pull, and looked back into the factory. "She's still alive. Whoever's hurt is still alive. Someone must be helping her, right?" Another scream cut through the air, and another whistle blast tried to cover it. Rosie pulled away from Pearl. "You go. I'm going to check on her. I know someone's there, someone's helping, but—"

"Don't go," Pearl pleaded, but her grip loosened. "Miss, please don't go. The factory's not safe at night, not for a girl like you. He's out there."

"Go on." Rosie broke away and into a run, following the echoes of the scream. Halfway across the factory, with only one more whistle-drowned cry to guide her. Someone was doing that deliberately, they had to be, and that could mean whatever girl was trapped *wasn't* getting the help she needed. Rosie cursed the weighty boots she wore, and stopped to kick them off after she careened into a long room with the belly of an airplane hanging from the ceiling. The cement floor felt rough under her feet, but at least she could move fast now.

But nobody lay hurt or screaming on the factory floor, or even tangled in machinery. Everything looked right: abandoned riveting guns, shut-down welding torches, drills and hammers, screws and nails. Someone's red kerchief was slung over a ladder's step, left behind in the expectation of a quick return. Tools of the trade, familiar items to Rosie's calloused hands.

And, bewilderingly, an old wind-up phonograph, hissing the song of an empty record as black vinyl spun endlessly on the wheel. It screamed as Rosie approached, and she shrieked too, then clapped her hands to her face in embarrassment. "What on earth!"

"I told you not to come, miss," Pearl said from behind her, miserably.

Rosie startled again, spinning to face the other girl. "You . . . you lured me?" she asked, as embarrassed by uncertainty as she'd been by her shriek. "You brought me to the break room so I'd be behind the others? So I'd hear the screaming . . . " She looked at the phonograph, then back at Pearl.

Pearl shrugged, sad motion emphasized by a lack of hope in her eyes. "He said he'd kill me if I didn't. I saw him the first night, see. When he took Tildy, the first Negro girl. I saw what he did and he . . . he said find him girls, or I'd be next."

"Next for what? What's he doing? Pearl, you can't—" Rosie reached for Pearl, ready to shake her until she started making sense.

The phonograph shrieked, not the recorded woman's scream but the high squeal of a needle scratching vinyl. Pieces broke from the turntable and the distinctive ping of metal bouncing against the concrete floor rang out. The record player itself thudded more loudly, its days as an entertainment piece ending with what Rosie guessed had been a sharp kick.

Pearl flinched and backed away with her hands clenched at her mouth. A spike of dread shot through Rosie's heart, breathtaking and cold. She turned to see the phonograph sprawled across the floor in pieces, and PFC Goode crunching the record beneath his feet as he approached.

He looked like Pearl, up close. They shared the same pallor, like neither of them had seen sunshine in far too long. Her eyes, though, were haunted, and his were dead. Rosie didn't see how he could inspire the lust Ruby and the others had felt, though she understood Pearl's fear well enough.

Then he smiled, and everything about him changed. Gauntness became slenderness, dead eyes became bright, his quick wink charming. Rosie smiled in return without meaning to, then, uncomfortable at having done so, shook herself and backed up a step. Closer to Pearl, in hopes the other girl would be made braver by Rosie's presence. "Whatever you're doing, Mr Goode, it has to stop. It *will* stop."

He grinned, full of fresh healthy American good looks. "'Mr Goode'? Jeez, miss, that's my dad. You call me Johnny, why don't you? What's your name?"

"Rosie." Rosie bit her tongue too late, astonished that she'd answered. Like she'd had to. Like she'd *wanted* to, even though she hadn't intended to give this oddly threatening man anything. "Mr Goode," she repeated, more firmly and maybe, if she told herself the truth, maybe more desperately. "Pearl says a lot of girls have gone missing, that you're responsible. It's going to stop."

"Shucks, Rosie, of course it's not. You're not even going to remember a bit of this, are you? It's just me and Pearl here, stealing a cig in the factory when we're not supposed to be." He came closer as he spoke, and Rosie forgot she'd meant to back up farther. Goode glanced beyond her at Pearl, offering the other girl a smile of her own. "Good job with this one, Pearl. She's got a lot of life in her. She might even finish the job for you."

"The job?" Rosie made her feet move, concrete cold through her socks. That helped her keep moving: as long as she didn't stay still long enough to warm the floor where she stood, she was doing all right. But Pearl was following her now too, boxing her in. Rosie edged toward the belly of the plane, trying not to look like she was running. "What job? Pearl's got a job here, she's a riveter like the rest of us . . . "

"Not that kind of job. Some of the blood splashed on me, see," Pearl whispered. "I thought it was my own, I'd cut myself earlier, so I stuck my finger in my mouth. But it was his, and now I just keep being hungry for more. I'm almost there, Johnny says I'm almost there, just a little more to drink, but he's gotta keep refreshing his own, too. You shoulda run, Rosie. You shoulda done what I said."

Bile filled Rosie's throat, though she barely understood what the other girl meant. She swallowed and forced a laugh. "Blood? What, you think he's a vampire? Sweetheart, you have to stop watching all those Dracula movi—"

Goode picked up a welding torch, twisted it into uselessness, and tossed it away. Rosie's words died in her throat. Cold drained from the top of her head to her fingertips, through her chest and all the way to her toes, numbing her body with disbelief. Half of forever passed before her heart started up again, a single thick beat that pushed back against cold. Not hard enough, though. Rosie just stood there, frozen with astonishment, until Goode spoke again and she jerked hard in response to his voice.

"Most of it isn't true. Turning to mist, turning into a bat, no reflection . . . " Goode brushed his hair with his fingertips, familiar action of a vain man. "Good thing, too. Nobody would cut a man's hair they couldn't see in the mirror."

"Vampires aren't real," Rosie said blankly. "They're not—you can't be . . . "

Goode shrugged and picked up another torch, flicking this one on. "Whether they are or aren't, I'm sure something, aren't I? Tell you what, Rosie. You start running, and if you get away, I'll never hunt you again. I'm not fast," he promised with an unnervingly sweet smile. "Go on, Rosie. Run."

Rosie's gaze flickered to Pearl, who nodded once. "He always lets them run," she whispered. She looked worse than pallid now. Fragile, desperate. *Hungry.* "Better go."

Rosie took another step back. It jarred her out of stupefaction, let her think again with the clarity of fear. The plane was above her now, burnished steel hanging too far overhead to touch. Ladders still leaned against it, abandoned by the women who had been working there not long before. Women who would find Rosie's own body, maybe, crushed in some machine's teeth. The other girls who had gone missing hadn't been found, though. She clung to that, reaching for an answer like it would save her life. "Where are they? The others, what did you do with them?"

Goode waved his torch, hissing blue flame making a short streak in Rosie's vision. "I ate them, Rosie. A man can't live by blood alone, you know. I made bread with their marrow." His eyebrows flicked together. "It's harder than it looks, isn't it? Making bread. My loaves are like logs."

Rosie's stomach turned, though macabre humor washed some of the sickness away. No wonder Goode wanted Pearl. A wife to cook and clean for him, just like every other man back from the war.

Except every other man couldn't bend steel, or dance his fingers through blue-hot flame the way Goode was doing now. Rosie's heart lurched again. Everyone had gone on break, leaving no one nearby to hear her scream. No one would save her. No one but herself. Her hand closed around a riveting gun. She lifted it, the familiar weight a sudden comfort, and Goode's voice dropped with disappointment. "Oh, Rosie, what are you doing?"

The riveting gun's weight steadied the jackhammer beat of Rosie's heart, letting her whisper, "There's nowhere to run and you know it. This factory's full of machines more dangerous than you are. I'm not going to let you chase me into one of them so I can be written off as a terrible accident."

"Pearl." All the niceness left Goode's voice, making him the unsettling man Rosie had first laid eyes on.

He might not have been quick. Pearl, though, moved way faster than Rosie expected. Quick with desperation, maybe. She veered wide of the riveting gun, springing at Rosie's shoulders from the side. Rosie spun, the gun's weight giving her momentum. To her own shock, metal hit flesh with a resounding *thunk*. Pearl collapsed to the floor, her temple already bruising. Rosie drew in a sharp breath, gaping, then snapped her attention back to Goode.

He gazed at Pearl with surprise before lifting his eyebrows at Rosie. "Guess I should've picked me more of a fighter for my first wife. You might just do instead, Miss Rosie." He took a step forward.

Rosie, though her cheeks hot with horror at having downed Pearl, hefted the riveting gun at arm's length with hands that remained cold and steady. "Not one more step, Mr Goode."

He smiled, almost recovering the mask of charm he'd worn before. The one that had almost drawn her in, that had made Rosie give up her name when she didn't want to. It wouldn't work again. Not with her heart fast with fear, not with Pearl a huddle at her feet. Maybe men at war felt this resolved, facing the enemy. Goode's smile widened, showing teeth, and he spread his hands. "Or what, Rosie? You'll shoot me? An unarmed man?"

Showing *teeth*. Showing a mouthful of too-long, hollow-looking *teeth*, like snake fangs except by the tens instead of just two. She couldn't see their bottoms, but they narrowed as they pressed against his lower lip, and Rosie just knew they ended in vicious points.

"You're something wrong, mister," Rosie breathed. "Something unnatural and wrong. Men might put up a sweet lying front, but they don't bend steel and they don't cup fire in their palms. I don't know what you are, but you are not a man."

"I was once," Goode said, and took one more step forward. Put his chest against the gun, and reached for its neck, to throttle the air flow and render it useless.

Rosie shot him.

The gun made the same sound it always did, a familiar, comforting *bam!* of air slamming a rivet into place.

Goode sounded nothing like airplane steel being punctured.

He made a soft sound, a wet sound, one that went with the sudden red mist and chunks of white that were things Rosie didn't even want to think about. He looked surprised in the instant before his hands splayed open and his whole body caved backward, away from her. Blood smeared first the air, then concrete. Goode was louder hitting the floor than taking the rivet, a *pop* like a hollowed-out grapefruit when his skull made contact.

Revulsion and relief tore through Rosie. Her hands shook, though she didn't release the gun, didn't even lower it. Couldn't if her life depended on it.

Her life *had* depended on it.

Rosie gave a short ugly laugh that did nothing to push away the dizziness sweeping her. Gold light unlike anything the factory had to offer danced around the edges of her vision. It coalesced above Goode like it was drawn to his blood, and gathered into a small dust devil that spun ever tighter. She took a step back, riveting gun still choked in her grip. The light comforted her with its warmth and beauty, but Goode had almost tricked her into believing in his beauty, too. She didn't know what happened to vampires when they died, but if she had to shoot the burgeoning light, too, then she would.

It became a column, spinning so quickly it wobbled. Goode's body arched as its pull lifted him a centimeter or two from the floor. A silver glow stained with blood eked out of his pores, drawn toward the golden column. Rosie wet her lips, knotted her finger around the gun's trigger, and waited in horrified fascination.

The bloodstains stretched and loosened, coming free from Goode's—*soul*, Rosie thought, and wanted to laugh at herself, but couldn't. The stains spiraled upward, taken into the whipping gold column, then spattered outward, cast away. Rosie's gaze snapped to follow them, but they disappeared before they reached her, even though she stood just a couple steps from the man she'd killed.

Unstained, unblemished, uncorrupted, Goode's soul rose after the blood, sucked into the column's vortex as well. But it shot upward when released, a bright streak reaching for Heaven. The column collapsed, and Goode's body fell to cold concrete.

Rosie edged forward. Under the hard factory lights, Goode had the skin tones and musculature of a youth who had been badly injured and a long time recovering. He looked handsome now, a cheeky all-American boy despite the trauma his body had seen. The horrible hollow-looking teeth shrank back into his gums as she watched, distending his mouth and then disappearing. With their retreat, his sickly pallor faded, more than just vitality fading in death's cool grip. It was as if a poison had been eradicated, thoroughly cleansing the young PFC of his life's misdeeds.

Whole, Rosie thought. He was whole, when he hadn't been before, and without knowing why, she dropped to her knees and cried.

THREE

The police found her there, serene with exhaustion. Horror had spun away with the golden column, leaving a deep, gentle regret in Rosie's breast. She had never wanted to hurt anybody, much less kill someone, but the peculiar certainty that she had done well made facing the police easier. They awakened Pearl, whose sob when she saw Goode's body cut through Rosie like a blade.

"He hit her," Rosie told the police, "and came after me. I had no choice."

Even through tears, Pearl's attention sharpened at the lie. Then she dissolved again, agonizing loss in each caught breath. She didn't, though, dispute the story Rosie had told. Better to be the victim than the accomplice. Better to escape the factory and face Rosie alone later than reveal her unnatural desire for Goode's blood. A calm space in Rosie's chest told her she would mete Pearl a similar fate, if necessary, but maybe it wouldn't be. Maybe with his inhuman lure extinguished, Pearl would return to normal.

"You weren't hurt, were you, miss?" One of the officers offered her a hand up.

Rosie took it gratefully, shaking her head as she stood. "Just frightened." She recounted what had happened—how she and Pearl had been chatting, lingering in the changing rooms when the alarm sounded. How they'd heard a woman's screams and followed them instead of leaving as they were supposed to. How they'd discovered the record player, and how Goode had attacked them. How he'd confessed to killing and—Rosie shuddered, theatrical but heartfelt—eating several women who had recently been thought to have left the factory's employment.

The officer paled, muttered, "Stay here," and went to get his supervisor. A few seconds later the older man's voice shot up: "*Eating* them? We got a God-damned lunatic *cannibal*—" He broke off, glancing self-consciously toward Rosie and Pearl, and through the calm haze of survival, Rosie almost laughed. The girls at the factory said saltier things every few minutes, but she supposed admitting that to a man born in the last *century* would only shock him.

He strode over and towered above them, a big man with a touch of black still coloring the hair visible beneath his hat. Most of the police looked rumpled in the night's heat, but his collars were crisp and his tie straight, and his shirt wasn't yet stained with sweat. It made him that much more professional, his expression that much grimmer. "I'm Detective Johnson. I'm sorry, girls. I know you've had a rough night, and I wish I could just send you home, but you're going to have to come down to the station so we can get the whole story."

Pearl shot Rosie a panicked look, but Rosie only nodded at the detective. The other girl had heard the tale Rosie had spun. The rest was up to her to deliver. Rosie hoped the police wouldn't find any of Pearl's belongings at Goode's home for her own sake as much as Pearl's, but if they did, she would amend her own story to another version of the truth. No one would believe the full truth, not even after she heard another officer say, "What the hell?" as he found the welding torch Goode had mangled.

"Could I change my clothes and call the USO?" she wondered aloud. "My friends were expecting me there tonight. Somebody could get a message to them."

"Soon as we get to the station," Johnson promised, and Rosie went with him, grateful to leave the dead man behind.

She hadn't been inside the police station since she'd gotten her driver's license. Not much had changed. The concrete walls painted cream were yellower than they'd been, maybe. The wide-open windows were stained with tobacco smoke and dirt, and the noise, even late at night, was consistent. There were fewer young men than there had been: all the

officers were past enlistment age, and some looked like they'd come out of
retirement. Johnson told the receptionist to let Rosie use the phone, but
she stood with its black earpiece curved in her palm and couldn't think
what she would say. Jean deserved to be told about Ruby in person, and
anything other than the truth would offer no excuse for Rosie's failure to
show at the USO. After a minute she put the phone down. The receptionist
pointed her at the restrooms so she could change clothes and wash up,
then, when Rosie came out again, showed her to a seat. "Want some coffee,
sweetheart?"

"Thanks, yes, please." Rosie sat watching Johnson talking to Pearl at
a desk halfway across the room. She could hear the detective's questions
but not Pearl's answers, which the other girl mumbled at her lap. Once
she dissolved into tears, and Johnson glanced Rosie's way with a frown.
She didn't pretend not to be watching, and when he finished with Pearl,
Johnson beckoned Rosie over. "You look like you're holding up all right."

"It's the coffee." Rosie smiled wanly and smoothed her skirt under
her thighs as she sat. "Good thing it's Friday, though. I'd never be awake
enough to work tomorrow."

Johnson looked toward the wall clock, ticking past one in the morning,
and nodded. "Saturday morning, now. I meant considering you just killed
a man."

The coffee turned acid in Rosie's stomach. She folded her hands over it,
pressing. "He was trying to kill us."

Johnson shifted in his chair, sitting back. It creaked, both springs and
leather needing attention. "Well, Miss Ransom, I must say you're a better
liar than Miss Daly is."

Rosie's gaze jerked up again, so surprised she didn't even feel guilty. "I
am? I mean, what? I haven't lied."

"Haven't you? Why don't you start at the beginning, Miss Ransom. I'll
tell you where you're going wrong."

She stared at him, heat flaming in her cheeks. Anybody would blush,
she thought, being accused of lying to a policeman. Her mouth dried up
and it took two tries to speak. "Pearl and I were lingering in the changing
room—"

"Right there," Johnson said, and Rosie broke off with another stare. Johnson waited a few seconds, then, gently, said, "She was his accomplice, wasn't she, Rosie? She as much as said so. You've got a good heart, trying to protect her, but it won't do her any good. My boys will find evidence they've been living together back at Goode's apartment. Why don't you tell me what really happened?"

"It happened like I told you," Rosie said after a long moment. "Except Pearl followed me through the factory, we didn't go together. And she tried to grab me so PFC Goode could—I don't know what. I hit her with the riveting gun, and he came after me anyways, and I shot him."

"That's it?"

"Isn't that *enough*? I *shot* somebody, Detective. I *killed* a man." Rosie's voice rose and broke, emotion surging up from a buried place within her. "And my friends are dead, girls I've known since school, and that monster *ate* them, and—!"

"Monster," Johnson murmured under her tirade. "Why do you use that word?"

The image of Goode's unnerving teeth retreating into his skull made Rosie snap her jaw shut. Breathing hard, voice still high, she said, "What else would you call someone who kills and eats girls?"

Johnson's shoulders sank a fraction of an inch. "*Monster*'s good enough for me. Miss Ransom, you lied to protect Miss Daly. Why?"

Rosie slumped in her chair. The station was too hot, even in the middle of the night with buzzing floor fans pushing a thick breeze through the big room. The heat dulled her thoughts as badly as emotion draining away did. All she had as an answer was the truth, and it couldn't be good if the truth seemed like a last resort. She offered it anyways. "Because I heard my friends talking about how he seemed to hypnotize girls. I thought maybe Pearl didn't have any choice, that she was stuck under his thumb and didn't know how to get out. I wanted to give her a chance, I guess. She didn't seem bad, just . . . scared."

"That's mighty noble of you, Miss Ransom. Foolish, maybe, but mighty noble." Johnson opened a pack of cigarettes and offered Rosie one. She shook her head. He shrugged, tapped one out for himself, and lit it before going on. "I'd like you to press charges against her. A lot of girls are dead and she had a part in all of it. We can probably make it stick without your help, but it'd be a lot easier if you were on the prosecution's side."

"I don't think it's a good idea." Pearl's visible hunger came back to Rosie, and she shivered. "I don't think you should hold her, Detective. I think you should let her go and . . ."

And let me deal with her. Rosie couldn't say the words if she wanted to. They were too absurd. She'd been lucky facing Goode: she'd had a weapon on hand, one that she understood, and she had been willing to use it. His strength, his resistance to fire, his horrifying teeth, they had all been enough to push her beyond the edge of civilized behavior. Rationally, she could never expect herself to do something like that again.

But that cool certainty sat inside her chest, calm and steady and born, Rosie thought, from the purity of light that had risen from Goode's body. She *knew* she could pull the trigger a second time, or that some other weapon would come to hand, if she again faced something like Goode had been and Pearl was becoming. That knowledge was nearly as frightening as Goode himself had been. Rosie pressed her eyes shut and after a long few seconds whispered, "I can't press charges. I'm sorry, Detective, I really am, but I just don't think it's a good idea."

She opened her eyes again to find Johnson watching her through a cloud of smoke, fiery end of his cigarette glowing and dimming. "What really happened at the factory tonight, Rosie?"

"Just what I told you," she answered quietly. "I'm lucky to be alive."

"That," Johnson said with a certain amount of force, "is true. What I do know is that Miss Daly's story corroborates yours, at least as far as you acting in self-defense, and I guess that means you can go. I'll get one of the boys to drive you home. Hank?" His voice rose in an impatient snap.

A man not too much older than Rosie stuck his head out of a side office. His yellow hair was cropped soldier-short and he looked fit. Rosie stared at him curiously as he called, "Yeah, boss?"

"This young woman needs a lift home. Get your coat, call it a night when you've dropped her off."

"It's too hot for a coat, boss." The man—Hank—disappeared back into the office anyways and came out a minute later with a fedora clamped against his head, a coat over his arm, and car keys jangling in one hand. "All right, doll, let's go."

He favored his left leg, limping as he headed for the door. Rosie watched him a few seconds, then stood, shook her skirt smooth, and followed him. Johnson's voice came after them both: "Don't leave town, Rosie Ransom. We're going to need to talk to you again."

"Where would I go," she said under her breath, and didn't say, *Pearl is here, and she'll need me—or I'll have to take care of her,* aloud at all. The door opened easily, creating a breath of slightly cooler air that faded as quickly as it had come. Rosie caught up to Hank in a step or two, glancing at his legs.

"Monsters." Hank didn't so much as look at her, just threw the word out. "Tore my damn knee out over in France. Got any other questions?"

Rosie's eyebrows lifted. "I didn't ask."

"You would have."

"I suppose everyone does."

He looked at her that time, eyebrows drawn down in appraisal. "Yeah. Unless I'm sitting on my ass when they meet me, then they ask why a strapping young fellow like myself isn't on the front lines. That's my car."

That was a long-nosed, narrow, curvaceous red two-seater with its top down. Rosie slowed, then stopped and wet her lips. "What is it?"

A smile crept over one corner of Hank's mouth. "SS Jaguar 100. She's a beaut, isn't she?"

Rosie swallowed, then put her hands over her cheeks, feeling the heat of a blush. She'd have to be dead to be from Detroit and not enchanted with the vehicle's low, lean lines. "It's beautiful. It's not American. The steering's on the wrong side."

"British. Hardly made any of 'em but my old man bought one. I brought it back when I came home."

"Your father's British?"

"Mom is. Proper romantic love-in-combat story there. She was a nurse in the Great War and followed him to Detroit afterward. Get in." Hank threw his coat into the back, waving Rosie around the car as he climbed in himself with no evidence of his knee bothering him.

Rosie hesitated at the door, which was scooped so low she might have stepped from the runner board into the car without risking her modesty. Hank, watching her, quirked a grin over the same corner of his mouth. It was attractive. *He* was attractive, in a clear-eyed Captain America kind of way. But he looked like he knew what Rosie was considering and betting she didn't have the nerve.

Swiftly, before she thought about it more, Rosie stepped over the door and into the car, tucking her skirt as she sat, and gave Hank a defiant look. His smile twisted further and he keyed the car on. "Where's home?"

She gave him the address over the engine's rumble. The Jaguar's seats were soft leather and still retained warmth from the day, even at two in the morning. Rosie glanced over her shoulder at its folded-down canopy, then eyed the hat smashed on Hank's head. "Won't that come off?"

"Hasn't yet. So you're a factory girl. Where's your husband, Europe or Japan?"

"My boyfriend is in Europe," Rosie said primly, then wished she hadn't sounded so stuck-up.

Hank noticed too, a grin in his reply. "Boyfriend, sorry. I knew you weren't married, anyway. No ring. You like the work or are you counting days 'til your soldier comes home?"

"Can't I do both?"

He gave her another look, more appraising, as they left the station parking lot for quiet Detroit streets. The Jaguar announced its presence for blocks to come, a big purr that would awaken light sleepers. Rosie closed her eyes against wind that slipped around the screen. It felt good in her hair, speed finally offering respite from the heat. If the car were hers, she might drive for what remained of the night, escaping not just the warm air but the memories of the past several hours. Maybe go down to the river and find a breeze, or head to some relatively high point to look over the city from, and try to make sense of the day.

Hank's question came as a surprise: "You in a hurry to get home?"

A thrill of cold ran through Rosie's hands. Smart girls—good girls—didn't go off on nighttime jaunts with boys they'd just met, but the question ran so close to her own thoughts that she said, "Not really," without hesitation.

"Great. I know a place on the waterfront." Hank changed lanes and sped up. Rosie turned her head away and bit her knuckles at her own boldness. No one knew where she was, though Detective Johnson knew who she was with, which might be close enough to the same. Besides, somebody working for the police oughta be trustworthy. Rosie tried the thought on for size and accepted it, but her heartbeat ran quick anyways.

"It's right next to a refrigerated shipping center and they're always leaving the doors open so it's usually about ten degrees cooler than anywhere else in the city," Hank yelled over the wind. "My favorite place in the summer. How fast do you want to get there?"

Rosie's smile split from behind her knuckles. "How fast *can* we get there?"

Fast enough that it seemed like the headlamp light pooling ahead of them should be overtaken by the Jaguar's smooth speed, it turned out. Hank handed her his hat and Rosie clutched it, tears and shrieks of laughter spilling from her as they raced through the empty streets. She hadn't thought she felt bottled up, but the chance to let so much emotion spill out felt like the cork coming off the bottle anyways.

Hank braked hard outside a tall set of gates, the car's tires squealing as it whipped around. Rosie caught a glimpse of company logos as the gates swung open, and pushed against the foot well, straightening up in her seat. "Hank, we can't come through, this is private property, it belongs to Vaughn Enterprises. They say Harrison Vaughn's a beast about security. I just got out of jail," she said with a weak laugh. "I don't want to go straight back in."

"You were at the police station, not in jail. Big difference. Anyway, don't worry. They know me here." Hank put the car back in gear and eased it through the gates, waving at the security guards who scurried to close it behind him. The Jaguar's engine echoed off steel-sided warehouses as they crept closer to the river, and the silence when Hank killed it echoed louder.

The air, as promised, was significantly cooler. Rosie took a few deep breaths, enjoying it, before giving Hank a curious look. "But you work with the police, not on the docks. Or is that how they know you, from the police?"

"These days, sure." Hank got out of the car, limped to a locked door, opened it, and took a bottle of amber liquid from within. "Want some? You've had a rough night."

"Not rough enough to drink with a strange man."

Hank's eyebrows shot up as he came back to the car and leaned against the driver's side door. "Then you are one tough broad, Miss Ransom. I'm impressed. I think my mother would like you."

"An Army nurse? No, she must be much braver than I am."

"Maybe. Don't think she's ever killed a man, though."

"I did—" Rosie broke off with a swallow. *I didn't kill a* man, she'd been going to say, but that sounded nonsensical. "I didn't have a choice," she said instead.

"That doesn't make it easier for most people. Did you see his soul?"

"I think so. It was stained with blo—" Rosie choked off her answer, gawking ashen-faced at Hank.

"Stained with blood," he said conversationally. "Stained with death and horror, and when you killed him, all the blackness siphoned away and his redeemed soul rose up free."

Rosie, staring at him, worked her mouth and made no sound.

"You thought I meant Nazis, when I said they'd torn my knee up," Hank said softly. "But I meant what I said, Rosie Ransom. I meant monsters."

FOUR

"They've been around since forever," Hank went on when Rosie couldn't speak. "Since people started being people. Since we started drawing pictures in the dirt and singing lullabies. They crawl inside human bodies, and the weak ones change the bodies until they don't look human anymore. The stronger ones can keep their human shape, and stay hidden. The ones that took out my knee were weak, for demons. They got inside our sentries and came back to camp with teeth and claws. They were fast as anything and we could hardly see them at night. A lot of men in my unit died. Three days out of seven I wish I'd been one of 'em. But then the people who saved me read me in when I survived and knew what I'd seen. No way I could think it was the Jerrys."

"Who?" Rosie hadn't meant to say a word except maybe *take me home*, but she blurted the question anyways. "Who—'read you in'? You mean I'm not crazy?"

"I'm betting you didn't think for two minutes that you were. I never saw a girl as cool as you, back there in the station. It got me to thinking about the stories they told me, about the Redeemers."

Pride warmed Rosie. She *had* been cool at the station, even if she didn't think anybody else had reason to notice it. But she didn't want to let that pride show, not with so many questions to ask. If this man who knew about monsters thought she could be led around by a compliment or two, she'd never get any answers out of him. "What are Redeemers? Who told you stories?"

"You sure you don't want some of this, Miss Ransom?" Hank offered the whiskey a second time, and this time Rosie took it.

Bottle in hand, she got out of the car and went to the waterfront, looking at reflected lights wobbling in the river. "Three days out of seven, huh? Is today one of the three?"

"It was, right up until you walked into the station."

"Then I reckon you don't need to be drinking this stuff right now." Rosie pitched the bottle into the river and watched it come down at a respectable distance with only a small splash. It caught a bit of light and turned it amber before water flooded the bottle's open top and it sank. Only then did Rosie face Hank again, satisfied at his slack-jawed astonishment. She didn't much care if he drank a lot or not, but it looked to her like he'd use the booze as an excuse to draw out answers, and she wanted as many as she could get, as fast as they could come. She set her own jaw, scared, but more determined. "Something awful happened tonight, mister, and I don't have time for your word games. You can tell me who your 'they' are, and you can tell me what a Redeemer is, or you can take me straight home and go find a bottle to crawl into, if that's what you want to do. I'm real sorry your knee got busted up, but it doesn't give you the right to play coy when you know what's going on with me."

Anger flashed in Hank's bright eyes. "You need me, Miss Ransom."

"I don't think so." Rosie stalked past the car toward the security gates, tossing the retort over her shoulder. "You already told me three things I didn't know five minutes ago. There are monsters, there are people that know about them, and you think I'm something called a Redeemer. That's enough to go a long way on, pal. I bet I can find out a lot, just knowing that."

She got a good solid thirty steps beyond the car before Hank's voice followed her: "Wait. Wait, Rosie. Wait."

Rosie turned, arms folded under her breasts, and cocked an eyebrow. Hank came after her, his limp more pronounced than it had been in the station. A single slug of hooch couldn't have affected him that much, that fast. Maybe driving aggravated his injury, or maybe he'd been playing it brave in the station. Either way, Rosie didn't have an inch to spare him, and he closed the distance until they stood ten or twelve feet apart. "They're called *Ex Libris.*"

He waited a second, like that should mean something to her. Rosie pursed her lips, guessing, "Library men?"

Something pained flashed across Hank's face before he buried it with something nearer to approval. "Close. It means *from the book*, and that's—it's important." He hesitated again, until Rosie muttered and turned on her heel, stalking away. She could find her way back to the gates, and if she apologized prettily enough, the security guards would probably forget they'd ever seen her.

"Stop! Look, we're not even supposed to talk about this. I don't know how."

"Well, start at the beginning and don't quit until you get to the end." Rosie turned back one more time, but she'd about had it. From the way his shoulders bowed, it looked like Hank knew it, too. He muttered, "I wish you hadn't thrown out that booze," then sighed like he'd given up on her, and limped back toward the car. Rosie followed before she knew it, the click of her heels echoing angrily off the concrete and warehouses. "Where do you think you're going, library man?"

"It's been a long day already, Miss Ransom. My leg gets tired. You can listen just as well with me sitting down."

Rosie snapped, "Not if you don't start talking," but she didn't walk away from him again. She'd give him another minute, she promised herself, and if he hadn't said anything useful by then, she knew the way out. Hank settled himself against the Jaguar's hood, shifting until he stopped wincing when he did it. "Try not to ask questions until I'm done. If I get off topic I'm never going to make it all the way through."

Rosie mimed zipping her lips. Hank smirked. "Thanks. *From the book* is important because there are demons in the world, Miss Ransom, and they can only be captured in art. Painting, music, sculpture, even literature. *Stop* it," he said as she caught her breath to speak. "I meant it. I'm not supposed to talk about it at all and it won't help if you interrupt. Demons—monsters—come from art. You ever read about art history? About how many artists seem to go crazy, or die young? How they even talk about the insanity of creation, like it's almost an outside force, driving them?"

"Muses," Rosie whispered.

Hank nodded. "It comes from inside, though. Art is—it's magic, Miss Ransom. Art *is* magic. You've seen a painting or read a book or heard music that makes you angry or laugh or cry, right? It's magic. It's the power of the artist reaching out, sometimes across centuries, to make you feel. Not every artist is powerful enough to make that kind of magic, the kind that affects people forever, but every artist has got magic inside them. And sometimes, it's bigger than they are. Sometimes, instead of making a piece of art that reaches across the centuries, that magic eats them alive. They lose control and go mad, and that madness can become . . . bigger. Bigger than the artist it's born from. It can claw its way out, like the artist was never more than a vessel to give birth to living magic. To a demon. Most of the time, it kills the artist."

"Only *most* of the time?"

Hank made a face. "Sometimes, the artist's body survives the transition, and when that happens, it needs blood for its human body and souls for its demon spirit. That's when you get vampires. Things like PFC Goode."

Angry disbelief thudded around inside Rosie's chest. "You're telling me that consumptive twerp was some kind of amazing artist?"

Hank's lip curled. "Probably not. Vampires—they reproduce the way they do in the stories, by biting a human. I think Goode was probably a scion, not an original. I *am* trying to explain, miss. Just . . . let me talk. Most demons are incorporeal." He glanced at her to see if she knew the word, and went on when she didn't question it. "They're living magic, but they can't survive without a host. They claw their way into living people and stay as long as the soul lasts. Most don't last very long with a demon gnawing on them, so the demons have to keep moving, finding new hosts. And it sounds counterintuitive, but it's the weakest demons, the ones who maybe only just barely survived birthing, who go through human hosts fastest. They don't have the control to keep the host alive. The strong ones, though, they can last for decades. They just nibble away at the soul until it's gone and the demon is all that's left inside, like a parasite. They have to move to a new host at that point, but they're patient and they've usually got somebody groomed for the job. Those ones are hard to find and capture."

"Capture?" Rosie felt like every word she spoke echoed something Hank had said, but she desperately wanted to understand.

Hank raised a finger, holding off the question. "I'm getting there. Demons who can take over a human body without destroying it aren't like vampires. They can reproduce like we do, *with* us. They father magical bloodlines, and most of those bloodlines are evil. Ex Libris stamps out every sign of them they find. Except one."

A chill wind off the refrigeration units spilled over Rosie's arms, raising hairs. "Redeemers?"

"Redeemers." Hank nodded. "Redeemers can kill demons, Miss Ransom. As far as I know, nothing else human can. But Redeemers don't just kill them. They cleanse the madness from the soul, destroying the demon and redeeming the human host's soul when they do."

"Wait." Rosie lifted her palms, eyes closed as she worked her way through Hank's lecture. "These demons are born from artists but usually kill them when they're born." A shudder twitched her spine and she muttered, "And they say childbirth is dangerous," before continuing. "Then the demons climb into other bodies. Do they have to be artists too?" She opened her eyes to see Hank shake his head and draw breath at the same time, like he might comment but thought better of it. "No, but I bet they *like* to find other artists, huh?" At his nod, she shuddered again and went on. "So a demon holes up inside a human and eats its soul bit by bit, and if it lives long enough it can have magic babies with normal humans. And if a Redeemer gets to it before it's finished eating somebody's *whole* soul, they . . . live?"

Hank grimaced. "They die, but they die saved. In most European religions, that means they're able to go to Heaven. In Buddhism, it means they enter the reincarnation cycle at a higher place, or in Shintoism, they take an honored place among the ancestors."

"What's Shintism?"

"Shintoism. It's—never mind. The point is that Redeemers are the only thing that can save a demon-infested human's soul. The rest of us can just capture them, if we're lucky. And we captu—"

"Wait." The cold off the fridges came back to stick against Rosie's skin, settling at her nape with a firm grip. "Wait, Redeemers are the *only* thing that can save the people demons . . . climb into? You mean if Ex Libris kills a demon, the person goes to Hell?"

"They would if we could kill them at all, but we only catch them."

"But that's horrible! How can a good person be damned to Hell just because they got stuck with a demon? That's awful!"

A sorrow-tinged smile slid over Hank's lips. "Yeah. Demons are nasty business, Miss Ransom. There are schools of thought, even in Ex Libris, that it must be that only the deserving get demon-infected. People who are going to Hell anyway, I mean. But I don't think that's true." He raised his shoulders like he was passing off a shiver, and glanced into the Jaguar at where he'd thrown his coat. But even with the fridge units blasting cooler air, the night was still warm, and he left the coat where it lay. "I think people just get unlucky. And there aren't many Redeemers, so hardly anybody finds salvation."

Rosie folded her arms around herself. "How do you capture them? How does Ex Libris stop them?"

"In art." Hank sighed. "They're drawn to art, and they can be captured in it. It's their weakness, and it's why the world hasn't been completely overrun by monsters. A painter or a sculptor or a composer can write or paint or carve the demon's essence into their art. Or a writer. You wouldn't believe how many dirty limericks hold small demons. The big ones, though . . ." He shook his head. "You don't want to know what the Sistine Chapel holds. Or *Ulysses*."

"You said *ex libris* means *from the book*," Rosie whispered. "Does that mean you're demons too? If you capture demons in art, and you're from the books . . . ?"

Hank shifted his weight like he'd gotten uncomfortable fast, and gave her a curious look. "No. We just write down everything we know, so our knowledge comes from the books. It's a pun." He tried a smile and Rosie gave him a flat look in return.

"Pretty hoity-toity, making Latin puns out of your secret society."

To her surprise, Hank's smile grew. "We take our humor where we can find it. Anyway, we write everything down, we learn from the books, so it doesn't get lost from one generation to the next. We don't often live very long, and with two wars in Europe back to back . . . a lot of art has been destroyed, a lot of monsters have been set loose, and a lot of us have died fighting them. There aren't enough of us around anymore, and the monsters are gaining ground. Which is why Redeemers could be important, and when I saw you glowing at the station, I remembered the stories."

"I'm glowing?" Rosie extended her hands, searching for a glimmer in her fingers.

"Not anymore. It faded."

"How come nobody said anything?"

"It doesn't show up unless you know how to see it. Besides, would you say something if you saw somebody glowing?"

"I guess not. Or, I don't know, maybe. Maybe." Rosie folded her arms under her breasts again. "The glowing, that's got to do with being a Redeemer?"

"Yeah. It's like a sign that they're one of the few who can save a demon-possessed soul. I don't know a whole lot else, honestly. There's not much in the literature about Redeemers. The Ex Libris don't think much of them."

"Let me guess," Rosie drawled. "The Ex Libris are *men*, and Redeemers are women?"

"Gosh," Hank drawled right back, "how'd you know?"

"Men never think much of what women can do, but look at us now, building the whole war machine. Must be scary, knowing we can. I bet your library men are afraid of Redeemers, too."

"I'm not."

A sudden smile blossomed across Rosie's face. "Neither am I. Heck, we might make quite a team, library man." She finally sat on the edge of the Jaguar's hood, feeling the engine's warmth rising beneath her, and got almost halfway through asking, "How come Redeemer magic is okay?" before a sharp, small laugh broke the words into pieces. "Listen to me," she said more quietly. "Magic and Redeemers and demons."

"Oh my," Hank put in softly.

The corner of Rosie's mouth curved up. "Oh my," she agreed, but she couldn't keep the smile going no matter how hard she tried. "It all sounds crazy. How come I'm not running away screaming? I killed somebody tonight."

Hank shook his head, hardly more than a twitch of motion. "You're an independent woman, Miss Ransom. You've got a job, I bet you don't live at home with your folks. But I bet you don't go out to the waterfront with strangers at two in the morning, either. I think you did run screaming. You're just dignified about it."

"I should be running harder now. You're the one who told me about the monsters."

"You already knew. Once you Redeemed PFC Goode, you knew. I'm just filling in the details."

Rosie let a deep breath go, imagining she could see it on the fridge-cooled air. "Are you always this calm?"

Hank grinned. "Part of my British heritage. Keep calm and carry on. Truth is you're not that rattled either, though."

"No. It sounds awful, but it felt right. Not killing him, I didn't want to have to do that, but afterward, I couldn't—I can't—regret it. Oh, gosh, I've got to go home and tell Mom and Pop before they see the newspaper. It's going to be in the newspaper, isn't it?"

"And on the radio."

Rosie slid off the Jaguar, shaking her skirt straight. "I have to go tell Jean, too. She can't find out from the radio. It'll all be there, won't it? All the missing girls? They'll be talking about all of it, oh, no. You've got to bring me to her house, please. I don't know what I was thinking, coming out here instead of going to tell them right away."

"There's a lot more I need to tell you, Miss Ransom."

"You'll have to tell me on the way, or bring me to your secret headquarters tomorrow and let your supervisor tell me. This can't wait." Rosie flapped her hand at him as she scurried to the passenger-side door. He edged off the hood more cautiously, frowning. Rosie took advantage of him not being in the car yet to step over the car door instead of opening it, and settled into the seat with a mixture of dread at facing Jean with terrible news and excitement at going for another drive in the low-slung convertible.

Hank climbed into the driver's seat, still frowning, and all of Rosie's anticipation, good and bad, crashed into foreboding. Her stomach felt squeezed, and she thought maybe the serenity she'd felt after killing Goode had been gone for ages after all: she'd been all highs and lows, either excitement or anger, since then. Maybe she was rattled after all, even if not as badly as she thought she should be. "What's wrong?"

"My supervisors . . ."

"They might not like Redeemers, but they've got to see I could help, right? You can't not tell them, after all. I'd think it'd be a feather in your cap, finding a Redeemer."

"No, you don't understand. It's not that I don't want to tell them. It's that there's no one to tell. I'm all alone out here."

FIVE

Hank explained, on the drive to Jean's house. At least, he kept talking, but the words whipped past Rosie, lashing her skin the same way stray hairs caught in the wind did. She only heard half of what he said, maybe not even that much. Something about Detroit being an outpost. Something about rumors of a—*daemon rex,* Hank said, and she glanced at him only to be told, as if the translation tasted bad in his mouth, "King demon." Something about a king demon in the Midwest, then. Something about his duty being to find that demon. "Not doing much of a job at it, are you?" she asked, but didn't think he heard, not with the wind snatching her voice away.

Earlier the drive had been a release, but the car felt like a prison now. She'd wanted to go somewhere that she could make sense of the day, and instead it made less sense now than it had before.

Except it didn't. It only made less sense if she thought she'd flipped her wig, and Hank had been right about that. She didn't for a minute think she'd gone crazy. She believed him about the demons. About everything, and that bothered her more than anything else. The world shouldn't be able to hide something as awful as demons without lots of people knowing the truth. "Only we do know, don't we? They're not really hidden. We have all kinds of stories about them. We just don't quite believe them. Not as *real* things, not things that walk the earth."

"What?"

Rosie shook her head and pushed her thumbs against her temples, where dried sweat made the fine hairs feel thick and rough. Her whole hairline felt like that where she pressed her index fingers against it, and the longer she held her hands there, the more hair came loose to tickle the backs of her hands. It'd be an awful mess later, and she had to get through a whole day, all of Saturday, before she could wash it again. Well, maybe she'd do it in the morning instead of waiting until Saturday night. That would feel good. Underneath trying to distract herself by thinking about her hair, she finished making herself understand why she believed Hank. She'd *seen* the demon, and Hank had explained it, and she could either figure that she'd gone nuts or that she now knew the truth. She had enough faith in herself to believe her own eyes and heart.

Hank kept going on about how America didn't have much in the way of Ex Libris anyways, even before the wars, because there were so many more demons in Europe and China. That didn't even make sense, if demons came from art. People made art and there'd been people in America forever, but her objection washed away before she said it. Men hated being challenged over details like that, and she still had to figure out what to say to Jean. *Ruby's dead, Jeannie, you were right, and I'm so sorry. But I killed the thing that killed her, and I'm not sorry about that at all.* It sounded awful. It sounded right. She didn't know what to say.

"Did you see anything when he died? Anything that could tell you about the daemon rex?" The wind died down as the car slowed, making Hank easier to hear.

Rosie twisted her hands in her hair, frowning. They weren't far from Jean's house now, and the Jaguar's engine sounded rudely loud among the quiet tree-lined streets. Half the neighborhood would be peeking out their windows, seeing Rosie Ransom driving around late at night with a strange young man. "Are Redeemers supposed to be able to read souls, too?"

"Not that I know about. I'm grasping at straws here, Miss Ransom."

"How do you know he wasn't the, uh. The *daemon rex* himself?" Rosie made a face. "That sounds stupid and highfalutin' coming from me. The demon king."

Hank glared at her. "Haven't you been listening? My superiors were glad I was from Detroit. It meant they could send me back here and have a local ear to the ground on the rumors they'd been hearing for years. Goode had just come back from France. He couldn't have been the daemon rex." His glare faded to a sigh and he conceded, "The king. He hadn't been here long enough."

It didn't seem right to say she *hadn't* hardly been listening, but he'd asked another question, so she didn't have to. "I didn't see anything in his soul. Just that it washed clean and rose up. No clues. Aren't you too junior to be hunting king demons?"

Bitterness flashed across Hank's handsome features. "Don't you mean too crippled?"

Rosie's eyebrows drew down in real surprise. "No, I meant too young. It seems like king demons would be a job for somebody with years of experience, not rookies."

"Like I said, we're spread thin," Hank said shortly. "Where do I drop you off?"

"You promised Detective Johnson you'd drive me home," Rosie said with a faint smile. "This isn't my home. Turn here. Jean's house is up there on the right, the one with the green Oldsmobile and the lights on." The tram stop near Jean's house looked strangely lonesome at night, a dark forgotten space beneath the trees. Rosie turned her face away and shivered.

"Your friend has a car."

Rosie's shiver slipped away into a scowl. "I'm about to go tell my friend that her best friend is dead. She's not going to be in any condition to drive. I was going to ask if you would wait, please, yes, but now I think I'll just tell you to, or I'll be calling the detective in the morning to tell him you're a lout."

"Fine." Hank pulled up behind Jean's Oldsmobile and killed the engine, sitting back with his arms folded across his chest as Jean burst out of her house with Irene a few steps behind. Jean caught the veranda strut and swayed, stark fear marking her face. "Ruby?"

Rosie vaulted out of the car in a flurry of skirts and ran up the steps two at a time to catch Jean in a hug before the other girl fell. Jean's weight pulled her to the porch, and they sank together with Irene collapsing to her knees behind them. Rosie huddled Jean against her chest, feeling tears run hot and soaking her dress. Jean smelled like Irene's perfume, depths of floral, and her dress crinkled under the pressure of Rosie's arms. Irene put her arms around them both as Rosie whispered, "I'm so sorry, Jean. I'm so sorry. It was Goode, and it wasn't just Ruby. Carol Ann, and some of the Negro girls too. But he's dead now." Rosie surprised herself with the vicious triumph in her voice. "He's dead now. I killed him."

Jean's head snapped up with such violence that she caught Rosie in the jaw and Irene on the nose. Irene cried out, clapping her hands to her face as Rosie's head bounced back against the porch post and she bit her tongue. Jean made a sound of dismay through her tears, patting ineffectually at Rosie and twisting to look at Irene, whose eyes were bright with tears as she tested her nose. "I'm okay," she reported shrilly. Rosie said, "Me too," on a swollen tongue, and Jean wailed, "I'm so sorry."

Rosie pulled her into another hug, suddenly laughing through the pain. "They couldn't have done that in the pictures if they'd tried."

Irene and Jean both giggled equally hysterically before tears and hiccoughs broke the laughter apart again. Jean lifted her head more carefully this time as she said, "You killed him, Rosie? You *killed* him?"

Rosie slumped against the porch post. "Do either of you know a girl named Pearl Daly? She lured me to him and he tried to—"

"He tried to what, Rosie?" Jean's color rose, tears in her eyes adding a glitter to her anger. "He did something, didn't he? I don't know what, but he had to do *something* to make Ruby fancy him. He wasn't—he wasn't her type, Rosie. You know he wasn't her type at all."

"But he was so darn handsome," Irene protested. "How could such a nice-looking man do—do anything awful?" She glanced toward the Jaguar and Hank as if she hadn't really noticed them before, then turned a worried frown on Rosie.

"He's with the police," Rosie said. "He's got to drive me to Mom and Pop's so I can tell them about Goode before the newspapers do. Jean, he tried to—to glamour me. I thought he was handsome too, Irene, just for a minute. But then I could see through it, and he wasn't any sheik, he was just a boy."

"See through it? You can't see through good looks, Rosie."

"You can if it's magic." Rosie hardly even heard herself say it. Hardly even wanted to hear herself, because she knew Jean and Irene would look at her the way they did, like she was a little bit crazy after killing someone. That hadn't even really sunk in yet, she could tell, and if they didn't really believe she'd killed Goode, she couldn't see how they were going to believe he'd been a vampire. A *demon*. Storybook monsters didn't just turn up working the night shift in a Detroit airplane factory.

"How did he die?"

The way Jean asked made it sound like Rosie hadn't been responsible for what she'd done, and somehow that got her back up. She straightened, took a breath to steady her voice, and said, "I shot him in the chest with a riveting gun."

Both girls recoiled, imagining the impact of a rivet on a man's body, but Jean leaned right back in with an angry grin stuck in her teeth. "Do you think it *hurt?*"

Rosie started to say she thought it had been too fast to hurt, that she thought he'd only been surprised, then thought of all the dead girls, and of how their bones had been made into bread. Goode had eaten them first, too, cut or bitten them to drink their blood, and bespelled or not, she bet anything that had hurt them. Ruby and the others hadn't died fast, with only enough time to be surprised. They'd felt it, and Jean didn't want to hear that Goode hadn't suffered. Rosie said, "Yes," quietly, and saw a flush of pleasure on Jean's cheeks before she began to cry again with wracking sobs.

"How could you do that?" Irene whispered. "How could you even think to do that, Rosie?"

"He was going to eat me, Rene. He killed and ate all the other girls. I'd have—"

"He *ate* them? He ate *Ruby?*" Jean's cry rang down the street, lights in other houses flickering on. Rosie caught Jean again, drawing her close and whispering hushes into her hair as doors opened and a few cautious women looked toward the commotion. Hank jumped out of the Jaguar and came up the porch steps in two bounds. "Miss Ransom, we're drawing too much attention."

Rosie glowered at him and urged Jean to her feet. "Come on. C'mon. Come on inside, Jeannie. I'll tell you when we get in. Goode was a monster, a straight-up monster, and I'm not just saying that because he ate people."

Irene breathed, "Swell," as Hank followed them inside. "By tomorrow morning the whole block will be talking about us going inside with a man at 2 A.M., especially with us still looking like the cat's meow."

"Well, I don't look so good," Rosie said, as if it would make a difference to the gossips. Hank muttered, "You look fine," and closed the door on the street. Rosie guided Jean-Marie to the couch, but Jean resisted sitting down, demanding, "How could he *eat* them?"

"He was a vampire," Rosie said bluntly. "That's how he made all the girls think he was such a dreamboat, and why he ate them."

Hank's jaw flapped. Irene whirled from peeking through the curtains at the neighbors, her eyes and mouth round with disapproval. "*Rosie!* This isn't the time to be making knucklehead jokes! How could you do that to Jean? How cou—" Hank snapped his mouth shut and momentarily silenced Irene into gaping at him. "You believe her?"

Jean's hands were ice-cold in Rosie's. "Rosie, what are you talking about?"

"PFC Goode was an honest-to-God monster and I can kill them. I didn't even know they were real until tonight, but even if I thought I'd been imagining things, Hank here walked me out of the police station and started asking me about them casual as can be. He works for people who hunt monsters and knows more than I do about it."

Hank grated, "Miss Ransom, you can't—"

Rosie cut him off with a glower. "I sure as heck can, library man."

"Demons are to be kept *secret*, Miss Ransom, so as to avoid widespread panic—"

"These are my friends. I'm not keeping secrets from them."

"Rosie, you can't expect us to belie—"

"Are they really real?" Jean's voice, so much quieter than Irene's, undercut her completely. Rosie nodded. Jean swallowed and finally sat, her round face gone pale. "A demon killed Ruby? And you killed the demon?"

"Yes."

An angrier kind of hope than Rosie had ever seen lit Jean's eyes. "Can you teach me how?"

Rosie shot a glance at Hank, who made a short explosive motion of exasperation with his hands, and shook his head. "Almost nobody can kill them, Miss. Only a special kind of warrior called a Redeemer. Miss Ransom is a Redeemer."

Jean's gaze swung toward Hank. "Then teach me how to hunt them like you do."

"You're a *girl*."

Jean surged to her feet, color flushing her cheeks. "I'm a woman and if this whole country doesn't know by now that a woman can do every damn same job a man can do—!"

"They catch them in art, Jeannie," Rosie interrupted. "He says demons are born when artists lose control, and the only way they can capture them is in music or paintings or books. I don't even know how you herd a demon into a sculpture. I guess that's what he's going to have to teach you."

"I'm not teaching anybody anything!"

Rosie gave Hank another flat look. "You're not going to teach me how to find them so I can Redeem them?"

"Of course I am. Ex Libris needs you. We don't need her—"

"Fine. If you won't teach Jean, I will."

Jean turned a heartbreakingly grateful smile on Rosie and sank back onto the couch to put her face in her hands. Rosie put an arm around her shoulders and whispered, "We girls have to stick together. That'll make it okay."

"Okay?" Irene stood by the window, her arms wrapped around herself as if it had gotten cold. "Nothing about this is okay. I don't believe there are demons, and you *killed* somebody, Ro. How can that be okay?"

"I don't know. I know I should be all torn up, Rene, but I'm not. The way I saw him . . . it was like he was already dead. The person was gone. All that was left was this awful stain, and when I shot him with the rivet, the stain lifted and his soul was . . . saved," Rosie said helplessly. "It sounds silly, I'm not a priest to go around absolving people, but—"

"No," Hank interrupted, more quietly than before. "You're a Redeemer.

Priests can only absolve mortal sins, Miss Ransom. Redeemers take on the immortal ones."

"I thought immortal meant not dying at all."

Hank shrugged. "Demons don't die except at the hands of Redeemers. It's a pretty small loophole."

"I think you're all crazy." Irene's voice sounded thin. "I'm sorry Ruby's dead, I really am, and I'm sick that Rosie killed somebody, even if he was bad. But I think you must be crazy to believe this story, Jean, even if it's so fantastical that it's easier than believing the truth, which is that Rosie's bananas and she's making things up so she doesn't have to think about what an awful thing she's done, and *this* creep is looking to take advantage of it. I don't think you should trust him, Rosie. I think you should go right home to your folks and take a while to get your head on straight, because you're all screwed up right now, honey. I'll stay with Jean."

Uncertainty creased Jean's forehead, wrinkles visible around the pressure of her fingertips. Rosie worried at her lower lip. She could argue all night and not come any closer to convincing Irene. "Your version makes a lot more sense," she admitted to Irene. "I can't help it if it's just not true. Jean, will you be okay? If Rene stays with you?"

Jean nodded without taking her face from her hands. Rosie stood reluctantly, patting her back again. "I'll come back in the morning to check on you."

"You should call a taxi, Rosie. Don't let this jerk drive you home."

Rosie judged the careful indifference in Hank's blue eyes and sighed. "He's okay, Rene. I know you don't believe me, but . . ." She turned her hands upward helplessly. "Try to get some sleep, okay? I'll . . . I'll see you tomorrow." Hank headed for the door, Rosie a few steps behind him, but she stopped in the frame to look back at Irene, whose eyebrows pinched with worry. "Thanks for looking out for me, Rene."

An unhappy smile pulled at the corner of Irene's mouth. "Us girls have to stick together, right? Be careful, Ro. Be really careful."

"I will be." Rosie followed Hank out to the Jaguar, smiling to see that this time he held the car door for her. "Trying to convince Irene you're not the bad guy?"

He closed the door behind her and glanced at the house, where the curtain twitched closed again, obscuring Irene from view. "Think it'll do any good?"

Rosie sank her fingers into her hair and pressed the heels of her hands against her temples, trying to decide if her head hurt or if she was just tired. "Not really. I don't know why I thought she'd just believe me."

"Because you believe yourself." Hank took the driver's seat and started the Jag, backing out of the driveway. "But there's a reason Ex Libris is a secret society, Miss Ransom. People don't take well to being told there are demons. Your friend Jean probably won't believe you by morning, either. Where are we going?"

Rosie looked east, as if she might find guidance from a sunrise still hours away. "Do you know where Pearl Daly lives?"

"Even if I did, they're not going to have let her go, Miss Ransom. She'll be at the station all night, maybe longer. Why?"

"But I told them I wasn't pressing charges!"

"Yeah, and if she's real lucky, that'll mean she won't get any jail time. She was Goode's accomplice, though, and there are a lot of dead girls that somebody's gonna have to answer for."

"They need to let her go. She said she'd gotten some of Goode's blood splashed on her. That it made her want more. Need more. *He* said my blood might give him enough to change her all the way. What if she's already had enough? She can't stay at the station. She might kill somebody."

"You telling me we gotta break a vampire out of jail so you can kill it?"

Rosie sat back, shaken by the idea. "Can't I Redeem somebody without killing them?"

"Not that I ever heard about."

"You've already said you haven't heard much," Rosie snapped. "I can't just go into the police station and kill the woman. There's got to be another way. Would they even let me talk to her?"

"Alone? No. Look, she'll be out by tomorrow evening if they decide they're not going to go after her as Goode's accomplice. Just hang on until then. You need to get home and get some rest anyway."

"I can't show up at my folks' at three in the morning and wake them up to tell them I killed somebody, library man. I have to wait until they're awake, at least. What am I supposed to do until then if I can't talk to Pearl?"

"Is 'home' with your folks?"

Rosie stared at Hank, not quite understanding the question, then shook herself. "Oh. No. No, you were right before, I don't live with my parents. I guess I just still think of that as home, in a way. Anyways, I'm not sure there's any point in taking me home. I don't think I can sleep.

"I think you'd be surprised. You get some rest, talk to your folks, and I'll call you when they release Miss Daly."

"And if they don't?"

Hank gave a sharp smile. "Then we'll figure out a jailbreak."

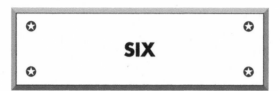

SIX

The idea of a jailbreak lingered as Rosie crept into the house she shared with Irene and four other girls. She didn't see how she and Hank could manage one, not really, but maybe if she talked to Detective Johnson again she could convince him that Pearl had been a victim too, and that the best thing for her would be to let her go home and try to get her life back together.

High heels, bleached of their color in the streetlight that flooded through the front window, lay in a tangle beside the door, indicating Rosie was the last one home after a Friday night out. Rosie slipped her own shoes off and padded to her bedroom, grateful that she could at least turn the light on without disturbing Irene. She wanted a bath so badly her skin itched, but noisy water running through the pipes would wake someone up and she didn't want to face the ribald teasing that would accompany her coming home so late.

Her side of the bedroom had a pair of black flats and some white Keds tucked into corners, and one of her dresses thrown over the back of the chair that sat in front of her vanity. Her closet door stood partway open, revealing the shoulder of her favorite blue shirtwaist. Rosie wedged the dress farther in and pushed the door shut, wishing she kept things a bit tidier, like Irene's side of the room. Irene always hung her dresses up and put her shoes away, no matter how tired she got.

At least Rosie's bed was made, neat and pretty with a checkered pink bedtop that matched the bedclothes on Irene's bed and complemented the deeper rose paint on the walls. Rosie closed the curtains long enough to change into her nightgown, then opened them again. The pale pink rayon curtains were thin enough to let the room brighten as the sun rose, but she couldn't risk oversleeping. Not when Pop would be up by seven, listening to the news radio as he waited for Mom to wake up and make his coffee. Rosie considered the alarm clock, but the bell rang so loudly half her housemates would hear it too, and none of them would forgive her for a 6 A.M. wake-up on Saturday. She'd just have to sleep lightly and wake up with the sun, assuming she could sleep at all. She lay down, ready to worry the rest of the night away, and a few seconds later, sunlight glowed warm and red through her eyelids.

She rolled to her feet without letting herself think about it, swallowing away the nausea of an abrupt awakening after too little sleep. The clock, ticking away so loudly it should have kept her awake all by itself, read a quarter after six. The sun hadn't hardly come up yet, not really. She'd been just as sensitive to it as she'd hoped. Rosie bumped along the wall all the way out of her room and to the bathroom to stare at her hollow-eyed reflection in dismay.

Fifteen minutes of cold water, hair curlers, makeup and tooth-brushing later, she reckoned she wouldn't scare the horses, although even with blush, she still looked nearly as pale as Pearl Daly. Back in her room, she found a red plaid shirt that she reckoned might help her color, and tied her hair up in a kerchief to match. Jeans with the cuffs rolled up, bare feet into the black flats, and she slipped out the front door without her housemates ever knowing she'd been home. She'd catch heck for that later too, but she didn't want to have to face anybody else before seeing her parents.

The sky lit gold all along the horizon, catching a low band of clouds that sprayed pink toward the river. The heat hadn't broken overnight, but it had cooled off just enough that early-morning mugginess felt nicely warm instead of like breathing a lake. Rosie nodded greetings or waved to the one or two other people out so early on a Saturday morning, but she had most of the walk to her folks' house to herself and the sunrise. It didn't help her figure out how she would tell them what had happened, but at least it made for a nice morning.

Their house looked quiet, just like all the others along their street.

A pretty little front yard with carefully kept flowers was bright after the night's relative coolness, not yet struggling with the day's heat. A car sat in the driveway, and curtains were pulled across the big front window to keep prying eyes from looking in at night. Rosie went around to the side door, letting herself into the empty kitchen. Another big window above the sink looked over the back yard, where two apple trees shaded a yellowing lawn. Rosie filled the coffee pot with water and wiped down an already-clean counter to make the white surface gleam, then twitched pretty yellow curtains over the smaller front window open. She had two cups of coffee ready when her father wandered in with the air of a man following his nose. "Blessed are the coffee sprites." He kissed her hair, then took a seat across the kitchen table and leaned in to first inhale deeply, then sip tentatively at the hot drink. "Perfect. You always use the right amount of sugar. What are you doing here so early, honey?"

"I knew Mom wouldn't be up yet and you'd be suffering without your coffee," Rosie said with a smile. "How are you, Poppy?"

"Content." He raised his cup to her, returning the smile. He didn't look so old, her Pop, dressed in checkered cotton sleeping pants that matched the robe he wore over them and a white T-shirt. His hair was still real dark, cut handsomely, and his eyes were bright and thoughtful. He'd fought in the first war. When he went back at the age of forty-six to volunteer for the second, they assigned him a 4-A, thanked him for his service in the Great War and told him he was too old now, and sent him home again. He'd come back both relieved and disappointed, but Rosie, who had just seen Rich off, had been nothing but glad. Her mom had been too: Rosie thought she'd aged five years the day Pop went to see about joining up. She still had silver in her hair where she hadn't before, and Rosie thought she'd been even more relieved than the younger women when the European war ended. It meant Pop was all the less likely to get called up, because the Japs couldn't hold out forever. They just couldn't, not with the Nazis defeated and the world setting itself back to rights.

Her expression must have gotten bleak, because Pop smiled again, more gently this time. "Worried about Rich, sweetheart? Don't be. He'll be safe at home soon. Is that what got you up so early today?" His smile grew teasing. "Or have you not been to bed yet? Ah, to be young and free . . .."

"I slept," Rosie said defensively. "No, it's not Rich, Poppy. Some crazy things happened at the factory last night and I wanted to tell you and Mom before rumor got around."

Pop put his coffee cup down, suddenly worried. "What happened, Ro? Are you all right?"

"I'm fine. I really am. I—"

"Don't tell me you finally learned how to make coffee, Steven." Rosie's mother emerged from the hall to blink sleepily at her daughter. "I should have known better. Good morning, sweetheart. What are you doing here so early?" Like Pop, Mom had dark hair and eyes, though Rosie had gotten some of Pop's height and breadth of shoulder. It hadn't been until she started working in the factory that her waist had whittled down so she had some of Mom's curves, too. Also like Pop, Mom kissed Rosie's hair before shuffling over to the coffee pot in her blue slippers to pour herself a cup. Her robe had frayed at the hems and worn thin over her bottom, like she'd spent a lot of hours in it. Pop's didn't show that kind of wear, but then, Mom bought Pop's clothes for him. Rosie bet she either hadn't thought of one for herself, or thought Pop would eventually buy one for her. He wouldn't, though, not unless somebody put it in his mind, because men didn't often notice that things like that needed replacing.

"You're up early," Pop said to her.

Mom's eyebrows rose. "I smelled the coffee and thought I must be dreaming. It's really not difficult to make, Steve."

"It's better when you make it."

"Everything is better when someone else makes it." Mom kissed Pop's head, too, then sat down beside him with her coffee. "Well, Rose?"

Rosie's heartbeat surged and she had to put her coffee down so it wouldn't spill. "First off, I'm all right. Okay? You see that I'm fine, right?"

Mom went pale, putting her own coffee down. "What happened?"

"One of the supervisors, PFC Goode, just back from Europe, went crazy at work. He attacked me last night." Her Mom inhaled sharply and Rosie rushed on, afraid she wouldn't be allowed to finish. "I had a rivet gun. I . . . I shot him with it. He's dead. And I thought you'd better hear it from me before it got out into the news."

Mom jumped up, knocking her coffee into a spin as she ran around the table to pull Rosie to her feet, inspecting her for injury. Exclamations of concern rattled out of her, so predictable Rosie hardly heard them through her own protests that she was fine. Pop, though. Pop only put his hand out, keeping Mom's cup from spilling entirely, and looked at Rosie with a terrible sympathy and regret in his eyes. Rosie found herself mouthing "I'm okay" at him around the louder promises to her mother, but his expression didn't change. He only shook his head, not enough to gain Mom's attention, and looked as if his heart had broken.

"—home *right now.* Steven, you'll just have to ask Paul down the street if we can borrow that big Chevy truck of his to pack Rosie's things into. We—"

"What? Wait, what, Mom? I'm not moving back home! This happened at the factory, not home, and even if it had, well, he's *dead* now, Mom. I'm fine."

"How can you say that so callously?" Mom demanded. "It's not that simple, Rose Anne! You don't just kill someone and walk away from it *fine.* You need to be at home, where people who love you can take care of you."

"Mom, I'm fine. Mom—*Pop,*" Rosie said desperately, but her Pop shook his head again, lines that had never been there before appearing in his face until he looked far older and more haggard than Rosie had ever seen him.

"I think you'd better listen to your mother, Roro. This kind of thing doesn't always hit you all at once. It's better if you're somewhere safe, with people who care."

Rosie bit back a protest, watching the changes come over him, then shook off her mother's hands and sat down again, suddenly feeling like she had to move and speak carefully. "You killed somebody, didn't you," she asked softly. "In the war. I mean you *know* you killed someone, not just . . ." She swallowed and made a helpless motion with her hands. Soldiers killed people. That was their job. Anybody knew that someone who'd been in war might well have killed a man, but it was different, knowing for sure you'd done it, rather than just figuring one of your bullets had taken a life. But Pop had never talked about it. Most of the veterans of the Great War didn't.

"It's not just that, Rosie," Pop said just as quietly. "It's seeing the men around you die, too. It builds up in a way you don't—you can't—understand, and I'm glad you never will."

"He killed Ruby McAnly."

Pop flinched back and Mom's voice shot up. "Ruby? Jean-Marie's friend Ruby? You *saw* him? Rose Anne Ransom, you are moving home *right now*—"

"I didn't see it. She died a few days ago. He didn't just go crazy and come after me, Pop. He's been killing girls since he got back. Everybody just thought they were quitting and going back to their men, but they're dead. Ruby, and probably Carol Ann McKay, and I heard that four Negro girls went missing too. It's not the same. I know it's not the same, Poppy, but people around me *did* die, and I stopped him from ever doing that again. He wasn't just a man, Poppy. He was a bad man. Not like soldiers. Mostly soldiers are just . . . they're just like you, aren't they? Even if they're Japs or Nazis or Russians or whoever. Most of them probably aren't *bad*. Most of them are probably just people. PFC Goode was bad. He *ate* them, Poppy. He ate Ruby."

"Oh my God." Mom's knees weakened and Pop stood to help her back to her chair. Rosie covered her face, reckoning she couldn't have found a worse way to convince her mother that she'd be safe living in the house she shared with Irene and the others.

"I'm okay," she said again, into her palms. "I really am. It was terrible, but I'm all right. Maybe I'm still too shocked to be shaken up, Mom, but I promise I'll come home and let you take care of me if I start falling apart. I really will. But right now—see, don't you see?" She lifted her face from her hands. "If I run right home and let myself be scared to death, then even if I didn't get hurt, he still wins. Mom, what would have happened if the suffragists had just given up when they got scared? We wouldn't be able to vote. We might not even be able to work in the factories, even if all the men *had* gone off to war."

"Oh, no," Mom said hoarsely. "You don't get to turn this into a suffragist movement, Rose Anne Ransom. It's not the same thing at all. Equality is one thing, Rosie. Killing someone—"

"Kept me alive," Rosie finished.

Mom lost all her color again and Pop put a hand over hers, gently reassuring. He never stopped watching Rosie, though. "I know you did what you had to, Roro. I know you wouldn't have gone that far if it hadn't been necessary. I won't push you to come home right now—"

"*Steven!*"

"—even though I think your mother is right. Just remember you can, sweetheart. Remember we'll be here when you need us."

"Steven Alexander Ransom!"

Pop said, "Beth," as quietly as he'd said everything else, and Mom's mouth closed into a thin line. Pop squeezed her hand and Mom looked away from Rosie, toward the sunrise spilling in through kitchen's front window. It caught glitters of tears in her eyes, though she kept them from falling.

Guilt clenched Rosie's stomach. "I promise I'll be careful, Mom. I promise I'll come home if I need help. But right now I'm okay, I really am. I just wanted to see you and tell you what had happened. And . . . I probably shouldn't have said that stuff about him eating Ruby. I don't think the cops want that bandied around. Don't mention it, please?"

Pop, dryly, said, "I don't think we were planning on talking about any of it much, Ro," and in spite of her upset, Mom looked at him disbelievingly.

"The whole block will be over before lunch, Steve. They'll hear it on the radio and want to know what really happened."

"What the radio says will be true," Rosie said. "John Goode attacked me and I defended myself and another girl. Tell them I used a rivet gun. That should be enough to keep them going for weeks." She gulped her coffee, suddenly tired.

"There was another girl?" Mom and Pop both sharpened, like that somehow made it all closer to okay. Rosie stared at them over the edge of her cup, then lowered it enough to speak.

"Didn't I say that? Yes, there was. But I'm not even going to tell you her name, because if they don't mention it on the news she sure as heck doesn't need to have people asking her about it, and if I don't tell you, you can't tell anybody else."

The tears in Mom's eyes faded as she took offense. "Rosie, you don't think we'd spread gossip like that, do you?"

"I think it'd be really easy to let it slip." Rosie stood to rinse her cup and put it in the rack beside the sink. "I also think if I'm here when the neighbors start showing up I'll never get home, so I'm going to go before it gets any later. I'll call tonight, okay? I swear I'll keep safe."

Her parents rose and came to hug her, their warmth and scent so comforting and familiar that Rosie wished, just for a moment, that she *could* stay and hide away from the whole world for a while. But she couldn't, not with Pearl Daly half-crazy with vampire blood and Hank's secret *Ex Libris* society to learn about and probably a million other things waiting on her. Rosie unwound reluctantly, kissed both her parents' cheeks, and slipped back out the kitchen door into the muggy morning.

Mr Raymond across the street lifted his hand in greeting as Rosie came out the door. She waved back and put on a burst of speed before he picked up his morning paper. Even so, he called after her when he read the headlines, but she pretended she hadn't heard and scurried down the block. Past old Mrs O'Donnell's house at a crisp walk, like the old lady would appear, leaning on her cane and shouting questions that the whole block would hear, because she never cottoned on to the idea that her deafness didn't affect other peoples' hearing. At least Milly Jane Jones lived at the other end of the street. She and Rosie had played together ever since they were babies without ever being friends. Milly would be stopping by the Ransoms' house later, just to look down her pointy nose and say of course that's the kind of thing that could happen to a girl who worked in a factory. Worst of all would be Rich's parents, whose worry might even outstrip Rosie's own folks', because who would want their son marrying a killer? Rosie couldn't imagine Rich letting them put the kibosh on their relationship, but then, that was a whole 'nother can of worms.

Imagining what everybody on the block would have to say got Rosie all the way to her own front door. The girls were still sleeping after their late

Friday night, and Rosie tiptoed through the house and fell onto her bed without even undressing.

Whispers woke her up what felt like two minutes later. She rolled over, pressing the pillow aside, to see all her housemates crowded into her doorway like an assortment of wildflowers stuffed into a small vase. One of them, Dorothy, shrieked when Rosie moved, then stuffed her knuckles against her mouth. "Oh my gosh. Don't kill me!"

All of them burst into nervous laughter, Barb elbowing Dorothy hard enough to make her wince, and Wanda's tall blond head poking above the others. "Did you really kill somebody, Rosie? It's splashed all over the papers. Did you really?"

"He was trying to kill me." Rosie put her head under her pillow, trying to remember if she'd closed the bedroom door before she collapsed into sleep. Marge, her calm voice deep enough to be distinguishable from the others even from under a pillow, asked something, and Rosie loosened the pillow enough to listen.

"I said, were you scared? What's it feel like to kill somebody?"

"Is it *awful*?" Wanda asked hopefully. "Do you hate yourself? Were you covered in blood? Are you going to *jail*?"

"I don't see how you could've done it," Barb said loudly. "I don't care what the papers say. You're just a girl."

"I'm a riveter," Rosie said into the bedclothes, "and there was a rivet gun. I used it. It was awful and scary and I don't hate myself and I didn't get covered in blood, and the cops know I was protecting myself, so they sent me home."

Four voices chorused, "You got *arrested*?!" in horrified glee. Rosie groaned and rolled away from them, pulling the pillow over her ears again. "I was taken in for questioning. I wasn't arrested. C'mon, girls, I haven't had any sleep. Can't you let it go?"

"*No!*" echoed into her room from all four of them, and then Wanda offered, "I'll make you breakfast if you get up and tell us all about it. C'mon, Ro. Heck, you're dressed already."

"What time is it?" Rosie edged her head out far enough to see the clock, which read a quarter after eleven. That meant about six hours of sleep, in bits and pieces. Not enough, but judging from the bevy of girls in the door, she wouldn't be getting more any time soon. "All right, fine, but there better be coffee."

She crawled out of bed and her housemates scattered back, giving her more distance to pass through the door than she could ever need. Barb even clutched her hands over her heart and curved her shoulders in, as if fearing Rosie's touch. Rosie looked at her own hands, wondering if the Redeemer magic would do anything to normal people. "I'm not dangerous, Barb. I'm the same person I was yesterday."

"Yesterday I didn't know you were a killer." The phone rang and Barb bolted for it, leaving Rosie without a response. She hadn't *been* a killer yesterday. She hadn't known she could be. Dorothy watched her like she'd become some kind of celebrity, but Wanda edged back too. Marge didn't seem too bothered, but then, as long as her paycheck made it to the bank on time, not much bothered Marge. Even so, she eyed Rosie with interest, no doubt counting on the gossip currency that the inside scoop would buy her. They trooped out behind her to the living room, spreading out in a half-circle as Barb extended the phone toward Rosie as if it had gotten dirty. "It's Irene. She says the cops are at Jean-Marie's house, and they're looking for you."

SEVEN

They'd found Ruby's things in Goode's apartment, Irene said. They'd come to Jean's house to ask her to identify them: dungarees and shirt and the red-checkered kerchief Ruby had worn around her hair on Monday. Irene hadn't said more before Rosie asked Marge, the only girl in the house with a car of her own—a blue Ford Standard sedan, years older than Jean-Marie's Oldsmobile and not nearly as expensive to start with, but still her very own—for a lift to Jean's house, and hurried out the door.

Jean's thin wailing could be heard from the street, and a black-and-white sat in her driveway. Rosie jumped out of Marge's sedan, thanked her for the ride, and ran into the house to find Irene sitting on the floor with her arms around Jean, for all the good it did. An uncomfortable police officer stood across the room, looking like he hoped the crying woman would forget he was there. Jean clutched Ruby's shirt, rubbing tear-soaked bloodstains against her cheeks and hands. She looked up when Rosie came in. "I have to tell her Nan. How am I going to tell her Nan?"

"Oh, honey." Rosie crouched beside her, stroking her hair. Jean curled over the shirt, sobbing anew, and Rosie met Irene's eyes over Jean's head. Irene wore one of Jean's shirts and a borrowed skirt, both of which were too big for her and neither of which did the gold undertones of her skin any favors. In fact, she looked yellow from exhaustion, and her eyes were dull with worry. "Did either of you sleep at all?"

Irene shook her head. Rosie tilted her head toward one of the bedrooms. "Go rest."

"Where? Jean is going to need her bed and I don't want to take Ruby's."

"Ruby and I shared a room," Jean whispered in a choked voice. "The other one's a guest room. They said there wasn't anything left, Rosie. There wasn't any body to identify. Just some bones, in her clothes. That was all that was left of anybody. Carol Ann McKay doesn't even have bones left. I hate him. I wish he wasn't dead, so I could kill him and kill him and kill him."

"I know. I know. I'm sorry, Jeannie. I'm sorry."

"Ro," Irene said in a low voice, "the cops were asking a lot of questions about what you'd said happened last night."

Rosie's hands turned cold against Jean-Marie's hair. "What did you tell them?"

Irene gave her a withering look. "That the supe attacked you and you shot him with a riveting gun and you were rattled and sick about it all and that I thought that creep Hank wanted to take advantage of you. I didn't tell them you'd gone crazy."

"Gosh, thanks."

"Here you go, Miss Diaz." Detective Johnson came out of the kitchen with a cup of coffee, crouching to offer it to Jean. "My wife says I make a mean cup."

Jean accepted it with shaking hands and took a swallow that left her coughing. "That's not standard-issue."

"Put a shot of whiskey in," Johnson confessed. "Might be why the old lady thinks I make a mean cup." A smile ghosted across Jean's face and Johnson jerked his chin in Rosie's direction, inviting her to stand. More like ordering her to stand, since she bet he wouldn't take it kindly if she refused. She squeezed Jean's shoulder and rose. Johnson gestured toward the kitchen and beckoned the other officer along.

Only a single cup's worth was missing from the coffee pot, and the whiskey Johnson had laced Jean's coffee with was nowhere to be seen. Rosie poured herself some coffee and opened Jean's fridge, looking for milk, as Johnson, behind her, said, "I wouldn't mind a cup of that myself, if you don't mind."

Rosie smiled. "Milk? Sure thing, Detective. Glad you take such good care of yourself."

Johnson chuckled and Rosie poured him a cup too. The crispness she'd noticed about him earlier had long since faded. His collar was rumpled and sweat-stained now, and his graying hair, though ringed where his hat usually sat, also looked like he'd been shoving his hands through it all night. The other officer looked fresher, although he wasn't any younger than Johnson. "Officer Moran," Johnson said. "He came on just before we got to Miss Diaz's place, so he's sharper than I am. Coffee, Moran? This is the young lady who defended herself and Pearl Daly last night."

"It's not right I should say congratulations, but I might anyway." Moran's tenor sounded like it belonged on a fourteen-year-old boy, not a man in his fifties. "Glad you got out of there safe last night, Miss Ransom."

"Me too." Rosie got Moran a cup of coffee, too, and sat at the table, feeling her limited sleep and thinking how much worse it was for Johnson, who hadn't gotten any at all. "Don't get me wrong, Detective, I'm glad somebody's here with Jean-Marie, but why are you still here? It can't take that long to check that those were Ruby's clothes."

"You're right. I wanted to talk to you again, Miss Ransom, and I thought it might be more comfortable outside of the station." Johnson sat across from her. Moran leaned against the kitchen sink, holding his coffee mug like he didn't know what to do with it.

Rosie sank her head over her own cup and sipped. "You're right. You do make a mean cup of coffee. What did you want to talk about?"

"Pearl Daly had a lot to say last night, once she showed us the mess at Goode's place. I wondered what you might say about it."

The coffee turned to hot lead in Rosie's belly. She swallowed carefully. "I guess that depends on what she said. I know I shouldn't have tried to protect her, but she seemed so lost."

"She said Goode had her in . . ." Johnson dug a notebook out and flipped it open, finding a page of scribbled notes in handwriting so awful, Rosie couldn't make out a word of it, upside-down. "'Thrall'. That was the word she used, *thrall*. Know what that means, Miss Ransom?"

"Like a slave?"

"That's right. Only she said it was magical." He emphasized the word. "Said Goode wasn't crazy at all, just a—" He consulted his notes again. "A vampire. And that's why he had to kill all those girls, to eat them to stay alive. She said she got splashed with some of his blood, and it made her have to do what he said."

Rosie's jaw fell open. "She said what?" *Irene* hadn't believed Rosie, not even with Hank there to back her up. She couldn't imagine what Pearl had been thinking, trying to tell the cops the truth.

"You called him a monster last night, Miss Ransom." Johnson's laborious note-checking and word-finding suddenly vanished into a keen look. "Why did you use that word?"

"I told you last night, Detective. He was killing girls and eating them. I don't know what else you'd call somebody like that, except a monster. Did she think you'd believe her?"

"She thought you would corroborate her story."

Rosie put her coffee cup down and stared straight at Johnson in a good show of offense and disbelief. "If I'd been involved with somebody killing and eating people I'd probably make up a crazy story about why I hadn't left, too, Detective. I'd probably do just about anything to make it look like I hadn't had any choice." Her shoulders slumped and she looked into her cream-colored coffee. "She was awful scared, Detective. I don't think she felt like she did have a choice. Sometimes girls get like that, you know? They get in over their heads with some jerk who's bad business and they can't get out again. She probably thought she was next if she didn't help him. In some ways she might even be worse hurt than the dead girls. She's gotta live with what she's done."

"Just like you do." Johnson tapped his pen against his notepad. "I've seen men kill people before, Miss Ransom. You're holding up awfully well."

"My parents think it just hasn't hit me yet and I'm liable to fall apart at any moment." Rosie glanced toward Moran, who had put his coffee aside and watched her without any of the discomfort he'd displayed earlier. Watching to see if she gave anything away. She wondered if she had, and shrugged, both at her own curiosity and the detective's waiting gaze. "They're probably right. I'm so tired right now I'm not sure any of it feels real. What're you going to do with poor Pearl?"

"She's got an appointment with a court psychologist this morning. He'll determine if she's fit to stand trial or if she's crazy, and if she's crazy, she'll be committed for her own safety. She probably should be anyway."

"At Eloise Asylum?" Rosie shuddered, no longer performing. "I've heard about that place. Poor Pearl."

"Poor Pearl," Johnson agreed with a shake of his head. "Good thing you're smarter than she is, Miss Ransom, or you might find yourself there too."

Puzzlement wrinkled Rosie's forehead. "Detective, I don't even know how I should take that. Do you think I'm lying to you? Do you think Pearl *isn't*?" A faint smile crept over her mouth. "Do you believe in monsters, Detective?"

Johnson flipped the notebook shut and finished his coffee in one swallow. "I believe there's something strange going on in this city, and I think you know more than you're saying. Come on, Moran. We're done here, for now. Give Miss Diaz our condolences. Tell her the police will be notifying Miss McAnly's family. She doesn't have to do that herself."

Rosie stood when he did, saying, "Thanks," uncertainly. She walked them out the front door, past Irene and Jean, who had at least gotten to the long blue living-room couch, and stopped on the hot porch to watch the officers head for their patrol car. "Detective?"

Johnson, halfway into the car, shaded his eyes against the glaring sun and looked up at Rosie with the door a barrier between himself and her. "Why do you think there's something going on here? Have there been other murders like Ruby's?"

The corner of Johnson's mouth turned up, like she'd asked a good question. "Police business, Miss. Nothing I can say. You call me if you remember anything else, Miss Ransom. You keep in touch." He got in the car and they drove away, leaving the heavy smell of gasoline fumes lingering behind them. Kids playing in the street scattered away, then returned to kicking the can and throwing baseballs, like it was any other Saturday morning.

Rosie pressed her hands into the porch railing, dropping her head to loosen knots that had appeared while the detective questioned her. She didn't have anything to hide, she reminded herself. She couldn't help it if the truth sounded crazy.

"The whiskey helped," Irene said from inside the front door. "Jean is half-asleep. I thought if I left her alone, she might drift off."

"Thanks." Rosie leaned her bottom against the railing and folded her arms. "I know you don't hardly know her, so thank you, Irene. You've been a champ. You should go home and get some sleep."

Irene came to lean her hips into the railing, looking at the yellowing grass in the yard. "Everybody at home read the papers already?"

"Yeah."

"Then I wouldn't get any sleep. I might as well stay here with Jean. I was really worried that creep wouldn't bring you home last night, Rosie. You don't know anything about him except—"

"Except he believed my story." Rosie tilted her chin up to look at the veranda ceiling. "And that Detective Johnson sent him to drive me home, and Johnson seems pretty solid."

"What'd he want?"

"Pearl told him the truth about Goode. He wanted to see if I was willing to tell the same tale."

Irene straightened in astonishment. "She told a cop there were vampires?"

"Shh." Rosie laughed quietly. "Yeah. I think he even half-believes her. He said—well, he didn't *say*—that there's something funny going on in Detroit. More than PFC Goode. Hank said something about a—a *demonus* . . . no, darn it. *Daemon rex*. A king demon, anyways, somewhere in the Midwest. That's what he's supposed to be trying to find himself, and I think maybe Johnson's on to it, a little bit. He knows something stra . . ."

She trailed off as Irene favored her with a hard look. "You can't let this guy's crazy stories take over your mind, Rosie. You gotta keep your feet on the ground. Detective Johnson doesn't think there are demons or monsters running around Detroit. At least, nothing more monstrous than men, which can be bad enough. I told you about Danny O'Brien back in Brooklyn."

"You did. I'm sorry I'm worrying you, Rene."

"But you're not going to change your story."

Irene held herself a little away from Rosie, the same way Barb and Dorothy had done at home. It hurt more when Irene did it, though, and Rosie whispered, "I'm still me."

"Maybe, but I see you different. Are you going to run off and find your new sheik, is that what happens next?"

"He's not my sheik, Irene. He's a cop, he's a . . ." Rosie sighed. "But yes, I am. Because he knows more than I do about what's going on, and I need to find out. I'll come back this afternoon and check on Jean, okay? I can bring you some clothes that fit . . ."

Irene brushed her hand over the yellow blouse she'd borrowed. "This is fine. Nobody's going to be coming over to see me, anyway. They'll be coming to help Jean as soon as word gets out."

"You're a good friend, Rene."

"The best." Irene's smile looked as forced as her voice sounded, but at least she'd made the effort. Rosie didn't make it worse by trying to hug her, and just went down the steps into the roasting afternoon sun. She'd wilted by the time a tram came, but for a small mercy, there were seats available, and she sank into one gratefully.

"Just off shift?" asked a sympathetic girl. Rosie smiled without answering and leaned her head on the window, letting the tram's motion, creaks and all, lull her into drowsing. Goode's face drifted behind her eyelids, first the arrogance of his sneer and then the surprise of his death. Rosie shuddered and sat up, focusing on the heat haze softening the skyline and trying to erase the images from her mind.

"Did you hear about the awful thing at the Highfield Road factory last night?" the friendly girl asked. "It's all over the papers. A supe went crazy and attacked a girl. She killed him with her riveting gun. How's that for a kick in the pants?"

"I heard."

"The papers say the police are investigating a lot of other missing girls from the same factory. I'm darn glad I work at Birch Walk factory. I'd be scared spitless to go back to work there."

"Why? The crazy supe is dead."

"But the girl isn't! Who knows what she might do! They say soldiers change when they've killed somebody. Maybe she'll become a maniac!"

"I bet she just wants some sleep." Rosie got off two stops earlier than she needed to and sat on the nearest bench for a minute, looking bleakly after the tram. Everybody gossiped. She knew that. She did it herself. But she'd never thought what it felt like to be in the middle of the gossip storm, not when something big had happened. It didn't make any sense, the idea that other girls might be afraid to go back to the factory. She'd think they'd feel safer, knowing the danger was gone. Except maybe never having seen it in the first place made it worse somehow. She pressed her hands against the warm planks of the bench and made herself stand up. Sitting there like a big baby wouldn't change anything, but maybe finding out what strange things Johnson had been talking about would.

The police station rose more imposingly in daylight, which didn't make sense either. Maybe she'd been too shaken up the night before to be properly cowed by it. She went inside and got an appraising look from the desk sergeant, whose paunch and bald head both put him at old enough to be her father. "What can I do for a pretty little miss like you?"

Rosie plastered on a smile. "I'm looking for Hank. Is he in?"

"The cripple? No, they said he was out all night squiring some girl around. Guess I would too, if I had the chance. He's got a great car, but who would want to play house with a guy who limps like that? I wonder what she saw in him." The sergeant looked Rosie up and down again. "What do you see in him, dolly? Moneybags?"

"Steve Rogers," Rosie said coolly. "Where does he live?"

"Aw, honey, Captain America was a wimp *before* he went to war. He didn't come home feeble. Anyway, he lives out on Lakeshore Drive. Hey, Millie, get her Hank's number, would you? Gotta give the poor sap every chance he can get if a pretty girl comes knocking. Unless you'd like to leave your number with *me*, sweetheart."

Rosie's smile strained until she thought her lips might crack. "'Sweetheart.' Gosh, that's what my pop calls me. I guess you must be about his age, huh? Fifty-five, fifty-six?" Her pop wasn't near that old, but it cleared the smirk right off the sergeant's face.

"I'm thirty-eight, you little—"

"Really?" Rosie widened her eyes. "Gosh, officer, you don't look it at all. I guess that's why they didn't take you in the army, huh? Afraid you'd have a heart attack or something? That must really sting, knowing all those other men your age are out there doing their part for the war effort and you're just stuck here behind a desk like some kinda patsy."

The secretary, a trim woman in her forties, stepped up to offer Rosie a folded piece of paper across the sergeant's desk. She held on to it longer than necessary, making certain Rosie met her eyes and saw the sparkle of approval in them. Rosie chirruped, "Thanks! Look, I'm friends with Pearl Daly and I heard she got herself in some trouble last night. Is she here?"

The desk sergeant snarled, "None of your business, you little—" while the secretary smiled and offered, "They've taken her out to talk to a psychologist. I think they'll be letting her go, though. This is all bad business and they won't want it aired around too much. Arresting a young woman in conjunction with the rash of missing girls and deaths would just bring too much attention to the whole mess."

"Millie! You can't go talking police business to any nosy little girl who wanders in here!"

Millie put her fingertips over pursed lips in a mimicry of apology, then snapped her fingers. "Oh, darn, I forgot to spell out Hank's last name for you. Give me that paper back, hon." She gave Rosie the gimlet eye as Rosie began a protest, so Rosie subsided and handed the paper back. Millie scribbled on it, then returned it to her. "Take care now, honey. Tell Hank hello."

Rosie smiled and unfolded the paper on the way out the door, then shot a surprised look back over her shoulder. Millie, watching, winked before going back to her desk, and Rosie left the station, smiling and smug, with both Hank's phone number and the building address where Pearl had been taken.

EIGHT

Two bakeries lay between the station and the psychologist's offices, and the scent of fresh pastries made Rosie's stomach cramp with hunger. She cast a glance at the sun—past overhead—and counted the hours since she'd last eaten. Enough that she could indulge in a doughnut. She scavenged the emergency dollar she kept folded in the pocket of every pair of dungarees, bought two doughnuts, and stopped at a corner pay phone to call Hank's number with the change. An English woman answered, told her Hank was sleeping late, and offered to take a message. "No, it's okay," Rosie said. "I don't know when I'll be near a phone he could call me on, so I'll just call back later, thanks."

"I insist. It's so nice to hear a young lady calling him."

"Um, okay. You could tell him Rosie's trying to meet Pearl at Harper Hospital, but I'm not sure what time she'll get out. Thanks." Rosie hung up and hurried down the street toward the hospital. A shaded bench across the street offered some relief from the heat and gave her full view of the front doors. Rosie tucked her feet under herself and nibbled doughnuts to keep herself awake while she waited for Pearl's release.

At least, she hoped it would be Pearl's release. If they kept her in custody, Rosie and Hank really would have to stage a jailbreak. The idea of tweaking the loutish desk sergeant made her grin, but she doubted Detective Johnson would look the other way if they got caught. Especially when he already thought she was lying about something.

The sun slipped farther across the sky, until the shaded bench sat in the full afternoon glare. Rosie squinted into the sun, unwilling to leave and risk missing Pearl, but wishing she had a bathroom, water, and more food. And a hat. She lifted her hands to block the sun, and startled as Hank spoke from behind her. "You're getting burned. I'll spell you for a while."

Rosie twisted to put her arms in the shadow of her body, checking their color. "Darn it. I've been working days so long I forgot about sunburn. Was that your mother I talked to? She has a nice voice."

"Very British," Hank said, sounding as British has she had. "She works to keep the accent." He sat down beside Rosie, extracting two Coke bottles from a bag over his shoulder. "You looked parched."

Rosie took a bottle gratefully and held it against her cheek to feel its chill. "Thanks. Except I can't drink this until I use the bathroom. Which one is your real accent?"

"They both are," Hank said, sounding American again. "I use *ske-jewl* instead of *shed-yule*, though, and *tomayto* instead of *tomahto*. Except when in Rome. They'll probably let you use the bathroom across the street there."

"I hope so." Rosie balanced the Coke bottle on the bench and jumped up to wait on traffic so she could cross over. Her legs tingled from the sudden change in pressure. Rosie groaned, bending to touch her toes and stretch the protesting muscles. "I've been sitting too long. I'll be back in a minute." She jogged across the street and up the steps, pulling the hospital door open. A secretary looked up and Rosie said, "Bad luck, having to work on Saturday. At least you have a fan."

"It doesn't do enough." The woman, whose hair was limp even in the breeze, smiled tiredly. "Can I help you? You've been waiting outside all day."

"Oh, you know how men are. He said he'd be there at noon, and it's three when he shows up. Do you have a bathroom I could use?"

The secretary glanced out the doors at Hank, who had sprawled across the bench, a Coke in one hand. "He's a dish, but is he tasty enough to wait three hours in the sun for? Sure, down the hall to your left. The lock sticks, so give it a shake before you cry for help."

Rosie laughed. "Thanks for the warning." The bathroom mirror confirmed her sunburn, reddening the tops of her cheeks and a V down her chest where her blouse buttoned, but her arms only looked strong and browned, not burned. She used the toilet, washed her hands, then drank a few palmsful of water from the faucet, reckoning the soda awaiting her wouldn't be enough. The lock didn't stick, and she left to say thanks to the secretary and to see Hank on his feet across the street, talking to Detective Johnson, Officer Moran, and Pearl Daly. Rosie ran for the door, but Hank flicked his fingers down low, by his hip, where it would hardly be noticed. She slowed and he dropped his chin in a minute nod, all without seeming to take his attention from Johnson. Rosie backed up and leaned in a window where she could see without, she hoped, being seen. Hank did a lot of talking, gesturing to Pearl, then around at the city, and offered Johnson a steady series of smiles and touches on the arm or shoulder. Over the course of a few minutes, Johnson's visible reluctance slowly turned to agreement. He spoke to Pearl, who lit up with disbelieving hope and then clung to Hank's arm as if he'd thrown a lifeline. Johnson clapped Hank on the shoulder, jutted his chin at Moran, and strode off down the street toward a distant patrol car. By that time the secretary had joined her at the window, peering out curiously. "What's going on?"

"No idea. He asked me to wait inside, so I did."

"You got a reason to avoid the cops, honey?"

Rosie shook her head. "No, my guy there is with the cops. I guess that was just business. You know. Nothing to worry my pretty little head over."

"Isn't it always. Who's the girl?"

"Friend of mine. I was waiting for her, really. She had a bad night and I'm hoping it's better now." Rosie smiled at the secretary. "Thanks for letting me use the bathroom."

"Anytime."

The woman went back to her desk, leaving Rosie to case the street and make sure Johnson had driven off before she came out and crossed over to Hank and Pearl. "What was that about?"

Pearl looked positively star-struck at Hank. "They were going to bring me back to the station, but he just talked them into letting me go. He said to think of the publicity and how they didn't want it getting around what had really happened and the detective started looking like maybe he was right and then started nodding and said I could go home now." Her joy crumpled into fear. "Except I don't know where home is anymore. I was living with—with—"

"Can you go to your folks?" Rosie asked as gently as she could. Pearl shook her head violently enough that Rosie didn't press it.

"I know a place. It's not the greatest, but you'll be safe there." Hank said, meeting Rosie's eyes over Pearl's head. A fist tightened around Rosie's gut as she understood why he hadn't wanted Johnson to see her. If she had to Redeem Pearl, if it killed her, the only thing saving Rosie from jail herself might be the fact that Johnson hadn't known she was there.

Rosie cast a despairing look over her shoulder at the secretary she'd left behind, and thought of asking Millie back at the station about Pearl. Johnson not knowing right now wouldn't save her. He'd find out soon enough, if things went badly.

"So it just can't go wrong," she said under her breath. Hank's gaze sharpened on her, but she shrugged it away. "Come on. Let's get Pearl somewhere safe. She's had a rough day."

"My car's down the street." Hank led them half a block while Rosie searched for the Jaguar's smooth lines, and frowned in confusion when he stopped at a dark blue Ford Coupe, one of the last that had come off the assembly lines before the war effort started. "The Jag's the Friday-night car," he said with a faint smile. "Even if I'm working. Mom takes it the rest of the time, so I get something more ordinary."

"Still pretty sweet to have your choice of two," Rosie said. "Most of us have to get along with one or none. Pearl, why don't you ride in front with Hank?"

"Really?" Pearl looked even more waifish by day than she had the night before, her pale skin nearly hollow in the sunlight, like the blood no longer came to its surface. Her eyes were worse, large and sad and almost empty, and she'd never changed out of her factory jumpsuit, which hung loosely on her small frame.

Rosie nodded. "Really." Mostly because she figured if Pearl got to ride in the back seat alone, odds were heavy in favor of her deciding to risk her luck on the streets and throwing herself out of the car. "Enjoy the view."

Pearl gave her such a pathetic, grateful smile that guilt surged through

Rosie. She climbed into the back seat just so she didn't have to meet Pearl's eyes again, and kept quiet while they drove into Corktown. Lots of folks ended up there, starting with Irish back in the day and just carrying right on until today, people from all over the place. Pearl wouldn't be much noticed in a part of town with all sorts living in it. Sometimes hiding in plain sight did the trick.

It took a long time, with Hank's limp, to get up the four flights of stairs to a one-bedroom apartment that almost overlooked the river. By the time they got there Rosie's curiosity overcame her caution. "Does this belong to your library friends?"

"Library friends? I thought you were a cop." Pearl sank down into a green leaf-patterned velvet sofa that looked like it'd been there for twenty years, but at least dust didn't rise from it. There were two other chairs, both green and trimmed with dark wood, but the fabric patterns and colors didn't quite match the sofa, and Rosie reckoned the whole suite being green with wood trim was luck, not design. She went to check out the kitchen, expecting it to have been decorated in the Roaring Twenties too, and it had been. Two straight-back woven chairs were pushed in around a small square table, and a hip-high fridge with a freezer unit on top, which meant it had been really swell when it was new, sat beside a green-and-white enameled stove on slender, curved legs. The enamel had worn off the stove's handles, and the top oven beside it didn't quite close anymore, but it was clean as a whistle and looked like it probably still worked. Rosie went back into the living room to squat in front of an ancient radio and turn the knobs to see if *it* still worked. It sat on a table of dark wood that matched the furniture's trim and had the same pretty curving legs as the kitchen stove, so it looked nice, but a couple seconds of fiddling with it didn't make it work. Rosie stood again and checked the legs of the coffee table, which matched the rest of the tables' legs. Maybe the furniture had been bought together, after all. She wondered who'd decorated it, library men or maybe their wives, and whether the wives knew what their husbands did.

Hank said to Pearl, "I read a lot," so blandly that Rosie laughed. "So it does belong to the library men."

"Yeah. They're not much for keeping the decor updated, but it's not bad, and they do keep some useful materials on hand for people like Pearl here."

What color Pearl had drained and she sat upright on the couch. "What's that supposed to mean?"

"It means demons. Vampires, in your case."

"She's not a vampire yet," Rosie protested. "She's awful close, but she's not one yet. Maybe I can save her without . . ." She swallowed and Pearl's whole demeanor changed, becoming as wary as a cornered beast.

"Without *what*? Are you gonna do to me what you did to Johnny?"

"I hope so," Rosie breathed, "only without the rivet gun. I think . . . I think maybe I can help you. I can try, at least."

"And if you can't?"

Rosie looked at Hank, who shook his head. Pearl mewled and skittered backward on the couch, not that she had far to go. "You're gonna kill me?"

Hank said, "If she has to," and Rosie burst out, "No! I sure as heck am not, not unless you put me in a corner, Pearl. But what's going to happen to you if I don't try?"

"She'll starve herself into madness, and if she's lucky somebody will put her out of her misery. At least if you do it, her soul will be saved, Rosie."

"What's he talking about?" Pearl looked about as big as a minute, crammed into the sofa corner like it could keep her safe. Rosie sighed and sat at the other end, hands folded in her lap so she didn't seem threatening.

"I guess you know vampires are real. Demons," Rosie corrected herself. Pearl gave a nod that looked more like a shiver, and Rosie nodded bigger. "So are the things that can stop them, and I'm one of them. When I killed PFC Goode last night—I saw it, Pearl. The demon got cleaned out of his soul. It's called Redeeming, and Hank here says it's the only way a demon-infested soul can get saved and go to Heaven."

"Or be reincarnated or released to Nirvana," Hank said. Rosie frowned, and Hank shrugged. "I'm just saying the Christian afterlife you're most familiar with isn't the only valid one, Miss Ransom. Cleansing a demon out of somebody's soul does even an atheist good."

"I thought atheists didn't even have souls," Rosie said tartly. "It doesn't matter, Hank. What I'm saying, Pearl, is that I think I can help you. I can try, at least."

"You mean maybe I won't end up a monster like Johnny? I didn't want to, Miss Ransom. I didn't mean to get all caught up in it. I just thought once I was, that I didn't have any choice. He said I'd die otherwise."

"He's right," Hank said heartlessly.

Rosie bounced to her feet and thrust a finger at the door. "You get out of here, mister. You're not any help at all. You're just scaring poor Pearl to pieces."

"Redeemers *kill* demons—"

"Maybe a Redeemer has never met one who hadn't turned all the way bad! I have to try!"

"And if you fail?"

"Then I'll draw a picture and put her in it until I can figure out how to help, mister library man, because I'm not giving up on her!"

"It's not that simple!"

"Why not? You know how to do it, don't you? Catch a demon in art? You'd better, or else what good are you? Out!" Rosie shouted. "Either get out or help me, because I'm *not* giving up on her!"

She'd been scared enough to be angry, back at the factory. That's how it had felt, so scared it had just clicked over into calm, like the punch-clock teeth biting at the time cards. Scared didn't feel half so strong now, except maybe scared *for* Pearl, not *of* her, but the anger came through just the same. It comforted her, like something she could work with. Like just another tool she'd learned to use at the factory. She turned away from Hank, kneeling in front of Pearl.

She could almost see *through* her, like the girl's too-thin body had lost its grip on being real and now mostly just housed a soul pocked and scarred with corruption. Rosie's anger helped her see that, although she'd have to learn to see it without anger, or she'd spend her whole life in a rage. Those dark clots retreated when she reached for them, gathering together into a coil around Pearl's heart. Pearl gasped, sweat beading on her lip and forehead, and she doubled over, wailing, "Stop it, stop, it hurts!"

"Shut up, shut up, I'm trying to think." Rosie hadn't done anything to Goode, or at least, nothing besides kill him, which she didn't want to do here. There'd been light, though, starting at the edges of her visions and rushing inward like it was drawn to Goode's spilled blood. "Give me a knife!"

Pearl screamed and Hank jolted forward with a pocketknife, the blade already exposed. Rosie grabbed Pearl's hand and poked the knife deep into the pad of her forefinger before the girl's thin strength jerked her away again with another scream.

Gold light streamed in at the corners of Rosie's eyes, spinning dizzily in her vision. She seized Pearl's hand again, snapped, "Hold her!" to Hank, and muttered, "Sorry," as she stabbed Pearl's fingers again and again, until blood welled from each fingertip. Hank swung around the back of the sofa faster than Rosie expected a man with a limp to move, and wrapped his arms around Pearl's torso as she screeched and struggled.

The light dancing in Rosie's eyes grew more agitated, diving toward Pearl's bleeding fingers, then swooping back up again. "It's not enough. Pearl, I'm *so* sorry." She didn't know enough about where blood ran to make a good deep cut that would bleed a lot without really doing any damage, and went after Pearl's other fingertips. "I'm sorry, I'm sorry, I just need enough blood for the demon to get *out!*" She sounded crazy even to herself, but Hank grunted, "Head wound," and wrapped his arm around the top of Pearl's head.

For a little thing, she fought like a cat, kicking and clawing, with blood spattering everywhere. Rosie got kicked in the belly so hard the Redeeming light faded. When she caught enough breath, she wheezed, "I've got a *knife*, you idiot, if you keep kicking I'm going to accidentally *hurt* you!"

Pearl's struggles ceased enough for her to shout, "You *are* hurting me!" and Rosie surged forward, carefully rocking the pocketknife's blade against the other girl's forehead. Blood poured free so fast, Rosie felt sick again, like she could see herself from the outside, and like what she saw was monstrous. Nice girls didn't go around cutting up other people, for Pete's sake. She and Goode suddenly didn't seem so different.

But the Redemption light shot back into view, filling the corners of Rosie's eyes and spilling forward to spin wildly over Pearl's forehead. Pearl gave up fighting and just sobbed, not even trying to wipe the blood out of her eyes. Hank jerked his coat off and wrapped it around Pearl's face, keeping blood from falling onto the factory jumpsuit Pearl still wore. Rosie pressed her hands into a steeple, almost praying without being sure what she should be praying for.

Just like with Goode, silver light eked out of Pearl's injuries, drawn toward the column of gold spinning above her. Silver, laced with black and brown and red, stains of impurity that took such a long time to shake loose. Such a long time, longer than it had with Goode, which hardly made sense, but as the minutes passed, Pearl's soul came cleaner and cleaner, until the blotches blurred into the whirl of golden light and the silvery substance snapped back into her body untarnished.

With the next breath, color flooded back into Pearl's cheeks, healthier than she'd ever looked before. Her fingertips healed, blood drawing back inside until they weren't even tender, and the thin line across her forehead sealed into an almost-invisible scar. Rosie slumped, serene exhaustion wrapping itself around her again. She passed a hand over her eyes, then lifted her gaze to find Hank staring at her in wonder, and Pearl extending her own trembling hands to gaze at them in disbelief. "I'm pink again."

She folded her hands over her heart, then her stomach, her eyes widening. "I'm hungry. I'm *hungry*, Miss Ransom! I haven't been hungry in weeks! Not for food! Oh my gosh. Oh my gosh, you did it, you helped me! You saved me! I won't be a monster now, will I? Oh, thank you!" She flung herself forward with as much ferocity as she'd fought with before, knocking Rosie backward with the force of her embrace.

"I'm really sorry," Rosie mumbled. Her bones were weary, like she'd just come off an extra shift at the factory. The deep satisfaction she'd had after Goode's death hadn't risen. All she could think was how badly she'd frightened Pearl, how she'd hurt her instead of just making it better. She'd been paralyzed with exhaustion after Goode's death, and she didn't want to move now, either, not even enough to sit up properly after Pearl released her from the hug. "I'm really, really sorry I scared you so much.

I didn't know what to do and I could've done it better, I'm really sorry and I'm glad you're okay."

"It's fine, I don't even hurt anymore, oh, I'm so *hungry*—!"

"She's not just okay," Hank said quietly. "She's a damn miracle, Miss Ransom. I never heard of anybody doing what you just did. If you can do that to a full-fledged demon, exorcise it without killing the host—" He sounded awed.

"I just about made a mess of it with Pearl. I don't reckon a full-on demon would let me sit and poke it full of holes so I could try. Pearl, I'm so *sorry*—"

"Oh, I don't care! I just want something to eat! A pastrami sandwich and an ice cream soda, a big pile of french fries, oh! I'm going to go straight to Big Bob's and try, oh, just everything!" Even her hair and eyes were gaining color, the straw-like thin blonde strands looking fuller with every moment and her eyes brightening to cornflower blue. "Oh, gosh, thank you, Miss Ransom, I don't know how to thank you!"

Hank limped to the bathroom while she rattled on, returning with a damp washcloth. "Start by washing the blood off your face, Miss Daly, and then Miss Ransom will make you a sandwich in the kitchen while you tell us everything you know about Goode and the Midwest daemon rex."

"What's a daemon rex?" Pearl asked through the washcloth as she scrubbed her face.

"It's a king demon, the boss." Rosie turned a flat look on Hank. "Make her a sandwich yourself. I'm too tired to move. Make me one too, for that matter. I've only eaten a couple of doughnuts today."

Offense curdled Hank's cheeks to deep red, and Rosie could just see him gearing up for an argument. She interrupted with "I bet you got eight hours of sleep too, library man, since your mom said you were sleeping when I called. I've had maybe six *and* I've Redeemed two souls in the last twenty-four hours. Stop being a twerp and go make some sandwiches."

Hank's jaw clenched, but he limped into the kitchen and started banging more things around than anybody could possibly need to, for sandwiches. Pearl turned a gaze wide with admiration on Rosie. "You sure are a modern woman, aren't you, Miss Ransom?"

"I'm sure a tired one, anyways. You should just call me Rosie, though. I don't think we should be formal when I've just cut your head open. I'm so sorry. I just never tried it before, I didn't know what to do, I shouldn't have been so scary . . ." Rosie curled forward, hiding her face in her hands. It shouldn't be harder to help somebody than to kill someone, even if she'd made a mess of it. Mostly a mess. Pearl was okay, at least, but Rosie's heart felt all twisted up and sick, like it was beating wrong. Maybe Hank had been right. Maybe Redeemers weren't supposed to help people like Pearl, stuck between human and demon. It probably didn't come up all that often anyways, not if what Hank said about how demons were made had any truth to it.

"Next time you'll be able to explain," Pearl whispered. "Next time you'll know what you're doing, so when you have to do something terrifying to save somebody at least you'll be able to tell them why. I knew what I was becoming. Miss—Rosie. I just didn't think there was any way to stop it. Johnny told me there wasn't, so I didn't have any hope. You gave me hope back. You gave me my whole life back. And next time it won't be so awful." She put her arms around Rosie carefully, not at all like the enthusiastic hug from before, and murmured, "Aw, honey," when a wracking sob shook Rosie's body. "Aw, honey. You saved me. You saved you. And if Hank there is right, you saved Johnny's soul, too. That's three out of three, Miss Rosie. That's batting a thousand. Even Hammerin' Hank only hits three hundred."

A shaky chuckle broke through Rosie's tears, though it didn't dry them up. She heard Pearl shoo Hank away, and heard sandwich plates go onto the coffee table, but the tears kept coming until she was red-nosed and her face felt swollen. Pearl went to rinse the washcloth for her, and Rosie looked up to find Hank sitting across the living room, obviously uncomfortable and just as clearly concerned.

"I didn't think about what it might be like," he offered. "Not really. The stories about Redeemers are just legends, like—like Joan of Arc, or the Amazon warrior women. I didn't think about how hard it would probably be, for a regular girl. Do you think you'll be all right?"

Rosie snuffled and rubbed her hand under her nose. "Yeah. It was okay with Goode, it really was. But I didn't want to h-h-hurt Pearl, and then it got all overwhe-eh-l-elming." She held her breath, catching sobs before they started again, and gratefully accepted the cold washcloth Pearl brought out. She mumbled, "I'll be okay," into it, scrubbed her face, then laughed when she lifted it to see Pearl cramming half a sandwich into her mouth at once.

"Ihth juhhht ho ghooo," the other girl tried, and Rosie, still giggling through sniffles, took up another sandwich to eat it less voraciously. "It *is* good," she said to Hank.

"Peanut butter and jelly is nothing special."

"It is when somebody else made it and you're hungry," Rosie disagreed. Hank rolled his eyes but went back to the kitchen to make four more sandwiches before the girls were done.

"There," Pearl said to her. "Nothing seems quite so awful now, does it?"

"Not quite." Rosie smiled. "Don't get me wrong, Pearl, but I like you a lot more now than before. How'd you even get mixed up with Goode?"

Pearl shook her head and glanced away. "I was working at the factory like all the other girls, and I thought he was the cat's meow."

"Just like all the other girls."

Pearl nodded. "Except I caught him going after Tildy, the Negro girl, I told you that. And I got splashed with his blood, and . . . and then I couldn't get away." She looked at Hank, who sat across the room again like he didn't want to interfere. "I know you want me to tell you everything he knew, but I don't think he knew much. He sure didn't say much to me, anyway. He loved the war. He wanted to stay in Europe, but they wouldn't let him after he got hurt. But he said they all loved it, everybody like him. They could get away with anything, under cover of the war. That's how he even got turned, some lady vampire in France who was going through his whole platoon. Mostly she was killing them, but she thought Johnny was so pretty she decided to keep him. He still wrote her letters, telling her about what was going on here."

Hank's gaze fastened on Rosie, then returned to Pearl. "Did he have any of those letters left unsent?"

"If he did, Detective Johnson's got them now. He's not Ex Libris, is he,

Hank? Because he sure thinks something fishy is going on. I can't hardly believe you got him to give up Pearl."

Hank's mouth pulled, and Rosie couldn't tell if he was pleased or unhappy. "I can be charming when I want to be. Pearl, were there any letters? To her, or from her?"

"Oh, gosh. Maybe from her. He thought she might like to come over here, except he said—he said to me once that there was already a big boss demon who owned America from Chicago down to New Orleans. I don't know if that was true, but he said they were making bank on the war machine, with all the money being poured into the factories to make airplanes and everything. He didn't know who the boss was, except somebody who'd been working in industry a long time." Pearl faltered. "I really don't know anything else. I wish I did."

"You're saying his loyalty was to some European demon? Not somebody here?"

Rosie's face fell. "Demons have loyalties? Really?"

"Only because some are stronger than others and can command it. The really strong ones, they can double themselves. Redoubling, we call it. They can take over more than one human soul at a time. It weakens them, but it also spreads them out so they're that much harder to capture. Unless you get the original host, you're basically just letting the demon go. The vampires are the only ones who don't do that, because they need flesh and spirit to survive. Most demons just eat souls."

"This keeps getting better and better."

"I could write to her," Pearl said slowly. "To Johnny's mistress. I could write and see what she knows about the boss demon. I could—I could make up a story and tell her the boss killed him, or something, something that might make her want to tell me anything she knows? I mean, she couldn't tell I was lying to her from across a whole ocean, right?" She looked nervously at Hank. "Right?"

"Can demons kill each other?" Rosie demanded over Pearl's question. "You said only Redeemers could kill them."

"Redeemers are the only *humans* who can kill them," Hank corrected. "Demons fight and kill each other sometimes. But we don't want demons declaring war on each other, Miss Ransom. Whether the rock hits the pitcher or the pitcher hits the rock . . ."

Rosie sighed. "Right. It's not good for the pitcher either way. But they can? So Pearl's story could work. And maybe we'd learn something about the king, which is more than you've managed to do so far."

"Thanks for the reminder. I'm doing what I can without many resources, Miss Ransom. There've been a whole rash of—" Hank clicked his jaw shut and Rosie sat up straight.

"A rash of what? Something that Detective Johnson knows about and they're not letting on the news? What is it?"

"Deaths," Hank said after a pause. "The past year or so, there've been a lot of deaths. Suicides, car wrecks, dead wives, that kind of thing. Stuff that looks mostly normal from the outside, except one thing. Their eyes are white. The pupils and irises are gone. It's a sign that a soul has been eaten by a demon, and there have been a lot of those here in Detroit. My counterparts over in Chicago haven't seen so many of them. I'll have to check in with St. Louis and New Orleans." He nodded to Pearl in thanks for the pointer, and she flushed with pleasure. "Johnson doesn't like it," he said to Rosie, "and I can't tell him what's going on. But what I don't understand is why I can't find any hint of their hideout. You said yourself that I'm young, Miss Ransom, and I am. But I'm still good at my job, and I should have found them by now. I'm afraid somebody high up in the city—and maybe in Ex Libris—is deliberately keeping me in the dark."

NINE

A cold drop spilled down Rosie's spine, making her sit up even straighter. "That's why you don't want to tell your superiors about me. It's not that you're all alone out here—"

"I am!"

"—it's that you think they're out to get you!" Rosie jolted out of the couch, hands snapping into the air in exasperation. "The boy who's part of a secret society thinks there's somebody out to get him! That's just rich! Gosh, mister, how much do they pay you to be this paranoid? And if you think your bosses are the bad guys, how come you brought us to one of their hideouts? You're nice to look at, library man, but I'm starting to think maybe you're not too smart."

"He makes nice sandwiches," Pearl whispered from the couch, like she didn't want to call attention to herself but couldn't help it at the same time. "He doesn't have to be so smart."

Insult flew across Hank's face, but Rosie laughed aloud. "I guess you'll make somebody a good wife someday, library man." Her laughter fled, and Hank's glare faded into satisfaction, like he thought he'd been dour enough to chase her laughter away. His satisfaction faded too, though, as she said, "Honestly, just give it to me straight, Hank, or I'm gonna start thinking Irene's right and you're just a creep trying to make time with me. What's your deal?"

"You don't really think that." Hank sank into one of the chairs and rubbed long hands over his face. "I *am* good at my job," he repeated, more quietly than before. "I have a knack for rooting out demon nests. I used to do it for them in Europe, get our teams pointed in the right direction. It's why they gave me an assignment this big to begin with. I should have dug up something by now, and I haven't, and that bothers me. So yeah. If I keep you out of Ex Libris's sights but give you everything I know, maybe you'll be able to see what I'm missing. You just being here already shed light on Goode killing girls, and that's something I should have known was happening. If I'm being blindsided . . ." He drew a breath and looked up, letting his hands fall between his knees. "Then I need help. And if I need help, I don't want to show my hand to Ex Libris. I want to keep you secret."

"Like a secret romance," Pearl breathed. Hank and Rosie both turned wrinkled eyebrows at her, and her eyes widened. "What? It's romantic!"

"Honey, I think you need some more to eat and some sleep." Rosie went past the sofa to the kitchen and made another sandwich for Pearl, saying, "Now was it so hard to say you needed help?" to Hank. "Couldn't you have just done that in the first place? Blond men shouldn't try to be mysterious, and girls don't need a big strong handsome man to lead them through danger without telling them what's going on. I'm the Redeemer here, mister. I'm the one you're going to want between you and trouble, anyways."

She brought Pearl's sandwich out to her and found Hank staring up at her from his seat in the chair. "I almost wish I'd known you before, Miss Ransom. I'd like to know if you were always this cocky, or if it's something that happens when you become a Redeemer."

Rosie shrugged. "Probably anybody who can punch rivets all day long gets pretty confident. Are you really on your own out here?"

"Largely, yes. There are passers-through, and my supervisor comes down from Chicago quarterly. He's due before the end of the month." Hank sat back again to pinch the bridge of his nose. "I'd like to have something before then."

"Something more than me." Rosie sat down too, using the pad of her index finger to pick up crumbs from her sandwich plate. "Is there anybody else in Detroit who might rat me—us—out?"

"Demons." Hank's hand moved to his knee, massaging it. "Sometimes there are informants. Someone willing to risk selling a more powerful demon out, in the hopes we'll overlook them in the name of bagging bigger game. Even the powerful do it once in a while, hoping to create an opening for themselves."

"And the librarians?"

Rosie bit her cheek to keep a smile inside as Hank sighed. "We're not librarians. We try to set it up so we nab the informer, too, either during our sting or soon after. But they'll stop offering information if we don't keep our end of the bargain, so sometimes . . ." He spread his hands.

"So sometimes, you let the demons go. Are you sure you're the good guys?"

"Lady, if you're ever out there with nothing between you and evisceration but a quaking kid with a piece of paper and a stick of charcoal, then you can talk, all right? Until then, zip it, sweetheart."

"Unless I can figure out how to carry a riveting gun around all the time, I might end up there. Do demons know when a Redeemer is around?" Rosie pushed her plate away, shivering. She kept asking questions like they were so normal, so reasonable, except they were about demons and her own ability to kill them. Maybe her parents were right and it hadn't really hit her yet.

Hank's mouth twisted in frustration. "I don't know. I told you, there's not a lot in the literature about your kind."

"I could ask Johnny's mistress. Maybe—maybe tell her the king had a girl soldier who was the one that killed Johnny?" Pearl asked hesitantly.

"No. That's setting Miss Ransom up as a target. If they can't tell when a Redeemer is near, pointing them at her is just asking for trouble. It's not a bad thought, though," Hank admitted as Pearl slumped with disappointment. She perked up, reminding Rosie of a puppy who'd been given a treat. The poor girl needed someone to take care of her, although it sure as heck couldn't be Rosie.

She glanced around the little apartment. "Hank, is there any reason Pearl can't stay here a while? More than a couple days, I mean. You said it's a safe place, and that you're the only active librarian—"

He opened his mouth and shut it again, resigned. Rosie grinned and kept talking. "—in Detroit. Can't she just stay here a while, where it's safe and she can get her feet back under her? She needs some time to find a place of her own. She's still got the factory job, if she wants to go back to it, and—do you have any savings, Pearl?"

Pearl shook her head. "I gave my paychecks to Johnny. He said he'd take care of us."

Rich would probably expect Rosie to do the same thing, if she could even keep her job after he came home. A hollow place opened up in Rosie's belly, but she pushed it down. "So you need a while to save some up. Please, Hank? Besides," she added quickly, as his face tightened like he was preparing to deliver bad news, "she's the first still-living person a Redeemer's ever, uh, Redeemed. Don't you want to keep an eye on her, make sure she's okay? Where better than in one of your own safehouses?"

Hank's blue gaze sharpened on her. "You play dirty, Miss Ransom."

"Don't I just." Rosie smiled at Pearl. "Six weeks tops, okay? You need to work hard and save up so you can get a place of your own." She turned the smile to Hank, whose expression softened. "Okay, so that's dealt with. If we don't know whether demons can sense me, do we know if I can sense *them?*"

"You ask a lot of smart questions, Miss Ransom. I wish I had the answers. Could you tell with Pearl?"

"Not until I got kind of angry and cold inside. I can't go around angry all the time."

"But it means the ability is there, so it can be trained. Ex Libris trains artists to capture demons. I don't see why I couldn't train a Redeemer to sense them."

The corner of Rosie's mouth quirked. "Except you can't find any demons here anyways, so who am I going to practice on? Look, as long as you don't go getting high and mighty about what you know, when it's not a lot more than I do—"

"I do have access to archives here," Hank said, offended again. "But the information about Redeemers is limited."

"Like I said," Rosie said dryly. "Anyways, we can figure it out. This is what we do know: your bosses sent you here because they heard about a king demon running the Midwest. Pearl says there's a boss demon that runs the whole Detroit River at least, so that's some, what do you call it, um—"

"Corroboration," Hank said.

Rosie's eyebrows rose. "I was gonna go for 'support', but okay, Mister Dictionary Man. Anyways, you say there's people turning up dead, demon-killed, but there's no sign of where they're at, and you reckon you're good enough at your job that you'd be able to find a, uh, what did you call it, a nest, if it was here, unless somebody's hiding it from you."

"And the only people who should know enough about demons to hide a nest are Ex Libris," Hank finished.

"Or demons," Rosie argued. "Pearl says there are industrialists involved. People come from a pretty good distance away to work in the factories, Hank. Maybe your nest isn't in Detroit at all. Maybe it's out in Flint, and they just come into the big city to hunt."

"My superiors would have *sent* me to Flint—"

"If they knew they should," Rosie said impatiently. "But you said you're shorthanded, that all your librarians are over fighting in Europe, and nobody knows what's going on here. Maybe they figured a big city's easy to hide in and a smart place to start, but if you can't find anything here, you might need to go farther afield!"

"They said my region was Detroit!"

"Well, jeez, mister, you say there's no sign of monsters in Detroit, so maybe you'd better show some initiative! Or did getting your knee chewed up wreck your ambition, too? You work for the police, so use that to ask around and see if anything's gone strange in Flint or, heck, down in Toledo!"

Hank spat, "I'm an errand boy for the police," and shoved to his feet, limping heavily toward the door. "I don't have a badge. I don't carry a gun. I'm just a shot-up local kid who needs a break, so they have me drive drunks home at three in the morning and fill out paperwork while the real officers get important work done." He leaned on the doorknob, angry face turned in profile to the women. "Pearl, you can stay here a while. I'll bring groceries in so you're not starved."

"Are you running away from me, library man?" Rosie demanded. "Is that how you solve your troubles? By getting out of Dodge? No wonder you haven't found anything to report to Ex Libris. Don't you walk out that door! Don't you—oooh!" She stomped her foot as Hank left, then spun toward Pearl, just about spitting with fury. "I'm going to go yell at that boy some more. Will you be all right here?"

Pearl nodded, eyes round with interest. "You have to come back and tell me what happens." She hesitated. "You will come back, right, Miss Rosie? I don't think I have any other friends left. I got kinda split up from them when Johnny came along."

Rosie's anger faded and she crouched to take Pearl's hands. "You bet I'll come back. And we'll see each other at the factory, Pearl. It'll be all right. You've been really brave."

"I was really dumb," Pearl whispered.

"People do a lot of dumb things for love."

"If I loved him why aren't I sad he's dead? How come I'm just glad I'm not?"

"Because he was a monster, and you're not." Rosie stood and stepped back. "Get some rest, all right? And maybe start writing that letter to Goode's mistress back in France." She hesitated. "If you think she might know something about Redeemers, ask."

Pearl nodded and Rosie chased out the door after Hank, her anger rekindling easily as she caught him hitching down the first flight of stairs. "So what is it?" she shouted after him. "Another one of those three out of seven days? So what if you're an errand boy? You're still with the police. Use it! Or are you afraid if you push hard on this, you'll fail, and then what with the knee and the errand boy and everything, you won't have anything left at all? So you got torn up, Hank. At least you came home alive. A lot of boys haven't."

"I shouldn't have either!"

"You want to tell that to your mom? Your pop? You want to tell that to anybody who loves you? Because I've seen a lot of girls who've gotten telegrams, Hank, and I don't think one of them would give a damn if their soldiers came home broken or changed, just as long as he got to come home."

Rosie sat down suddenly on the top stair, face in her hands as the fight ran out of her. "I can't know what it's like," she said, muffled, then dropped her hands. Hank stood at the landing, leaning on the stair rail. He looked slimmer without the coat, afternoon heat sticking his button-down shirt to his shoulders, and the line of his undershirt making a wrinkle along his shoulder blade. "Watching the men in your unit get killed by monsters, and making it out of that yourself, I can't know what that's like. But I guess I know what it's like to find out too late that there *are* monsters, and things that can stop them. I guess I know what it's like to feel like now the only thing you can do is try to stop them yourself, in memory of your friends. And I guess I know what it's like to have somebody look at you and figure you're not worth spit, whether it's because your knee doesn't work anymore or if it's because you're a woman. So don't you get angry at me, mister. We can be angry together, that's fine, but don't you dare walk out on me, because I might be brassy, but if demons *can* tell when a Redeemer is around, then the truth is . . ." Rosie trailed off, then finished more quietly. "The truth is that without your help I'm not going to last a week. I can't walk around with a rivet gun all the time."

Hank turned around as she fell silent, looking up the stairs at her. His hair, wet enough from sweat to be brown at his temples, needed to be combed. He looked younger with it messy, and sounded younger still. "Are you scared?"

"No. Yes." Rosie thinned her lips and glanced at the wall beside her. Child-sized handprints and dents from knees or furniture marred it with ordinary little scars. "I'm not scared or upset by what I did, even though everybody thinks I should be. I'm scared to death of running into another demon and being unprepared. If there are others here, more than just Goode—"

"There are. There have to be," Hank said with a certainty that sounded like he hoped to convince himself.

Rosie nodded. "Then I want to help find them, and save them if I can, like I did with Pearl. And if I can't . . ." She sighed. "Then I want to make sure they don't hurt anybody else. So even if *you're* scared, library man, I'm going to need you to push, because nobody's going to tell me anything."

"I *am* scared. I'm afraid I've been put here because they figure I'm a good patsy. Crippled kid back from the war, of course he couldn't be expected to find anything, so when there's an uprising, they've got somebody convenient to blame."

"You really don't trust your bosses, do you?"

"It's not that I don't trust them. It's that I do trust myself. If there are demons here, Rosie, I should be able to find them. If I can't, then something else is happening. I can't explain it. I just know it's true."

"Say I believe you. It could be something simple. Something like they're not *in* Detroit. That means we need to start looking in other places."

"It could be. I'd just like to think the men who sent me home to protect my city know enough to be certain it's the source of trouble. But if they do know that much, and I still can't find it . . .."

Rosie nodded. "Then either you can't trust them, or you can't trust yourself."

"And I've known myself a lot longer."

Rosie smiled, and Hank studied her before offering a bleak smile in return. "You know, you could just tell me to go to Hell. Walk away, leave all this behind you. Nobody would blame you."

"I would. If somebody else died, if I could have stopped it? I'd blame myself forever. Besides, you need help. Even if the demons are right here in Detroit, you're still just one man. A nest is like a whole army, right? A whole army of demons that are almost impossible to kill. Those aren't very good odds."

"You're going to level the playing field? You and me against the demons, that makes it fair?"

Rosie lifted her arm to flex her biceps. "I'm tough, mister. You said so yourself."

A better smile crept across Hank's face. "Yeah. You are. Look, Rosie. I've got a family dinner tonight that I can't get out of, so let me give you a lift home and we'll start fresh tomorrow. This infestation, wherever it is, isn't going anywhere. A good night's sleep won't hurt us."

"You can drop me off at Big Bob's. I want to go check on Jean, and I should bring food in case she hasn't got any. Speaking of which, is there enough food in there for Pearl until tomorrow? I didn't check the fridge."

"There's powdered milk and corn flakes, at least. She'll be all right. I'll bring her some cash, too, so she can get out if she needs to."

"See," Rosie said, standing to come down the stairs, "you're not so bad, library man. We might just make a good team."

✪ ✪ ✪

It took most of an hour to get dropped off at the diner, wait on burgers, fries and milkshakes, and then wait for the tram to take her over to Jean's house. She tapped quietly on the front door before letting herself in to find Jean sleeping on the couch under two blankets despite the heat. Rosie slipped into the kitchen to make coffee and put the milkshakes in the freezer, then went back to the living room while the coffee brewed. She curled up in one of Jean's armchairs to wait for it to finish, and woke up a while later to Jean nudging her arm and offering a steaming mug to her. Rosie took a deep breath of its scent, then curled her hands around the cup and cleared her throat. "Sorry. I meant to have this ready for you, not the other way around."

"It's okay. The smell woke me up and for a minute . . ." Jean's face crumpled. "For a minute I thought Ruby had come home and made me coffee."

"Aw, honey." Rosie put the mug aside and stood to draw Jean to the couch, where they sat down as Jean cried in Rosie's arms. Eventually her sobs became shivers, and Rosie wiped her cheeks. "C'mon, Jean. I brought dinner, too."

"I'm not hungry."

"I know, but you need to eat something. Gosh, I sound like my mom. There are milkshakes in the freezer."

Jean offered a wan smile. "If I'd known your mom kept milkshakes in the freezer I would've come over to visit more often."

Rosie smiled. "There you go. You'll be all right, Jean. You want me to bring the shakes out here to thaw while I heat up the food?"

"Yeah." Jean nodded. "Please."

"All right, honey." Rosie went back into the kitchen, where the coffeepot sat two cups shy of full. Beside it stood a half-empty bottle of whiskey that hadn't been there earlier. Rosie got the food in the oven to reheat, then tightened the whiskey's cap and put it up before she rescued the milkshakes from the freezer and brought them into the living room. Jean's whiskey-rich coffee was half gone by then, but Rosie reckoned she deserved whatever took the edge off. She squeezed one of the milkshakes, impressed with how firm it had gotten. "That's a good freezer in there."

"It's a Philco. Ruby—Ruby thought if we were going to buy one, we should get one that would last." Jean took a shuddering breath. "She was my whole life, Ro. What'm I gonna do without her?"

"I don't know, sweetheart." Rosie sat down with Jean again, folding the other girl's hand into her own. "I can't imagine losing Irene, and I haven't known her half as long as you and Ruby were best friends."

"Best—" Jean pulled her hand out of Rosie's to grab a handkerchief and wipe her nose. Behind it, she said, "Yeah. Best friends," with more anger than Rosie had ever heard from her before.

Rosie's eyebrows lowered in confusion. "Well, you were, weren't you? Oh, Jean, did you two have a fight before she—before?"

"No. No, we didn't fight, we . . . Yeah," Jean said again. "Sure. Best friends. Just forget it, Rosie. Can you check on the food?"

"Sure. Okay." Rosie got up again, but stopped at the kitchen door, looking back. "I don't know what I said wrong, but I'm sorry. I want to be here to help, not make it worse."

Jean's shoulders dropped and she shook her head without meeting Rosie's gaze. "It's not your fault, Ro. It's really . . . it's really not. I'll explain it sometime, maybe. Just . . . can you check on dinner?"

Rosie whispered, "Okay," and fled into the kitchen. The cheese wasn't even re-melted on the burgers, but there'd been so much loss and defeat in Jean's posture that she didn't want to return to the living room until she could at least offer the salve of food. Like she'd told Irene, she couldn't remember a time when Ruby and Jean weren't together, through thick and thin. Losing Ruby had to be like it might feel for Rich to not come home from Europe, only worse maybe, because Jean had been a lot more certain of wanting to stick with Ruby than Rosie felt about staying with Rich. At least Jean didn't have that guilt, not that anything would happen to Rich, with the European war over.

"Jeez, Ro," she whispered to herself. At least she hadn't gone off talking about Rich like that out loud at Jean, who didn't need Rosie's love life quandaries landing in her lap right after she'd lost her best friend. The burgers finally started smelling good, and she pulled them out of the oven to shovel onto plates, followed by fries that had crisped up nicely on reheating. She added extra catsup to both plates, balanced a salt shaker on one of them, found some flatware just in case, and brought the whole mess out to the coffee table. "You don't have to eat a lot," she promised Jean, "but you need to eat something. A cup of coffee and nothing else will just make you feel sick."

"If there's enough booze in the coffee after a while I won't even feel sick." Jean ate, though, first a fry or two, reluctantly, then more before picking up her burger and sinking her teeth in. Her eyes closed momentarily, and around a mouthful she admitted, "This is good. You went to Big Bob's?"

"Hank dropped me off there. I came here because I thought the girls at home wouldn't get off my back about what happened at the factory if I went there. I hoped you'd want company."

"Got a new beau there, Rosie?"

"He's a looker, isn't he?" Rosie smiled but shook her head. "I don't think so. He just knows more—a little more—about what's happening to me."

"So I didn't imagine all that stuff you said about demons last night," Jean half-asked. "I was thinking a lot of crazy things. I thought . . ."

Rosie pushed a fry around her plate, collecting salt. "Would it be easier for you if you'd imagined it all? Because we can pretend that, if it helps."

"No. I just want to know what I can do to make a difference so this never happens to anybody else."

"I don't know yet. I—" Rosie jumped as the telephone rang. "Gosh. Wow, it's been quiet. I'm surprised, now that it's ringing."

Jean, wiping her hands on her dungarees, got up to answer it. "I only put it back in the cradle when you went to get dinner. It rang all afternoon before you got here and I couldn't take it anymore. Ruby's Nan . . ." Her eyes filled with tears again and she dashed her hand over them before picking up the phone. "Hello?" She glanced at Rosie, saying, "Yeah, she's here," to the phone. "I'll tell her. Okay as I can be, I guess. Rosie brought food. Okay. Thanks. Tomorrow. Bye, Rene. That was Irene," she said to Rosie as she hung up the phone. "She says your supe's been calling all afternoon and wants you to come in as soon as you can. He just called again and she thought to call here."

Rosie looked around for a clock. "It must be past eight. He can't need me to work an extra shift. What does he want?"

"I don't know, but I'll drive you over to find out when we're done eating."

"Are you sure?"

"I think I need to get out, and the tram is busy and smelly. I'm sure. And I should get Ruby's things from the factory. I don't want anyone to throw them out."

"I can get them, if you want. I have to go in anyways."

Jean shook her head. "I'd rather get them myself. There might be some private stuff in there."

"Sure." Rosie offered a tentative smile that Jean returned briefly before finishing her meal. Rosie, mumbling something about nothing being worse than coming home to a messy kitchen, then hating herself for the insensitivity of the remark, tidied the kitchen while Jean put on cleaner clothes, and had to help the other girl as she started trembling at the threshold.

"I haven't been out since I found out for sure."

"I know. I know, hon. You're doing great, Jean. We can sit on the steps a while if you want to catch your breath, but you're doing okay. It's only been a couple days. Not even that," she said, thinking back. "Is it only

Saturday night? Gosh. Wow." She sank down beside Jean on the steps, leaning into her. "I think you're amazing, to even try getting out tonight."

Jean knotted her arms around her waist, bending until her forehead almost touched her knees. "I don't know if I really can. I thought I could. I thought . . ."

"Jean, it's okay. Ruby's things will still be there in the morning, and I bet the supe will be too. Whatever he wants can wait. Come on." Rosie rubbed Jean's back, then stood and pulled her up. "Come on. Things will look . . . just as awful in the morning, probably," she finished with enough honesty to make Jean laugh tearily.

"Thanks. That's better than somebody saying it all happens for a reason and things will look brighter tomorrow."

"I'll stick around," Rosie offered. "I can take the tram to the factory tomorrow."

"We'll see how I am in the morning." Jean hesitated at the door to her bedroom, too, finally shaking her head. "I can't. I can't sleep in there without Ruby."

"It's so sweet you girls shared a room. You must have expected to take on housemates after the war ended and us girls weren't making so much money, huh? It's okay," Rosie said gently. "You sleep in the other bedroom, Jean. I'll take the couch."

Jean turned a silent, flat look on Rosie for the second time, though she didn't seem so angry this time. "We didn't think we'd need housemates."

"You're good about saving up money, aren't you? You bought the house and everything. Still, better safe than sorry, right?"

Jean passed a hand over her eyes. "Right. Right, Rosie. Look, I'm going to bed. Take the phone off the hook so I don't have people calling all night."

"Sure, Jean." Rosie called the factory first, leaving a message for Superintendent Doherty that she'd be in first thing in the morning, then put the receiver on the table and set about cleaning up the living room before settling on the couch with an old *Life* magazine. A folded print slid out from where it had been used as a bookmark, and Rosie unfolded it to smile briefly at an Art Deco image of a bare-breasted mermaid beneath a layer of ice and looking up in delight at the girls skating above her. Rosie tucked the print back into place, wondering what the French words beneath the mermaid said, and thought she would try to remember to ask Jean the next day. A smile caught her off guard. If demons were real, maybe mermaids were too. She turned the lights off and curled up on the couch, drifting to sleep on that cheerful thought.

TEN

A knock awakened her the next morning, with two worried faces peering through the panes in the front door. Rosie let Jean's parents in and, surprised, accepted embraces from both of them. "Rosie," said Mrs Diaz. "We haven't seen you in a long time."

"Not since graduation. Jean's still sleeping. Can I get you coffee?" She led them to the kitchen, glad she'd cleaned it the night before and even gladder she'd put the bottle of whiskey away. "How are you?"

"How's our daughter?" Mr Diaz asked at the same time. He was shorter than Rosie remembered him, with dark hair and light eyes that reminded her of Jean. Mrs Diaz was rounder than she'd been, but from the way she barely sipped the coffee Rosie made and refused anything to eat, Rosie thought that roundness might fall away soon.

"She's heartbroken," Rosie answered. "She and Ruby were such good friends."

Mrs Diaz nodded over her coffee. "We were here all afternoon yesterday, until she sent us home. I called this morning, and when there wasn't any answer . . ."

"Oh." Rosie glanced toward the phone guiltily. "She asked me to take it off the hook last night. There's nothing wrong. Nothing worse than before, anyways."

"She said the police were here," Mr Diaz said.

Rosie nodded before realizing he hoped she might tell them more, and ended up shaking her head. "They found Ruby's clothes at the murderer's apartment."

"She said he's dead. She said—" Mrs Diaz's brown gaze met Rosie's, then skittered away as a blush darkened her cheeks.

Rosie put her coffee down to steeple her hands in front of her mouth. It would be like this a long time, she reminded herself. For years, maybe. She'd better learn not to hate it, or it would ruin her. "She said that he's dead and I killed him? It's true. He attacked me and I defended myself. I didn't mean to kill him but I'm not sorry I did."

Mrs Diaz's eyes flashed with the same angry passion her daughter's had. "Neither am I. Ruby was a good girl, the best friend our Jean-Marie could have, and I'm glad that bast—"

"Maria." Mr Diaz put his hand over his wife's, stopping her outburst.

"What? Why should I not be glad that justice has been done? How easy it might have been for it to be Jean instead of Ruby! How close have we come to mourning for our own daughter instead of someone else's? Ruby was *like* my daughter, Peter! Like ours. We loved her." Mrs Diaz pushed tears away, about to speak again, when Jean, from the doorway, said, "I know you did, Mama. We all did. Have you seen her parents yet? They wouldn't talk to me when I called. Her mother blames me."

"How could she?" Rosie whispered in astonishment, as Mr Diaz stood to embrace his daughter unhappily.

"They wouldn't let us stay. There was too much family to deal with, they said, but . . ." He shrugged, and Jean said to Rosie, "If it weren't for me, maybe she'd have gotten married to some nice boy already and stayed home with babies instead of working at that factory where she was in danger."

"That doesn't make any sense," Rosie protested. "Lots of the girls are married and are still working while their mothers take care of the babies."

"I don't think they care very much about sense right now. I don't either." Jean spoke so rigidly that Rosie couldn't help but remember that Jean had believed her about Goode being a demon, and then couldn't help thinking the whole world didn't make very much sense anymore. She nodded instead of arguing, then quietly backed out of the room to let the Diazes spend some time together without her presence making things more difficult.

A while later Jean came out of the kitchen, pale and hollow-eyed but with her jaw set. "Mama and Papa are going to stay a while. Mom's going to cook something for lunch while I bring you to the factory."

"Are you sure, Jean? I can take the tram."

"It doesn't run as often on Sundays. I can do it. Ruby. . . . She wouldn't want me holing up in the house hiding, even if it's only been a couple of days. She'd want me to go see her parents and her Nan, too, so I just have to do that, Rosie. I have to."

Rosie's eyes filled with unexpected tears. "You're so brave, Jean."

"I'm really not," Jean said softly. "Come on. Let's go before I lose my nerve." She held Rosie's hand hard as they left the house, but they made it past the steps, and a minute later they were on the road to the factory. Jean drove more carefully than usual, but the roads were clear on a Sunday morning, so it took hardly any time to get across town. Jean pulled into the parking lot and sat with her hands on the wheel, staring bleakly out the big windshield at the factory's windowed facade.

"Last time I saw her was Monday night, when I dropped her off to work. She looked so cute, Rosie. Her hair was in pin curls and she had that kerchief tied around it to keep them in place, and she was wearing that polka-dot shirt I liked so much, and a pencil skirt. She blew me a kiss from the door. That was the last time I saw her. It all looked different to me then. It looked happy and safe, not like . . . this."

Rosie saw what Jean meant. Girders lay in heavy stacks near the doors, with pipes and lengths of rust-colored rebar leaning against them. Boxes of screws and rivets and bolts were piled against the walls, hiding some of the windows, and a girl emerged from the maze the whole mess made, dropping her cigarette guiltily when she saw someone watching from the car. Even the factory building itself looked grim, bleached instead of brightened by the morning sunlight. It hadn't seemed like a dangerous place before, but Jean had it right: it wasn't friendly anymore. "You want to come in with me or stay out here?"

"I'll come in," Jean said resolutely. "I need to get Ruby's things from her locker. But I'll meet you back in the car, Rosie. I don't want to wait in there."

"I can't imagine I'll be long." They got out of the Oldsmobile together, Jean giving its hood a pat like a promise she'd be back soon. Rosie wavered at the factory's front door, reaching for Jean's hand for support.

"It's okay." Jean sounded a lot stronger and more certain than she had for the past couple of days. "You did a good thing, Rosie. You don't have any reason to feel wrong about going back in."

Rosie, biting her lip, hugged the other girl hard before they went in together, not letting go of one another's hands until Rosie had to turn toward the supervisor's office and Jean had to keep going to the changing room. Jean cast a last look over her shoulder at Rosie as Rosie knocked on the supe's door, and Rosie wiggled her fingers in nervous support. A woman's voice called for Rosie to come in, and she stepped inside to smile uncertainly at the secretary, Vera. "The supe asked me to come in. Is he here?"

"For a wonder," Vera said tartly. "I've never seen Doherty here so late or so early, but you really shook things up around here, Rosie Ransom. The cops have been all over the joint and Doherty looks like he's lost fifteen pounds and three nights of sleep."

"It's only Sunday morning. That's two nights."

"I'm just telling you like I see it, hon." Vera tilted her head toward the second door. "He's waiting for you."

Rosie nodded and navigated her way around Vera's desk, file cabinets, and another stack of rebar and small girders that made the bare-walled office seem more industrial than it had ever looked before. All those things had always been there, she knew that, but it all felt different now. Except it wasn't the factory that had changed. Rosie sighed, knocked on Doherty's door, and waited for his peevish "Come in" before she pushed the door open and went inside.

His office looked worse than Vera's, with a dirty glass window overlooking the factory floor and papers strewn everywhere. A pin-up girl calendar hung on the wall with June's picture still up. After a second glance, Rosie realized the calendar said 1944, and wondered if he just especially liked the rocket-riding girl in the picture. Doherty himself stood at the window, hands folded behind his back like he imagined himself to be some kind of Howard Hughes, surveying his domain. Except where Hughes stood slim and handsome and dapper in well-cut suits, Doherty had gone soft a long time ago and probably never wore a good suit in his life. Vera hadn't been wrong, either: he looked paunchy and pale instead of robust, like he was a couple cigarettes short of a heart attack. There were bags under his eyes when he looked at Rosie. "Please sit down, Miss Ransom."

"Sure, Supe." Rosie sat in one of the wooden chairs that faced Doherty's desk, then scooted it backward several inches as he came to lean on the near side of the desk and look down at her. Pasty or not, he looked imposing from that angle, and her heart lurched from new nerves. "What's going on, sir?"

"You've caused quite a stir here, Miss Ransom. We try to keep the factory free of accidents, of course, but we've never had to consider what to do if a murder is committed on the grounds."

Rosie flushed. "It was self-defense, Supe."

"Of course it was, but a man was still killed on the premises."

"And at least five girls!"

Doherty smiled ingratiatingly. "Well, now, we don't know that they were killed *on* the premises, Miss Ransom, do we?"

"Well, what does that even matter? It was one of your employees killing them, and if I hadn't stopped him, *I'd* be dead! And maybe others, too!" Rosie started to rise in self-righteous indignation, but Doherty's voice snapped out: "Sit down, Miss Ransom."

Rosie sank back into the chair, her face hot. Doherty looked at her impassively. "The fact remains that you've committed a dramatic act of violence on the property, Miss Ransom, and the whole floor is talking about it. The girls are frightened."

"There's nothing to be frightened of anymore. Goode is dead."

"But you're still here."

Rosie stared up at the flabby superintendent in bewilderment. "I work here."

"No, Miss Ransom, you don't. Not anymore."

It felt like a rivet had plunged into *her*, not Goode, after all. Rosie's breath escaped her and wouldn't come back, leaving her heart to hang between beats in a hollow where her chest had been. She even looked down, sort of expecting to see another mist of blood and bone from the impact of Doherty's words. When she saw she was whole, it took an effort to lift her head again. Her question was only a shape, not even a sound: "What?"

"Miss Ransom, the owners are unanimous in agreement on this. We can't have a killer running around the floor, frightening the other girls."

"But you had one for months!" Rosie cried. Her breath came back in a rush, hurting as badly as the emptiness did. "I stopped him! There's nothing to be afraid of anymore!"

"They didn't know there was something to be afraid of before," Doherty said almost gently, as if his crazy logic would make sense if only Rosie listened carefully enough. "Now they do, and what they're afraid of is you. We can't have that. We're happy to offer you a very generous three months' wages as compensation, but this is the last time you'll be permitted on the premises, Miss Ransom. You're fired."

"You can't . . . you can't do that. I didn't do anything wrong. I didn't—!"

"Of course we can. For the morale and comfort of our other employees. Besides." Doherty's lip curled. "I'm sure you have a young man who will be home any moment, Miss Ransom. Three months' pay is probably more than you'd end up with when he expects you to quit so he'll have a job himself."

"I never planned to quit!"

Doherty laughed. "Don't be silly, Miss Ransom. Things will be going back to the way they were soon. You might as well accept it gracefully. There's nothing less attractive than a sullen woman, and you'll want to keep your solider happy by smiling for him when he gets home."

"You don't know anything about what I want." To her horror, Rosie's voice shook and tears threatened. "What I want is my *job,* I don't deserve to lose my job—"

"Life isn't fair, sweetheart, and you're just a girl. Get over it, and go home to make yourself pretty for your soldier."

"No! I'm not going to just let you do this, I'll—I'll find a lawyer, I'll sue you for my job—!"

Doherty laughed again. "You do that, Miss Ransom. You find yourself a lawyer who'll take on a girl riveter who murdered a shot-up war hero over a job, and see how far that gets you in the court of public opinion. I look forward to it. Now, I have a lot of other business today, so do I need to have you escorted off the premises or can you find your own way?" He pushed away from the desk and went around behind it, sitting to pull paperwork toward himself and dismissing Rosie from his attention entirely.

After a few seconds Rosie pushed herself up, trembling, and whispered, "This isn't over, Doherty." Biting her cheek to keep tears from falling, she walked carefully to the door and left, getting it closed behind her before a sob broke through her tightly compressed lips.

Vera looked up, her expression shifting from surprised confusion to resigned comprehension inside a heartbeat. "Oh, no. Oh, dangit, Rosie. I didn't know. I swear I didn't know. I'd have warned you going in."

Rosie pressed her knuckles against her mouth, fighting to keep sobs inside, and nodded as tears streamed down her cheeks. Vera offered a handkerchief that Rosie knotted around her fist until her fingers went cold, and she kept biting the inside of her mouth until the pain overwhelmed the feeling of a hole punched through her whole body. It didn't help, though: the tears kept coming until the door behind her opened suddenly and she fell backward toward Doherty.

He caught her and pushed her forward again with the distaste of a man who'd found something unpleasant stuck to his shoe. "I told you to get off the premises. Vera, call security. Now!"

Vera, agonized, reached for the phone, but Rosie cried, "No!" She ran from the office to careen through familiar, fond halls that were no longer where she belonged. It took hardly a minute to crash through the factory's front door, stumble a step or two into the maze of girders and boxes, then fall to her knees and sob helplessly with her forehead bent all the way to the ground. Tears collected dust, then disintegrated from drops into damp spots as Rosie smashed her fists on the ground and struggled to hold back shrieks of hurt and anger and frustration. Another girl stealing a smoke break emerged from the mess of girders, gasped, and scurried past Rosie without offering any solace. A horrible laugh scraped from the back of Rosie's throat and turned into more tears that sent her rolling onto her side, curled up with her knees against her chest.

Everybody had been right. She'd just been waiting for it to hit her, except they'd been wrong about what could break her. Not Goode, not Pearl, not anything about demons or Redeemers, oh no. Losing her job, *that* broke the camel's back. *That* turned out to be more than she could take. All her independence, gone in a snap, because Doherty had one thing right: finding another job when the soldiers were coming back would be just about impossible. She had plans in place, she'd even been accepted at one of the community colleges, but she'd counted on a few more months of employment, maybe even through the end of the year, to make it all work. All of a sudden it seemed like *nothing* would work, like she'd lost it all.

Rosie knew she should get up off the ground and stop crying, but she couldn't make her arms unlock from around her knees, or untuck her head from the tight ball she'd rolled into. She bet Jean felt just like this right now, but worse, since Rosie had only lost a stupid job and Jean had lost her best friend. She still couldn't unroll herself, only lie there in a knot on the ground and cry.

"Aw, the poor little Redeemer is so sad. Poor creature. No wonder you things don't last very long, if you fall apart so easy. You're not legends at all, just scared little girls." A woman's voice spoke above her, sweet tones rolling around the walls made by girders and factory equipment before a booted foot caught Rosie in the kidney and turned her sobs into a scream. She rolled onto her back, then scrambled backward in a crab-walk until she crashed into a stack of girders and had to gape upward at the woman standing over her.

She worked in the factory, obviously: she wore coveralls and heavy boots and, right now, a smirk that broadened as she kicked Rosie across the jaw, then squatted to say, "You call that a scream, Redeemer? Let me show you what a real scream sounds like."

Her jaw unhinged, dropping horrifyingly far, and the sound that ripped from her throat made the air wobble around them. It hit Rosie like a fist, knocking her head back, and the woman—the demon—laughed. "That was fun. I haven't gotten to let loose in so long. God, I *felt* it when Johnny died, did you know that? This terrible shiver, like everything he was had just come apart. And next thing I knew, everybody was talking about how Rosie Ransom from the day shift had killed a supe, and I knew. I knew if I just waited you'd come back, and I'd get the chance to be the one who killed the Redeemer. Oh, honey, your ears are bleeding! Isn't that a thing!"

Another scream shattered the air, reverberating off the steel until Rosie couldn't tell where the sound came from. Wetness trickled from her ears and her nose, and the scream's weight kept her pinned in place like it had mass of its own. She struggled to lift a hand, but the screaming demon laughed and rolled back on her heels. "Well, I'm hardly gonna let you lay hands on me, am I, Redeemer? Not if I want to live. Oh, gosh, your eyes, sweetie, they're all bloodshot. I haven't screamed anybody to death from this close before. This is swell!"

"Wh . . ." The word wouldn't even shape itself in Rosie's mouth, but the demon cackled with pleasure anyways.

"What am I? I was a symphony, baby. I was an aria, dying to get out. Oh, heck, no, I got that wrong." Her voice dropped into deadly flat tones. "*Killing* to get out. I'm the music my maker couldn't hold, and now I can destroy you with sound. Isn't that something? I bet one more scream will do it. I think your head might explode. I can't wait to see."

Rosie jerked her hand up, trying to reach the woman, but the demon's jaw fell open again and her cry slammed Rosie's hand backward again, bruising it against the girders. It hurt, like a distant surprise that couldn't really get through the pain in her head. Her tears were thick and dark and not really tears at all. Blood, its redness almost black right against her eyes like that. Dark crimson ate at her vision, reducing it to nothing, and then the screaming demon made an ugly short sound and silence fell.

Rosie wiped blood from her eyes, blinking frantically to see Jean's blurry form standing above the demon with a long piece of rebar shoved through the demon's back. For a heartbeat or two, Rosie just stared at the rage and triumph contorting Jean's features. Then she lurched forward, slapping her hands on either side of the demon's head and letting her fear turn to righteous rage. In seconds, power swept through her, pouring into the demon and whipping around, separating its essence from the human soul until the one breathed a soundless sigh of relief and faded, and the other turned to black dust on Rosie's hands, disappearing against her skin.

She fell back against the girders, relief and gladness washing through her, and Jean, standing above her, let go of the rebar to fall onto her butt on the concrete. They stared at one another across the body, both breathing hard, until an awful, proud grin twisted Jean's features. "Oh my God, Rosie. What are we gonna do with the body?"

ELEVEN

"We're gonna call the police!"

"Really?" Jean's awful grin stayed fixed in place, like skewering the demon had been cathartic. "You really want to call the cops and tell them you've killed somebody else on the factory grounds inside of three days? Or did I kill her?"

"No, you . . ." Rosie stared at the woman's body. Her jaw hadn't re-hinged itself and her face looked horrible. Rosie glanced away again, pressing her knuckles against her mouth. Behind them, she said, "You stopped her long enough for me to Redeem her. I think she'd have . . . gotten better, if I hadn't. I mean, not like . . . *better* better. Not human again. But I think she would have healed and come after us again. We can't not call the cops, Jean. . . ."

"Bet we can. Bet we can bug right out of here and nobody's gonna know any better. Do you want to explain *that* to that detective?" Jean gestured sharply at the woman's face.

"No, but I—I—I could call Hank," Rosie stuttered. "Maybe he'd know what to do. I don't know what to do."

"Where's the nearest payphone?"

Rosie looked helplessly beyond the girders they were hidden among. "I don't know, around the back of the factory? Except no, I remember Ethel grousing that some jerk had yanked the cord free and nobody had come to fix it yet. Half a mile? I don't know, Jean."

"So you think we should leave her here, go find a phone, call your pet cop, come back here, let him show up with the rest of the cavalry, and explain it all to them then? I say we run while the running is good, Rosie."

"Somebody will figure out it's me anyways! I just left the factory two minutes ago, Jean! And I was upset, and I already killed someone, and they'll put it all together!"

"Then we better take the body with us." Jean stood, her round face set with determination. "Think there's a hose around here we can wash the blood away with? It'll only take a few minutes for the ground to dry, in this heat."

"No." Rosie swayed, even though she hadn't gotten up. "No, I'm gonna stay and face the music, Jean. You better go, though. You better not get involved."

"How can I not be involved? I stabbed her!"

"They don't have to know that. I can say I did it. I can say—"

"That you were leaving the factory and thought some girl needed to be stabbed in the back for kicks?"

"Well, she looks like . . ." Rosie fluttered her fingers at the woman's face, which was slacker now, as if the idea of being dead had caught up to her. It made the distortion of her jaw even worse, loose and wobbly-looking. Rosie could see unnatural ridges near the back of her throat, and wondered if they amplified the creature's screams.

"I couldn't see her face. I just saw her standing over you, screaming like that."

"I've already got the bruises to prove I was in a fight with her," Rosie said stubbornly. "Really, Jean, you should go. At least back to the car where you can say you didn't see anything." She looked around, confusion rising in her chest. "Where is everybody? Half the factory should've come running at those screams."

Jean glanced around too, uncertainty replacing the determination she'd shown in the past few minutes. "Maybe the steel baffled the sound somehow?"

"I don't think anything could baffle it that much." Rosie finally tried pushing herself up, gasping as pain bounced around her torso and finally settled in her kidneys as a sharp throb. She faltered, using the girders to hold herself, and Jean surged forward to get under one of Rosie's arms, helping her to stand.

"Never mind where everyone is. I couldn't leave you here even if I wanted to, could I? You can hardly move. You need to get checked out at the hospital, Ro."

"Hospital. Cops. What's next?" Rosie wheezed with the effort of moving. Back in the beginning, she'd been sore from hefting a riveting gun and working muscles unaccustomed to hard labor, but that had been a long time ago and turned out to have nothing on the pain of being beaten up.

"Being arrested for murder," Jean muttered. "Come on. I'll get you into the car, back it up to the steelworks here and drag the body into the trunk, and we'll go call your friend Hank."

"Jean," Rosie said in despair, but Jean had the strength Rosie lacked just then, and Jean half-pulled, half-carried her along to the Oldsmobile, then all but dropped her into the car's big back seat. Rosie fell against the tan leather with a whimper, then gritted her teeth as Jean scrambled into the driver's seat and backed the car up to the stacks of girders, just as she'd threatened to. "Jean, don't. If we leave her here, then maybe—"

"Then maybe the cops will think she looks so scary they'll bury the whole thing instead of investigating? Maybe, or maybe she'll blow the whole lid on there being demons in Detroit. I'm just going to do it, Rosie. Yell at me later, if you can catch your breath enough to."

"I *will* yell at you," Rosie whispered through her teeth. The pain hadn't really faded. More like she'd started getting used to it, she thought. She started to sit up, just to see if she could, then realized it might be better if she stayed down, where nobody could see her. "I'm thinking like a criminal," she whispered to the Oldsmobile's ceiling, then crushed her eyes shut. By anybody's lights *a criminal* pretty well defined her right then. The light changed as Jean opened the Oldsmobile's trunk, and the car echoed with a dull thud as something heavy—heavy enough, anyways— got dropped inside. Jean closed the trunk gently and disappeared for a few minutes, leaving Rosie to listen to a rush of water that sprang up suddenly, then drained away.

"Found a hose," Jean muttered in triumph as she got into the car. "There wasn't much blood. I thought there'd be more. You okay?"

"Nothing a couple of aspirin and some whiskey wouldn't cure." Rosie pressed her lips together as Jean put the car in drive and left the parking lot at a perfectly sedate pace, like she hauled bodies in her trunk every day. Once they were on the road Rosie pulled herself to sitting, taking deep breaths to test the pain in her back and ribs. "It's not quite so bad now."

"Good. Where's your friend live?"

"Hank? I've got no idea, Jean." Rosie pulled another deep breath, then squirmed over the back of the front seat to sit by Jean. "I've only got his number."

"So we'll find that pay phone. Stop looking at me like that, Rosie. This is the only smart thing to do. They find out you're involved in another death, and at the best, they'll be on you like a hawk, watching everything you do. What if you have to fight another demon? How can you do that with the cops watching?"

"What if they find out anyways? This is all—this is real bad, Jean. What we're doing here, it's . . ." Rosie shook her head, but Jean barked laughter.

"Which part of it? Hiding the evidence? Or demons trying to kill you? Demons managing to kill Ruby and all those other girls? I believed you anyway." Jean's fierce tones went thin. "Maybe because I wanted to, because maybe it's easier to accept a real true monster killed her than just some awful person. That'd almost be worse. So I believed you anyway. But seeing that thing, Rosie . . . What was it?"

"I don't know. Some kind of screaming demon. Like you couldn't figure that out yourself," Rosie said softly. "I don't know. I'll ask Hank. The pay phone is up there."

"Don't ask him on the *phone*!"

Rosie gave Jean a withering look as she pulled the car over. Jean waved it off and sank back in the driver's seat to wait for Rosie to make the call.

The nickel dropped with a clunk that reminded Rosie of the time clock at work. Tears sprang to her eyes again, and she gripped the phone's heavy black handset, staring wide-eyed down the street so the tears wouldn't fall.

She'd just killed her second person in three days, but losing her dumb *job* made her cry. The whole world felt turned on end.

The pleasant British accent that answered the phone didn't help that either. Rosie startled, almost dropping the handset, like she'd forgotten she'd even been making a phone call. The woman said, "Hello?" a second time before Rosie got her throat clear enough to say, "Hi, is Hank home?"

Delight filled the woman's voice, just like it had last time. "I do like hearing a girl calling for him. Just a moment, I'll get him for you."

"I'm not . . ." Rosie shaped the words more than said them, and sighed, pressing her forehead against the phone box's scarred surface. At this time of day, it hadn't heated up to sizzling yet, and the steel felt almost cool against her skin. It smelled like warm metal, though. Warm metal and too many hands touching it. Rosie straightened, repulsed enough that she didn't feel like crying anymore.

"This is Hank."

"Oh! Hank, thank gosh. It's Rosie. Rosie Ransom. I have to see you right away."

"Rosie?" Surprise filled Hank's voice, although he tempered it right away. "I'm glad you called. I've been looking forward to hearing from you. What can I do for you?"

Rosie frowned at the phone, astonished at how casual he sounded, then realized his mother might be nearby and eavesdropping. "I can't tell you on the phone, but it's an emergency. Can you meet me somewhere? Somewhere private?"

Hank chuckled. "There's an offer a guy doesn't get every day. Sure. You could swing by here if you wanted to."

"Are you sure? It's kind of a big mess."

"No, it's fine, no trouble. Come on by. Let me give you directions. Got a pencil?"

"No. Is it hard to get there?"

"No, just come on up Lakeshore and turn at the marina. You'll see it. Got that?"

"I guess I'll find another phone and call if I don't. We'll see you in a while." Rosie hung up as the operator blared that she would need to deposit another nickel soon, and got back in the car to rattle directions off to Jean before she forgot them.

"Nice part of town," Jean breathed. Rosie nodded and rucked her shirt up to look at her ribs, which hardly hurt at all anymore. A faintly yellow stain, edged with green, made a block between her floating ribs, with no evidence of the black discoloration she expected to see rising. She prodded at the kidney she'd taken the hard kick in and winced but didn't get dizzy from pain. Jean glanced at her. "How's it look? Hospital first?"

"No, I'm . . . fine?" Rosie twisted, keeping her shirt pulled up as she displayed her ribs and lower back to Jean. "Am I fine?"

Jean glanced at her again, then over her shoulder to check traffic before pulling back onto the road. "Old bruising there, like you got hit really hard a week or ten days ago. Rosie, twenty minutes ago, you could hardly stand up."

Rosie felt her back again, then peered down at her ribs a second time. "I know. That was real, right? I . . . I could hardly stand up." She kept feeling the bruises, tenderness vanishing under the pressure. "I think I'm healing really fast. *Really* fast. Holy bean, Jean. Hank didn't say anything about this!"

"If you ever say 'holy bean, Jean' again, Ro, I'll . . ." Jean shook her head, falling short on threats. "Count yourself lucky, I guess. You should be laid up for a week, with the beating you took."

"I guess it'd be pretty crummy for a demon slayer to get so beat up, she couldn't fight back," Rosie whispered. "I guess that's not a problem."

"Oh, you're a slayer now," Jean said with a faint smile. "Very impressive."

"Redeemer sounds so . . . it sounds so . . . it sounds okay when someone else says it. It sounds silly to say it myself."

"But 'demon slayer' sounds okay?"

Rosie blushed. "No, that sounds pretty silly too."

"Besides," Jean said, more fiercely. "I slayed that one. You just . . . you just finished the job."

"I don't know how you can slay something and need somebody else to finish the job," Rosie protested, but she nodded anyways. "You did. You saved me, Jean. Thank you."

"You got Goode for me." Jean spoke in a near-snarl. "Call it even."

Rosie nodded again and folded her knuckles against her mouth, looking out the window. Detroit looked hazy in the morning light, sunshine not yet able to burn it off, or more likely, coal dust from the factories hanging too heavily in the air for a clear day. Somehow days like that made the heat seem worse, but it hadn't rained in ages and the sky seemed yellower every time the sun rose. "They fired me," she said to the window, and Jean startled so hard the big Oldsmobile wavered on the road.

"They what? Why?"

"Having a killer on the floor is too frightening." Rosie kept pressing her knuckles against her mouth even though it muffled her words. It kept her from crying, too, which felt more important.

Jean's silence drew out forever, until she finally said, "That's about the stupidest thing I've ever heard. I'm sorry, Ro. What're you gonna do? When does Rich come home?"

Rosie let out a short cry, not a sob and not a shout but the worst parts of both of them, a sound too big to fit in her chest that hurt coming out. Jean flinched enough to hit the brakes and Rosie covered her face with her hands. "I'm sorry, I'm sorry. I don't know, Jean. I don't know when he's coming home and I don't know what I'm going to do but him coming home isn't the answer to that! I love him, I do, but I just—I just don't want that to be all I get or have or do in my life! I don't want to depend on a man. I love my life, Jean. I . . . loved it. And it's all gone now."

Jean gave her a side-eyed glance. "You love him so much but you don't want to depend on a man. Are you *in* love with him, Ro, or do you just love him?"

"I don't know that anymore either," Rosie said miserably. "I was in love like crazy when he left, Jean, but that was such a long time ago. Everything's different now. People change. They want different things than they used to. Don't they?"

"Yeah." Jean slid another glance Rosie's way. "Rosie, don't get me wrong, but you're so determined to make it on your own and not have to rely on your solider coming home. . . . Are you the sporty type?"

"The sporty type?" Rosie's eyebrows drew down. "Gosh, I don't know.

I went to football games and things in high school and who doesn't follow the Tigers, but I don't really think so?"

The corner of Jean's mouth quirked. "No, I guess not."

"Are you? I guess you're pretty determined to get by without a soldier too."

The car rolled to a stop at a sign as Jean put one hand over her mouth like she was trying to wipe away a smile. "Yeah. Yeah, Rosie. I'm the sporty type."

"What teams do you like?"

Jean burst out laughing and put the car back into gear while Rosie blinked at her in astonishment. Jean glanced her way, laughed again, and turned her attention back to the road, still smiling. "I like the Tigers too, Ro. Who doesn't?"

Rosie smiled uncertainly and Jean's own smile faded away into something sadder. "That's the first time I've laughed since Ruby died. I didn't think I would so fast. Thanks, Ro."

"You're welcome," Rosie said, still uncertainly.

Jean leaned over to squeeze her knee. "I mean it. Thanks. And I'm sorry I asked about Rich in regards to what you're going to do. I ought to know better than just about anybody what it's like to have people expect you're going to turn around and rely on a man when it's the last thing you want to do. You'll land on your feet, Rosie. I'm really sorry they fired you, that's just dumb, but you'll land on your feet. Wait, what road are we supposed to turn on?"

"He just said the marina. Did you see a sign for it?" Rosie looked out the window, searching for landmarks.

"Yeah, just another few minutes. I hope your new friend knows what to do."

"He will," Rosie said with confidence born of having no other options. A minute later Jean turned the car down a tree-lined avenue, both of them glancing up in admiration before keeping an eye out for their next turn. It came later than Rosie expected, and the drive meandered a distance toward the water before a corner brought them up to a set of steel gates half again Rosie's height. A familiar, stylized *V* had been cut out of the gate bars, right at the center, so it would split in half when the gates opened to offer admission.

Jean killed the engine and they both stared at the *V* until Jean found her voice. "Your boyfriend is Hank *Vaughn?*"

"He's n . . ." After the breath of protest, Rosie didn't bother, just stared again, and finally smacked her head back against the headrest. "Son of a . . . He didn't . . . I didn't know, Jean, I swear I didn't kn . . . But he . . . Oh, that . . . Oooh!" She stomped her feet in the foot well, feeling like a kid who'd been tricked out of a treat. "He brought me up to the river on the Vaughn factory grounds on Friday night, well, Saturday morning, I guess, before I came to see you, and he said they knew him there and I thought it was because he was with the cops but *oooh!* The rat! That rat!"

"Well, but didn't he tell you his last name? And you didn't put it all together?"

"But he didn't! Detective Johnson just called him Hank and I never got his—oh, the gates are opening, oh, gosh, Jean, what do we do? I could kill him, I swear, Jean!"

"Maybe he just wanted to get to know you without having the Vaughn family name hanging over it all." Jean started up the car again and they crept forward through the gates. "I mean, it's probably not every day he meets a nice girl who doesn't have a bunch of notions about what a Vaughn ought to be like and who also kills demons while she's off shift from the factory."

"But I wouldn't have any idea what a Vaughn should be like!"

"Yeah? What's Harrison Vaughn like?"

"A womanizer," Rosie said promptly. "Smart and suave, rich as sin and doesn't care who he steps on to get what he wants. He gives enough to charity to look good but you can bet he's keeping millions more where nobody's looking."

"Sure," Jean said with a brief smile. "No notions at all."

"Well, but—but that's different! He's in the papers all the time!"

"And if your dad was in the papers like that all the time?"

Rosie muttered and gave Jean a brief, baleful look of understanding her point before they reached the house. It had to be three times the size of the place Rosie shared with five other girls, never mind the pretty little two-bedroom home she'd grown up in. Jean stopped the car again and they both gazed out its windshield, counting windows and balconies. "It's three stories tall," Rosie whispered, and Jean, obviously fighting off a sudden bout of giggles, grabbed Rosie's hand like it would help her stop laughing. The main building, at least, stood three stories tall: its two wings were only two stories, but the whole flat-roofed building gleamed white with black accents, beautifully imposing. Huge windows lined the wings, though on one side the second floor had doors that opened onto a broad deck kept safe by sharply decorative railing. The top of the main wing had the same kind of railing, suggesting a deck up there, too.

The front door—doors, they were double and recessed under a pillared entryway with a curling facade—swung open and Hank Vaughn came out, looking fresh and handsome in a blue-and-yellow knit shirt and tan trousers. At home and informal, he didn't wear a hat, so his gold hair gleamed in the midday light, and he came down the three or four steps leading to the front door so easily it took Rosie a few seconds to realize he'd come down them in a way that favored his right knee but still looked fluid and flawless. The limp was more in evidence as he crossed to Jean's car, and his surprised gaze caught Rosie's through the windshield before she got out of the car. "You didn't tell me you were in company."

"I said *we* would see you in a while. You remember Jean, right, *Mister Vaughn*? Jean-Marie Diaz?"

An expression of pain flickered over Hank's face as she emphasized his name, but he smiled briefly for Jean. "Of course I do. I'm glad to see you out, Miss Diaz. How are you?"

Jean shrugged one shoulder. "I wouldn't be here if Rosie didn't need me."

Hank nodded. "And it seems both of you need me. What's wrong?" He glanced over his shoulder, smiling, then turned a much grimmer expression back on the girls. "My parents will want you to come in, and if you're not in quick, they'll come out here, so what is it?"

"Are they watching?" Rosie asked in alarm.

"I doubt it. We've had a visitor over the weekend and they're saying their goodbyes now, but he'll be out shortly and so will they. What *is* it, Miss Ransom?"

"Show him, Jean."

Jean got out of the car to open its trunk. Hank followed her, his forehead marked with a frown line that worsened as he got a look inside the trunk. "Good God. Close that. What happened?"

"I got called to the factory, got fired, and got attacked by a screaming demon when I left. She said she'd been waiting for the Redeemer to come back and she'd be legendary for killing me." Rosie shuddered suddenly, the impact of that threat finally hitting her.

"She beat the hell out of Rosie," Jean carried on, "and I came running and shoved the rebar through her chest and Rosie Redeemed her and we cleaned up—well, I did, because Rosie couldn't hardly move—and we called you. What *is* she?"

"You cleaned up?"

"I got the body into the car and rinsed down the ground. There were drains around, all the blood went into them, and the ground will be dry by now."

Hank, sounding very English, said, "Well done, Miss Diaz," then passed his hand through his hair, ruffling the tidy golden cut. "We call her type *ochim*."

"More Latin?" Rosie muttered.

"Hebrew, actually. It means—well, it means *doleful beast*, but the root comes from a word that means crying or howling." Hank shifted his shoulders in something between embarrassment and a shrug as Rosie gazed at him in disbelief. "You asked, Miss Ransom. Are you all right?"

"Fine," Rosie whispered. "I guess I healed right up. You know anyth— no, you don't, do you," she guessed from the way his eyebrows elevated again. "I'm going to have to learn everything about being a Redeemer the hard way, aren't I?"

"Not if we can get what's going on in Detroit sorted and I'm able to request access to the full archives without betraying your presence here. Miss Diaz, I can . . . take care of this, but I'll have to borrow your car, which means we're going to have to concoct a reason for you to be lending it to me at noon on a Sunday. My parents are somewhat removed from the tedium of the working-class life, but I doubt either of them would think a mechanic is working on Sunday afternoon."

"We could just be coming by to pick you up for lunch at the diner," Rosie pointed out. "You don't have to drive off mysteriously in Jean's car. We could all go."

"Do you really want to go with me to dump a body, Miss Ransom?"

"I thought the idea was to get you away from your parents without them suspecting why, Mr Vaughn. What we do once we're past your long, impressive driveway doesn't really matter, does it?"

"You're mad at me, aren't you. Look, Rosie, it's just that people always—they expect things of me when I'm Harrison Vaughn, Jr. It's just . . . It's nice to be my own man once in a while."

Beside Rosie, Jean caught her breath like she'd say *I told you so,* but Rosie snapped, "Just not so much of your own man that you don't take advantage of dropping by the Vaughn factories in the middle of the night for some quiet time by the river," over any chance Jean might have of making commentary.

Hank's shoulders dropped. "Would you be less angry if I'd taken you somewhere that someone might overhear us?"

"Detroit's a big city, Hank. There are a lot of quiet corners that don't include your daddy's property."

"Fight about it later," Jean said quietly. "They're coming out. Everybody smile, kids!"

Funnily enough, they did, all three of them, like suddenly they were best buddies. Jean pushed her hands into her pockets and leaned against the Oldsmobile's trunk, while Rosie folded her hands behind her back and smiled up at Hank, who grinned at both the girls like they'd just said something funny.

A four-door Cadillac, its enormous engine rumbling deeply enough to shake the ground, pulled up the driveway as two men and a woman came down the steps outside the house. Rosie recognized all three of them: Harrison and Valentine Vaughn from the society pages, and the third man from somewhere she couldn't place. He was thick and tall, with a square-jawed, oily handsomeness that looked like he worked at it. His black hair shone with tonic and his olive skin looked sweaty in the early afternoon heat, even from a distance of several yards. He seemed too young to be jowly, but he carried it well, taking advantage of its hint of gravitas.

The Vaughns looked straight out of the pictures, especially Mrs Vaughn, who wore her sunshine-blond hair in shoulder-length waves a decade out of style but perfect for her high cheekbones and long jaw. Her tailored day dress made her waist look spannable by two hands. Harrison Vaughn, taller and sandier-haired, had a nervous energy about him, suiting a strong build that reminded Rosie he'd been an amateur boxing champion in his youth. Rosie couldn't help looking between the son and his parents, seeing elements of both of them in him.

"Here's your car," Mr Vaughn said as they came down the steps. "I'm glad you were able to take time out of your busy schedule to visit this weekend."

"For the Vaughns, anytime. But the car can wait. Who are your friends, Hank?" The big man passed by Mr and Mrs Vaughn to approach Rosie and Jean, an uncomfortably wide grin spread across his face.

"Rosie Ransom and Jean Diaz," Hank said. "Rosie, Jean, I'd like you to meet Senator Coby Haas."

A blush soared up Rosie's cheeks as the senator shook her hand with damp fingers. "Gosh, I knew I recognized you but I couldn't think why. How embarrassing. It's a pleasure to meet you, Mr Senator, um, Mr, oh, fiddlesticks. Senator Haas."

Haas chuckled, deep and rumbling. "I'd be pleased if you'd call me Coby, Miss Ransom. It can never hurt a politician to be on a first-name basis with pretty women."

Rosie withdrew her hand from his and tried not to wipe it on her dress. "That's very generous of you, Senator, but I couldn't presume."

"It's not a presumption if I ask," Haas insisted, but shook Jean's hand, too, rather than press Rosie any further. Jean's gaze skittered to Rosie's, her eyes widening as the senator clasped her hand with his sweaty one. Rosie struggled to keep a moue of disgusted agreement from her features, mostly because the Vaughns were watching. "A pleasure," Haas repeated. "I hope

I can count on you girls voting for me in the next election. Now, I really must run, but if you ever need anything, why, Harry there has my direct number and I'll be darned if he shouldn't hand it over to two such fine young constituents as yourselves. Harry, Valentine, until next time." He climbed into the waiting Cadillac and it drove away, leaving Rosie looking after him in astonishment.

"Well, now we have to go through this whole rigmarole all over again," Harrison Vaughn said as he approached with his wife. "Coby's always jumping the gun, doing his best to get introductions before anyone else has the chance. I suppose I would too, if I was thinking about running for President. Those personal connections can make the difference, I'm told. I'm Harrison Vaughn, and this is my wife, Valentine Lewis Vaughn."

He offered a hand that Rosie took nervously, still wanting to wipe her fingers after Haas's handshake. Harrison Vaughn's hands were warm but not slick, and a smile of relief swept Rosie's face. "Rosie Ransom. This is my friend Jean-Marie Diaz."

Mrs Vaughn offered a trill of dismay. "Oh, dear, you poor creature. Not the Rosie Ransom the papers have been talking about, surely? What a trial for you, Miss Ransom! How *are* you holding up?" Rather than shake Rosie's hand, she offered a delicate embrace, then slipped her arm around Rosie's shoulders. "You must come in and have something to drink rather than stand around in this dreadful heat. What a good friend you are, Miss Diaz, helping Miss Ransom in her time of need."

Rosie said, "Actually," and Jean caught her eye, shaking her head swiftly. Mrs Vaughn turned an expectant look on Rosie, who fumbled for something to say and landed awkwardly on "Actually, we were hoping we could steal Hank away for lunch at Big Bob's. There's a Sunday special, see, Big Bob's Burger Challenge, where if you can eat the whole burger you get it for free. It's as big as Hank's head and I bet Jean he couldn't finish it and that I'd buy everybody lunch if he did." She clamped her lips shut and tried not to meet Hank or Jean's eyes, knowing they'd be gawking at the elaborate lie.

"Well, we could never keep a young man from his diner duties," Mrs Vaughn said with a smile. "Perhaps you might come back to visit us this afternoon or later in the week. We so rarely get to meet Hank's friends."

"We'd be delighted," Rosie promised before she caught Hank's wince, but that just served him right for fibbing about who his parents were. Or avoiding the truth, anyways, even if he hadn't outright lied.

Mrs Vaughn smiled and slipped her arm through her husband's. "Oh, I know! Why don't you take the Jaguar? Then you'll have to come back for your car."

"We'll have to come back to drop Hank off anyway," Jean pointed out with a faint smile, and Mrs Vaughn trilled another laugh.

"Oh, yes, of course. Well, run along, then, children. It's lovely to have met you. Do try to not eat the entire burger, Hank. It would be ungentlemanly to make Miss Ransom pay for lunch when you could do it yourself."

Hank, smiling crookedly, said, "Yes, Mother," and escaped into the Oldsmobile before she could offer any more advice. Rosie and Jean, both smiling, followed suit, and a moment later, they were off, following the dust from the Senator's Cadillac.

TWELVE

"Head south," Hank said to break the overwhelming silence in the car. "We'll find a stretch where we can dump it in the water. Hopefully by the time it surfaces it'll have lost enough pieces that no one will be able to put its face back together."

"That's horrible."

"What did you expect me to do, Miss Ransom? If I let Johnson see that thing, it'll raise all kinds of questions nobody can answer."

"You can."

"Questions nobody really wants answered, then," Hank said irritably. "Do you want to be dropped off somewhere first? So you're not party to this?"

"Would it do any good? I wanted to call the police in the first place."

Hank leaned forward, draping his arms over the back of the front seat so he could gawk at Rosie. "And tell them what? You're having a run of bad luck and keep being obliged to kill people?"

"That's what I said," Jean murmured.

Hank gave her an approving look. "Thank God somebody here is sensible. How did she know you were the Redeemer, Miss Ra—"

"You might as well call me Rosie. Mr Vaughn."

Hank sat back suddenly enough that Rosie looked at him, surprised to see his jaw set as he frowned out the window. "I wasn't trying to deceive you, Mi—Rosie. And I'm not ashamed of being Harrison Vaughn's son. But when your father's an industrialist, people have certain expectations of you. Sure, it's too bad the Vaughn boy got shot up, but at least he can follow in his father's footsteps, right? Make a profit even if war cost him the life he wanted to have."

Rosie caught her breath on asking what life that was, and Hank continued unabated. "But then it turns out the son would rather take a clerk's job at the police station than take part in the family business, and people just don't understand that. He can afford it, sure, but someday, he'll go back home to where the money is. He's just playing around in the gutters for a while. When a soldier who really *needs* a job comes home, well, the Vaughn kid better know enough to get out of Dodge. No point in getting his hands dirty, never mind that there's a hell of a lot of dirt involved in making war machines. But that's different, when you're just the overseer. Can't help it if there's money to be made in killing people, right? Might as well make the money yourself. Somebody's gotta, after all."

Hank transferred his attention to Rosie, startling her with the intensity of his blue gaze. "But I came home tired of blood, Rosie. I'd rather my money wasn't stained with it either, if I can avoid it. So I noticed, yes, when Johnson didn't call me *Vaughn* the other night. I noticed I had a chance to not be Harrison Vaughn's son, for a while. My mistake was probably in imagining I could deceive myself into thinking the family name might not matter, not that I could trick you into thinking I was somebody else." He looked back out the window, apparently no longer interested in the conversation.

Rosie turned around and frowned out the side window, speechless for a long while. When she finally found something to say, she thought it might be too late, but there wouldn't ever be a better time, either. "I guess most of us are swimming in blood money, Hank. I guess that's the only reason I have—had—a job at all. I guess you can walk away from it if you want, but maybe instead you might think about seeing if you can wash all that money clean. Maybe it doesn't matter so much how you got it. Maybe what's important is what you do with it." She pressed her lips together and wrapped her arms around her ribs. "And I guess maybe I would've treated you differently if I'd known you were Harrison Vaughn's son, and I'm sorry about that, because it's not fair. Not any more than being talked down to because you're a woman is fair."

"Oh good," Jean muttered. "Now you can kiss and make up while I dump a demon into the river. Did you have somewhere in mind, Hank?"

"There's an abandoned quarry with water at the bottom, not much farther down the road. We should be able to weigh it down and drop it there." All the stiff offense left Hank's voice, leaving him sounding like he was discussing what to have for lunch after all, not hiding bodies. Rosie sank deeper into the Oldsmobile's bench seat, trying not to hide her face in her hands. Jean and Hank seemed suited for this kind of thing, but up until a few hours ago she'd never broken a law in her life. Well, a few days, if she counted shooting Goode, but that didn't hardly count. He hadn't been human, anyways.

"What do we do if somebody sees us out there?"

"Pretend we're making out," Hank said so blandly that Rosie twisted around to gape at him. He pulled a faint smile into place. "No?"

"Well, for one thing, there's three of us, mister!"

"I spent time in France," Hank said, still blandly. "Ever heard of a *ménage à trois*?"

Jean shot him a sharp look in the rear-view mirror, and Rosie, who hadn't, figured out enough to blush. Hank's smile turned into a grin, and Rosie kept her mouth shut the rest of the drive out to the quarry.

It should have been hard, Rosie thought later. Dumping a body should be hard. But the old rock quarry looked like it hadn't been visited in a decade, and Jean backed the Oldsmobile up to its lip like she'd been doing it her whole life. She wouldn't get out of the car, though, shaking her head violently when Rosie climbed out. "I can't look over that edge. I'll throw up. It's bad enough having the car this close. It makes me want to vomit already."

"Scared of heights?" Rosie asked in astonishment, and Jean gave her such a dark look, Rosie decided not to tease her. She hadn't imagined *she* would be the one helping to weigh down the demon's pockets, though, and muttered, "At least she's in coveralls, or we'd be tying rocks into her skirt." Hank looked at her and she said, "Women's clothes hardly ever have pockets. Why do you think we like wearing dungarees so much?"

"I thought it was because you knew how great you look in them."

A smile crept over Rosie's mouth. "That part doesn't hurt." Then, horrified, she realized that sounded like flirting—on both their parts!—and not just flirting, but doing so over a dead body. There had to be whole sections of Hell set aside just for that kind of thing. She bit her bottom lip, finished filling pockets, and with a thin wail, helped Hank pitch the demon's body over the edge of the cliff.

They didn't throw it quite hard enough, and it bounced off a narrow ledge before rolling down the quarry's side until it splashed into the lake. Rosie watched through her fingers, but Hank stood there, frowning down at it with a cool professionalism, until he finally nodded. "Hardly any bubbles, and no hint that it's coming up any time soon. Good. Let's get out of here. Does that bet on the burger still stand?"

Rosie, sick to her stomach, looked at him through her fingers. "Are you serious? You could eat?"

"One thing the Army teaches you is to always eat when somebody else is buying." They got back into the car, and Jean put it into gear with more force than necessary, getting them away from the cliff's edge as fast as she could. They were a good five miles out of the quarry again before she started to get her color back, and by the time they'd driven back into town, she said she could do with some lunch. Even Rosie, reluctantly, admitted to hunger, and not too much later conceded she would buy everybody's lunch, while Hank Vaughn leaned back in a red booth at Big Bob's and groaned over eating too much.

Bob came out of the kitchen to whip them up ice cream sundaes that he brought to the table himself, with a shake of his balding head at Hank. "Mostly it's the young pups who put those burgers away, and usually only after a game. I don't know if I oughta be horrified or impressed."

"If I eat that sundae, *I'll* be horrified," Hank said. "Is this the reward for eating too much? More food?"

"Nah. It's a break for a couple kids having a rough weekend. Sorry about Ruby, Jean. She was a good girl." Bob pressed his big hands against Rosie and Jean's shoulders for a moment, then ambled back to the kitchen, where his deep voice echoed comfortably off the walls as he called out orders.

Jean bit the inside of her cheek and didn't look up from her ice cream for a long time. Not that she ate any, any more than Rosie could right then. She just looked hard at it, eyes bright, until she finally dug the spoon deep into the ice cream bowl and came up with a giant bite that she shoveled into her mouth. A dribble of chocolate squirted from the corner of her mouth and her eyes popped, cheeks chipmunk-round. Rosie clapped a hand over her own mouth and giggled. Jean tried a smile around the huge bite of ice cream and more squirted free, until she grabbed a napkin to keep it all in as she laughed. She managed to swallow it, wiped her mouth, and whispered, "Ruby used to do that all the time to make me laugh," before pushing the sundae away and putting her head down on the table.

Rosie reached over to touch her hair, and Hank got up from the table. "I'll get the tab."

"No, I said I would."

"Hey." Hank gave her a faint smile. "Let me. At least I've still got a job. For a while, anyway."

"You have a strange way of comforting people, library man." From the way Hank's smile strengthened, Rosie figured he recognized she'd forgiven him, and he went off to pay the bill without any more argument from her. The diner had filled up while they were eating, lots of well-dressed women with children in their Sunday best, coming out for a treat after church. It made the joint comfortable, if not homey. It couldn't really be homey with the chrome highlights and red leather seats and gleaming white tables, and the black-and-white checked tile pattern on the floor would overwhelm any home kitchen with its size, but it felt like a good place. Friendly and safe, where, if everybody didn't know each other by name, they at least knew they were among like-minded folks.

Jean snaked a hand out to find a napkin without lifting her head, and sniffled and wiped her eyes at the table's edge, then sat up to take Rosie's attention away from the other diners. "I'm okay now," she said hoarsely, then shrugged. "You know. 'Okay.'"

"Atta girl." Rosie squeezed her hand, then dropped her voice. "I forget if I said thank you for saving my life, so . . . thank you."

"You did," Jean said with another sniffle. "You can say it again a few more times, though."

"Thank you thank you thank you—" Rosie kept going until Jean giggled again and Hank came back to the table to peer at Rosie curiously. Her last thanks petered out into a breathless wheeze and she got up to say, "Thank you, too. For lunch."

"You're welcome. Look, if you want to run me home, I'll get out of your hair—"

"Out of our hair?" Rosie asked. "Are you crazy, mister? I think we need to be in each other's hair. Have you gone to see Pearl today? We need to bring her groceries. More than peanut butter and jelly, anyways."

Jean asked, "Who's Pearl?" as Hank shook his head, and they all headed for the door. Hank and Rosie exchanged glances as Hank held the door for them, the girls ducking under his arm, and neither of them answered until they were in the car.

"Pearl is the other girl who was there on Friday night," Rosie said carefully. "She was sick with Goode's blood and I . . . well, I guess I Redeemed her. Hank didn't think it could even be done, but she's not sick anymore. Or dead."

Jean put the key in the ignition but didn't turn it. She just sat there, in fact, then said in a low, dangerous voice, "What do you mean, *the other girl*? What was she doing there? Was she helping him? Rosie, is Ruby dead because of her?"

"No." Rosie swallowed. "Ruby is dead because Goode was a monster. Pearl was just another girl in trouble because of him, Jean. A different kind of trouble, but it would've killed her just as dead."

Jean gave her a flat look. "You're splitting hairs, aren't you?"

Rosie thinned her lips, then glanced away and nodded. "Yeah. But it's still not Pearl's fault, Jean. You said yourself Ruby was all dazzled by Goode. Pearl couldn't have done that. It was all him. She did try to . . . lure . . . me to him. And I guess it worked, but it wasn't the same. Ruby and the other girls, they were already besotted with him. Pearl brought me to him because I was asking questions. She didn't get Ruby killed, Jean. Just Goode did that."

Jean twisted to look hard at Hank, who nodded. "She's right, Miss Diaz. Pearl was another victim. She just got lucky that Rosie was there and able to save her from Goode. She got lucky Rosie insisted on trying. I would've just . . ." He shook his head. "Let's just say if I'd had a piece of rebar handy, it would've ended differently."

"I don't think I want to meet this girl," Jean said in measured tones. "How about I bring you two back to Hank's place, and then you can get his car and go do whatever it is you need to do."

"My parents' place," Hank said, but Rosie nodded and Jean drove the Oldsmobile back through the increasingly attractive streets until they'd reached the Vaughn estate again.

Mrs Vaughn appeared in the huge house's double front doors as if she'd been waiting for them since they left, and came lightly down the steps to open her arms like she'd embrace all of them even before they got out of the car. "Do come in," she offered. "I'm sure you lovely young women have a great deal of social activity to keep you busy, but I would so appreciate just a little of your time. Oh, you must come in too, please, Jean. You mustn't just run off. Five minutes, and I'll make you a cup of tea."

"You mean Bertha will make us tea," Hank said as he got out of the car and held Jean's door for her. Mrs Vaughn shrugged agreeably, and Jean cast Rosie a frustrated glance before reluctantly emerging from the car. Rosie got out before Hank could get to her door, and Mrs Vaughn clucked at him for ungentlemanly behavior.

"It's all right," Rosie told her. "He got lunch. I can handle a car door."

"Oh, you did!" Mrs Vaughn's disapproval fell away into a delighted smile for her son. "Thank you, darling. I knew you remembered your manners, somewhere under all that crusty police business. Five minutes," she promised Jean a second time, and escorted them into a foyer that stopped both the girls in their tracks. Rosie breathed, "Golly," and Hank crinkled his face in something barely shy of a wince, muttering, "It's something, isn't it."

"Golly, I guess so." The foyer rose three stories, overlooked by curving stairs that led to balconies separating into two distinct wings of the house. A dark-skinned Negro maid with her hair in a bun carried linens up to the top left balcony and disappeared down a hall. Afternoon sunlight chased her a little way and fell down the balconies, creating shadows and streaks of brightness that didn't dare highlight dust in the air, not in this house. Rosie thought the balconies must be carpeted, because the maid's footsteps had been silent, but the stairs and the foyer floor looked like caramel-swirled marble. An impressionist painting of a woman with a parasol hung on the foyer wall, with orange lilies offering color beneath it. Rosie let out a breath of laughter and turned to Hank's mother. "I think I need to go home and change into something fancier to come any farther in, Mrs Vaughn. Gosh, this is beautiful!"

"It's kind of you to say so. Please, come in. The sitting room is this way. Oh, dear, the living room. I never will learn to use those American phrases."

"You shouldn't," Rosie said with a smile. "It's more fun to hear rooms called what other people call them than the same-old-same-old that we use all the time."

"You're playing it up, Mum," Hank murmured as he passed Mrs Vaughn on the way to the living room, and she followed him with a fond smile.

"He's right, you know. I am. But it's so rarely that I get to meet his friends, and I feel that I ought to do my best to offer some of that old-world pizzazz."

"I thought the British were supposed to be very reserved." Even Jean seemed reluctantly charmed by Mrs Vaughn, whose eyes sparkled as she tucked her arms through both the girls'.

"Perhaps Americans have rubbed off on me more than I care to acknowledge, then. I have lived here a long time, after all."

"How long is that?" Jean asked.

"Oh, dear, I couldn't say without betraying my age, could I? Is it enough to admit that Hank was born here?" Mrs Vaughn smiled again as color crept up Jean's cheeks.

"I'm sorry. I didn't mean to be rude, Mrs Vaughn."

"No, no, not at all. Oh, Hank, you've asked Bertha for the tea, good lad. Girls, please do sit down?" Mrs Vaughn escorted them down two steps into a deep living room with a bold diamond-patterned rug covering most of the hardwood floor. Big couches and armchairs would have overwhelmed any house Rosie knew well, but fit right in to the over-sized room. The ceiling rose to ten feet or so, not all the way to the house's roof, but the sunken floor made it feel like it went that high. Rosie sat in one of the armchairs and gazed upward in silent astonishment. Crystal light fixtures caught the sunlight and gleamed, casting bright shadows around the room. She followed them around with her gaze until she found herself looking out the windows at a view of a far more extensive yard than Rosie had seen, coming up the drive. "Gosh, I could live here forever without getting tired of that view!"

"You should see it at night, when it's lit up with the garden lights," Mrs Vaughn said with another smile, then brought her hands together in something to refined to be a clap, but still expressed enthusiasm. "Oh, you *must* see it at night, and we have the perfect excuse. Hank, you must bring the girls to the gala Tuesday evening. A little soiree for charity, nothing too much, although between you and I, Daniel Franklin will be there. He's only just finished filming his latest movie—oh, what was it called, Hank?"

Hank muttered, "*Mom*," in embarrassment, and Mrs Vaughn's expression filled with mock dismay.

"Oh, dear, I've horrified him and he's punishing me by using that dreadful American *Mom*," which she said with such a long O it sounded nasal and made both Rosie and Jean smile. "*Uncertain Stars*, that's it. Errol had intended to play the role, but there was all that terrible business with that young woman. Fortunately, Daniel was able to step in. Anyway, he's a delightful man, so very handsome, and single too. I simply must have the opportunity to introduce you. The party is themed, of course. 'The Way We Were.' A perfect chance to dress like it's the Roaring Twenties, or the glamorous thirties, before things changed so much with the war. Do you darling girls have beaus? You must. Soldiers home from the war?"

Rosie exchanged a glance with Jean, who looked down with the air of someone determined not to be drawn into the conversation. A wry smile curved one side of Rosie's mouth as she looked back at Mrs Vaughn. "No, ma'am. No one home from war yet."

"Then Hank can escort you," Mrs Vaughn said in delight. "You will come to the party, won't you? Of course you will. Oh, you must be looking forward to your soldier coming home, Rosie. It will be a relief, won't it? To put all this unpleasantness behind you. The business at the factory, and all the strain of being a working woman. I don't know how I would manage in your position."

"But Hank said you were a nurse in the Great War," Rosie said with slow astonishment. "An independent woman, yourself. How can you not imagine carrying on that way?"

Mrs Vaughn laughed. "With Harry to take care of me? Goodness, dear, why would I want to? Oh, Bertha, there you are. Is that coffee I smell? Hank, I asked for—oh, you Americans. And you brought tea for me, didn't you, Bertha? Thank you."

The maid, a small, light-skinned Negro woman with a downcast gaze and a polite smile, nodded to Mrs Vaughn and poured tea and coffee for everyone before quietly leaving the room. Rosie picked her coffee cup up, looking after the maid. "I've never even met anybody who had staff before."

"Oh, only two for the house, and the cook, of course. And the gardener and the driver, not that Harry ever lets anyone drive him around," Mrs Vaughn said. "You Americans have driving in your blood, I think."

"Well, we did invent the car. Here's to Mr Ford." Rosie lifted her coffee cup an inch or two, then sipped the hot liquid. "Say, this is really good. I wish I'd told Bertha so."

"Anyone can make a good cup of coffee if they have quality beans." Mrs Vaughn dismissed the topic with a sniff. "Now, do you girls have costumes for the gala? Oh, dear, you wouldn't, would you? You'd have been children in the twenties and hardly more than that in the thirties, wouldn't you? Well, I'll just have something sent over. It won't be any trouble."

Rosie hesitated, a thought striking her as she glanced first at Hank, then at his mother again. "Mrs Vaughn, we couldn't impose—"

"Nonsense. There will be dozens of stuffy old people here. A little youth will lighten things up and ensure Hank enjoys himself. You must invite a few other friends as well. Young ladies, to get the older gentlemen onto the dance floor and make them happy to write some checks for charity."

"Irene would be thrilled," Jean murmured. Rosie shot her a dirty look, but Mrs Vaughn smiled.

"Indeed, invite your friend Irene. Please do, girls. Does she have a solider coming home?"

"No, ma'am. She only wishes she does."

"Then a party will be just what she needs. You just call me tomorrow morning with all your measurements, girls, and I'll get you sorted out. It should be lovely, girls. A chance at some old-fashioned romance. I wish you girls could remember what it was like before the Great War. Things were so much more peaceful then, with everyone having such a settled sense of place. Of course, I was very young myself, but I hope so much the world will calm back down to how it was. Perhaps a soiree like this will help people to remember, and help us to return to that happier time as we recover from this terrible war."

"But . . ." Rosie set her coffee cup aside, gazing at Hank's mother in astonishment all over again. "But women didn't even have the vote then, Mrs Vaughn. At least not in America. I don't know about England," she admitted.

"Oh, it came in stages at home, from just before the end of the war up through the twenties, but really, my dear, with a home to take care of and a husband to care for you, what real need is there for such nonsense? I hate to think of women getting involved in politics. It's just not appropriate."

"But you were a nurse," Rosie repeated. She sought first Jean, then Hank's, eyes for support, and found them both studiously examining their coffee. *Traitors*, she thought, and turned her attention back to Mrs Vaughn. "You must think education is good for women, if you were a nurse. And if education is, why not politics? Why not anything a man can do? We've sure as heck proven ourselves working in the factories! In your own husband's factories!"

"Oh, dear." Mrs Vaughn smiled gently at Rosie. "You're a real modern girl, aren't you, Rosie? Well, I admire that. I just hope it doesn't break your heart. Hank will pick you up at seven on Tuesday, won't you, Hank? Very good. Now, if you'll excuse me, girls, I'm afraid I have some old-fashioned household business to attend to. Oh, yes, even on a Sunday. A woman's work never ends." She rose with a smile, leaving Rosie and Jean to scramble to their feet and say goodbye.

Hank kissed his mother's cheek, then turned an apologetic expression on the girls once Mrs Vaughn had left the room. "I'm sorry about Mum. You don't have to come to the party. It really will be full of dull old men and their pinch-faced wives."

"And Daniel Franklin," Jean said. "Irene's got a crush on him like you wouldn't believe. If she misses the chance to meet him, she'll never forgive us."

Rosie wrinkled her nose at Jean. "Whose side are you on?"

"Irene's," Jean said with a brief smile. "And a party might be good for me too. I feel like I better keep busy or I'll just fall apart forever."

"Aw, honey." Rosie slipped her arm around Jean's waist. "Come on, it's been a crazy day. Why don't we go home?"

"What about Pearl?" Hank's voice dropped to secrecy levels and Rosie stomped her foot.

"Oh, darn it. All right, Pearl and then home."

"Forget it, Rosie. I'll see to Pearl. You head back with Jean. Rest up and I'll come by later so we can finish yesterday's conversation."

"Yeah." Rosie pursed her lips. "Wait a second. Senator Haas was visiting? That was the family thing you couldn't get out of?" Hank shrugged one shoulder and Rosie huffed at the strangeness of it all. "I guess that's how the other half lives. All right, library man. Next time I see you, I expect you to tell me how to save the world."

THIRTEEN

Jean dropped Rosie off at home. Irene came running out the door before Rosie even got to it, and flung a worried hug around Rosie's neck. "Where've you been? Did you go to the factory? I expected to hear from you hours ago, Rosie! Your parents have called three times and the third I could hardly keep them from coming over to make sure I wasn't hiding you from them or something. The girls are all agitated—"

The girls were, in fact, hanging around the doorway, making no bones about listening in. Only Marge remained out of sight, not that the other three left much room for her to watch too. Rosie hugged Irene, mumbling, "I'm fine, I'll call Mom and Pop in just a minute—"

"You can't, Marge is on the phone with Evan right now—"

Rosie muttered, "I wondered why she wasn't in the door with everybody else. Well, as soon as I can, then. I was with Jean. We got lunch and things." She sighed and let Irene guide her through the door before confessing, "I got fired, Rene."

She might've dropped a bomb, the way the room fell silent. Even Marge, curled up on the floor between the couch and the wall, where she could pretend she had some privacy, stopped talking into the phone and looked toward Rosie.

Barb, who'd led the pack of questions earlier—*yesterday,* Rosie thought in dismay. It had been a whole day of chaos since she'd seen her housemates. Anyways, Barb broke the silence with a sharp "But how're you gonna pay rent?"

"Barb!" Irene snapped. "Gosh, can't you think of anything else but rent and bills? Rosie, what happened? That's just awful!"

"It's not awful," Dorothy whispered loudly. "It's no surprise. She's a killer. A real killer-diller, just like the gangster girls back in the twenties. I bet she coulda run with Al Capone and everything."

"But I'm not," Rosie protested. "Not like that. And I have some savings, Barb, plenty to keep paying rent while I find another job."

"There's not going to be another job," Marge put in, in her deep voice. "Come on, Rosie, you know that." She hung up the phone, having said good-bye to Evan under the others chattering, and got up from the floor. "Factory work is slowing down already, and as soon as the boys get those Japs dealt with we'll all be out of work anyway. What're you thinking, that you'll go wait tables at Big Bob's? Like you're sixteen and want extra cash for the pictures or something?"

Rosie lifted her chin, suddenly as angry as she was scared. "That's not a bad idea. Not for a full-time job like working in the factory, but—but I was gonna quit this fall anyways, and go to college," she blurted. "Working part-time at Big Bob's might be real smart. I—"

"*College,*" said three voices at once, including Irene's. The others fell silent as Irene continued, "You never told me you were thinking about college! Gosh, Rosie! What's Rich gonna say?"

"What's it matter?" Barb stuck her nose in the air. "Rich isn't going to want to marry a murderer anyway."

"Oh, my *gosh,* Barb," Irene said in shock. "She didn't murder anybody. He was plumb crazy and trying to kill her. She was just protecting herself, and Rich is gonna understand that just fine. Oh, sweetie," she said to Rosie, whose eyes had filled with tears again. "It's gonna be just fine. How could you?" she barked at Barb, and put her arm around Rosie's shoulders to guide her into their bedroom. "It'll be fine," she promised again, as Rosie sat down on her bed and put her face in her hands. "Gosh, hon, they fired you?"

"For being dangerous and making the other girls uncomfortable."

Irene closed the door and leaned on it. "But that doesn't make any sense, Ro. You weren't the dangerous one."

An awful little laugh burst through Rosie's fingers. "Everybody keeps saying that. Everybody but the supe. He didn't care. I'm a bad influence and a distraction and I give the factory a bad name and I'm welcome to try to do something about it but they're never going to take the word of a factory girl over the story about the poor wounded solider just barely home from wa-aa-aaarr . . .!"

"Oh, *honey!*" Irene ran from the door to Rosie's bed, sitting to pull her into another hug. "Oh, honey, they're right, aren't they? You're just going to come out looking awful if you push it, and that's just wrong! But I don't know what to tell you to do. At least—" She caught her breath and popped her lips shut, loud enough for Rosie to hear it over sobs and give a snotty, unhappy laugh.

"At least Rich is coming home? That's all anybody says. It doesn't help, Rene. It doesn't help at all."

"I managed not to *say* it. . . . I'm sorry, Ro. I know that's not the answer you want. Especially if— College, Rosie? For real? How come you never told me?"

Rosie's shoulders slumped. "I thought everyone would say I was crazy. Who do you even know who's gone to college?" At Irene's hesitation, she said, "See? And I bet the ones you do know are all boys. And I'm not book smart, Rene, I know that. I'm not *dumb*, but I listen to Hank and all his big words and the things he knows and I know I'm not like that."

"But that's just education," Irene protested loyally, then ducked her head against Rosie's shoulder and smiled. "I guess that's kind of the point, huh? Wow, Ro. You've got hidden depths! College plans! Oh my gosh," she said after a moment. "Oh my gosh, you're not going to marry Rich, are you? What's he going to think of an educated *wife?*"

"I don't know," Rosie wailed, then took a shaking breath, trying to regain control of her emotions. "I don't know, Rene. I haven't talked to him about this. I haven't talked to him about anything! What was I supposed to say in a letter that wouldn't seem like I was throwing him over? I don't want to dump him, Rene, I just want time to figure out where things stand, to see whether we still fit together! And I'm scared to death he'll hate me going to college, but I can't give that idea up either, not and still feel like—like I'm being *me*!"

"Okay. Okay, hon. We won't talk about Rich right now." Irene hesitated, casting around for something to say, and they both looked up as voices sounded in the hall outside their room. Irene made a face. "I'm sorry Barb's such a beast, jumping all over you for rent like that when she knows you've been saving like crazy, just like all of us. How much *do* you have saved up? Not for rent," she said hastily. "For your own peace of mind, sweetheart."

"Just about three grand." Rosie straightened, the number giving her some confidence. "No, wait, Supe said he'd pay me three months' salary to keep quiet and leave, so just a bit over three grand."

"Three— Rosie, you could rent this house all by yourself for five years with that!"

Rosie laughed quickly. "Not if I want to go to college. I want a four-year degree, Rene, something that means something. That'll cost most of what I've got saved, between rent and tuition and food, but if I can find another job, I think I can do it."

"You've been thinking this out," Irene said with admiration. "Gosh, I wish I had half your discipline! You'll find *some* kind of job, I just know you will, even if it *is* at Big Bob's. Can you type?"

"No, but I'll learn if I have to. I'd rather rivet. Can you imagine them keeping girls on—or hiring them fresh—to build cars? I bet that would be fun."

Irene shook her head. "You have a crazy idea of fun, hon. All right, listen, here's what I'm going to do, Ro. I know you don't need me to, and you can pay me back under the table, but I'm going to go tell that awful Barb that I'll cover your rent until you're back on your feet again, just to smooth it out. *I* still have a job, so she can't complain about that, and if she does, I'll get New York tough on her, you hear? I know I look like a doll, but I'm tough underneath."

Rosie laughed and hugged Irene's ribs. "Of course you are. You lit out, didn't you? Came all the way out here to Detroit instead of marrying that wife-beater boy your mother wanted you to. Just because you're pretty doesn't mean you're a pushover. Oh, *Irene!* Oh, wait until I tell you! We got invited to a party, a really classy affair, you and me and Jean, and guess who's going to be there!"

"Daniel Franklin. Jimmy Stewart. Gary Coo—"

"Daniel Franklin! You got it in one!"

This time, Irene laughed, elbowing Rosie hard enough to remind her she'd been kicked in the ribs a few hours earlier. "You're a riot, Ro, you— you're pulling my leg?" she finished uncertainly as Rosie's eyes sparkled.

"Not even a tug. Honest, Rene. It's a charity ball at Harrison Vaughn's house and we're invited and Daniel Franklin is going to be there!"

"At Harrison *Vaughn's* house? Ro, how could we even get noticed by somebody like that? You're joshing me. What a strange girl you are."

"Hank the creep is his son."

Irene's mouth formed an O, then closed into a purse as her eyes widened. "Oh my gosh. Oh my gosh. Oh no. And I said he was a jerk! I didn't know he was rich!"

"I think rich people can still be jerks." Rosie smiled, though, as astonished color flooded Irene's cheeks. "I think that's probably what I looked like, too, except I was sitting in Jean's car at his giant monogrammed driveway *gate* when I found out. So we met his parents and Senator Haas and Mrs Va—"

"You met a *senator?*" Irene's voice shot up and she clapped both hands over her mouth. "Did he seem, I don't know, wise and powerful?"

"That's the wizard of Oz, Rene. No, he seemed kind of slimy." Rosie rubbed her hand against her dungarees, remembering. "He sweated a lot and his hands were oily. And he wanted us to vote for him."

"Are you going to?"

"Maybe." Rosie smiled ferociously. "If he can find me a job. Anyways, so Mrs Vaughn invited us to their charity ball on Tuesday and told us to bring our friends along. I'm not bringing those girls," Rosie said with a glare toward the living room, even through the closed door. "Not after that. Rene, you don't think I'm some kind of crazy killer now, do you?"

"Of course not." Irene sounded less certain than Rosie wished she did, but at least she'd said the right thing. "Are we really going to meet Daniel Franklin, Rosie?"

Rosie smiled. "You are. I'll just hang around in the background and watch him fall crazy in love with you."

"He wouldn't." Irene looked dreamily at the ceiling. "But he might!"

"Stranger things have happened. And Mrs Vaughn said she'd send over clothes for us and everything. It's a costume party, Roaring Twenties and glam thirties. She said we're supposed to call with our measurements."

"I take it all back," Irene said. "Hank the creep isn't a creep at all. He's handsome *and* he's rich, and if you're not stuck on him, I might decide I am."

"Unless Daniel Franklin falls in love with you."

"Well, sure, honey. Then all bets are off." Irene laughed and hugged Rosie. "Come on. Let's go out to Big Bob's and get something to eat."

Rosie groaned. "I've eaten there twice this weekend already and the last time was only a couple hours ago. I'm bushed, Rene. All I really want to do is get some sleep, even if there's a million other things I should be doing."

"Like what? If you're not hungry, after the weekend you've had, I think sleep is the only thing you need to do."

"Call my parents?"

"Oh, right. Darn. I forgot about that."

"I need to talk to Hank again, too. He was supposed to check up on someone and I want to make sure she's all right. And . . ." Rosie trailed off, not wanting to press Irene's patience beyond what it could handle. She didn't believe Goode had been a demon, and there'd be no telling her about the screaming demon from earlier in the day. *Jean* believed. Rosie could talk to Jean about the awful thought she'd had while talking to Mrs Vaughn, a thought she didn't dare mention to Hank: that Pearl Daly thought industrialists were mixed up in Detroit's demon problem, and that Harrison Vaughn, Sr. stood at the top of the city's big-industry rankings. Maybe that explained why Hank couldn't see the heart of the demon trouble. Maybe he wouldn't let himself look that close to home.

Which meant Rosie had to look *for* him and be darned certain before she presented him with any arguments against his father. Mrs Vaughn had shanghaied them into coming to her party. Rosie might as well make the best of it.

"And what?" Irene finally asked. Rosie frowned, then shook herself.

"And I don't know. Call my parents, talk to Hank, and sleep. I should call Ruby's parents," she added more quietly. "To say I'm sorry and to find out when the funeral will be."

"That can wait until tomorrow," Irene said firmly. "You do need to call your folks or they'll flip their lids and move in here, but can't the rest wait? You look awful, Ro. Blue shadows under your eyes and your skin looks dry."

"Gosh, thanks." Rosie rubbed her eyes. "I think the thing with Hank can't wait, no. There's too much . . ." *Strange and awful going on*, she wanted to say, but kept it behind her teeth. "I'll go call Mom and Pop, and then decide about the rest."

"I'll tell Barb I'm paying your rent." Irene kissed Rosie's hair and left the room. Rosie took a few deep breaths, nerving herself up to go, then followed her, expecting a gauntlet in the living room and surprised to find it abandoned instead. Low, tense voices came from the kitchen, though: it sounded like the whole crew had gone in there to argue with Irene. Rosie got the phone and, huddled in the same small space between the wall and the couch that Marge had been in, called her parents to say she'd been fired and reassure them that she was all right.

Or to listen to her Mom lecture about how she *wasn't* all right, as it turned out. The whole neighborhood had been by for gossip and scolds and sympathy, each of them with a worse story about what happened to "a girl like Rosie." Rosie sat with her eyes closed, less hearing the dreadful tales than the concern and love in her mother's voice. She finally begged off by saying her housemates needed the phone, and got up wearier from the one-sided conversation than she would have guessed possible. Barb and Dorothy flounced out of the kitchen, gave Rosie glares both baleful and distressed, and went out the door. Marge came out a few seconds later and shrugged, as if matters were out of her hands. Tired worry twisted in Rosie's stomach and she stood with the phone clutched in both hands, waiting on Irene, who emerged after another minute with Wanda trailing after her.

"Everybody thinks it's swell if I pay your rent," Irene said with false brightness. "Isn't it nice that's all settled? How are your folks?"

"They still think I should move home."

Wanda's eyes widened, but she ducked her head and scurried to the room she shared with Marge rather than saying anything. Rosie, sighing, watched her go. "I probably shouldn't have said that where she could hear."

"It's going to be fine, Rosie. It has to be. Did you call your rich boyfriend?"

Rosie shot her a startled look that faded almost before it had begun. "Oh. I thought you meant—Rich, boyfriend, and I thought, Rich isn't home yet, is he? You're the one who stopped thinking Hank was creepy when it turned out he had money. Maybe he should be *your* boyfriend."

"I'm still not sure he's not trying to take advantage of you. Those stories you two were telling, Rosie . . . "

"That's what I need to talk to him about."

Relief swept Irene's face. "Oh, gosh, oh, good. I knew you'd come to your senses, honey. It's not your fault. It's been an awful few days. Look, maybe you shouldn't talk to him at all, just stay away. We don't even have to go to that silly party, his mother can't really expect us to come anyway . . ."

Rosie smiled. "What, and lose you your chance to meet Daniel Franklin? I couldn't do that to you. No, I need to see Hank, Irene, but thank you. I'll—" She nearly jumped out of her skin as the phone, still clutched in her hands, rang sharply. The receiver fumbled in the cradle, lifting and pushing down again so the call was answered and hung up on all at once. Rosie swore and set it down on the coffee table, both girls staring at it as if it might strike like a viper. After a few seconds it rang again, startling them both a second time, and Rosie snatched the receiver up. "Yes? I mean, hello?"

"Rosie? This is Hank. Can you meet me?"

Rosie glanced around for a clock. "It's almost seven, Hank, and I haven't had much sleep. What do you need? Did you go see Pearl?"

"She's fine. I brought her groceries. She was eating all of them when I left. Are you sure you can't meet me?"

"Is it an emergency?"

"You mean, are—" He took a breath where *demons* would be in the sentence. "—involved? No, I just—"

Rosie's voice sharpened. "Did you see another one?"

"What? No."

"Then it's not an emergency. Can it wait until morning, Hank?"

An exasperated sigh came down the line. "I suppose, but I do have to work, Miss Ransom."

"Thanks for rubbing it in," Rosie answered sharply. "Besides, I thought you worked late."

"Just on Fridays, when they have a lot of drunks who need to have it walked off."

"Well, call in sick if it's so important." Rosie bit her tongue on pointing out he didn't need the money anyways. "I *will* be sick if I don't get some sleep."

"Fine. Capitol Park on Michigan Avenue tomorrow at eight."

"In the morning or at night?"

Hank sighed again. "In the evening. It's better if I don't call in sick."

"All right. I'll see you then." Rosie hung up to find Irene frowning intently at her. "Don't look at me like that."

"What's going on?"

"Hank wants me to meet him, but I'm no good tonight. It'll wait until tomorrow." Rosie stood, shaking herself. "Let me make you some dinner, Rene, and then I'm hitting the sack."

"I already ate, but thanks, hon."

"In that case, I might just go straight to bed." Rosie clutched her hair suddenly. "Or take a bath, gosh, I haven't had a chance with all the craziness. That sounds swell."

"I'd wait until the girls are all out of the house in the morning," Irene said almost dreamily. "Then you could soak as long as you wanted."

"Now *that* sounds swell!" Rosie gave Irene a quick hug, made herself a sandwich, and didn't even care that she dropped into bed before nine o'clock.

FOURTEEN

Irene getting ready for work woke her in the morning, and the smell of coffee tempted Rosie from her bed. Only tempted, though. She thought about Dorothy's furtive looks and Barb's nasty comments, and rolled over again, head buried under the covers until the house gradually grew quiet. Then she rose to make herself some fresh coffee and draw the bath she'd missed over the weekend. She ran it hot even though the day would be hot, then sank into it with her coffee, the cup held barely above the water's surface. Washing her hair, getting the sweat out, felt wonderful, once the coffee was done. Then she tied it up in pin curls and sank as deep into the tub as she could, drowsing as the water cooled around her. She finally got out when she was wrinkly, betting she'd been a kid the last time she'd taken a bath that long. At least getting fired had one tiny benefit, not that she could linger in the bath all day every day.

There were probably a thousand things to do. Rosie pulled on a boxy-shouldered flower-print dress that would be cooler than dungarees and tied a scarf over her damp hair: there. That counted as one of the thousand things, at least. She had to find work, too, but that wouldn't be so easy.

Signing up for unemployment, though. That would be easy, and with years of factory work under her belt, she didn't see how they could turn her down. Most unemployment paid out twenty dollars a week, just over half what she'd been earning, and that would sure be enough to shut Barb up. Rosie grabbed her purse, making sure it had everything she needed in it before hurrying out to catch a tram. It didn't smell too bad, with most folks already at work.

The older lady at the unemployment office handed over paperwork for Rosie to fill out, and widened her eyes when she saw Rosie's name written on the page. "Aren't you the girl—"

"Yes, ma'am, and they fired me for it."

All the curiosity drained from the woman's expression, until her whole face, from the thin line of her mouth to the little muscles around her eyes, looked like she'd been beat down dozens of times and was just waiting for another hit. She took a pen and signed off on the paper Rosie had filled out, then slapped it into a processing box. Rosie startled. "Aren't you supposed to ask me questions?"

The woman just barely shook her head. "My momma got put in jail for shooting my poppa after he'd come after her and us girls with his fists or worse. They all said it took two to make a fight, but I know better, and that newspaper article says that soldier killed a bunch of other girls too. Protecting yourself's no thing to get fired or worse for. You have any problems collecting your unemployment, Miss Ransom, you come see me. I'm Ida Mae Bartlett, and you come see me." She gave a short, sharp nod and sent Rosie out the door.

Things wouldn't always go that easy, Rosie reminded herself on the way out. Mostly they wouldn't. Still, it felt good to have someone, a stranger, on her side. And knowing the unemployment money would come in made having to look for another job less scary. Worse came to worst, she could manage on unemployment until school started in the fall. At least she wouldn't be dipping into her hard-earned savings. Plus Superintendent Doherty had promised three months' severance. Maybe she ought to find a lawyer anyways. Doherty might be right that she'd never get the job back, but she might get a few months' more severance. Rosie turned around and went back into the unemployment office to ask Mrs Bartlett if she knew any lawyers for that sort of thing, and, to her surprise, came away with a number. She stopped at a pay phone, called the number, and next thing she knew, she had an appointment for the next week to talk about her situation. "Don't sign any paperwork yet," the man on the other end of the line said. "We'll talk about it before you do."

Nobody could say she hadn't made an effort at getting her life in order. Rosie dusted her hands together and, glancing down the street at thickening heat waves, thought she deserved an afternoon movie. An Abbott and Costello film was hanging on at the theater, and there might even be a new Gary Cooper movie out. And even if nothing good was on, the theater would still be air-conditioned, which Rosie figured was worth the price of admission. There were sure worse ways to while away the afternoon, and she didn't have to meet Hank until eight. Popcorn and some M&Ms made a nice treat and filled her up enough to not have to worry about dinner when she emerged, squinting, into the evening heat. She got an ice cream and walked, slowly, to Capitol Park, thinking it had been a pretty good day, all things considered.

She saw Hank from half a block away, leaning on the hood of the Ford Coupe he'd parked beneath the shade of trees yellowing in the relentless heat, and not far from the tram stop. He wore a button-down shirt and slacks, his hat tilted well over his eyes to protect them from the sun, and didn't look one bit cooler than Rosie felt. Rosie finished her ice cream and hurried toward him, her heels sounding especially loud against the sidewalk.

He glanced up at the sound, then tilted his head at the car. "Mind going for a ride? I want to show you the library."

"I know where the library is, Hank."

"Not this one." He pushed away from the car's hood to open the passenger side door, his limp more pronounced than it had been earlier.

"Gets worse with the heat?" Rosie asked. He glanced at her, at his knee, and back at her again with a scowl.

"Or when I'm tired. You don't leave it alone, do you?"

"I never met anybody who got his knee eaten by monsters before," Rosie said as she climbed into the car. "Makes a girl curious."

To her surprise, Hank gave a snort of laughter, just audible over the closing of the door, and said, "I guess when you put it that way," when he got in the car. "Most people pretend I'm not hurt, or get sticky-sympathetic."

"Which do you prefer?"

He considered that a minute as he drove. "Neither. Even if they ignore it, I figure people are doing the sticky-sympathy thing behind my back. I'm not used to somebody just asking me about it."

"Oh. Well, I guess I wouldn't if I thought it was just a regular old war injury. I know my pop doesn't like talking about the Great War. But you're different. Monsters are different." Rosie looked out the window, watching streets roll by. "What library are we going to? Mom would scold me for getting into cars with strange men all the time."

"Oh, come on." Hank smiled crookedly. "I'm not that strange."

"You're pretty strange, library man. Oh! *That* library?"

"Yeah." Hank turned down an alley too narrow to imagine itself a street. Not even tram tracks had been laid in it, and there were tracks everywhere in Detroit. "It's not much of a location, but it doesn't draw attention, and that's most of what I need. Hang on, I have to get the door." He pushed the car door open almost wide enough to let himself out easily and squeezed past the vehicle up to the alley's cinder-block back wall. With a quick grin over his shoulder, he sank his fingers into the wall, twisted something, and pulled a smoothly rolling door open.

Rosie laughed in astonishment as the cinder blocks swept past, revealed as nothing more than a terrific paint job. Beyond the door a deep black room gaped. Rosie lifted her eyebrows and pointed to the driver's seat. Hank stepped out of the way, and she scooted over to ease the car into the garage. Hank came inside, pulling the door closed again. Lights came on overhead as it clicked shut, and Rosie squirmed out of the car. "A secret hideaway! You have a secret hideaway in downtown Detroit!"

Hank grinned fit to beat the bank. "It's all right, isn't it? We're behind the Industrial Building, and we're about to go below it. The architect who designed it built our house, too." He edged past the car—the garage wasn't much wider than the alley—and pressed open another door without a visible handle. Rosie paused to examine it, finding an indentation where pressure made the latch slip open, before she followed Hank down a set of well-kept concrete stairs into a daylight-window basement split into two spaces.

One side—the bigger side—had mats, punching bags, bull's-eyes and weaponry that included everything Rosie could think of, plus some, except maybe for rebar. Squares of light from the dirty windows made mottled spots over everything so it looked old and badly used, but the smell reminded Rosie of a new car: fresh and sharp and clean.

The other side had two brown leather armchairs and a broad wooden table, none of which looked like they should have fit down the tiny staircase. Shelves lined the walls over there, dozens of books with leather bindings stacked on them, and fewer, more-modern-looking books piled on the corner of the table beside a handsome desk lamp that matched a tall floor lamp. Two more chairs, these ones metal and folding, leaned against a wall, and in the corner sat a counter with a sink, a coffee pot, and a small refrigerator next to it. Rosie studied all of it, then looked at Hank, who gave her a droll smile.

"Welcome to the Ex Libris Detroit headquarters, Miss Ransom."

Rosie turned, taking in the space again. "How can this be here without anybody knowing about it?"

"People don't go poking around in basements very much, and there are a lot of people in Detroit. All sorts of strange things slide by without much notice."

"Like killing a couple of demons."

"As a casual example, sure."

Rosie gave him a faint smile and went to the bookshelves. "There's stuff about Redeemers in these?"

"Let's find out."

❂ ❂ ❂

Half an hour later, sitting in one of the leather chairs with a semicircle of leather-bound books open on the table in front of her, Rosie pulled a hand over her mouth. "So far I haven't found much more about Redeemers than we've figured out already. Not even as much, if you want to look at it from me Redeeming Pearl—nothing about how a demon horde might hide from a library man who was looking for them. And I still don't understand why half the factory didn't come running when they heard that—what did you call it? Oshim?—screaming yesterday."

Hank sprawled in the other chair, his bum leg bent over its arm and the other foot stretched along the floor. He held a small book in his hands, examining it with the intensity of a man who needed glasses. He looked a lot more approachable that way, Rosie thought, like he'd thrown off some kind of formality he'd never been comfortable with. He glanced up at her last comment, and Rosie swore his finger went to the bridge of his nose, like he'd push up spectacles he didn't wear. "Ochim. In some ways, it's just another word for demon, but we use it to describe the ones who use sound as their primary offensive. Ochim create a dampening effect when they scream. It's in . . . that book up there behind you, the one with the yellow crack on its spine. No, with the red horizont—yeah. The explanation goes on for a while, but it boils down to they suck all the ambient sound in the area into them and project it as an attack. It might've gotten strangely quiet inside the factory for a minute, but they sure wouldn't have heard the screams."

Rosie thumbed through the book he'd directed her to take down, opening it to a page with a drop-jawed monster like the one she'd faced. A block of cramped, handwritten text sat opposite the drawing, with notes scrawled across the sketch. "This isn't even in English, Hank."

"Well, of—oh. Most of them aren't. Mostly French. Some Latin."

"*Latin?* And there I was, thinking of an engineering degree," Rosie said under her breath.

"They're old. Before the Great War, they had people working on translations, but the efforts have fallen by the wayside. I'll teach you French, if you want."

"I guess you're going to have to."

Hank nodded, turning his attention back to the small book he held. "The more ambient noise there is, the stronger an ochim's screams are. Backing up to a factory like that, she must have been deadly. You're lucky Miss Diaz was there."

"She wants to help, you know." Rosie put aside the French book and laced her fingers under her chin. "I'd say you're not going to be able to stop her, so you should adapt to the times, mister library man, and start teaching her French, too."

"Henpecked," Hank said under his breath. "You're going to keep me henpecked, aren't you?"

"And you'll be the cock of the walk. That shouldn't sound too bad."

Hank glanced up again, this time with a faint smile playing on his lips. "You've got a way of turning things around, don't you, Rosie Ransom?"

"I guess I'm trying. Look, Hank, this is a pretty nice setup you've got here, but if I can't read the books and nothing in them is about Redeemers anyways—"

"This one is." He lifted the small volume he held. "Some of it, anyway. It talks about Joan, who was probably the most famous Redeemer there's ever been."

"Joan? Of Arc? Was a Redeemer?" Rosie stared at Hank, momentarily shocked into disbelief before the obvious struck her. "Who was the demon?"

"We believe it was John of Lancaster." Hank shook his head once at Rosie's blank expression. "King Henry the Fifth of England's brother. Our records indicate that even at the time, the Tudors had been suspected of harboring a demon for decades, probably without ever knowing it. All the illnesses and madnesses and ambition, though. We think those were caused by the demon, which is why the family members were afflicted at such wildly different times in their lives. It only moved when one host became too weak to maintain it. And we know for certain that the Siege of Orleans was demon-ridden. Dozens, maybe hundreds of demons were part of the English army, and France was near to falling to England's army, under John's rule, until Joan came to fight. John had her put to death after the siege, but she broke his hold on France and changed the history of the world. Who knows what might have happened, if she hadn't been there."

"Wait." Rosie hadn't followed the half of that, unfamiliar with nearly all the history Hank mentioned, but one part made sense. "She broke the siege but he lived to put her to death? Does that mean she Redeemed him, the way I did Pearl?"

Hank gazed at her sightlessly, then snapped his little book shut and rose all in one smooth motion, striding with only the faintest limp to the bookshelves. He took down a tome as large as Rosie's torso and thumped it onto the table, riffling through old, dusty pages with no more care than he would with a dime novel. A page went by and he stuck a finger in, flipping the pages back to a colored sketch of a beak-nosed man in long-armed robes and a heavy cloak. "John of Lancaster, Duke of Bedford, et cetera, held Orleans, et cetera . . . but there's no evidence she ever laid hands on him, Rosie. She was reputed to have never killed anyone."

"Said who?"

"She did."

Rosie rolled her eyes. "People keep telling me I should be upset about killing a man, Hank. I'm not, because I didn't kill a *man*. Goode was a monster. I can split that hair pretty easy and I don't even hear voices. Dang it." She sank back into her chair, frowning at the drawing of John. "I hoped she'd be like me. Or I'd be like her, I guess. That someone else had Redeemed someone without killing them."

"It might only be possible on people like Pearl, anyway, Rosie."

"But if she didn't Redeem him, how does Ex Libris know he was the demon?"

"We fought there too." Hank turned pages until another sketch was exposed, a horde of grim-faced men in much less elegant clothes than John had worn. They carried pikes and swords and—strangely, to Rosie's eyes—a variety of instruments ranging from flutes to drums to something that looked sort of like a big-bellied, four-stringed guitar. "Ex Libris saw her Redeem again and again, in the nine days she fought at Orleans, but one Redeemer couldn't stop *that* many demons. We fought too, and we captured several demons. All the information we got from them pointed to Lancaster as their leader."

"Only he got away. And Joan didn't. How did her reputation for not killing anybody stay in place if she was Redeeming?"

"I told you, you glow." Hank's voice dropped suddenly, enough to make a shiver run over Rosie's skin. "I didn't see you until what, an hour or two after you'd Redeemed Goode? And I could still see the glow. It's like looking into a foggy sunrise, Rosie. It's beautiful and powerful and peaceful, and she'd already turned a dynastic succession battle into a religious war. There were thousands of believers fighting there that week, and she Redeemed *so* many demons in those nine days. I think that glow probably never faded. I think it was probably strong enough for almost anyone to see. If Lancaster was there, it's no wonder he didn't allow himself to get near her. He'd have known. Every demon on the field would have known."

"Then why didn't they run?"

"Because if they won at Orleans, all of France would have fallen to them, and if France fell, they could move on to Spain, to Prussia, to Italy, anywhere. They were fighting to rule our world. Even facing a Redeemer on the battlefield must have seemed worth the risk for the hope of a demonically ruled Europe."

"So nothing's really changed," Rosie whispered. "Hundreds of years later, and we're still fighting to keep Europe in human hands? Joan would be disappointed in us."

"Not in you." Hank's voice sounded strange. He straightened away from Rosie, closing the book and returning it to the shelf. "I think she would be impressed with you. Anyway, this book talks about her." He went back to the smaller book he'd left in his chair, collecting the volume so he could sit, open the pages again, and say, "It's in French, so forgive me if I read slowly. Um, let's see. *'Joan carried only her banner, never a sword, and ran...'* Well, where angels feared to tread, more or less. *'Where she laid hands on the enemy, they cried out and separated body from soul in a great haze of purity and light.*

"'In the aftermath, she spoke of the voices that guided her, naming the saints...' We know all this, et cetera... *'was seen to be healed of the wounds she had taken, one to her foot that had stymied her for most of a day, and a second to her shoulder that seemed not to slow her at all. Though she would not carry a weapon, she lifted a man's weight with ease'*—so Redeemers are stronger than usual—"

Rosie made a face. "Wasn't she a farm girl? I'm stronger than usual too, from lifting a rivet gun. I bet she'd done plenty of hard work that toughened her up."

Hank's mouth pinched, but he continued. "'... *traveling to court, twice she seized, crying out that the saints were speaking to her, and twice she turned from these seizures to lay hands upon a man close to her, and from his body parted his soul.'"* He fell silent, meeting Rosie's eyes as she steepled her fingers over her mouth, almost breathless with suspicion.

"Does that mean she sensed them getting closer? Hank, if I can do that—"

The blond man fought down a grin until nothing more than a hint of pleasure tugged at his mouth. "Then maybe you'll be able to see through whatever's blinding me to the demon horde here. Assuming," he allowed, "that they're here in Detroit and not down in Toledo or somewhere else. But, Rosie, two things. One is that Joan had Redeemed . . . I don't know how many demons, by then. Dozens, at least. Maybe hundreds. If it takes that many before a Redeemer learns to sense them—"

"Then I might be dead before I learn," Rosie said flatly. "I get it, library man."

He flinched. "That wasn't what I was going to say at all. Just that it could take a long time. And the other thing is, if I'm right, if there's something masking them from me, it might be able to mask them from you, too."

"Redeemers are rare, right? Rarer than library men, even if there aren't all that many of you, either." At Hank's nod, Rosie went on. "We might as well assume that something masking them from you won't affect me. I'll just let you know if I start hearing voices."

Hank's expression became alarmed and Rosie laughed. "Well, I hope I don't, but she did. Does it say anything else?"

"Mm." Hank looked back at the book. "Not really. It's not much to go on."

"It's something," Rosie said. "She learned to sense them. That's a lot. It makes me feel less helpless. If I know they're coming, I have a better chance. And no offense to Joan, but I'm not going to go around carrying a banner instead of a weapon." Her gaze darted to the larger part of the room, with the mats and weaponry. "There must be something over there I can learn to use and that'll fit in a purse."

"In a purse?"

"Look, it'd be easier than a rivet gun, but I still can't go around Detroit carrying a sword everywhere, now, can I? I need something small."

"Like a derringer?"

"Don't they only have one shot? Fat lot of good that would do me if there were a bunch of demons nearby, especially since it firing would draw attention. What do you use? You can't just run around with a pen and paper hoping you can draw a demon into captivity before it kills you. . . ."

"Even if I could, I don't draw that well. I do have a gun," Hank admitted. "And a couple of knives I carry most of the time. Conventional weaponry slows them down enough to get them to an artist—"

"Or unconventional weaponry," Rosie interrupted, thinking of the rebar.

Hank crooked a smile to say he'd heard, but continued, "—at least, most of the time. Some of the time," he hazarded.

Rosie flattened her mouth at him. "Most, some, once in a while?"

"Most. Some. It depends on how powerful they are. Most demons . . ." He sat back in his chair, speaking his fingers wide. "The really strong ones come from genius-level artists, Rosie. Beethoven. Da Vinci. Hokusai. You'd like him," he said to Rosie's lack of recognition of the third name. "I'll show you some of his work later. And for the record, none of *them* became demons. The really famous ones who've died young, they're usually the ones who lost control of the power. Keats. Shelley. Young geniuses often become the strongest demons, while great artists who can master their output—their muse, whatever you want to call it—retain their sanity and never become demons. But it's not just geniuses who make demons. There are a lot of bad artists in the world, Rosie, and they make for a lot of low-level demons. We're lucky there are comparatively few really powerful ones."

"So you can put a piece of rebar through a weaker one and keep her down long enough to Redeem or capture, and the stronger ones . . . how do you hold them long enough to paint the Sistine Chapel, Hank?"

"You hope it's redoubled, so you can snip away pieces of it at a time. You have an artist with you, always, when you're hunting it. Sometimes, if you're lucky, it's drawn to the artist."

"That doesn't sound lucky for the artist."

Hank shook his head. "You're right. It's not. But it's the closest thing we've got to an ace in the hole, see. They usually like the kind of art they once made. Music, words, paintings. Sometimes we can match the artist with the demon, to lure it. It's dangerous, but it's our only advantage."

"Unless you've got a Redeemer."

"Unless we've got a Redeemer." Hank hesitated. "Rosie, do you . . . sense me, in any way? If you close your eyes or look away, do you know I'm here without . . . knowing it?"

Rosie's eyebrows furled even as she smiled and closed her eyes. She turned her face away, trying to stretch out her—her soul, she guessed. Something that wasn't physical, anyways—toward Hank, to see if she had any sense of his presence. Then she laughed and shook her head, opening her eyes again. "I already know you're there, so I just feel silly. I guess I wouldn't be able to tell anyways, would I?"

"I . . . I guess not. I guess I thought maybe it stood to reason that if Joan knew when a demon was near, she might know when a human was too. Like there might be a difference of some kind." Hank exhaled noisily and sank deeper into the chair, like he'd failed to convince himself with his explanation. "Do you know how to fire a gun?"

"Not unless it shoots rivets."

"Yeah. You're pretty good at that. Well, I'll have to take you out to a firing range to teach you how to shoot a real one. We can't do that here. Knives and arrows. I can teach you those, here."

"You're going to teach me how to shoot a bow and arrow?" Rosie asked, amused. "Do you library men get a lot of call for using those these days?"

"You're the one who pointed out guns are loud," Hank said. "Arrows aren't. Carrying a bow isn't subtle, either, I admit, but . . . we do a lot of our hunting at night, Rosie. We're trying not to draw attention to ourselves."

"What happens when you do?"

"Things get awkward. Sometimes we bring people in. Sometimes they choose to forget what they've seen."

"Wait, for real? Like magic?"

"Like self-preservation. They decide it's better to pretend that never happened, so they can go on with an ordinary life that makes sense."

"Like I couldn't."

Hank nodded. "And sometimes . . . often . . . people who get caught in the crossfire end up dead, Rosie. Like most of my unit. I got brought in because I saw, and I couldn't make myself forget, not any more than you could. And because they thought I could be useful. American kid, home territory a town they thought trouble was brewing in."

"Comes from money," Rosie said softly, and though Hank's face tightened, he didn't disagree. "Hank, what kind of crossfire do people who don't get read in and can't forget end up in?" Hank looked away and a knot formed in Rosie's stomach. "You're not really doing a great job convincing me you library men are the good guys, you know that?"

"I will never harm a human being," Hank said in a low, thick voice. "That's about all I can promise you, Rosie. I'd never hurt a person. Whether my superiors would or not . . ." He shook his head. "I don't know, all right? I don't know for sure. I just know I think it's better for people to join up or forget. Mostly it doesn't matter. Mostly people who get mixed up in this war either die or decide to forget. If more people could handle it, maybe we wouldn't be so overwhelmed. Maybe we'd be able to push forward instead of barely holding the line. Instead of retreating," he admitted after a grim silence.

Rosie took a deep breath, stood, and went to crouch in front of him. "Look at me. Hey. Library man. Look at me."

Hank did, his blue eyes looking older than somebody his age had any right to. Fine lines that hadn't been obvious earlier were visible now, around his eyes and the corners of his mouth, and cords stood out in his throat. He reminded Rosie of Jean over the past couple of days: like he couldn't do anything but keep going, without any real hope of relief any time soon. Only Hank looked like he'd felt that way a long time, like Jean might in a year or two, if she couldn't get over Ruby's death.

"Listen," Rosie said, hearing determination creep into her own voice. "You know what, who knows, maybe the guys you work for really are creeps. Maybe they're the bad guys, just in a different way, or maybe they're not. Right now you feel like you've been hung out on a limb, but look, you're the only limb I've even got. I'm trusting you, okay? We're in this

together, so we're going to find this demon nest and take care of it. After
that we'll figure out if Ex Libris is good or bad."

"And if they're bad?"

Rosie took a deep breath and stood up. "Well, then, I'm a Redeemer,
and if they want me on their side, they're gonna have to straighten out or
watch me start a new branch of the library."

FIFTEEN

She talked big, Rosie thought later, but she didn't have a clue how to follow up, not really. She and Hank stayed up late at the library, poring through books to find any scrap of information about Redeemers—Hank wrote the word down in French, Latin, German and even Greek, although there were only two books on his shelves written in that language, so she could scour the pages—until Rosie finally caught herself jerking awake over a page she hadn't turned in ages.

Hank pushed his own studies away at that point, too. "I'll drive out to Toledo in the morning. I'll talk to the cops, see if there have been any unusual deaths, anything that points to a demonic presence, and I'll hunt around for hints of a nest. I'll feel like a right prat if it's been out there all this time."

"Like a what?" Rosie laughed. "*British* library man. I should go with you."

Hank shook his head. "Not a chance. You haven't learned to sense them yet and we don't know if they can sense you. If there is a nest out there, I don't want you walking into it unprepared. If I lose you, I don't have anything." He cleared his throat. "I mean, nothing to help me figure out if I've been set up here. Besides, you'll want your beauty sleep for the party tomorrow night."

"Are you saying I need beauty sleep more than you do?"

Hank blushed. Rosie grinned over that the whole drive home. A light shone in Marge and Wanda's room, but not the main house, and Rosie slipped in quietly, just as happy not to deal with any of her housemates except Irene. But even Irene had already fallen asleep, leaving Rosie to climb under her covers, where she slept better than she expected to. She woke up early Tuesday morning, early enough to slip out of the house again without having to see Barb or Dorothy, and went to the public library, sitting on its front steps in the morning haze until it opened.

The librarian, short, plump, white-haired and grandmotherly, with sparkling eyes behind her glasses, and who had been old as long as Rosie could remember, smiled when she saw Rosie waiting on the steps. "Goodness gracious, Rosie Ransom. I haven't seen you sitting there like that since you were a little girl, in a hurry for another story."

"I'm in a hurry for more now, I guess, Mrs Deforest. Let me get that." She took Mrs Deforest's purse and a large bag of books while the old lady unlocked the doors and peered curiously over her shoulder at Rosie.

"What kind of stories? You used to like adventures."

"I still do. Stories about women like Joan of Arc. Women soldiers."

"Oh." Mrs Deforest clicked her tongue. "There aren't so many of those written down, Rosie. Mostly, they're legends, like Athena. But there are a few. Boudicca was one. I remember reading about a woman called Artemisia, after the goddess. There must be others."

"Those are a good start. Thanks, Mrs Deforest."

The librarian laughed. "You're all grown up now, Rosie. You can call me Emily."

"I'm not sure I can." Rosie smiled and went to pull books on the women Mrs Deforest had mentioned, not really expecting to learn anything about Redeemers but hoping there might be an unexpected hint or two hidden in popular lore, now that she knew to look for it. After a few hours of reading, nothing had sprung to her attention, but it had seemed worth a shot. On the way out of the library, she called Jean, offering to bring lunch over, and stopped at a deli for sandwiches that were only a little wilted by the time she arrived. Jean greeted her at the door with a cup of coffee, and Rosie could smell that Jean's had whiskey in it. She handed the sandwiches over and took Jean's coffee cup in exchange. "Eat these before you drink any more of that."

"The funeral's on Saturday," Jean said bleakly. "I don't think I can stand it if I don't keep drinking."

"We'll be there for you," Rosie said. "We'll go to the party tonight, take your mind off it a little—"

"I'm not going."

Rosie took a breath to argue, held it, then blew it out again. "Okay."

Jean's shoulders hunched in surprise. "Okay?"

"Well, what am I gonna do, honey? Drag you out by your hair? It's enough of a mess already."

Jean put one hand to her hair before glaring at Rosie. "That's a dirty trick."

"That's some dirty hair," Rosie said. "Sit down and eat, Jean. I'm not going to make you go to the party if you don't want to, but I am going to call your folks or even Ruby's Nan to come stay with you."

"I don't need anybody here!"

"Of course you do," Rosie said gently. "Being alone and blotto isn't going to help. At least be with someone if you're going to get drunk. That way your friends know somebody's taking care of you."

Jean whispered, "Ruby was supposed to take care of me," and curled into one of the chairs. Rosie took the sandwich bag and went to the kitchen for plates, returning again with the food and glasses of water to go with them before risking saying anything.

"I know she was, but she'd want the rest of us to try now when she can't, Jean. You know she would. How's her Nan?"

"Old," Jean said. "She didn't seem old last time I saw her, but she's old now, Ro. She loved Ruby so much."

"Just like you did. So it'd be good for you two to be together and take care of each other for while, maybe. Should I call her?"

"No." Jean took a few bites of sandwich, then put it down. "No. Call my folks, I guess, if you have to call somebody. I wish you'd just leave it alone, though."

"You know I'm not going to do that." Rosie did call Jean's parents, and Mrs Diaz's gratitude at being needed, if not welcome, more than made up for Jean's sullenness about asking her. "They'll be over in about an hour," Rosie said when she hung up. "What time is the funeral?"

"One o'clock."

"We'll be there."

"We who? You and your new boyfriend?"

"Maybe." Rosie smiled as Jean jerked her gaze up to Rosie's. "Hah, I got you. He's still not my boyfriend, but I surprised you, anyways. How are you?" She finally sat on the couch across from Jean's chair. "Not about Ruby. I can see how you are there. But what we did, what *you* did at the factory on Sunday, did that . . . make it worse?"

The surprise that had been in Jean's eyes changed to a different kind of flash, this time more ferocious. "It helped. It made me feel like I could do something. *Something*, at least. I know I should be sick over killing somebody, but—"

To her own surprise, Rosie laughed. Offense flew across Jean's face, but Rosie shook her head. "No, it's just I know exactly what you mean. People keep saying how upset I should be, but all I'm really upset over is getting fired." She took a sharp breath after that, trying to quell the pinch of nausea at reminding herself, and sympathy shadowed Jean's features.

"We're a hell of a pair, aren't we," the other girl asked, and Rosie exhaled again, a hard little jolt of agreement. After a few seconds of uncertain silence, Jean said, "But we're going to be okay, right?"

"Yeah." Rosie leaned across the table, offering Jean her hand. "Yeah, Jeannie, we are. Believe it or not right now, we're going to be okay."

Jean took her hand and held on hard, even though she looked away with her eyes crushed shut. "I believe it." Her face crumpled and she pulled her hand back to press knuckles against her mouth, but she nodded again and repeated, "I believe it," hoarsely.

"C'mere." Rosie reached for Jean's hand again, tugging her to her feet and around the table. Jean sat beside her and Rosie wrapped her arms around her, bowed her head over Jean's, and felt tears leak down her own face as Jean cried, almost silently, for a long time.

They were both half asleep with exhaustion when the Diazes arrived, Mrs Diaz sweeping in with an expression of heartbreak and concern as her husband hung back looking worried and uncomfortable. Rosie smiled wearily at both of them, promising they were all right, then extracted herself from Jean's embrace so Mrs Diaz could take her place. Mr Diaz looked even more helpless, and Rosie gestured him toward the kitchen, where she couldn't help but smile at his nervousness. "Can you cook at all, Mr Diaz?"

Affront chased nerves from his features. "Of course not!"

Of course not. Rosie struggled to keep her smile in place. "Maybe now would be a good time to learn. Think how much they'd appreciate it, Mr Diaz. Now let's have a look at what Jean's got here." She popped cupboards open until she found a jar of wieners and a box of Kraft macaroni and cheese. "Perfect. When it gets near to dinnertime, around a quarter to five, you just come in here turn the heat on the burner, like this, see?" She showed him how, cajoled him into trying it himself, then turned it off again and dug around for a frying pan and two pots. "These will do. Now, first you'll start the macaroni and cheese, because the water takes a few minutes to boil. You follow the instructions strictly, you hear, Mr Diaz?" She smiled at him and he nodded uncomfortably. "The most important thing to remember is once you put the macaroni in, you turn the heat down so it doesn't boil over, and you give it a couple of stirs. Got that? Once the macaroni is in, you put a bit of margarine in the bottom of the frying pan and let it melt, then put the wieners into it and fry them up until they're hot, it's just a few minutes. Turn them over a couple times, and while they're cooking, you can take this . . ." Rosie opened the fridge and made a sound of triumph. "Take this broccoli, it's already even all cut up, and put it into a pot and turn the heat on under it until it boils too. The whole thing won't take more than half an hour, and they'll be so impressed, Mr Diaz. You'll be a regular hero. A regular hero, taking care of his girls when they need him." She patted his shoulder and left the kitchen wondering how men survived without women in their houses. Some of them *must* learn to cook or clean. Either that or they starved and lived in squalor. Still shaking her head over it, she hugged Jean good-bye, then waited in the heat for the next tram, thinking of a sponge bath when she got home.

Finding the house empty came as a shock. For a moment she couldn't understand why, before she realized everyone else wouldn't be home from work for two or three hours yet. Delighted, she took another bath, cool instead of hot this time, and, mindful of having teased Jean about her hair, borrowed Irene's hair dryer to set fat waves into her chin-length brown hair. A clip kept her bangs to one side, and the result in the mirror looked 1920s enough to satisfy her. She left the bathroom just as Barb and Dorothy arrived home.

They stopped short upon seeing her, then both giggled as if they'd been caught doing something they shouldn't. Dorothy grabbed Barb's hand and they ran to their room, where another burst of giggles reminded Rosie of teenage girls being cruel to another. She held still, trying not to let it affect her, but heat crept up her cheeks until her eyes prickled. At least she hadn't put any makeup on yet. She went to her room to sit on the edge of the bed and wait for her breathing to calm.

Irene came in a while later, hot and pink from work, and started gaily telling Rosie about the day before cottoning on to Rosie's careful posture and fixed gaze. "It's that nasty Barb, isn't it," she said. "Don't pay attention to her for a minute, Ro. You look swanky and you're only in a day dress. Just wait until your sheik gets here with the costumes. Where's Jean?"

"She decided not to go. Her parents are with her right now. Oh, Rene, your hair looks swell!" Irene had undone her white hair kerchief to reveal big curlers, and as she unwound the curlers, long waves fell around her shoulders in auburn ripples. "Daniel Franklin's going to swoon at your feet! Want me to do your makeup? And then you can do mine when my face isn't so puffy anymore."

"I could just kick that Barb for making you cry," Irene snapped, but her pleasure over Rosie's approval of her hair swept her irritation away. "You should do your own makeup, though, after you do mine. You're better at it than I am. A real artist. *You* should go to Hollywood, Ro! You could do makeup for the stars!"

"Maybe if you're one of the stars." Rosie smiled and did Irene's makeup with thin eyebrows and lips, then washed her own face with cold water again and, after drying it, did her own with bow lips and smoky eyes, to go with the Roaring Twenties bob she'd created for her hair. "I hope our dresses are right for the makeup."

"I hope our dresses are right for our skin tones!"

"Irene, you look good in everything. It's one of the advantages of being beautiful."

"Rosie?" Marge's deep voice called from the living room. "There's a man here to see you. He's got clothes with him."

"Hank!" Rosie jumped to her feet and ran to the living room with Irene trailing behind her. Wanda, in dungarees with her bare feet on the couch, peered over the edge of her book at Hank like she didn't want to be noticed looking at him, but Marge, still holding the door, examined him with interest, then whistled as she saw Rosie and Irene.

"You two look swanky. Going to a party?"

"Hank's mom invited us to a dress-up party. Gosh. Hank. Wow. Wow!"

He handed their dresses over, then spread his arms as if seeking approval. "Will I do?"

"Holy heck, will you ever! Turn around, let me look at you!" Rosie laughed as Hank cocked an eyebrow but did as she asked, turning slowly to show off a short-waisted tuxedo with tails. His hair was bright and glossy and smoothed over in a parted wave. In his right hand he carried a cane of golden wood that Rosie swore came within an inch of matching his hair. "You clean up good, mister. Marge, Wanda, this is Hank. He's with the police."

"Ladies," Hank said gallantly. Wanda blushed and Marge let go a deep bark of laughter.

"Try not to eat him up while we get dressed," Irene breathed. She and Rosie went back to the bedroom together to finish getting ready, with Irene wiggling into an ivory gown she needed Rosie to zip, and Rosie slipping a straight-cut crimson flapper dress on without really looking at it. She zipped it under her arm, then snugged Irene into her dress before stepping back to look at her.

"Oh, Rene."

"*Ro*," Irene said in the same tone, and turned her to face the tall mirror in their room. Rosie protested, still wanting to gape admiringly at Irene, then fell silent as she saw them both in the mirror. Irene's sleeveless gown fit flawlessly through the bodice and loosened at the hips to fall in shimmering satin waves to the floor. With her hair in thick waves, she looked like a redheaded Veronica Lake, porcelain-skinned and perfect. Rosie towered over her, but she didn't look big, just *different*. More Clara Bow than Veronica Lake, with black fringe whispering over crimson silk on a dress short enough to be scandalous.

"There's a headband," Irene said, and tucked it over Rosie's hair, catching the waves and pinning it in place with the clip Rosie had put in earlier. "Rosie, you look *swell*."

"You look like Hollywood." Rosie hugged Irene, and, clutching hands, they returned to the living room, where Hank, who had taken a seat in their absence, jumped to his feet, then stood there speechlessly while Marge let out a low whistle and Wanda's jaw dropped.

"Look at you two," Wanda said in astonishment. "There better be a photographer at this party, because you two need to be recorded for posterity. You three!" She nudged Hank's leg with a bare toe, startling him into speaking.

"I think I'd better say thank you right now for letting me be the guy who walks you in to this party. My whole life is going to be a disappointment after that. Nothing will match up. You look beautiful."

Irene laughed and hugged Rosie's arm. "I guess we're not too shabby. Oh, gosh, Ro, do you think we'll need coats?"

"Wraps," Marge said firmly. "I'll lend you a couple of mine—"

"I have some in the car," Hank said in embarrassment. "I forgot to bring them in. I'll go get them."

"Don't worry. We can wrap them around ourselves in the car. Oh, shoot!" Rosie glanced toward the window. "You don't have the Jag, do you?"

"Mum thought I should bring it, but I thought you might have taken some trouble with your hair and wouldn't appreciate it getting blown all over the place."

"You were right." Irene stepped forward to put one hand on Hank's arm and gathered her skirt in the other, encouraging him to escort her out the door. He shot a conflicted glance over his shoulder at Rosie, who smiled and shook her head. Irene's skirt brushed the floor, and Rosie would have to crawl to risk tripping on *her* skirt, so she didn't need the support as much. They also made a beautiful couple, with Irene small and curvy and ivory beside Hank's tall, slender, gold-clad form. Rosie couldn't imagine she'd look so good with him, even if her dress did shimmy when she moved. Marge said, "Have fun," as they went out the door. Rosie, smiling, waved at her, and tried not to remember she intended to spy on Harrison Vaughn all night, at his own party.

SIXTEEN

A band of Negro musicians in white tuxedo coats, occasionally visible through a throng of people so beautifully dressed Rosie could barely look at them, played at the back of the Vaughn's huge foyer. Doors were flung open all over the downstairs, not just to the living room Rosie had been invited into earlier, but to a dining room big enough to be considered a dining *hall*, and to another room with hardwood floors and all the furniture cleared away so the room's center was left open for dancing, and to a third space like a living room only more formal, where Rosie caught a glimpse of Daniel Franklin holding court amid a bevy of admiring women. She caught Irene's hand and nodded toward Franklin, gratified to hear her friend's almost-soundless squeak of excitement. It made her feel less alone and overwhelmed by the casual wealth and beauty on display in the Vaughn home. She bet every pearl, ruby, and diamond she could see was real, and that, unlike her dress, none of them had been borrowed.

"There you are!" Mrs Vaughn slipped through the crowd to embrace her son, then, with equal charm, first Rosie and then Irene. "You must be Irene. I'm so sorry Jean couldn't make it tonight, although it's certainly been a difficult time for her. Do tell her I was thinking of her, will you not? Rosie, you were absolutely correct about Irene's size, and you both look perfectly lovely. Now, let me introduce you to a few people, and then I'm sure you'll be able to make your way quite well on your own. I want you girls to enjoy yourselves. Hank, darling, I need you to go be charming. People have been asking about you all evening. I told them you were collecting more guests, of course, but I wish you hadn't gone to that silly job today. It was inconsiderate, knowing I had so much to do for the party."

"I know, Mum. I'm sorry." Hank kissed Mrs Vaughn's cheek, glanced apologetically at Rosie, and went to do as he'd been told.

"Men," Mrs Vaughn said with a shake of her head. "I can't imagine how they'd get by without us. Speaking of which, I promised you an introduction to Daniel, didn't I. Let's begin there." She slipped her arms through both Rosie and Irene's and walked them into the third party room, with the crowd parting easily to let them through even though they were three abreast. "Daniel, Danny, darling, I have some young ladies to introduce you to. Rosie Ransom and Irene Fandel, who were so good as to come to the party on virtually no notice."

"Miss Ransom. Miss Fandel." *Photoplay* claimed Franklin got by on his smile, which could smolder as easily as it could make him seem like the boy next door. Under its full weight, in person, Rosie struggled not to giggle like a schoolgirl, while Irene smiled up through her lashes at him as if suddenly stricken with shyness. Franklin, bowing over her hand, took a step back and opened his arm, so Irene's dress and figure could be seen to their best advantage. "Miss Fandel, I know six producers and two studios who would give you a contract for that smile. Tell me your speaking voice is as dulcet as your gaze, and together, you and I shall conquer Hollywood."

"I'm a New Yorker, Mr Franklin," Irene said with no hint of Brooklyn in her accent. "I don't think we're known for dulcet tones."

"Oh, better still," Franklin cried. "She speaks directly, a woman who knows her mind and calls the shots even as she devastates with a glance. Would you like to be the next Katharine Hepburn, Miss Fandel?"

Irene shot Rosie a wide-eyed glance that sent Rosie into another laugh, which brought her—momentarily—to Franklin's attention. "My God, another beauty I'm neglecting. Forgive me, Miss Ransom. The pleasure is mine." He bowed over her hand as well, making her realize, as he straightened, that he stood almost exactly her height, far shorter than she'd imagined him to be from seeing him on screen. He caught her glance toward her own heel-clad feet and put on a rueful smile. "I know, I know. I'm shorter than you expected. I always am. What's a man to do, when he's been seen on screen twenty feet high, and he proves to be only mortal upon retreating to the real world?"

"Rely on killer charm," Rosie said with a smile, and he struck a hand over his heart.

"She understands me! Please, Valentine," he said, suddenly addressing Mrs Vaughn, "leave these young ladies with me. I'll do my best to ensure they have a splendid evening. I'll introduce them to everyone who's anyone, and I'll steal at least one of them back to Hollywood with me, thus ensuring my career as a talent scout when they inevitably discover I cannot in fact act at all."

"Oh, but that's not true!" Irene burst out. "I've seen all your movies, Mr Franklin—"

"Daniel, I insist."

Irene blushed prettily. "Daniel. And you *can* act! You broke my heart when you played Lieutenant Wilson in—"

Franklin put his hand over his heart again. "You *have* seen all my films! No one ever mentions poor Lieutenant Wilson! You're too kind, my dear, far too kind, and let me introduce you to—no, not him, he's much too handsome and might take your eye from me. Here, Mr Driver, he's old and terribly boring, just the sort who can't threaten to replace me." Old, boring Mr Driver couldn't have been more than a dozen years older than Franklin, and if he didn't share the actor's classic features and sun-blond hair, neither was he unattractive, and Franklin muttered, "Of course, he's awfully rich," as if the other man had committed a sin by being so, and Irene, laughing, accepted Driver's kiss on her cheek gracefully. Franklin drew her deeper into a crowd of men and women alike, offering introductions and looking positively smug as Irene charmed and flirted. Rosie watched from the outside of the circle, then, confident Irene was happy and in good hands, slipped away from the noisy group to explore the rest of the party.

People from the society pages were everywhere, laughing and talking, sipping sparkling wine from glasses that made prisms when the light caught them right. A waitress offered Rosie one, and she took it with a murmur of thanks, mostly to tap her finger against its rim and hear the crystal's sweet chime. She paused near groups of people a few times, listening in on conversations. Mostly the speakers ignored her, or nodded an acknowledgment that neither expected nor forbid her to join in.

No one idly mentioned being a demon, or hiding a nest of demons in Detroit, and Rosie, finally realizing she was listening to hear just such a confession, laughed at herself and drank her wine, surprised at its sweetness. Another waitress offered her a thumb-sized bit of pastry from a tray, and she tried it, startled to find it proved savory. She wished she'd taken a second, but the chance would come again: innumerable staff circulated through the crowd, easy to pick out because of their black skin and sharp, white-clad shoulders. Rosie thanked the next waiter who offered her something, nibbled it, and listened to wealthy men argue about whether the war in Japan would continue or whether it might be better to start shutting down the production of airplanes and bombs and retooling for vehicles again.

"They can't hold out forever," Rosie said into one of those conversations. "But I bet a lot of women would be happy to get the training on building cars instead of airplanes. It might mean they'd still be able to hold jobs, if they've been trained to skills that the men coming home haven't been."

All three of the gentlemen holding the discussion turned toward her, no less astonished than they might have been if the table behind them had started talking. Then the oldest chuckled and shook his head. "That's just nonsense, sweetheart. I suppose a little slip like you who's used to having the men off at war might think that way, but no sensible woman is going to want to get greasy building cars when she could be at home with her children."

"I'd want to," Rosie objected, and the humor in the older man's face went flat.

"You'd better get used to not getting what you want, then, little girl."

Rosie bit back saying *I'm not a little girl,* knowing it wouldn't help, and turned away from the trio, who laughed very much the same way Barb and Dorothy had earlier that day. Rosie put her champagne flute aside and worked her way through the crowd, finding doors and trying them, in hopes of locating a bathroom to regain her composure in. One door, off the dance hall, let into a quiet, dim room, and she pressed the door shut behind her, eyes already closed, to take a breath of cooler air and stand in the comparative silence for a while. She kept her eyes shut against the faint light until she felt less shaky, then opened them and straightened up, preparing to go back into the party.

A dozen feet ahead of her stood a boxing ring, set above the floor like someone had built it for competition in the Vaughn's spare room. The only illumination in the room hung above it, a bare bulb meant to throw harsh light on anyone in the ring. A punching bag hung in one corner of the ring, making Rosie squint past the light to see the heavy exposed girder that held its weight. A smile curved the corner of her mouth. Harrison Vaughn had been a lightweight contender in the twenties or early thirties, a fact she'd been reminded of when she'd seen him in his well-cut suit the day they'd met. She hadn't imagined he maintained a boxing ring, though it probably made keeping his fine form easier. Without thinking it through, she crossed to the ring, toed off her shoes, and climbed up to the canvas, slipping between the ropes to walk silently to the punching bag.

It had taken plenty of beatings, dents and knuckle-marks deep enough to catch the hard light. She pressed her fingertips against one of the dimples, then shot a grin over her shoulder, as if someone might catch her, before stepping back to throw a punch.

The canvas bag barely moved, but her knuckles protested the impact with its solid filling. Rosie laughed almost silently and tried again, then backed up a few feet and danced up onto her toes, throwing punches like she imagined a boxer would. It felt good, like riveting did: strong and powerful, like she could take care of herself. After a minute she threw her arms up, pretending she'd won the round, then shrieked and fled to the ropes when applause echoed through the gymnasium and Harrison Vaughn said, from the shadows, "Not too bad, Miss Ransom. You drop your left, even when boxing imaginary opponents, but not too bad."

"Oh my gosh." Rosie could barely hear herself. "Oh my gosh, Mr Vaughn, I'm so sorry. I didn't even mean to come in here. I was looking for the bathroom."

"As long as you didn't use the ring for one." Vaughn swung himself up into the ring, sliding between the ropes with the ease of long practice, even if he wore a tuxedo and shining shoes right now. "This room is supposed to be locked during parties, but I may start keeping it unlocked, if it lures pretty young women in to try their strength against shadows. Have you ever punched someone?"

"No!" Rosie hesitated. "Maybe a couple of boys in grade school."

Vaughn laughed. "Why?"

"One stole my mitten and wouldn't give it back. Another grabbed my arm too hard and wouldn't let go, so I socked him in the stomach. Then I ran away."

"Running away is the best possible resolution for conflict. Nobody gets hurt that way. Let's see what you've got, Miss Ransom." Vaughn lifted his hands, making invitations of his palms, and cocked a challenging eyebrow. He looked a lot like his son with that expression in place, and Rosie grinned with shy excitement.

"Really?"

"Absolutely. If for no other reason than I'd love to see a flapper throwing a real punch. No, see, your stance is too square. Stand more like I am, one foot a little forward, one foot back. You want to be able to get your hips into it, even your thighs. A good punch comes all the way up from the floor through your fists. Whoof!" The last sound exploded in surprise as Rosie followed his instructions and threw a roundhouse punch into his left palm. Vaughn dropped his hands a few inches, grinning. "You're a riveter, right? Got some strength in you!"

"I was a riveter." Rosie threw another series of punches, faster this time, as Vaughn lifted his palms to take their impact. "They fired me." She hit again, harder, until her knuckles felt swollen and thick. Vaughn stepped back, dropping his hands as an indication to stop.

"I'm sorry to hear it. I'm sure it's for the best, in the long run. I'm sure you must have a soldier coming home soon."

Rosie gave him a bleak look. "Do you really think a girl who decides to climb in a boxing ring and knock out some shadows is the type who just wants her soldier to come home and take care of everything?"

Vaughn looked down at her thoughtfully. "I suppose not. What do you want, Miss Ransom? You can't be a contender." The words were said with a smile, to take away the sting, and Rosie backed up a few more steps, finding somewhere else to look.

"I want to take care of myself. After what happened at the factory—it was scary, Mr Vaughn."

"Call me Harry."

Rosie looked at him dubiously, but went on. "It was scary. I had a tool handy that I knew how to use, but most of the time, well, who carries a riveting gun around? The only thing I've got with me all the time is me. I'd like to be able to fight, at least some. I'd like to be able to rely on myself, if I need to."

"You're unlikely to ever need to again, Rosie."

"Does that stop you from coming in here and practicing?"

A slow smile spread across Vaughn's face. "No. No, it doesn't. Tell you what, Rosie. If you want to learn to box, I'll teach you. Come out here a couple of days a week and we'll see what you can do. It might even get Hank back in the ring. He used to be pretty good, you know. Before—"

"Before his knee got hurt?"

Vaughn nodded. "He told me when he came home that it wasn't his gun or his army training that got him out of there, just good old-fashioned fisticuffs. He knew how to take care of himself. And now he won't get in the ring at all."

"It must be hard, being less able than he was before."

"Everybody changes, Rosie. Some days, we're all capable of more than we are at other times. Sometimes it's a change that lasts forever, and sometimes it only lasts a few minutes. You were able to save yourself when it mattered, and it seems to me that's a change that's lasting, in you." He smiled suddenly, putting seriousness away. "Now, if you want to put your shoes back on, I might like to ask you to dance. And I'll be careful of stepping on your toes, because I already know you can throw a mean right punch."

Rosie laughed and climbed out of the ring to put her shoes back on. "You're not what I expected, Mr Vaughn."

"Harry. What did you expect?"

"I don't know. A cold, calculating businessman, or a . . ." She couldn't exactly say *a ruthless demon looking to take over Detroit, middle America, and then the world,* so shook her head and finished, "I don't know."

"Good. I like to keep people on their toes. And myself off yours." He held the door for her, emerging into the dance hall. Rosie blushed, realizing how her appearance with Harrison Vaughn, from a private room in the house, could easily look to someone with a nasty mind. But in fact, Vaughn swept her into the dance so easily that even she half-imagined they'd been dancing all along, and enjoyed herself as they spun around the room. Vaughn lifted her hand, eyebrows raised as he examined her knuckles. "I expected more bruising, after those punches you threw."

"Oh." Rosie's heart stuttered. "I guess I was careful?"

"Evidently so. Just as well. It would have been difficult to explain bloody knuckles to my wife, who notices that kind of thing."

"I bet a lot of people here would," Rosie said wryly. "Everybody's so fancy."

Vaughn laughed. "Well dressed and monied, at least. It's not quite the same thing."

Hank Vaughn, once again startlingly handsome in his tuxedo and slick hair, appeared abruptly to tap on his father's shoulder. "Mind if I cut in?"

Harrison chuckled and stepped back. "Of course not. I'm sure you two will look far smarter together than I could. Enjoy the evening, Rosie." He left the dance floor and Rosie smiled after him before looking up at Hank, whose jaw was set and whose blue eyes were angry.

"What were you doing with my father?"

"Dancing," Rosie said in surprise. "What's wrong?"

"You really expect me to believe you were just dancing with my father? When I saw you come in from the gym together?" Hank pulled her into the dance steps less gracefully than Harrison, but at least they were moving and not holding up the other dancers. Not until Rosie stopped, anyways, staring up at Hank in genuine offense.

"I went in there looking for a bathroom, Hank Vaughn, and I found the boxing ring and I threw a couple of punches and he caught me. He said I wasn't bad, and I said I'd like to learn to fight so he offered to teach me, and then we came out here and danced." She dropped his hand and shoved the other one off her waist, backing up in outrage. "What kind of girl do you think I am? What kind of *idiot* do you think I am? How dare you, you nasty, small-minded jerk!" It took everything she had to keep her voice quiet, but that didn't stop people around them from noticing the altercation. Rosie spun away and stalked out of the dance hall.

She caught a glimpse of Irene perched on the arm of a chair with half a dozen admirers, including Daniel Franklin, who appeared entirely smitten. A thread of gladness coiled through Rosie's anger, but she didn't want to be near Hank Vaughn or even at the party, and walked outside still in a fine fury, hoping the night air would calm her down. Mrs Vaughn had been right: the yard, lit up at night, looked astonishingly beautiful, like fairies had come down with sparkling wands to spread points of brilliance across the lawn and trees.

"Rosie?" Irene spoke behind her, sounding concerned. "I saw you come out here like a storm cloud. Is everything all right?"

"Hank Vaughn is a jerk, just like you said, that's all."

"Oh." Irene hesitated. "Well, come back in with Daniel and me. He's fun, and the people with him are mostly nice."

"Daniel, huh?" Rosie smiled at her. "It's Daniel already, is it?"

Irene blushed visibly, even in the darkness. "He kept insisting."

"I bet he did." Rosie's grin broadened as Irene's blush deepened. "All right. I'll come back in. I want to watch him fall in love with you."

Irene whispered, "Stop that," and leaned on Rosie as they went back inside together. Franklin made much of Rosie's return, although he gave no indication he actually remembered her name, and her anger at Hank slowly faded into enjoyment of the party. Both Valentine and Harrison Vaughn stopped by to check on them more than once, and Rosie watched them a while, noticing how they isolated one or another wealthy attendee, working on him with charm and flattery until the checkbook came out and a donation was made to charity. "What charity is it, anyways?" she wondered.

"American Legion," Hank replied, at her elbow. She startled, then frowned, her anger not that deeply buried after all, but she hesitated, then nodded when he said, "Rosie, may I talk to you for a minute? Outside, maybe? Where it's quieter?"

They went out, Hank wisely not offering his arm on the way. Once outside, Rosie folded her arms under her breasts, glared up at him, and awaited what he had to say. He sighed and ran a hand through his hair, making a mess of the careful waves. "I'm sorry about earlier. I mean it. Really sorry. It wasn't even you I was angry at. It was Dad. He's got—"

"A reputation?" Rosie said when Hank stopped abruptly and didn't seem likely to start again. "You think I didn't know that? You think I'd just . . ." She lost the ability to finish too, and Hank sighed.

"No, I don't, but I think Dad would in a heartbeat. Like I said, it's him, not you, I was angry at. So I'm sorry. I should have—" He half-smiled, apologetically. "I guess I should have asked *you* if I could cut in, and snapped at *him* while we danced. Look, let me come over tomorrow afternoon. I'll take you back to the library and I'll start teaching you to fight. Really fight."

Rosie's glower faded until she had to look away. "Darn it, Hank Vaughn, you make it hard to stay mad at you."

"That was kind of the idea. I really am sorry, Rosie. I'll do better next time."

"Next time I dance with your father?"

Dismay crossed Hank's face. "Are you going to make a habit of it?"

"I don't know. He at least danced with me, which you didn't."

Hank drew a deep breath and offered his hand. "Well, would you like to dance with me now? I'll probably step on your feet. I'm tired and my knee hurts."

"That's all right. You can tell me if you found anything in Toledo. Or did you really go to work this morning?" She hoped not, because she hadn't found anything amiss at the party, even though she'd been convinced she would. At least she wouldn't have to broach the idea that his father was the demon hiding things from him in Detroit.

Hank's face fell. "No. I mean, I did, and found an excuse to drive down to Toledo. I talked to the cops there. No strange marks on bodies, no unusual murders, no centers of bad behavior besides the trouble kids usually get into. I drove all over the place down there, too, Rosie, trying to get any kind of sense of—" He stopped, not wanting to use the word *demons* aloud, but Rosie nodded her understanding. "There's more sense of it here. I guess I didn't even know that until I went someplace else, someplace that really *is* clean. I'm on the right track here, Rosie. Maybe they didn't send me astray after all. This *is* where I'm supposed to be hunting. I just need to figure out what's blinding me." As he spoke, headlights glared in the driveway and he lifted his hand, blocking the light and muttering, "Besides that, I mean. Who's arriving this late? It must be three or four in the morning."

"Probably your friend, Senator Haas," Rosie said dryly. "He seems like the sort to show up late to a party."

"You're right about that," Hank admitted. "But he was borrowing our driver and car, and they're here tonight. Maybe it's one of Dad's friends." He offered Rosie his arm and they walked down the steps together, both of them shielding their eyes against the light. The car pulled up and the driver killed the lights, making the driveway seem suddenly flooded by light from the house washing through the windows and creating soft shadows everywhere. Rosie lowered her hand, smiling curiously, and murmured, "I guess he knows how to make an entrance, whoever it is."

"It'd be more of one if he'd shown up at dawn while everybody was leaving," Hank argued, and Rosie laughed as the driver got out of the car.

Tall, broad-shouldered, in military uniform, he took a couple of steps toward the house, then said, "Rosie?" uncertainly.

Hank looked at her in surprise. "You know him?"

"No. I don't think so? I think—" He looked a little familiar, like someone she'd known in childhood but hadn't seen in a long time. Dark-haired, handsome in the complicated way soldiers just home from war could be: overwhelmed with joy at being home, but older and different from who they'd been when they left, and no longer certain of where they belonged. A sad kind of attractiveness, but not one that made any sense when she tried to pin it to someone she knew.

Not until the *car* suddenly looked familiar. More familiar than the man: *it* hadn't changed all that much since she'd seen it in his family's driveway.

A little more rust, maybe, and a few extra dings. The soldier, though: he'd been tall but still slim, not yet filled out to a man's breadth, and his jaw had been softer, still a boy's. Now with his dark hair cut short and the uniform emphasizing the trim lines of his body, he looked like someone else, but he was, after all, someone she knew.

"Oh my God. *Rich*."

SEVENTEEN

"Rosie." Rich took a couple more uncertain steps, then came up the stairs to her at a run, catching her off Hank's arm and into an embrace hard enough to press her breath away. He even smelled different, some kind of new foreign cologne over the sharp, hot scent of traveling a long time. Rosie hugged him cautiously, then put her hand against his chest, pushing him away a little. He went easily enough, taking her shoulders in his hands and looking down at her with adoring, concerned eyes. "Rosie, you're okay. Thank God you're all right. I got back Stateside and somebody handed me a Detroit paper. I saw the whole story about the trouble at the factory and called your parents the minute I got back into town."

"What time was that?" Rosie whispered. Her heart felt like it didn't know which way to go, out of her chest or into her stomach. Either way made her cold with sweat and surprise. "Two in the morning?"

Rich laughed, a nicely embarrassed sound. "I guess it must've been. Your mom sure sounded confused. And I was an idiot to call them anyway, because I have the number at your house. I just forgot. Habit, you know? Your mom didn't know where you were, of course, so I had to call your housemates anyway. God, Rosie, I'm so glad to see you."

"I'm . . . I'm glad to see you, too, Rich. I didn't even know you were coming home." Rosie's hands were icy and her cheeks were hot, confusion surging through her with every breath. Rich standing in front of her didn't make any *sense*. She couldn't keep up with the idea of it, like it ran right over her and left her trampled and stunned.

His smile lit up, bright and startlingly beautiful, and Rosie's heart twisted again "I got the orders last week. I thought I'd get here almost as soon as a letter, so why spoil the surprise?"

"Sure. Right. Why . . . why spoil it." She'd heard women at the factory talk about their surprise when their soldiers came home unexpectedly, how they didn't know how to react. She wanted to be happy—she *was* happy, she was *relieved*—but that felt distant from her, cushioned by shock. "How did you . . . I don't think we even told the girls where were going. How did you know to come here?"

Rich's grin broadened. "Checked the society pages after that girl with the deep voice—Marge?—said you were all dolled up in a flapper dress. You look terrific, Rosie. You look amazing."

Rosie glanced down at herself, then toward Hank, who had fallen back a step or two and watched her with a sardonic twist to his lips. "Thanks." She swallowed and looked back at Rich. "Thanks, I guess it's fun to dress up. You look . . . you look real handsome, too, Rich. All grown up." A laugh broke from her throat. He did look handsome, and *so* grown up. Like more of a familiar stranger than she'd ever imagined, and she'd thought she'd imagined it all pretty well.

"That's what they say the army will do for you. There was only one party worth mentioning tonight listed in the papers, so I drove out here and here you are, Ro. Here I am."

"Here we are." Rosie bit her lower lip, head swirling with uncertainty, then took a step back. "Um, party. This is one of the hosts, Rich. Hank Vaughn. Hank, this is Rich Thompson."

"Your soldier, back from the war." Hank took a limping step forward and offered his hand. "Welcome home, Rich. Glad to see you made it back in one piece."

Rich smiled again and shook Hank's hand. "Thanks. I'm glad to see it, too. It's nice to meet you too. You're not just back. Hair's too long."

"March '44. My knee got . . ." Hank shrugged, and a flash of sympathetic understanding crossed Rich's face.

"Glad you made it home. Hell, Rosie," he said, turning back to her, "I'm glad *you* made it home. What the devil happened—listen to me. Forgotten how civilized people talk, haven't I? What happened at the factory? God, I'm glad I'm home to take care of you now."

"She's doing a pretty good job taking care of herself," Hank murmured, and Rich's smile didn't exactly fade, but it got stiff around the edges as he looked between Rosie and Hank.

"Is that so?"

"Turns out I'm pretty tough, Rich," Rosie said with a pained smile of her own. "It was awful, at the factory, but I'm okay. Mom and Pop wanted to take care of me, too, but . . ." She shrugged, then, too late, realized Hank had just done that himself. Her shoulders dropped in resignation, and Rich's smile got that much stiffer. Rosie forged on, trying to make it better. "But I'm getting by, honest. I've got plenty of savings to live on while I look for work, and—"

"Look for work, Ro? *I'm* going to be looking for work, or maybe going to sch—well, maybe while I go to school. I guess there's no sense in keeping an independent-minded woman out of a job while I take advantage of the GI Bill, huh? At least until we have—"

A shiver ran through Rosie, right from her middle all the way out, and Rich broke off at her expression. "Well, this isn't the time to talk about that, is it. It's a party, and it looks like I'm spoiling the fun."

"Not at all," Hank said. "I'm sorry. I should have invited you in. It's a charity ball for the American Legion. A soldier coming home to his sweetheart is just what we need to top off the night."

"Hank," Rosie said quietly. "Hank, don't."

He gave her a smile with a bit of nastiness underlying it. "Come on. Mother will eat it up, and anybody who hasn't written a check already will have his wife crying in his handkerchief and adding a few zeroes. You wouldn't want to deny the Legion that, would you?"

"No, but—"

"Then come on in." Hank took two steps up, backward, then turned and went into the house, his limp more pronounced than it had been all evening. Rosie, mindful of her lipstick, pressed her fingers against her lips less hard than she wanted to as she watched him go, and startled more sharply than she should have when Rich spoke. "You didn't tell me you'd moved on, Ro."

"Oh my gosh, Rich, he's a cop. I met him Friday night, during the mess at the factory. I haven't—he's not—I'm just surprised to see you, Rich. I didn't know you were coming home so soon. I didn't . . . I wasn't . . ."

"You didn't what? Want me to? You weren't ready? Rosie, I've been waiting for you for years. I thought you were waiting for me, too."

The only thing worse than the hurt and confusion in his eyes was the twisting and thumping of her heart, choking back all the things she knew she *should* say to ease his unhappiness. But that wouldn't help her own at all, and might make things worse. Rosie shook her head once, then again, harder. "Rich, can we not do this right now? We *can't* do this right now. Hank's in there making a fuss over you coming home and we're going to have to go in and smile for them all."

"I don't really think we do have to. I'm sorry I spoiled your fun, Rosie. I should've warned you I was coming home." He moved off the steps, then slipped his hands into his pockets and looked up at her, all handsome shadows and sorrow. "Maybe I'll come by and see you tomorrow, huh? When we've both had some sleep, and we're not springing surprises on each other. Or maybe you'll just give me a call, when you want to see me again."

"Rich, no, don't . . . don't be angry."

"I'm not angry, Ro. Just . . . I imagined this going differently. Give me a call, when you're ready." He stopped once more, at his parents' car door, and said, "I'm glad you're okay, Rosie. I really am."

"I'm glad you are too," Rosie whispered, and sank down to the steps to put her face in her hands when he had driven away. Her heart still banged around inside her chest, hurting every time she took a breath, every time she remembered the surprised upset on Rich's face. He hadn't deserved that.

Neither had she. Rosie bit the heel of her hand, trying to keep herself from crying. Rich *hadn't* deserved that, but neither had she. Heels clicked on the steps behind her and she turned her head as Irene came to sit down, carefully, beside her. "What just happened, Ro? Hank came in like a big deal was going down, said your soldier had just come home from war, and everybody started applauding but you didn't come in. What happened?"

"Rich did come home, and he saw me standing here with Hank, and he got the wrong idea, and Hank—I don't know what got into him, but he got nasty and went inside and did that. He shouldn't have done that."

"Oh, honey. You really don't know what got into Hank?" Irene rubbed Rosie's back. "Where's Rich?"

"I don't know. He went home."

"You let him go? You let him go thinking that—"

"No! No, I told him—but it didn't matter. It was awful. It was awful, Rene. And it wasn't just my fault. He shouldn't have just come back like that, without warning me."

"Why wouldn't he?" Irene said quietly. "You never told him you weren't sure about you two. I told you, Rosie. I told you you needed to tell him."

"Well, I guess he knows now," Rosie snapped. "I don't really need an *I told you so* right now, Irene. I just—I want to go home." She stood up, shaking her dress so the fringe fell straight again. "I just want to go home."

"I'll call the car for you." Hank Vaughn spoke from behind them, his voice tight. "I'm sure you'd prefer that to me driving you home."

"How could you be so mean," Rosie said without looking at him. "Why would you be so mean?"

"It had been three years, Miss Ransom. A man's a certain kind of fool if he thinks a woman will just wait, no questions asked, for that kind of time."

"Yeah?" Rosie, flushed with anger, looked at him after all. "Were you that kind of fool, library man?"

"Oh, heck, no. I knew I was coming back a cripple. I let Alice go before I even got out of hospital. I knew better."

"But what if you hadn't gotten hurt?"

"Doesn't matter. Didn't happen."

"Sure it matters. Did you ever even see her? Did you ever ask what she wanted? Maybe she wouldn't have cared about your knee, Hank, if you'd ever given her a chance to decide herself. That's all I want, is a chance to decide. Now, after everything's changed. *Everything* has changed," Rosie burst out. "Not just the war, not just the job, *everything* has changed for me. And he shouldn't have just come back without warning me, but you shouldn't have been such a jerk!"

"I'll have the car sent around," Hank said again, and limped back into the house. Rosie strangled a scream at the back of her throat that made Irene jump, then frown.

"I gotta hand it to you, hon, you really know how to handle a man. I never saw anybody lose two suitors in as many minutes before."

Heat burned along Rosie's jaw as the muscles there clenched, but she bit back a snarled answer and looked away. Anything she said about Hank would be protesting too much, and Irene had a point about Rich. But she wanted to fight, not be reasonable, and Irene probably didn't deserve to bear the brunt of that.

"Really, Ro? You got nothing to say? What are you going to say to poor Rich?"

"I don't know. I don't *know*, Irene. Drop it. I don't want to talk about anything right now."

Irene sniffed. "As if that's going to help." She folded her arms, though, and turned away, shutting Rosie out. Rosie slumped, but she'd gotten what she'd asked for. Trying to make up to Irene might mollify her, but it would stick Rosie with a conversation she'd just said she didn't want to have. Everything she said right now turned out to be a disaster. Better to keep her mouth shut. *Maybe forever*, she thought bitterly.

The car Hank had promised came around, a driver dark enough to be almost invisible in the night getting out to open the door for them. Rosie climbed in with a sense of the absurd. The people she knew didn't have drivers or parties with movie stars or gates on their driveways. The people she knew worked in the factories owned by Hank's kind of people. But she got in the car like she did it all the time, and stayed quiet the whole ride home, not even looking at Irene, who held her tongue until they got into the house, then turned on Rosie with her eyes snapping. "Know what? It's not going to help, and I'm not going to just sit here and let you be all self-righteous when you're *wrong*, Rose Anne Ransom. You treated Rich *awfully*, and you should be ashamed of yourself."

"Do you know what, maybe I did. That doesn't make it all right for him to just show up—"

"But why wouldn't he? You never told him you were having second thoughts, and most girls would be thrilled to have their soldier home safe from war!"

"I *am* glad he's home safe! But my whole life has changed, Irene. I don't want to just be the little wife anymore. I don't even know if I ever wanted that. I just didn't know there was another choice."

"Not until the war and boys started going off to die so we had to work for them!"

"You say that like I'm glad the war happened. I'm not, I never wanted anybody to get killed, but it *did* happen, Irene, and I'm not the same person I was before. I'm not even the same person I was last week!"

"Because you're a killer now?" Irene's eyes widened and she steepled her hands over her mouth, so shocked at herself that Rosie blushed.

"Because I'm a Redeemer! Because—"

"Oh, *Rosie*. Rosie, you can't just go around saying nonsense like that. Honestly, if you want Rich to take you back, y—"

"Who said I want him to take me back? Who says *he* has to take *me* back? Why can't it be my choice, Irene? Why shouldn't it be?"

"Well, because what kind of boy is going to want a girl who goes around—" Irene paled this time, silencing herself.

Rosie's eyebrows shot up. "Goes around what, exactly, Irene?"

Irene hissed, "Sleeping around," and her cheeks went from pale to scarlet.

"Oh, gosh, Rene, you're going to have to decide which is worse, sleeping around or killing somebody, or does it all just make me the devil's harlot? Even if I did, so what? Boys do it."

"I bet Rich didn't."

"Are you gonna ask him?"

Irene's cheeks turned redder still, and Rosie gave a sharp little smile.

"I didn't think so. And he's not gonna ask me either, because even if he thought there was a reason to, why would he want to know? I don't want to know what he did, over there."

"But he went away! You're still—"

"Still here? Still me? Yeah, but I'm not the same person I was, either, and besides, why should the rules change if you go away? It doesn't count if it's not at home?"

"Well, at least there's nobody to talk about it if it's not at home!"

Rosie folded her arms and gave Irene a flat look. "Who's talking."

"*You* two are!" Barb flung her bedroom door open and stomped out, Dorothy following wanly in her wake. "My *God*, Rosie, what is your problem? It's six in the morning and you two are out here screeching at each other like a couple of harpies. Some of us are trying to *sleep*, you know."

Dorothy fumbled at Barb's nightgown. "Shh, Barb. Stop it. Don't make her mad. She might—"

"I might what," Rosie asked incredulously. Dorothy blushed and wouldn't answer, but Barb lifted her chin.

"Well, you've already killed one person, haven't you? Who knows what you might do. You're some kind of freak, Rosie Ransom. Nice girls don't do that kind of thing."

"I guess nice girls just let themselves get killed," Rosie snapped. "I can't believe you really think I'd hurt anybody."

"You did it once!"

Rosie bit back snarling *twice!* at Barb, instead stalking past her toward her own bedroom. "Sorry we woke everybody up." She got the flapper dress off, hoping Irene would get one of the other girls to help her out of the starlet gown—they were still out there fighting, although more quietly now—and flung herself onto her bed, pulling the pillow over her head to block out sunlight and muffle her own hysterical gasping. She'd had enough of crying, even if she'd earned every tear that had fallen. Knots twisted her stomach, making breathing hard enough that her whole body felt weak. She curled around the pillow instead, trying to slow her breaths, and didn't notice when sleep took her.

✪ ✪ ✪

Marge's deep voice and a knock on the door woke her what felt like only minutes later. "Phone call, Rosie. It's Jean."

Rosie rolled out of bed, grabbing a robe as she stumbled toward the door. She'd managed to pull it on, if not tie it, by the time she reached the phone, and sat down hard on the couch without really opening her eyes. She hit the arm with her hip, thick dull pain radiating into the bone, and whimpered as she brought the phone up. "Yeah, Jean, are you okay?"

"Are *you*?"

"Yeah, I just bashed my hip. Are you okay?"

"Yeah. How'd the party go?"

"Great! And then bad. And then awful." Rosie fell sideways into the couch, mashing her face into its cushions. "What time is it? I'll come over and tell you about it. It was . . . a lot of awful. Rich is back."

"Almost noo— What? But that's good, Rosie, that's— Isn't that good?"

"Of course it's good, but it's awful. Look, I'll explain when I get there, it's too awful for the phone. How are you doing?"

"Okay. Mom and Dad left a couple of hours ago. It was the strangest thing, Ro. Dad cooked dinner last night. Mom didn't think he even knew how to turn the stove on."

Rosie smiled into the couch. "That's great. Okay, look, do you need me to bring food over or anything? I can be there in an hour or so. I don't really know how often the midday trams are. I'm usua . . ." A pang hit her, and Jean finished what she'd been going to say.

"Usually at work. Yeah, I know. Sorry. I had breakfast, so you don't need to bring anything over."

"Breakfast. Coffee. I should have coffee, at least. All right. I'll be there in a while." Rosie hung up and went to the kitchen to find an inch of old coffee in the bottom of the Chemex brewer. It smelled too sharp to drink, like it had been sitting there since that morning. She poured it out and cleaned the Chemex while the water boiled in a kettle, and, a few minutes later, coffee mug in hand, went to get dressed. Irene hadn't moved from her own bed, a tired lump who didn't stir when Marge called, "Somebody's here for you, Ro," before Rosie had more than changed her underwear.

Rosie muttered, "Who?" under her breath, drank the coffee in three gulps, and pulled on dungarees and a white blouse before leaving her room, still barefoot. Two steps out her bedroom door she realized she hadn't even looked at her hair, and decided maybe she just shouldn't. She backed up for a checkered kerchief instead, tying it around her head as she headed for the living room.

Rich Thompson sat on the edge of the couch, head down, elbows on his knees and big hands dangling. Rosie stopped short at the end of the hall, shooting Marge a look of confusion. The other woman shrugged and went into the kitchen, where the kettle started to roar again. Rich glanced up, then stood, his hands making a nervous motion like he would fiddle with the hat he'd already hung on the coat tree beside the door.

He looked gorgeous in daylight, Rosie had to give him that. He wore a boxy green shirt with slightly darker pinstripes set wide, and trousers so sharply creased they had to be brand-new. So was the shirt, for that matter. Rosie had never seen it before. It struck her that he'd grown, wider shoulders and more height, so probably none of his old clothes fit him at all. Even his shoes were new and shiny. It'd take forever for his hair to grow out of regulation-short, but it looked good now that she could see it better, in daylight and not half-hidden under a cap. He looked more real, somehow, than he had the night before, and Rosie's chest filled with an ache she hadn't felt then. She wanted more, now, to hug him and not let go, but none of her hesitations had vanished with the morning, and that kept her in the hall entrance, one part of her eating him with her gaze and another part confused at his presence. "Rich, what . . . are you doing here?"

His eyebrows drew down. "You called this morning. Mom said you—" His mouth twisted in sudden understanding, distorting his face before the expression fell away again. "You didn't call."

Rosie, bewildered, shook her head. "I didn't even wake up until twenty minutes ago. I don't know—" She looked over her shoulder, but Irene hadn't gotten up yet either, and Rosie couldn't really imagine her calling Rich, no matter how angry she was with Rosie.

Barb, on the other hand. Rosie remembered the other girl's brazen anger narrowly masking fear, and wondered how much of the early-morning fight with Irene Barb had heard. Enough to figure out that calling Rich would make Rosie's life more complicated, almost certainly. She said, "Barb," under her breath, then went to sit on the armchair kitty-cornered to Rich, a knot of defeat in her stomach weighing her down. "I'm sorry, Rich. I had a fight with Irene this morning when we got home and I think one of my housemates called your mom to get even with me for waking her up. And because of what happened at the factory, and . . . a lot of things."

Rich didn't sit, only looked down at her. "So I should go."

"No, you're here." Rosie glanced up with a wan smile. "I don't know when I'd have been brave enough to call you, so since you're here, you should stay."

"You were always brave." Rich sat carefully, not quite as much on the edge of the couch as before, though he leaned forward again, hands loose. "I'm sorry I surprised you last night, Ro. I thought . . ." He sighed. "I thought it would be romantic."

A small laugh escaped Rosie. "Soldiers do. An awful lot of the girls, though, are just shocked. An awful lot of them come back to work—or to quit work—and all they can really say is 'I hadn't washed my hair' or 'I was in an old dress.' It's different, Rich. It's different being the one who's been at home the whole time. Even if that was the only difference, it's . . . not always all that romantic. I'm glad you're home." She reached across the corner of the coffee table to take his hand briefly, and to squeeze it hard. "I really am glad you're home safe, Rich. I'm sorry if it doesn't seem that way."

"But it's different," he echoed emptily, then ducked his head and gave a laugh hardly more than a breath. "Don't know why I didn't think of that. Nobody stays the same over three years, I guess. I haven't."

"Because everything being the same is what we're promised. All of us. It's what you're supposed to come home to. It's what us girls are supposed to be glad to return to. But it's harder than that. I love working, Rich. I love being independent. That's what my life is now."

"And me showing back up means it's supposed to go back to the way it was. And that's what I want, Rosie. I want to get married. I've been thinking about that for the last three years. I know we never said anything formal, but we talked about it, didn't we? And that's what's kept me going. I know you love working, you said so in your letters, but I never thought you might love it more tha—" Rich bit the words back and Rosie flinched, sickness in her belly turning to unhappy heat along her cheeks.

"It's not that I don't love you, Rich. It's just . . . how can I even say I know you anymore? Or that you know me? Because even if I wrote a hundred letters, everything's changed. Even if it was just the job, I've changed, but in the past few days it's gotten so much more complicated."

Rich rolled his jaw. "How much of the complication is that guy?"

"What gu—" Rosie snapped her teeth shut on the question, a flush of anger replacing her discomfort. "Hank? I told you last night, I met him less than a week ago. He drove me home from the police station after they were done talking to me about PFC Goode. None of this has anything to do with him, not the way you're thinking. He's been a pal and is helping me get through this—"

"That's supposed to be my job."

"You weren't even here! And even if you were—" Rosie bit back finishing that sentence, too, because it wouldn't end anywhere happy. "He's seen people go through things like this before, that's all, Rich. He knows . . . what to do."

"You think I haven't seen someone go through killing somebody, Rosie? You think I couldn't help with that? At least understand a little?"

"You weren't here," Rosie said again, more quietly. "That's not your fault, Rich. It's not mine, either."

"So what am I supposed to do? Start over?" Bitterness filled Rich's face as he offered a hand, voice sharp with sarcasm. "Hi, I'm Rich Thompson, nice to meet you, wanna go on a date?"

Rosie looked away. "That's not how you'd start with somebody new, Rich. You're kinder than that."

"Am I? Maybe I was. Maybe that's changed too."

"You still are. Or you were last night, when you maybe should have been maddest."

"Sometimes a guy has to think about it to build up the right head of steam. Last night I was floored, Rosie. I didn't know what to do. Causing a scene didn't seem right."

Rosie's mouth twisted. "You did cause a scene. Just indoors, where you didn't see it. I was floored too, Rich, but I'm not saying start over. Just . . . we can't start where we left off. *I* can't. So we either have to find somewhere else to start or we . . ." Her heart thumped shockingly hard, taking her breath, and she had to swallow before she could whisper, "Or we call it quits."

"Is that what you want?"

"I really don't know." Tears stung Rosie's eyes and she pushed the heel of her hand across them, trying to get her breathing back to normal. "I just know I can't do what everybody expects, not anymore. So if you still think you want to marry me, Rich, you're going to have to give me time and maybe help me figure out how to make it all work. I'm sorry. I wish it was different. I wish I was different, or the same, or—oh, I don't know!"

"Aw, Ro." Rich sighed, scrubbing his hands over his face, then looked up with a brief smile. "Look, I guess I've been waiting three years, right? I can hold on a little longer." His smile disappeared. "But Rosie, you've got to tell me. I can hang on, but not forever. Don't keep me in the dark. I already feel like I've been blindsided, so . . . don't keep me in the dark. Fair?"

Rosie nodded, a sharp, jerky motion, and wiped her eyes again. Rich sighed, stood, and took her hand to pull her to her feet, whispering, "Then c'mere for a minute, Ro. Last night was a mess. I didn't even get a homecoming hug from my best girl."

She stumbled coming to her feet and blurted a confused laugh as Rich tugged her into his arms. He felt familiar but not: he was more solid than she remembered, bigger and stronger. Rosie felt herself relax into him, comfortable in a way she hadn't been in a long time. She and Rich had fit so well together, and all of a sudden it seemed like maybe it hadn't been so long ago after all.

Rich chuckled into her hair. "You're like a brick, Ro. A curvy brick. You hug like a stone crusher now. You've changed a lot, haven't you?"

"I was just thinking that about you." Rosie smiled up at him, trying not to let tears overflow. "I guess we've both changed a lot. Rich, I really am so glad you're home safe."

"I know." He pulled her close again, bending his head over hers. "We'll get through it, okay, Ro? It'll be crazy, but I guess everything's crazy these days, isn't it?"

"You always did look on the bright side, didn't you. I'd forgotten. I like that about you." Rosie's smile grew stronger as Rich chuckled again.

"Glad you remember some things you like. Look, you want to go out for lunch? I'd just about kill for one of Big Bob's burgers. I can't remember the last time I had a decent burger."

"That sounds gre—oh, darn it, I can't. I just promised Jean I'd come over. You heard about Ruby?"

Disappointment flashed across Rich's face, but he nodded. "Yeah, and Carol Ann. How's Jean doing?"

"She's a wreck. Maybe I can wash my face and you can drive me over. I know she'd like to see you again. Gosh, I guess it's been since graduation, huh?"

"Yeah. All right, go wash your face. I'll wait." Rich offered another brief smile and Rosie hurried to the bathroom to splash cold water on her face before risking a glimpse in the mirror.

She still looked worse than she'd hoped, too, when she finally did. Puffy eyes, red snotty nose, white tear tracks through hot-colored cheeks. She didn't mind Irene being prettier, but she wished like heck she could cry like Irene did, without swelling up. It took a couple minutes with a cold washcloth to make her coloring start looking normal again, and she took another few minutes afterward to put her makeup on. She didn't dare look at her hair, just left it under the kerchief. Feeling almost able to face Rich and maybe even the rest of the world, she went back toward the living room and, for the second time in a row, stopped short at the end of the hall.

Hank Vaughn stood in the house doorway, glowering at Rich, who asked, "What's he doing here, Rosie?" in a strained voice as Rosie stared in astonishment at Hank.

"Picking her up for a boxing lesson," Hank said shortly. "Or did you forget, Rosie?"

Rosie's shoulders dropped and she turned a helpless look at the ceiling, as if the blue paint up there that matched the living room's accents could save her, and said, "I did forget," in a voice that sounded defeated even to herself. "I completely forgot. Is it one o'clock already?"

"Five 'til."

A string of curses that wouldn't have been out of place at the factory rose to her lips, and Rosie stifled them until she could say, "Gosh darn it," so mildly even the boys could tell she'd rather be saying something else. "Rich, I'm really sorry. I have to go do this."

"Why? I thought you were going to go see Jean."

"Hank is going to have to take me there to see her first," Rosie said through her teeth. "He's teaching me to fight because of what happened with Goode, Rich. I don't feel safe anymore."

"It's not like that's going to happen again," Rich said incredulously.

"Oh, my gosh. You've really put your foot in it this time, haven't you, Rosie?" Irene, voice thick with scorn, spoke from down the hall behind Rosie, who turned to see her roommate leaning in their bedroom door. She'd been awake long enough to pull on a wide-collared print dress that nipped in perfectly at her tiny waist, and to get her hair into soft curls that looked modern and old-fashioned all at the same time, thanks to the styling from the night before. "Two dates at the same time and you're about to blow the wrong guy off. I swear, Rosie Ransom, nobody's going to feel sorry for you when you end up old and alone and sad." She pushed out of the bedroom door, passed Rosie, and offered a hand to Rich. "Hi. I'm Rosie's roommate, Irene."

Rich smiled automatically and shook Irene's hand. "She's mentioned you in her letters. She said you looked like a movie star, but I didn't expect Maureen O'Hara. It's nice to finally meet you."

"You too. Look, let me get you some lemonade, how's that sound, Rich? Rosie, you go do your important world-saving stuff. Rich and I will be fine here."

"I'm not trying to save the wo . . ." Rosie sighed and got her purse. "Fine. I'll see you later, Rich. Ready, Hank?"

The blond man smiled sharply. "I was ready ten minutes ago. See you later, Irene. Nice to see you again, Rich. Promise I'll bring your girl back safe and sound."

Rosie muttered, "I swear to God, Hank," and stalked past him out the door.

He followed her out, smirking, to ask, "You sure you're all right with leaving them there together?"

"Why wouldn't I be?"

Hank smirked. "No reason. Just wondering."

Rosie stared at him, then at the sunlight reflecting off the house's big picture window and obscuring the people inside, then got in the car and slammed the door. "Just shut up and bring me over to see Jean before we go learn to fight."

EIGHTEEN

"Wow." Jean leaned in her own front door, watching Rosie stalk up the steps. "Who snapped your cap? And what's he doing here?" Hank hadn't gotten out of the car and, in Rosie's opinion, didn't need to. She hugged Jean, took a deep breath, and hugged her again, trying to let go of her own anger. Jean returned the hug, then tilted her head at the house. "Come on in. Are you all right?"

"No. Rich showed up and things were less awful and then Hank showed up because I'd forgotten he'd promised to start teaching me to fight—"

Jean sharpened. "Hank's teaching you to fight? I want to learn too."

"Fine by me. So we left and he wanted to know if I was okay leaving Rich with Irene and I *was* until he *asked* and I shouldn't have a problem with it now but we had a huge fight this morning—"

"You and Rich?"

"Me and Irene, and she thinks he deserves better than I treated him, and what if she thinks she's better?"

"Doesn't matter unless Rich agrees, and if he does, *you're* better off without him."

Rosie snapped her mouth shut on another spill of complaints, then barked a laugh and hugged Jean again, harder and more abruptly. "You're right about that."

"Besides, I thought you weren't too sure about what you wanted."

"It's worse than not knowing, Jean. I know exactly what I want. I want to not get married right now. I want to go to school." Rosie curled her fingers in frustration, like she'd shake something. "I also wanted to have a chance to talk to him about it, and I imagined—I imagined we'd be able to see each other again and think about who we are now and what we might do, but instead he just showed up out of the blue because he thought it would be romantic, and instead of getting to talk I was just floored *and* it looked like I was on a date with Hank and now Rich is angry and—" Rosie cut herself off with a click of her teeth before blowing air out noisily. "And I can't blame him for being mad. I just . . . none of this is turning out the way I thought it would. It's all a lot worse."

"Yeah." Jean's voice dropped to almost nothing. "I hear you."

Rosie echoed, "Yeah," and gave Jean a third hug. "All right. Okay. How are you?"

"I'll feel better if I can learn how to hit something. I just wanted some company. I don't have to be here to have it, and doing something will help. Let me change into some trousers and we can go." She untangled from the hug and headed for her bedroom.

"Hank's probably not going to like it," Rosie called after her.

Jean's laugh came back like a blow. "Do you think I care what he likes? Besides, it sounds like he went out of his way to make you feel bad, so I vote we go out of ours to make him uncomfortable." She returned in dungarees and a blouse enough like Rosie's to make her grin. "Look at us, in Redeemer uniforms."

"You need a kerchief." Rosie tried to ruffle Jean's hair and got her hand knocked aside for her troubles as they headed out the door.

Hank, true to expectation, looked like he'd sucked a lemon when he saw Jean behind Rosie. "What does she think she's doing?"

"She thinks she's coming with you to learn to fight demons, and that if you talk about her in the third person again she'll kick your cane across the room." Jean climbed into the back seat, leaned back, folded her arms, and cocked a challenging eyebrow at Hank as Rosie got in the front of the car.

"You can't. You're not a Redeemer."

"So what. Neither are you. Drive, James."

"I'm not going anywhere with you in the car."

"Then I'll get out of this car, get in my own, and follow you wherever you're going," Jean said evenly. "Or you could stop wasting our time and just drive us all there."

Rosie bit the inside of her cheek to fight off a smile and turned her gaze toward the window. She felt Hank looking at her like he expected her tacit support, and kept her attention out the window until he said, "Tell her she can't come, Rosie."

"I say she can. She's the one who stuffed the rebar into that . . . omar . . ."

"*Ochim.*"

"Right. The ochim. And gave me a chance to kill it. I'd be dead without her, so I definitely think she should come with us. I bet there's nothing in your rule book that *says* girls can't hunt demons."

Hank threw the car into gear with such aggravation that Rosie lost her battle to stay solemn and grinned broadly out the window. Jean made a sound of satisfaction that turned Rosie's grin into a laugh, and Hank, plainly furious, said a few things no gentleman would say in front of ladies. But they weren't ladies, Rosie thought. They were Redeemers and demon hunters, and that changed everything.

The drive to Hank's library went faster when she knew where they were going, and Jean managed to contain her curiosity until they drove down the blind alley. Even then, all she whispered was "What the . . . ?" before biting back the same kind of delighted squeal Rosie had let loose with when Hank had opened the hidden garage door. A couple minutes later they were beneath the Industrial Building, where light poured through the half-height windows and lit dust motes in the air.

Hank had changed things since Rosie's last visit. A punching bag hung in one corner now, and a tall stump with stubby, padded arms stood across from it. A balance beam stood six inches off the floor, held up by concrete blocks, and a vaulting horse lay near it. Rosie hopped onto the balance beam and ran along it before stopping at its far end to turn and look at Hank. "What are these for?"

"Improving your balance and learning to jump using whatever leverage you've got. You're going to need every advantage you can get. Run back and forth on that until you fall off, then get up and run for the vault and jump it."

"What, just like that?"

"I want to see if you can."

"Can *you*?"

Hank gave her a withering look and thumped his right leg, reminding her of his injury. Rosie made a face and did as she was told, managing half a dozen scurries along the beam before she missed a step and slid off with a painful thump. Jean stepped on it behind her as Rosie scrambled to her feet and ran for the vault, feeling both ridiculous and like a kid again. The vault's back stood higher than she expected. She slammed into it rather than sailing over, and crashed to the floor with an embarrassed laugh.

She hadn't gotten up yet when Jean, who hadn't fallen off the beam at all, launched herself at the vault, planted her hands firmly on its back, and cleared it with casual ease. Without breaking speed, she ran for the punching bag, spun, and kicked it hard enough with her heel to send it swinging, then punched it hard twice when it swung back to her. Rosie, gaping from under the vault, rolled over to see what Hank thought of that, and found him tense-jawed with reluctant approval. "Great," Rosie said with a grin. "You've got one natural and one Redeemer. Too bad they're not the same person."

"You'll learn."

Rosie heard the thin smile in Jean's voice as she said, "And I'll keep you alive in the meantime. What's next, Vaughn?"

"One fancy kick doesn't mean you know how to fight. Come on, Rosie. Let's see what else you've got."

Forty minutes later, Rosie had had enough, not that Hank had any intention of letting her stop. She could throw a punch, and it turned out she could throw a knife better than Hank could. Even her first few throws matched his accuracy when he demonstrated, and she got better with each try after that. Jean kept picking up swords and axes that Hank made her put back down, muttering that they would always have their fists with them and swordplay could come later. He showed them footwork for boxing, moving more heavily than either of them did, then put them in gloves to throw a few punches at one another so they could experience hitting another human being.

Rosie ducked Jean's first punch and threw a fast left that crossed Jean's eyes. Hank barked in surprise, stopping the fight, and gave Jean a quick once-over to make sure she hadn't been badly hurt. "Either she's got a glass jaw or you hit like a pile driver."

"I've been using a riveting gun for three years." Rosie gave Jean an apologetic smile. "You okay?"

Jean rubbed her jaw. "I've been riveting for three years too, and I'm bigger than you. Just you wait." She balled her fists again, but the flurry of blows she rained on Rosie were nothing like the hits Rosie had taken from the banshee. Bare-knuckle and feet versus boxing gloves accounted for part of it, but somehow they felt easier to take, like she'd toughened up inside. She ducked out of the hits and threw a punch of her own, remembering how much the kidney shots had hurt, and yelped in worry when Jean gasped and dropped to the floor. Hank, mouth pinched with approval, helped Jean to her feet, then took the gloves off her to put them on himself. "Don't worry," he said dryly as he lifted his hands so she could lace the gloves, "if you can hit a girl, I'm sure you won't have any problem hitting a cripple."

"*I'm* a girl," Rosie muttered, as if it made a difference, and caught a glimpse of his sour smile before she threw a series of punches, every one of which he blocked. They fell back, nodded, and tried again, until Rosie finally got a glancing blow in past his guard.

To her surprise, Hank nodded. "Not bad. Now try to block me." He threw a punch so fast she didn't have time to get her hands up, much less block it. Her eyes crossed as his fist stopped half an inch from her nose, the scent of sweat and leather strong. Hank dropped his hands, said, "Try again," and threw the same blow, to the same effect. Rosie lost count of how many times they went through it before she got her fists up in time and ducked out of the way, but when she did, she struck back, nailing him with much the same blow she'd taken Jean's breath with. Hank gave a startled, pained gasp that contrasted with an approving grin, then beckoned Jean to go through the same exercise. Rosie stripped her gloves off, gave them to Jean, and backed up, watching them both intently and copying Hank's moves, even if she fought an imaginary opponent.

Jean had more natural talent, simple as that. She learned to block and hit faster than Rosie had, even advancing on Hank a few times, though when she landed a blow, Hank didn't reel the way he had when Rosie had hit him. Rosie shadow-boxed behind them, trying to mimic Jean's speed as much as Hank's expertise, but gave it up when Jean finally fell back with a sweaty, satisfied grin. Hank, hardly grudging at all, said, "I admit it, you've got potential. We're going to need to do this daily, though. You're going to have to figure out how to work around it."

"Before work or after," Jean said with a shrug. "Both, at least for me, once I go back to work, if it has to be four hours a day like we've done today. Rosie doesn't have to worry about that right now."

"Gee, thanks for the reminder." Rosie picked the gloves up, returning them to the pegs they'd hung on, then shuddered from her spine out as a deep chill ran through her. She took up the knife she'd thrown earlier as if she'd done it thousands of times. One moment, it lay on its pegs nearby, and the next, it was unsheathed and ready to throw.

Glass shattered behind her. Rosie spun at the same time, throwing the blade with an almost-casual expertise. With crystal clarity, she watched it tumble end over end, passing within a hair's breadth of Jean's face, until it came to an abrupt stop in the eye of a woman sailing through falling glass toward them all.

Jean screamed more piercingly than Rosie thought she could, with Hank's shout registering a few octaves below. Rosie's hands felt icy but her heartbeat stayed calm as she watched gold and silver coalesce over the fallen body, drawing darkness out of the woman's corrupted soul. It shouldn't be a relief, watching someone die, but she couldn't feel much else. Regret, maybe, but a distant tired kind of regret, like remembering something sad from a long time ago. A shudder ran through her as the last of the foulness drained away, and her knees lost their strength until she sank to the floor, folding her arms around herself as if she could hold on to the strange serenity of the demon's death. Jean's screams were mere echoes by then, nothing more than memory. Hank looked at Rosie in astonishment. "How did you do that?"

A thin laugh escaped Rosie. She mimed picking up a knife, throwing it, and Hank's expression shifted from astonished to irritated. "I meant how did you know *to* do it."

Rosie laughed again, more body to it this time, but still not much real humor. "I don't know. I got a chill and picked the knife up and threw it and then she was there. It was there."

"That's great! It means you can sense them!" Hank smiled like a schoolboy, but Rosie only stared at the body.

"Does it mean they can sense me, too? Because how did it know I was here? I'm guessing you haven't had demons crashing through the windows up until now."

Hank's smile went slack. Rosie put her face in her hands, then looked toward Jean, who hadn't yet moved. "Are you okay, hon?"

"I never saw anybody move like that," Jean whispered. "You were so fast. I think it would've gotten me if you hadn't been so fast."

Rosie and Hank both studied where the demon had fallen and where Jean stood before Rosie exhaled softly. "Wow. Yeah. Yeah, I think . . ." A vision of the blade glinting between Hank and Jean as it flew magnified itself in her mind and she curled her arms around herself again, fighting off another shiver. "I think it's a good thing you didn't move."

Jean's eyes widened in horror. "I didn't think of that. Great. Great!"

Hank rolled the body over, making it obvious that hardly any blood had spilled. That seemed wrong to Rosie, but then, the ochim hadn't bled all that much either. Maybe demons didn't. A lot of blood had misted from Goode's chest, but Hank said vampires were different from other demons. Rosie knotted her knuckles in front of her mouth like it would stop her galloping thoughts. Hank jerked back from the body like it had burned him and his voice rose in horror. "I know her. Christ, I know her. Her name is Helen Montgomery. She, um. Knew my father. But she wasn't a demon. I met her. She *couldn't* have been a demon then."

"Why couldn't she have been? Is there some kind of sign you're not telling us about?" Rosie didn't even believe that herself, and could hear it in her own question. Hank might be kind of a twerp, but he'd been pretty straight with her, and if he knew how to pick demons out of a lineup, he would have told her.

"I wish there was. No. I just know she couldn't have been."

Rosie bit her lower lip. "Hank, Pearl said there was an industrialist involved in the demon presence here. Your father . . ."

"My father's not a demon!"

"How do you *know*?"

"Because I can sense them!" Color flushed Hank's jaw and he spun away from Montgomery's body, limping halfway across the basement before slowing like he'd lost his way, rather than because he wanted to. He cast a glance at the girls, then slumped before continuing wearily to the tables. Rosie and Jean exchanged startled looks before Jean pulled Rosie to her feet. They followed him a few steps across the room before stopping in confusion. He glanced back again, face twisting bitterly, and limped to the liquor cabinet to pour a glass of dark red liquid, sipping before he even tried to speak. "I'm a monster, Rosie. I'm one of the bad guys."

"Well, that's just silly. You're part of Ex Libris. You fight the demons. How can you be a monster?"

Hank shrugged, putting on a show of not caring that the strain in his voice belied. "It happened in Europe, after the attack. I was soaked in blood, but I didn't realize I'd . . . ingested any. But it started almost immediately. I could tell what people around me were feeling, more than what anybody can tell. Anybody could tell the sergeant was always angry, but I knew, I *knew*, it wasn't just anger. He felt guilty and helpless because soldiers under his command were dying and he thought he should have been able to stop it. That drove the anger. It wasn't just that Sam, the soldier in the bed next to mine, was afraid. We were all afraid. But his fear got worse when one of the medics came around, because Sam was falling in love with him and knew he shouldn't." Rosie gasped, shocked, and Jean huffed a sharp, pained breath. Hank gave them both hard looks and kept talking. "It just kept going. I knew everything like that about everybody around me, before Ex Libris came for me. And when they did, I knew it wasn't just that they needed bodies. They were *desperate* for them. Anything to keep their part of the war effort going. They were dying too fast. None of it was words, all of it was just feelings. I thought I was losing my mind.

"But then they explained about the demons, about Ex Libris's rules and laws, and I knew then that I wasn't just a survivor. I was a monster. And all I could do was hide it and hope I could stay alive long enough to prove I was worth something. With my torn-up knee and my demonic empathy. I wasn't worth sh . . ." He turned his head, not far enough to see the women, but enough to remind himself they were there, that he was talking to girls, not other men, and didn't finish the word. "The first time a demon came near me after the attack, I knew it was there. I could feel it, its . . . emptiness. No emotion, just bleakness. I got the drop on it, even with my busted-up knee. Impressed everybody. Didn't tell them how I'd managed it, either. Just lucky. And I kept just getting lucky, until they sent me here."

He finally sat, moving like an old man. "My father's not a monster, Rosie. I know he's not. And I know the demon army isn't here in Detroit, either, because I'd be able to feel it if it was. And I know Ex Libris would kill me, if they knew that for sure."

"Why didn't you just tell me?" Rosie waved away the look Hank gave her, understanding that he'd just explained, but shook her head anyway. "I'm not Ex Libris, Hank. I— hey! Is that how you got Detective Johnson to let Pearl go? Can you . . . empathize the other way? Make people feel things?"

Hank thinned his lips and looked away. "I told you I can be charming when I want to be."

"Charming," Jean echoed. "That's *terrifying*. How can anybody around you know if what they're feeling is real?"

"Like I said," Hank muttered as Rosie bugged her eyes at Jean, trying to silence her. "I'm a monster."

"For heaven's sake, Hank, you're not a monster," Rosie said in exasperation. "A monster wouldn't have just told us he was one."

Jean returned to the dead woman's body, looking between it and Hank. "Is Rosie a monster too?"

Guilt flashed across Hank's features, making cold drain through Rosie. "Jeez, am I? I mean, do your library men think I am?"

"The jury is out on Redeemers," Hank said quietly. "Generally, yeah, but there are so few of you and you don't usually—" He caught his breath, and Jean, in a hard voice, said, "They don't usually live very long, do they? So they're useful enough for the little while they're around that you sons of bitches overlook them being by-your-definition monsters."

"I don't think Rosie is a monster. I don't *feel* that she is." He turned his attention to Rosie. "You don't feel blank, like demons do. There's not an emptiness where you are. You feel human."

"Well, so do you! I don't get a warning when you show up like I did with—with that, with her. And if I'm useful, then you must be too. Jeez, Hank, they're fools if they don't want to know you can sense demons. Empathy, how's that bad? Doesn't it mean you understand people better? Doesn't—" The words clogged in her throat as she remembered, too clearly, his sarcasm over Rich expecting Rosie to wait for him. She'd thought—well, she hadn't known *what* to think, but now she couldn't help wondering if he'd only been reflecting her own emotions, reflecting a streak of nastiness she didn't even know she had.

Her expression must have changed, or maybe just her emotions, because deep lines of regret appeared around Hank's mouth. "There," he said. "See? You just started wondering about me too. Not if I'm a monster, probably. That's not really like you. But you're doubting me, and yourself. Now add a fear of demons infiltrating the Ex Libris ranks to your paranoia, and ask yourself if you might not think it's safer to kill me after all."

"Never mind that," Jean said. "We're not going to kill you unless you come after one of us, which you're not going to do. Why didn't you know *she* was here?" She pushed a toe toward the body, making sure not to actually touch it.

Hank shook his head. "I don't know. I should have. Rosie was faster, but I should have known. I wish you hadn't killed her. She could have told us something."

"She has told us something," Rosie said shortly. "She made you tell us the truth. That's worth something. What if Ex Libris does know, Hank? You said you think they're hanging you out to dry. What if they know you've got power and they sent you here because only a . . . what do they call people who do what you do?"

"An empath."

"Okay, so what if they sent you here because only an empath could find the demon king they think is roosting here? If you can't find him, maybe they've got the wrong city."

"Or maybe they're protecting him."

"But why would they do that?"

"Even secret organizations need money." Jean edged away from Montgomery's body and went to get a drink of Hank's alcohol straight from the bottle. She made a face, wiped her mouth, and said, "There's an industrialist involved, right? Somebody making money off the war. Maybe they're letting your, uh, your demon king, have some free rein so they can skim off the top or get a kickback. But I don't know why they'd send an empath to hunt demons here if that's what they're doing."

"So they can look like they're on the up-and-up. Or maybe it's just that the left hand isn't talking to the right. It's more likely the left hand is obscuring what it's doing from the right. Ex Libris isn't big, but it's big enough to have factions. I told you," Hank said to Rosie. "Sometimes we bargain or let smaller demons go to get to bigger ones. Some of us think we shouldn't do even that. If some of the bargaining types cut a deal with a daemon rex . . ."

"If they can bargain and deal with demons I don't see how they can think *you're* a monster who should just be killed," Rosie muttered. "Anyways. Let's stop guessing and do something. How did she find us? You're pretty well hidden here."

"You can sense her. I'm guessing she could sense you."

"And jumped through a window to kill me?"

"That other one thought she'd get a lot of brownie points with the king if she took you down, Ro," Jean pointed out. "Maybe you're just such a tempting target they get stupid."

"Great. Maybe all I have to do is go stand in Times Square and shout,

'Come on, demons, I'm a Redeemer, come get me!' and we'll just see who turns up. It's kind of what Joan did, isn't it?"

"Joan who?"

"Of Arc."

"Oh. Sure. Joan of Arc. Of course." Jean stared at Rosie. Rosie looked at Hank, whose mouth turned up at the corner.

"It is kind of what she did, at Orleans. But the daemon rex didn't come after her. Monsters that powerful are usually smarter than that. I could ask Dad," he said more quietly, and with visible reluctance. "I could ask Dad who Helen knew. Worked with. I don't know. See if we can find a lead."

Jean pursed her lips, glancing between Rosie and Hank again, and spoke with a soft note Rosie didn't expect. "We don't need to ask him. We just need fifteen minutes and a pay phone We know her name. I bet there's only so many Montgomerys in the phone book. Where's yours?" She went to the shelves and found one, flipping the pages to find the names she wanted. "No need to involve your dad, Hank."

A surge of gratitude made Rosie smile at the other girl as relief sagged Hank's shoulders. *He*, Rosie reckoned, didn't want to get his father involved because he believed in Harrison Vaughn's innocence. *She* preferred not to just in case the older Vaughn turned out to have demonic ties after all, even if Hank's empathic sense ruled him out as the demon king. "Great. It's worth trying, right?" Her face fell as she looked at the body. "What are we going to do with her?"

Hank sighed and limped to the bookcases, searching them. "I'll take care of it as soon as I find something to wrap her in so she doesn't stain the trunk. You two—do you really think you can learn something, Jean?"

"Can't hurt to try. There are five Montgomerys in here. We can call them, so we're doing something instead of just worrying about the cops finding her wherever you dump her."

"Jean," Rosie said, faintly shocked.

Jean, writing numbers down, shrugged. "It's what he's going to do, Ro. We did it ourselves with that woman at the factory. I didn't know all of this was going to lead me into a life of crime." She didn't sound distressed, though Rosie cringed.

"I don't want to be a criminal."

"I don't want to be a wi—" Jean snapped off the word, her jaw tense. "We aren't getting a lot of what we want right now, Rosie. I'm trying to make the best of it instead of hiding under the covers and sobbing, so help me out."

"Help *me* out." Hank came back from the shelves with a stretch of canvas. "I've got to get this body into the trunk of the car and I can't do it alone."

Rosie stared at the canvas even as Jean prodded her into motion, and together the three of them rolled Helen Montgomery's body into it and helped Hank heft the corpse over his shoulder. He limped toward the door, and Rosie said, to his retreating back, "Do you always keep sheets of canvas lying around? Just in case you need to move a body?" Hank shot her a look that answered the question and went out the door, leaving Rosie to whisper, "What's happened to my life," to herself and then gather herself to nod at Jean. "All right. Okay, Jeannie. Let's go do this."

NINETEEN

Hank dropped them at a pay phone closer to Rosie's house than his secret library, and drove off to deal with the Redeemed body. Jean stood at the edge of the road like a sentry as Rosie pushed coins into the phone slot. The first number rang without an answer, and the second two came up duds. She shook her head at Jean, who stepped back from the sidewalk's edge as cars went by, and wiped her wrist across her forehead. "He better find somewhere cold to hide that thing, or it's gonna start stinking real fast."

"Jeez, Jean!" Rosie hissed. "Shush!" Not that Jean had spoken loudly, or that anyone was around to hear, but who knew, the operator might be listening in as the line connected. A man picked up with a gruff "Hello?" and Rosie burst into her best bubble-headed impression of Irene's Brooklyn accent for the fourth time. "Hi, is Helen Montgomery there?

Her eyes widened and she gestured to Jean as the man's voice cleared, like he'd just woken up. "No, she's working. Supe at Highfield called her in for some extra hours today. What can I do for you?"

"Oh, good, she's working, I really sort of wanted to talk to you anyways, Mr Montgomery," Rosie babbled, a knot of discomfort tight in her throat. "You're a star. Look, can I ask you something? Has she been acting different lately? I don't know, it just seemed to me she got kind of cool toward me around, I don't know, a while now, maybe around—"

"Christmas," Mr Montgomery said with a sigh. "Her mother died about this time last year and it seemed to really hit her around Christmas."

"Yes, that was so awful about her mother." Rosie agreed unhappily, and made a face as Jean's eyebrows rose. "And, gosh, yes, I'd say she seemed to

change around Christmas, too. I just wanted to make sure the fella closest
to her thought she was doing okay."

"We'll get by," Montgomery said. "I'll let her know you called. What's
your name again?"

"Oh, don't you worry about it, I'll just give her a call again later.
Thanks!" She hung up and slumped against the pay phone, feeling sick to
her stomach. "That was awful."

"Really?" Jean sounded admiring. "You lied like a pro. I didn't think
you had it in you."

"I wish I didn't! That poor man has no idea his wife is—" Rosie couldn't
even say the word, half-afraid someone would hear her even though they
were alone on the street. "And I just grilled him for information! What
kind of monster am I?"

Jean's eyebrows lifted again. "The kind that fights real ones. Come on,
Ro, get over it. Did you learn anything besides whatever that was about
her mother and Christmas? You sounded real sincere about that, just like
you knew what he was talking about."

Rosie sank down to sit on the sidewalk's edge, her knees drawn up and
her arms wrapped around them as she stared down the street. "She started
acting different around Christmas. And she works at Highfield and got
called in today to cover for somebody. Me, maybe. Or Irene. Rene swapped
to a late shift so she could go to the party last night." She could hear herself
talking to keep her thoughts away, but hardly knew what she'd even said.
The street had emptied out, late afternoon turning to dinnertime. Families
were gathering around their tables for dinner instead of kids playing
while parents headed home. It felt lonely, even if dozens of people weren't
more than a stone's throw away. "I don't think I'm cut out for this kind of
business. You should have been the Redeemer."

"Maybe, but I'm not, and you did pretty good there." Jean sat beside
her. "Hank can be the brains, you're the muscle, and next time, I'll be the
sneak."

"Our own little holy trinity." Rosie made a face, then rubbed it out
with her hands. "We should have asked Hank *when* his dad knew her, to
find out if she was already a demon then. PFC Goode was at the factory,

that ochim thing was there, Mrs Montgomery worked there . . . it all comes back to the factory. I wonder who owns it now. Probably Henry Ford built it, but it could belong to Harrison Vaughn now, for all I know. Only don't let Hank hear me say that."

"I can't blame him for not wanting it to be his dad." Jean dangled her arms over her knees, fingertips tapping together. "But we should find out who owns it. If Harrison Vaughn does, it's just too much coincidence, him having an affair with Mrs Montgom—"

"An *affair*? Jean, you can't go around saying things like that! Oh my gosh! What if Hank heard you?"

Jean leaned back until her fingers locked around her knees and studied Rosie. "Are you serious, Ro? What did you think he meant when he said his dad knew her? Didn't you see how uncomfortable he was?"

"I don't know, but he—" Rosie bit down on her protests as she remembered Hank's tension. "Oh, no. No, that just can't be right, Jean. His dad had an affair with a demon? How could he not know?"

"Which one of them?" Jean asked sourly. "Lots of men think women are crazy anyway, so what's the difference if he's screwing a demon or not? Or do you mean Hank?" She shook her head. "I don't know. Do you think that empathy thing of his is for real?"

"I don't know. *He* does." Rosie wet her lips, frowning at the dust on the road. "I'm parched. Let's walk up to the house and get a drink." She stood, offering Jean a hand, and pulled the other girl to her feet. "I guess I want to believe him. It makes me be not the only one, and I *have* to believe me. But I don't know how you can tell that somebody's a . . . an empath . . . for real. I don't even really know what it is, except what he said. How do you tell if somebody really knows what you're feeling?"

"I guess you run some tests somehow." Jean shoved her hands in her pockets as they walked under trees spaced too far apart to offer any real relief from the heat or shade from the slanting sun. "Maybe you pretend hard to have a feeling, until it gets real, and you see if he can figure it out."

Rosie laughed. "Yeah, but if you're standing there pretending to get mad until you do, I can just see that, can't I? You getting all red in the face and tight-lipped and all of that."

"So do it on opposite sides of a wall. That way he can't see you."

"I don't think he'd like it. Having to prove it, I mean."

Jean stopped short in a puddle of her own shadow. "Who cares? If he's on the level, it shouldn't be a problem. He's got to know how crazy it sounds, so he should be willing to try and prove it. If he can't, then there's no reason to think he can tell when a demon is nearby, either, which makes him—"

"Not useless," Rosie disagreed, even if Jean hadn't actually said it. "Come on, we're not getting any less hot standing here. He does know more about demons than we do, and he can read all those research books in all those different languages, and we can't, so he's not useless. He just wouldn't be useful in finding them, so we're no worse off than we are right now." She giggled suddenly. "Listen to us, Jean. Talking about finding demons and empathy and magic like we haven't flipped our wigs."

"Part of me has." Jean sounded hollow, but she kept her voice steady and her eyes stayed dry. "I'd have to be crazy or dumb to not know I'm hanging on to all this craziness because it gives me something else to do. If I think too much about Ruby, I start flying apart. That's the part of me that's going crazy, Rosie. The part that looks crazy, all this demon stuff, that's all that's holding me together. Her funeral is on Saturday. It'll be a whole week then. More than a week. I don't think I can stand it."

"I'll be there," Rosie said helplessly. "We'll all be there."

"I know. I just want every demon in Detroit dead before then." A smile pinched her mouth. "That's not too much to ask, is it?"

Rosie reached out and took her hand, squeezing it. "We're batting a thousand so far. None of the ones we've met have made it out alive."

Surprise tweaked Jean's smile into something better than it had been. "There is that." She squeezed Rosie's hand in return, then let it go, looking toward the slowly setting sun "It's already past seven and Hank's probably gonna be busy for a while. Tomorrow we should put him through his paces, but in the meantime, should we go up to the factory and find out who knows what about Helen Montgomery?"

"I don't think they'll even let me on the grounds. Maybe Irene can find something out."

"Do you really want to tell her there's another dead body with your name on it?"

Rosie's eyes popped. "Jeez, put a cork in it, Jean! Keep your voice down! And no, I guess not. I guess if we went up and grabbed coveralls, we could blend in okay, as long as the supe didn't see us coming in." Rosie frowned at patches of changing sunlight through the widely spaced trees. "She worked night shift, so anybody who knew her wouldn't be there yet. Maybe I should get dinner and look at the help wanted ads until Hank turns up again."

"Rosie . . ." Jean trailed to a stop, her steps as slow as her words. "You know it's going to be darn near impossible to find work now. Especially—I mean, Rich is home."

"Oh, not you too. Not that."

Jean shook her head. "I'm with you, but you know what people are going to say. 'She's still working? With her soldier home? How does he like her taking his job?'"

"Well, who am I going to tell that my soldier is home, anyways? My new supe? Why would I do that?"

"They'll ask if you're getting married."

"And I'm not." Rosie folded her arms under her breasts and walked away, scowling at the sidewalk. "Not any time soon, anyways. Everything's different now, and who knows if he'll want to marry me, in the end?"

"Or if you'll want to marry him." Jean caught up, measuring her steps by Rosie's shorter ones. "I'm just wondering if you've got a fallback position."

"I really am going to college, Jean. I still want to find part-time work, but that's what I'm gonna do. I'm gonna go learn how to design the cars all the men will be back to build, or something like that, I don't know yet. But I'm going to college."

"Holy moly," Jean breathed with a smile. "You said school earlier, didn't you, but I don't think I really heard you. Really? That's what you're going to do? Good for you. Does Rich know yet?"

"I haven't had time to tell him. I don't know what he'll think."

"Does it matter?"

"No. Yes." Rosie sighed. "I was so crazy in love with him when he shipped out, Jean. But it's been years and I don't know anymore. It matters because maybe we're still meant to be, maybe it'll work . . . but at the same time, it doesn't, because this is what I gotta do for me. So I hope he'll think it's great, but if he doesn't . . ." She shrugged helplessly. "Then I guess I know how it works out between us."

"Good." Jean offered a brief smile at Rosie's glance. "You're stuck on having your independence. I'd hate to see that just wash away when the going got tough."

"Well, I don't know what could be tougher than this." A superstitious thrill ran down Rosie's spine and she muttered, "Probably something," to ward it off. "I'll figure something out and spit in their eye."

"Atta girl. I'm going to catch a tram home, Rosie. You give Hank a call tonight and tell him that tomorrow we want to test and see if his empathy is real, okay?"

"I still think he won't like it."

"None of us like any of this." Jean ducked under the tree at the tram stop, taking what cover from the sun she could, and shooed Rosie along.

✪ ✪ ✪

Lights were on in the kitchen and voices spilled out the open window as Rosie walked up to the house a while later. She hesitated on the porch, listening until she'd identified Barb and Dorothy and Wanda. Marge usually worked a swing shift and Irene had taken that shift today, too, so the three who'd become least friendly to Rosie since Saturday were the ones at home. She might avoid them by going straight to her room, but that would mean not getting any dinner, either. And she'd paid for her fair share of that food, since they all went in together for groceries, spreading their money farther that way. Jaw set, Rosie pushed the door open and marched in to be met with a sudden silence. Dorothy giggled nervously. Wanda elbowed her, but Barb tossed her hair. "Well, what do *you* want?"

"Dinner," Rosie said as steadily as she could. "Is that potato salad?"

"Macaroni," Wanda volunteered. Barb shot her a daggered look and her shoulders hunched, gaze dropping to the table.

Rosie smiled, even if it felt more like baring her teeth. "Sounds nice. Maybe I'll fry up some wieners. Anybody else want some?"

"We didn't make enough macaroni salad for everybody." Barb tossed her hair again.

"Really. I can't ever make more than enough for everybody. I don't think I've ever been able to make just *a little* macaroni salad in my whole life." Walking across the kitchen under the weight of everybody's gaze made Rosie move stiffly, but she'd be darned if she'd give up now. "Gosh, Barb, there must be eight cups of this stuff besides what you've got on your plates! How much more do you reckon you need tonight? Maybe I could dish it up for you."

Dorothy squeaked, "No!" and shot Barb a wide-eyed look when Barb glared at her. "She might *poison* us or something!" Dot hissed.

"Dot," Wanda protested weakly, but went quiet again as Barb's filthy look returned to her.

Rosie felt her smile begin to slip. "So I guess that means you don't want me to fry you up some wieners, Dot. Anybody else?" She got a jar down instead of watching them look at each other, and fried up her hot dogs with an itch between her shoulder blades. She didn't dare look over her shoulder to see if the three girls really were watching her, but they sure as heck didn't go back to talking among themselves while she cooked. Chin held high, she put food on her plate and sat down at the table.

It didn't take hardly two minutes for the others to clear out. Even Wanda, who never left dirty dishes, left her plate and fork by the sink in her hurry to get away. Rosie watched them, trying to look like she thought they were funny, but the moment they were gone she put her fork down and her face in her hands, trying to hold back tears. After some deep breaths and a reminder her wieners were cooling, she got control of herself and ate dinner. Then she scooped some extra macaroni salad onto her plate, got a glass of lemonade, and retreated to her bedroom feeling like she'd fought hard enough for one night. Irene had a copy of *Forever Amber* on her bedstand. Rosie borrowed it, reading while she ate the rest of the salad and lemonade, and fell asleep without brushing her teeth.

She heard Irene come in hours later, but only pulled the pillow over her head, not ready to wake up or talk to anyone. By the time morning and almost twelve hours of sleep had rolled around, she couldn't pretend not to be awake when Rene got up, or when everyone else banged around the house. She didn't make much effort to leave the room, though, except to brush her teeth, until most everybody had left for the day. Marge probably hadn't, but Marge liked to sleep late, so once the other girls were gone, Rosie felt safe enough leaving the bedroom.

"Safe," she whispered as she got coffee. She shouldn't have to sneak around to feel safe in her own house. Maybe her folks were right and she *should* move back home, although with Rich back, even her parents would probably think she ought to just get married. Well, that just wouldn't do. She poured another cup of coffee and flipped the paper open, the ink's sweet, acrid scent mixing with the coffee's richer smell. There were plenty of jobs if you could type or wanted to waitress, but she kept looking, as if searching the pages again would turn up an ad that read *Wanted: Rosie the Riveter, for construction & mechanical work.* No, those jobs were for men coming home from the war. After a while she pushed the paper back and rubbed her hands through her hair, too late realizing she had newsprint on her fingertips. Well, now she probably had it on her face, too. She gave her forehead an ineffectual swipe, then got up to wash her face and look at herself in the mirror.

Even early in the day, her cheeks were awfully pink from heat, although washing up with cool water helped. Her eyes still looked tired, despite catching up on her sleep. But the weariness reflected back at her ran deeper than a lack of sleep. "It's all crazy," she whispered to the mirror, and, since she was talking to herself anyways, added, "You're gonna have to learn to type, Ro. It'll be helpful for school. You'll be able to type up your papers faster, and get a job being a secretary or something until you have your degree, because you gotta face it, nobody's going to hire a girl riveter anymore." She pulled a few pin curls into place, then gave a short laugh. Look at her, fixing her hair, worrying about a job, when her housemates wouldn't talk to her, and last night, Hank had gone out to dump the body of the third person she'd killed in a handful of days. Even if they weren't really people anymore. It seemed like she had bigger worries than her hair, but she still kept fussing over it.

Pearl Daly had bigger worries, too. Rosie patted her face dry and marched out of the house to go visit Pearl. She didn't much know what she could do for Pearl other than let her know she hadn't been forgotten, but that might be enough, and it gave Rosie something to do until she could call Hank, either at home or work, and set up testing his empathy. A tram full of factory girls shining with sweat brought Rosie close enough to Pearl's apartment to walk the rest of the way. She stopped at a five-and-dime store for a couple of ice creams even if it was only nine in the morning, then hurried up four floors to knock on Pearl's door.

The smaller girl opened it cautiously but lit up as Rosie thrust the ice cream at her. "Eat it quick before it all melts! I got vanilla, I figured nobody could object to that."

"I was just trying to decide what to have for breakfast." Pearl beamed at Rosie and gave the dripping cone a quick lick as she stepped back to let Rosie into the apartment. She'd gained some weight, and her color, which had improved instantly when Rosie Redeemed her, looked better still. "How come you're here?"

"I wanted to check on you. I said I would." Rosie came in to sit on the couch and finish her own ice cream. "How are you doing?"

Pearl curled into the armchair, nodding. "I'm okay. I think I'm okay. I wrote a letter to Johnny's lady."

Rosie blinked. "Oh. Oh! I'd forgotten you were going to do that. Thank you." Jean would never get her wish of all the demons in Detroit being dead by Saturday if they had to wait on mail to France, but then, that wish had never been going to come true, anyways. "Have you gotten out of here at all?"

"Well, I went to the post office." Pearl smiled and shifted her shoulders. "I've gotten the paper and called about some jobs. I need to learn to type."

Rosie looked at her hands. "Yeah, me too, I guess. I got fired," she said to Pearl's questioning glance. "I was a bad influence on the girls, and frightening."

"*You* were—! But—!"

"I know, but what could I do?" Rosie finished her ice cream and got up to wash her hands.

"I could tell them . . . something . . ."

"No, don't. Don't get yourself any more into this mess than you are, Pearl." Rosie smiled ruefully over her shoulder at the other woman. "Thanks for the offer, though. Are there any typing classes in the ads? I didn't think to look."

"A couple, at different schools. Some are for shorthand typing, and those take a while, but just learning to type is a six-week class, and they swear you'll find a job if you learn there. It doesn't cost too much, so I'm trying to find some other job in the meantime. I guess I haven't been *fired* from the factory, but I haven't been in in days, and even if I've still got a job, I don't want to go back." Pearl shivered more than the ice cream accounted for, and Rosie nodded sympathetically.

"Well, I'm not going to let Hank throw you out of here, so if it means taking the class and finding a job, then that's just what's going to happen. And you oughta be able to apply for unemployment, Pearl. I did." Rosie came back to sit down again, realizing as she did that Pearl wore the same blouse and dungarees she'd had on the last time Rosie had seen her, the ones she'd been wearing under her work coveralls. "You don't have any other clothes, do you?"

Surprise and guilt turned Pearl's cheeks pink. "Everything was at Johnny's."

"And Hank didn't think of that. Heck, neither did I. Well, we're just going to have to find you a few outfits, I guess. Dorothy at home is slight like you, I'll see if I can't talk her out of a couple blouses and jeans, and I'll buy you a new dress for interviews."

Pearl's eyes rounded. "Oh. Oh, no, you couldn't do that."

"You can pay me back when you're not flat, but for now, you want to put your best foot forward, right? So let me help. I guess all of us who know what's going on here should stick together."

"You're an awful nice lady, Miss Ransom. Especially considering I almost got you killed."

"You were trying to protect yourself. I guess I know what that feels like, now. I don't hold it against you." Rosie grinned. "But don't do it again!"

"That's a deal."

Rosie, still grinning, stood up again. "All right. Look, I don't think I gave you my phone number. Let me do that, and you can give me a call and we'll go shopping this week. Not on Saturday, but it's only Wednesday." She wrote her number down. "Give me a call tomorrow or Friday and we'll figure it out. In the meantime, look, here. Take this, just so you've got some pin money." She took a ten-dollar bill out of her purse and offered it to Pearl, whose fingers opened and closed reluctantly.

"I shouldn't . . ."

"You can pay me back for this, too, sometime. I'd just feel better if I knew you had some cash, Pearl. I want to be sure you're eating okay."

Pearl took the bill carefully, unable to meet Rosie's eyes. "Thank you again, Miss Ransom."

"I told you to call me Rosie." Rosie hugged the other woman, taking care to avoid the last bites of ice cream cone in Pearl's hand, and waved herself out with Pearl's smile following her.

TWENTY

Rosie stopped at the five-and-dime again to call Hank, who wasn't home, and then the police station, where it took a couple minutes and some more nickels for the phone to get him on the line to say, "I can't get away until after work."

Rosie puffed her cheeks at the sky. "Not even for lunch?"

"No. Regular desk sergeant sprained his ankle and can't get in. I'm covering for him." Hank chuckled. "The secretary says he hurt himself because some pretty girl twitted him about his figure, and he overdid it on the exercise."

Rosie clapped a hand over her mouth to hold back a laugh. "The tubby sergeant who's going bald?"

"Yeah, you know him?"

"I was the girl."

"Oh." Hank sounded suddenly cheerful. "So it's your fault I can't make it until this evening."

"I guess so. All right, see you then." Rosie hung up, called Jean to say she wouldn't be over until evening, then put her hands on her hips and looked up and down the street, trying to figure out what to do with the day. Maybe visit her folks again. Maybe go to Hank's library and practice throwing knives. Or see if she could figure out how to fix the window in there, since it couldn't be good to have people able to look in and see his secret library. Well, at the least, she could board it up, if she got measurements. Whistling, she caught a tram and went downtown, letting herself in to the library just like she belonged there.

Hank had obviously come back the night before, because the window already had cardboard over it. Rosie dragged a chair over and climbed up to measure the space, examining the seals while she stood there. "Yeah," she said aloud, to herself. "I can do this." It might take a library book on how, but she could do it. Whistling again, she left to get glass cut and a how-to book from the library, and spent most of the afternoon using the kind of salty language that would probably make Hank blush to hear it from a girl. But by dinnertime, the window had been replaced, and Rosie, looking at the bright light it spilled in compared to the other windows, splashed it with water and threw some dirt on it to grime it up properly. After that it hardly looked any different from the other windows, from either inside or out. Satisfied with herself, she cleaned up, found a phone, and told Jean she'd be there soon.

"Bring dinner," Jean said. "I don't have enough for three. I haven't gone shopping since . . ."

"Okay. I'll go to Big Bob's again." Rosie hung up the pay phone, wrinkling her nose at the late-evening sun. She'd blow through all her savings if she kept eating out like this, but she hadn't eaten much that day except ice cream herself, and dinner sounded like a great idea. She headed for the nearest tram stop, mopping sweat off her neck. A breeze came up, just enough to tease promises of cooler air, but the rattling car still felt like an oven, and by the time she reached her stop, she didn't care if she spent every cent in her bank account, as long as she got a cold soda and some extra ice to wash her face with.

For a hot Thursday evening, a lot of people had crowded into the diner. The counter didn't have a single empty seat, and people were tucked by groups into the booths. Even most of the meant-for-two booths sported four, and a familiar laugh greeted her over the sound of the chiming door bells as she walked in. Rosie peered around, looking for Irene, and found Rich instead, or at least, found him first. They were in a corner, almost out of sight from the door, one of the few couples instead of crowds in the booths. Irene couldn't hardly have been off work more than half an hour, but there they were, all settled into a booth instead of waiting. Rich leaned in, smiling at Irene, who looked pretty as a picture even in the heat, with her cheeks all flushed and baby curls escaping around her nape and temples. Rich looked almost as pretty, even if *pretty* wasn't a word for boys, with his good grin and the confident, military set of his shoulders. He said something and Irene laughed again, and instead of heading over to say hi like she'd been going to, Rosie stopped short, feeling like an intruder just by seeing them.

A pink-cheeked waitress stopped breathlessly beside Rosie. "Hi, hon, I don't know how long it's going to be before I can get you a seat. Got any friends here tonight you can join?"

Rosie bit her lip, looking toward Irene and Rich, but shook her head. "No, I just wanted to get something to go. Can I do that?"

"Oh, gosh, sure. I wish I could offer you a place to take a load off while you wait, but it's just crazy here tonight. Too hot to cook!"

"No, it's okay. I might even wait outside, at least there's a breeze out there. Can I get a glass of water while I wait?"

"Coming up," the waitress said with a smile. "Know what you want to order or do you need a menu?"

"I can order." Rosie did, got the water, and went outdoors to hide under the canopy with half a dozen other people while she drank it. They had everything in the world to talk about, it sounded like, and she let their chatter wash over her, closing her eyes as she listened to talk about the war and the possibility of Japanese surrender along with complaints about the baby not nursing in the heat and whether or not Hammerin' Hank would take the Tigers all the way through to the Series in the fall. It all sounded so ordinary that tears pressed against the insides of Rosie's eyelids. She took a couple fast sips of water, trying to freeze the emotion away, and instead swallowed an ice cube that set her coughing until the tears ran down her face. For a moment, everybody around her set aside their conversations to pat her back and look at her in concern, but as she recovered, they drifted back into their own ordinary worlds. Rosie sat on the window ledge, wiping her eyes carefully, and finished her water as someone else came out of the diner to join the little crowd under the veranda. The group shifted to accommodate them before a pleasantly surprised woman's voice said, "Rosie?" and the crowd moved more, letting Valentine Vaughn through.

Rosie stood, making a gesture with her water glass that invited Mrs Vaughn to sit where she'd been perched. Valentine glanced down at her own perfectly trimmed cream-colored dress, and up again with a smile. "Perhaps you and your dungarees are better suited to window sills than I am. How are you? Didn't I see your friend Irene inside? That's a handsome young man she's with. Her beau, home from Europe? My goodness, won't Daniel Franklin be disappointed." A sparkle came into her eyes. "Kind of you to give them some time alone. I'm sure we'd all rather be inside than out on the sidewalk."

"I'm fine, thank you, Mrs Vaughn. What are you doing here? I'm sorry." Rosie blushed. "It's just Big Bob's doesn't seem like your . . ." She stopped, uncertain of how to say anything else without giving offense.

Amused confidentiality pursed Valentine's lips and she leaned in to murmur, "Don't tell anyone, but even a well-bred English woman likes the occasional burger." Her smile turned to laughter and she shook her head. "Harry has a terrible weakness for bacon cheeseburgers, and he asked me to stop and get him one while he's in a meeting. Usually I would let our driver take care of such things, but the car is absolutely stifling and I thought I'd feel better with a walk."

"You're not in the Jaguar?" Rosie asked in surprise. "I'd think on a day like today, you'd be driving around with the top down and the wind in your hair."

Valentine touched her careful blond curls. "Not after I've just had it set. Oh, I've gotten terribly old and dull, haven't I? I'll have to insist Hank take the car tonight and bring you out somewhere, Rosie." She laid her hand on Rosie's arm, emotion deepening her voice. "It's so nice he's making friends his own age. He's been so isolated since he came home from Europe, and I've been worried about him. He was always bookish, but the past year . . ." She sighed, shaking her head. "But that's the price of war, isn't it? We all change so much."

"Bookish? I thought he was a pugilist like Mr Vaughn."

"Oh . . ." A line appeared between Valentine's eyebrows. "Yes, I suppose so. I suppose we often see our children the way we want to, don't we? He did box. Quite well, in fact. But I remember him sitting on the window ledge, surrounded by books. I suppose that's my favorite way to think of him. I hope friends will help him settle back down. Perhaps your friend Irene and her young man will get him in a more permanent mood."

Rosie glanced through the diner window, unable to see Rich or Irene, and nodded without meaning anything by it. "What about you, Rosie? Oh, but no, you said you didn't want to settle down, didn't you. Well, perhaps Irene will get you in a settling mood, too. I'm glad she's got a nice local young man. Daniel is a darling, but really, he's such an actor. Wealthy, of course, and charming, and very handsome, but a girl could hardly rely on him. It's much more sensible to keep things in perspective."

"But you were a nurse," Rosie said. "That can't be practical, can it? Going off to serve and help in a war when you didn't have to? You must have really wanted to. You must have followed your dreams to do that. Don't you think Irene should? Or any girl?"

Valentine sighed. "I thought that when I was a girl, of course. It's different, when you've been to war. Well, you must understand that now, Rosie. After what happened last weekend," she said with significance, leaving Rosie glad she didn't spell it out for everyone chatting around them. "You must want the comfort of a family in your future, after all you've been through."

"I have a family," Rosie said stiffly. "My parents are doing just fine."

"Oh, darling." Valentine smiled. "You know that's different from having a husband and children of your own. I do hope you'll be spending some more time with Hank, Rosie. Not that I'm matchmaking," she said with a laugh that made Rosie struggle not to wince, "but I think spending time with some nice young people is just what he needs, and I'm sure you'd like that too, right now."

"I'd like a job right now, Mrs Vaughn." She'd started to get used to confessing to friends that she had college plans, but that seemed like more than she needed to tell Valentine Vaughn. Besides, Mrs Vaughn would probably hear it soon enough from Hank.

Valentine's eyes lit up at someone down the street and she smiled again, first at Rosie, then, as Rosie turned, at Harrison Vaughn, who strode toward them at a brisk walk, as if wholly undisturbed by the warm air. He hadn't even broken a sweat, Rosie saw as he joined them, and promptly wondered if some demons were impervious to weather.

"Here's the man you need to talk to, then, Rosie," Valentine said mischievously. "Harry, you remember Hank's friend, Rosie Ransom. Rosie is absolutely determined to keep working, Harry. This is one young lady who insists she won't give up her dreams. You must have a position for her somewhere, mustn't you?"

"Rosie." Harrison Vaughn smiled and offered a big cool hand that Rosie shook nervously. "Val can't talk you into the domestic life, hm? I'm impressed. I thought she could convince anyone of anything."

"Except you not to call me 'Val'," Valentine said. "Really, Harrison."

"If you really minded, I'd stop." Vaughn kissed Valentine's cheek, then regarded Rosie. "I'm sure I could fit you in somewhere, Rosie, if you're that determined. I won't even hold it against you when you get married and leave me in the lurch. Can you type?"

"No." A spark ran through Rosie. "But I know someone who's taking classes now, someone who needs a job more than I do. If you could give her a break, Mr Vaughn, just a chance to get up to speed while she learns, I'm sure she'd do a good job for you."

Vaughn's eyebrows rose. "We have a Good Samaritan on our hands here, Val. Now are you asking me for *two* jobs, Rosie?"

Rosie threw her shoulders back and met his eye with as steely a look as she could manage. "No, sir. Like I said, my friend Pearl needs work a lot more than I do."

"Not Pearl Daly," Valentine said in surprise. Rosie looked at her, astonished, and she waved long, elegant fingers. "Hank mentioned her in connection with the whole incident this weekend. Really, Rosie? From what I understand—"

"She's a nice girl who got in a lot of trouble," Rosie said fiercely. "She needs help getting back on her feet, and she's real shy, not likely to put herself forward, so if you're willing to help out, Mr Vaughn, won't you help Pearl? Won't you—" Her gut seized as it struck her that Harrison Vaughn might be the last person on earth it would be safe for Pearl to work for. She swallowed hard and finished, "—find somewhere in one of your offices she could work? Somewhere not too important, while she learns, and if she's any good, she could move up, couldn't she? She deserves a chance, Mr Vaughn. She didn't do anything wrong."

A smile a lot like Hank's tugged the corner of Vaughn's mouth. "I'll see what I can do, Miss Ransom. And in the meantime, don't think I've forgotten about those boxing lessons I promised you. I like a girl who can take care of herself."

"*Boxing* lessons, Harry?" Valentine examined both her husband and Rosie with dismay. "You can't be serious. For heaven's sake, what is the world coming to. When I was a girl, no polite young lady would even consider something so crass and violent as boxing. I wish the world could be the way it was then, Harry. I find this all very distressing."

"Change is inevitable, Val."

"So is dinner," the breathless waitress announced, arriving with several bags of food that she handed to both the Vaughns and to Rosie. "I'm sorry this took so long, we're just so busy. But here you go, fresh and hot!"

Harrison Vaughn dipped into a pocket and came out with a five-dollar bill that he tucked into the waitress's apron pocket. "Thank you—Clara," he said, tipping his head to read her name tag. "Thank you, Clara. I appreciate a job done with politeness and enthusiasm. Good luck with the rest of the evening in there."

"Gosh, thank *you*, mister! Thank you!" Clara ran back into the diner, leaving Vaughn and Rosie smiling openly, and Valentine with a smile of rueful tolerance.

"Honestly, Harrison, left to your own devices, you'd give every penny you make away. Rosie, do you need a lift anywhere? We have the car."

"No, I couldn't ask you to go out of your way. The tram goes right where I need to. Thank you, though."

"Of course. Tell your friend Irene and her handsome soldier hello for me, won't you, dear?"

". . . sure." Rosie watched the Vaughns leave before looking in the window again at Rich and Irene. They were laughing again, Irene's hand on top of Rich's on the booth table. They didn't look as nice together as she and Rich did, Rosie thought with a pang of uncertainty. She and Rich both had dark hair and light eyes, like they'd been made as a matched set. But then again, maybe Rich did look better with Irene, with her red hair and brown eyes. Maybe they were less ordinary together than Rosie and Rich were.

Well, she hardly needed to worry about that right now. She and Rich had a whole lot to talk about, and she could hardly blame him for having dinner with Irene when she'd made it plain that she wasn't ready for a big commitment. A queer knot of jealousy, hard to swallow down, still twisted the breath out of her. Lips pressed together, she turned her back on Rich and Irene, and went to catch the tram.

She'd gotten most of the way to Jean's house when she realized that she hadn't gotten any sense of danger off Harrison Vaughn's approach or presence. She'd felt nothing like the thrill that had warned her before Helen Montgomery's attack. She sagged against the tram window, clutching the bag of hot food against her belly, and wished she felt better about eliminating the only lead they'd had.

✪ ✪ ✪

"Yeah," Jean said over her burger and fries as Rosie explained it all to her, "yeah, well, there's no telling if sensing Montgomery was Redeemer magic or just some kind of luck, anyway. Maybe you just saw a shadow at the right time. The only way to know for sure is if we find another demon to test it out on."

Rosie pushed her own food away and folded her arms on Jean's kitchen table so she could rest her forehead on them. "How are we going to do that?"

"They've been coming out of the woodwork. I guess we wait a day or two."

"That's a terrible plan."

"I know, but I don't have another one. Are you going to eat those fries?"

"Yes." Rosie sat up and pulled her food back to herself protectively. A knock sounded on Jean's door and Rosie stood, eyeing Jean. "That's probably Hank. No stealing my fries."

"Mmhmm." Jean took one as Rosie left, and laughed at Rosie's expression. "I just wanted to see you make that face," she called after Rosie, and Rosie, shaking her head and smiling, opened the front door to a bedraggled Hank Vaughn.

"I wish you'd told me you'd be here. I'd have saved myself twenty minutes of driving and ten minutes of bad flirting from that tall housemate of yours." Hank pushed his way past Rosie and threw himself into Jean's couch, unbuttoning the collar of his shirt. "Damn, it's hot. How can you be eating burgers?"

"Because ice cream sundaes would have melted on the way over. I got you one."

"A sundae?" Hank pushed out of the couch again, and still headed for the kitchen when Rosie muttered, "A burger." He reached for one of Jean's fries on the way past, got his hand slapped, and stole five of Rosie's instead. She protested and he shoved them in his mouth without guilt. "Where are the plates?"

"Second cupboard from the sink, and you can get yours yourself. I should've drunk your soda." Rosie sat and glared over her burger as Hank poured his food onto a plate and joined them at the table.

"There's soda? Cold soda? You're an angel, Rosie Ransom."

"In the fridge," Rosie said, mollified. Hank jumped up again to get his, and Jean said, "So Rosie cleared your dad of wrongdoing while you were out."

"I think I did. Maybe."

Hank said, "I told you," when Jean had finished explaining. "I wish it didn't leave us with no answers, but I told you."

"Still," Rosie said, "we want to test your empathy, Hank. It's hard to believe any of it's real. What if Jean's right and I was just lucky with Helen Montgomery? You didn't know she was there, so—"

To her surprise, Hank's eyebrows rose with intrigue. "How are you going to test me?"

"By going into another room and trying to feel things you can't see on our faces. How far away does your empathy work from?"

"I don't know exactly, but far enough that driving around in Europe, I'd know if we came within, say, a quarter mile? Across a room is easy.

Walls don't stop it, if that's what you're asking. This will be interesting. I've never had anyone to run tests with. But I don't know how well it works if someone's trying to feel the emotion. I don't know if that's real enough, if you take my meaning."

"We'll find out. We should put wax in his ears, too," Jean said to Rosie. "So he can't hear anything we do or say."

"Do I get any say in this?" Hank asked dryly, but after dinner, he submitted to the wax ear plugs without objection, and sat in the living room, his back to the kitchen, where the women remained.

Despite his ears being plugged, Rosie lowered her voice. "How are we going to do this?"

"The best way I can figure is something like this." Jean thew a punch straight into Rosie's stomach, so hard the dinner she'd just eaten came halfway back up. Rosie made a sick sound and dropped to her knees, tears in her eyes, and from the living room Hank said, "Pain. Anger. Nausea. Rosie is hurting."

Rosie, struggling to draw a breath, lifted an astonished, tear-filled gaze toward the door. "Disbelief, amazement," said Hank. Rosie met Jean's guilty eyes and accepted her help in getting up.

"Now you do me." Jean braced like she was getting ready for a hit. Rosie stuck her fingers in Jean's armpit and wiggled them. Jean swallowed a shriek and batted at Rosie's hand, fighting off startled laughter.

"Surprise," Hank reported. "Something else. Humor, kind of. Mostly surprise. Oh. Sadness. Jean . . ." He sounded sad, too, as Jean pressed a hand over her mouth, unable to stop tears from spilling over.

"Sorry. Sorry," she said hoarsely. "I was ready to get punched, and then you know how sometimes you can't tell if you're laughing or crying, and I just miss Ruby so much, and it just hit me again, I didn't expect it . . ."

Rosie pulled her into a hug, forgetting about the experiment. "It's okay. It's okay, hon. Cry all you need to. You've been so brave."

"I don't feel brave at all."

"Compassion," Hank said from the living room, softly. "Fear. Loneliness. You're both tired."

"That's enough." Rosie's voice cracked. She lifted it, trying again, hoping Hank would hear her this time. "That's enough, Hank. Shh," she said more softly, to Jean. "Shh, it's okay, hon. It's okay."

"It's not okay! How can it be okay, Ruby's *dead*!"

"It's okay to cry," Rosie amended. She pulled Jean down to the floor, hugging her. "I know it's not okay, none of it is okay, but it's okay to cry. You don't have to be brave all the time."

"Anger," Hank said, now from the doorway. His eyes were closed, unhappiness etched in lines on his face. "Futility. Loss. Emptiness. Love. I'm sorry, Jean. I really am."

"Just shut up now," Jean said hoarsely. Hank nodded and stepped back from the door, leaving Rosie alone with her again. "The worst part is I keep living," Jean whispered. "I keep right on living without her and I don't even want to be doing that. Sometimes I forget, already, for a whole minute or two. I get distracted and I forget, how can I already forget, she hasn't even been dead a *week* and sometimes I *forget*—!"

"You're not forgetting her. You're never going to forget her, Jean. It's okay to be alive, though. To keep on breathing and forget for a minute that she's not here anymore. It's hard to get used to the idea that she's not. Forgetting that she's not isn't the same as forgetting her, not at all."

"It hurts so bad when I remember she's gone, though." Jean's voice came in raw gasps. "It hurts all over again, just like new."

"I know. I know. C'mon. Come on." Rosie helped Jean to her feet, helped her out of the kitchen, past Hank in the living room and toward the bedrooms. "Which room are you sleeping in, hon? You need to lie down and rest for a while."

"Mine. Mine. It didn't help at all, trying to sleep in the other room. At least I can still smell her perfume in my room."

Rosie left her curled around a pillow on the big double bed, with a light blanket pulled up over her and the curtains tugged closed. Hank sat on the edge of the armchair, fingers knotted together and his head dropped, gaze locked on the floor, although he looked up when Rosie sat wearily in the couch. "Did I do that? Did I make it worse?"

"No." Rosie sank back, pressing the heels of her hands into her eyes. "No, she's just been being real tough all day, all *week*, and it caught up to her. She misses Ruby so much. They were so close." She dropped her hands, looking at Hank. "You're the real deal, though, aren't you? You really can sense emotions."

"Yeah." Consternation writhed across Hank's face. "What happened in there? That wasn't false emotion, that pain and anger I felt from you."

"Oh." Rosie slid her hands over her stomach and chuckled thinly. "She punched me, the witch. I thought I was going to vomit."

"She—!" Hank laughed, though he kept it as low as their voices were. "It was sure effective."

"She hits like a tank! I thought I was strong, but Jean's a tank! You teach her to fight, Hank, and she'll be better than I'll ever be."

"No. I watched you yesterday. You've got something special, Rosie."

"Magic." Rosie half-laughed the word. "Magic doesn't count. Jean's got natural talent."

"Magic counts for a lot, in this fight."

She glanced at him, mouth pressed in a thin line, before she nodded and looked away. "Yeah. I guess it's got to. Oh. Oh! We found something out about Helen Montgomery. She worked at the same factory I did. It's a hotbed, Hank. That's three demons we've run into who are associated with it. Have you spent any time out there? Maybe there's something you can sense."

"I haven't prowled through it. Maybe I should. Maybe I'm trusting how far I think my reach is, too much. Maybe I need to be closer."

"Or slower. You've been doing a lot of driving around, hunting, right? Maybe it's just too fast, when people are always moving too. Think how easy it is to miss somebody you're looking for in a crowd when you're sure they're there. They could just be stepping the wrong direction at the wrong time. If hunting demons is like that, only bigger . . ."

Hank smiled faintly. "Then maybe it is my own incompetence, and not some conspiracy within Ex Libris."

"That's not what I was going to say."

"No, I know. You're generally kinder than that." He frowned toward the bedroom. "Should we go check the factory out, or do you need to stay?"

Rosie glanced over her shoulder, as if the back of the couch didn't block her view of the hall and bedroom door. "I think she'll probably sleep, but I'm not sure I can get on to the premises even if I'm being sneaky, Hank. I know a lot of the girls, even some of the night shift, and they all know I've been fired. Maybe you should go by yourself."

"I'd feel a lot better with a Redeemer at my side."

A smile curled Rosie's mouth. "Really?"

"Swear to God. Even in the best of circumstances, we try not to hunt demons alone, Rosie. It's hard as hell to capture one by yourself. For some strange reason they'd rather kill you than let you read them into a book or catch them in a drawing. And I'm a terrible artist."

Rosie let go a startled little laugh. "But I bet you read well. I bet you can do your mom's accent and sound all foreign and exotic."

"Sure, if I'm reading something somebody else wrote, but when you're trying to catch a demon, you're trying to write their essence onto the page, not read someone else's words. An Ex Libris–trained artist can . . . *see*, I guess, is the word. Can see into the infested shell and write or draw the demon's . . . personality. I don't write that that well or that quickly. Especially when something is trying to kill me."

"Can people really do that? Write, or draw, or—or whatever—when a demon's fighting for its life? Can they do it fast enough? How? I'd think they'd be too busy being terrified."

"We try to capture them first. They don't really change shape or anything, so if you can chain one up or throw it in a cell, generally they can't go anywhere. They can redouble, but only if they get close enough to touch someone, and we're mostly smart enough not to let that happen." Hank smiled faintly. "Mostly. Anyway, usually they've been captured, so they're holding still while the artist works. But the great artists can do it on the fly. Compose music, or sculpt soft wood, sometimes even stone, so fast that even while we're fighting the demon, it's weakening. Its essence is being stripped away, drawn into the art. They say da Vinci could do it, and I've heard Rosetta Tharpe can."

"Ros—Sister Rosetta Tharpe? The singer?" Hank nodded and delight bloomed in Rosie's chest. "So women *can* fight demons."

For an instant Hank looked like he wanted to argue, but it faded into resignation. "It's dangerous for singers. Worse than usual, I mean. I saw . . ." He shook his head. "He wasn't anybody. Just someone who worked for Ex Libris, but he could sing. We fought an ochim one night, and we were losing. Badly. Jacques began to sing, and he—he wasn't a composer, you understand. He wasn't writing it down. That's the trouble with dance and song, to capture them. They're easy to do in the moment, but they're ephemeral. There's no physical prison that holds them. But Jacques made himself the prison. He sang it into himself. It couldn't resist. His voice was so beautiful, and his song . . . it went into him, the demon did. And then, before it could take hold, he blew his own brains out. It was the bravest thing I've ever seen anyone do. He saved five of us that night."

"Oh my God." Rosie hesitated. "I thought humans couldn't kill them at all."

"Humans can't kill a demon, but they can still kill themselves. Jacques had the talent to draw the demon into himself, and the bravery to move incredibly fast once it had moved in. I said they start to eat your soul right away, right? Your humanity doesn't die all at once. But most things want to live, even if it means living with a demon infestation. So to do what Jacques did . . . you have to be totally sure of yourself. You have to be completely unafraid to die, to do what Jacques did. Hardly anybody has what it takes. I don't think I do. And I think I'm glad." He took a breath. "Some hero I am, huh?"

"I think you're doing all right." Rosie steepled her hands in front of her mouth. "I was going to ask Irene if she could nose around at the factory and maybe find out something about Helen Montgomery. Jean thinks telling her somebody else is dead is a bad idea, and she's right, and so is involving her in this any more, but if we had some idea of who her friends were there, we might be able to narrow down our search. Not waste so much time when we go in looking."

"You're both right. I'd hate to involve her any more, but the information would be helpful. Maybe you could not mention she's dead."

Rosie made a face. "Her body is going to turn up eventually, isn't it?

Or it'll be in the papers that she's gone missing, so Irene will hear about it or figure it out eventually. I'd rather not lie to her if I'm going to ask her at all."

"I can't blame you. How fast do you think she can learn anything?"

"Not before tomorrow. Mrs Montgomery worked night shift, and I bet Irene's not going to be so agreeable that she'll just run right over to the factory tonight. So tomorrow night at the soonest. Which means we won't be able to do anything with what we learn until Saturday, probably. Ruby's funeral is on Saturday," she added more quietly. "It doesn't matter what else is happening, Hank. I have to go to that." A horrid thought struck her and a word or two of it escaped: "Unless we're—"

Hank nodded. "Unless we're all dead by then."

TWENTY-ONE

Barb leaned in the door, watching Hank drive away after he dropped Rosie off. "Got yourself a gimpy sheik there, hm, Rosie? What's his secret, he likes violent girls?"

Rosie climbed the front porch steps and slipped past Barb. "Are you the tall housemate he mentioned?"

A smile twisted Barb's mouth. "Maybe. What'd he say?"

"That he had to endure ten minutes of bad flirting before he could get out of here, earlier." Rosie didn't even stop to watch Barb's reaction, just went down the hall to her own bedroom, where she fell backward on the bed, arms spread wide, in the faint hope she would cool down. Valentine Vaughn's offer of the convertible crossed her mind and she let out a breath of laughter, wishing there had been some chance for Hank to get home and hear that offer himself. In between work and empathy tests and figuring out how to hunt down clues about demons. Well, it had been an appealing thought.

She slept, because the next thing she knew her back was sore and her throat dry from lying on her back, and Irene was slipping out of her shoes and skirt beside the mirror. Rosie lifted a hand in greeting to let the other girl know she'd woken up, then rolled over with a groan. "I'm awake. You don't have to be quiet."

"I guess I wasn't quiet enough anyway."

"You were fine." Rosie pulled her pillow close and buried her face in it before lifting her head and tucking the pillow under her chin. "You and Rich have a nice time at Big Bob's?"

Irene fumbled her clothes hanger and sent it clattering to the floor, where she stared at it guiltily. "I swear it wasn't anything, Rosie. He came by the factory near the end of shift to talk to the supe about you."

Rosie blinked. "About *me*?"

"He wanted to say he thought it was rotten, what they'd done to you. Firing you like that. He thought maybe if you'd be ridiculed for trying to sue when the bad guy was a former soldier, maybe having another former soldier on your side would help. He was trying to get your job back for you, Ro."

"Jeez," Rosie whispered. "I gotta call him."

"You should," Irene said almost urgently. "We just saw each other at the factory and got to talking, and he asked if I'd like to get something to eat, and I said sure, and then do you know who we saw, we saw Mrs Vaughn, can you believe she eats at Big Bob's? But she does, and she stopped and said hello and I introduced her to Rich, and she was just so nice and we got to talking some more, Rich and me, I meant, after she left and next thing I knew it was nine o'clock and we'd been there all day and I swear it wasn't *anything*, Rosie."

". . . so you had a nice time," Rosie said after a moment. Irene blushed and picked the hanger up, folding the skirt over it carefully as she nodded. Rosie nodded too, the strange twist in her belly again. "That's . . . that's nice. I saw Mrs Vaughn, too. She said she'd said hello, but you looked like you were having fun, so I didn't want to bother you."

"You could have bothered us. You should have! Gosh, Rosie, why didn't you? Why wouldn't you?"

"Well, I had to go see Jean. And you were in a booth for two. He's nice, isn't he."

"He's so nice, Rosie. I swear you're practically all we talked about. He told me about what he'd been doing at the factory, and I wanted to tell him about all the craziness you've been saying but I didn't. I didn't think it would be right. I thought it might sound like—like—"

"Like you were making him try to think his girlfriend, or whatever I am, was crazy so you would have a shot?"

"Oh my *God*." Irene faced her, blouse off but clutched against her chest. "Rosie, I wasn't, I wouldn't, I *swear*—"

"I know, Rene. But that's what telling him would seem like, right? And if it worked that would be especially awful. It's okay, Rene. I don't think you're trying to move in on my man, if he even is my man anymore, and I don't even know that." Rosie put her face back in the pillow for a few seconds before looking up again. "Do you know a Helen Montgomery at the factory?"

Irene sagged, clearly glad to be off the topic of Rich, and answered swiftly. "Sure, she's the one having the affair with Doherty, everybody knows that. Why?"

Rosie sat straight up, pillow falling away. "She's what? He's the one who fired me!"

"Well, somebody had to, I guess, I mean, if they were going to. I don't see what that has to do with the price of eggs. Honestly, Rosie, how can you not know this? The swing-shift girls say she's away from her job half the night most nights, and nobody likes her because they have to do her job. But who are they going to complain to when she's seeing the supe? Don't you ever listen when people talk?"

"I guess not." Rosie checked to make sure the bed hadn't started swaying, but the dizziness came from inside her. "I had no idea."

"Why did you want to know?"

Rosie hesitated. "More craziness."

Irene pulled her nightdress over her head and paused, shaking it into place, to frown at Rosie. "Oh, no, Ro. Not more of this. Honestly, if you don't stop this, somebody's going to have to tell Rich."

"And you're just the girl for the job, huh?"

"I didn't say that!"

"Then let me worry about whether he needs to be told, Rene. Things are complicated enough as it is."

"They're only complicated because you'd rather tell yourself that cockamamie story than face up to what really happened. Have you talked to your pop any more, Rosie? Or anybody but Hank Vaughn?"

"Not much." Rosie rolled over to look at the alarm clock beside her bed. "And it's too late to call Mom and Pop now, although you're right, I should give them a call so they don't worry. Oh, jeez, they're going to want to know what's going on with Rich."

"Do they even know he's home?"

"Yeah, he called them the night he got in, before calling here. Old habit." Rosie crooked a rueful smile. "Maybe I'll just tell them he's dating you now."

"Rosie! I told you, it wasn't anything!"

"Then why are you getting so upset about it?" Rosie got up to put her own pajamas on, glanced at her hair in the mirror, and sat to start winding rags into curls. They wouldn't hold as well now as they would if she wet her hair, but it would be better than nothing. Irene sighed and came over to help, her fingers quick and deft enough that after a few curls, Rosie let her own hands drop.

"I'll tie them up nice and snug and you can go stick your head in the sink to soak them," Irene offered. "Sleep on them and tomorrow you'll be pretty as a picture. I don't know why I'm so upset, Ro. He's such a nice guy."

"You're upset because you like him and he's my boyfriend. . . ." Rosie shrugged. "Or was. Or something. So you think you shouldn't like him."

"Well, don't you?"

"I think it'd be nice if my boyfriend and my best friend got along." Rosie watched Irene part sections of hair and wrap curls more tidily than she could do it herself. Well, at least on her own head. She could do Rene's curls up lickety-split, just as Irene did now with hers. "And I guess if he turns out to not be my boyfriend anymore, I don't have any room to complain."

"Yeah, but you can't be happy about that."

"I don't know what I am, Rene. I got kind of jealous, seeing you with him, but you said there's nothing going on, and why shouldn't I believe you? I don't think either of you are that mean. I bet it'd take at least a week for you two to hook up if Rich and I called it quits for good."

"Rosie!" Irene tugged Rosie's hair. "Give me some credit." She paused. "I'd wait at least a month out of respect for you."

Rosie giggled. "See? I knew you were a good friend." She fell silent, then met Irene's eyes in their reflections. "You like him, huh?"

"He's a really good guy," Irene said again, more solemnly. "You shouldn't let him go, Rosie. Think real hard about what you're doing."

"I will. I am."

"Okay." Irene patted Rosie's tied-up curls. "Now go soak your head, hon, and I mean that in the best way."

"Want me to do yours when I'm done?"

Irene turned her head this way and that, examining her reflection in the mirror. "I don't think so. I've got plenty of bounce left."

"You always do." Rosie went to run her head under water, letting it soak in to the curls, then wrapped a towel around them to keep the worst of the drips at bay. Between the sun having set earlier and the water trickling around her ears, she felt cool for the first time all day. She climbed under her sheet with the towel still wrapped loosely in place, figuring it would come off during the night, and despite her nap, fell into a comfortable sleep.

✪ ✪ ✪

The paper boy's bad aim woke Rosie early, an all-too-familiar sound of newspaper thudding against the wall just beneath her window instead of onto the porch. She lay in bed a while, eyes closed against the encroaching light, then got up to pull a robe on and get the paper so she could look at the help-wanted ads. It had been noble and all, trying to get Pearl a job, but it would have been smart to look out for herself, too. Not that she wanted to work for Harrison Vaughn, if she could avoid it. It seemed too much like asking for favors, what with having just gotten to know Hank.

She put the paper on the table and got coffee started before shuffling back to unroll the paper. Somebody else in the house got up, bathroom water running and the toilet flushing while Rosie poked at the ads. Nothing better than there had been yesterday. Rosie drank her coffee and tapped the pen against the newsprint, smearing lines here and there where the ink had gone on too thickly. At the bottom of one page were ads for typing classes and a couple of "girl wanted for office work" requests. Rosie circled one without enthusiasm, but didn't push the paper away. Marge came in for a cup of coffee, said, "Anything interesting?" and left again before Rosie had a chance to answer. A minute later, Dorothy followed her in, stopped in the doorway when she saw Rosie, and retreated without even getting coffee. Rosie looked after her in disbelief, then got up, got coffee for Irene, and went back to their room.

Irene sat on the end of her bed, brushing her curls out, and eyed the coffee suspiciously. "What happened?"

"I chased Dorothy out of the kitchen just by being there. I thought maybe I should leave."

"Like heck," Irene said. "She's the one acting crazy, Ro. Don't make it easier for her to feel right. Did she say anything?"

"No. Probably just as well. You know, people always say they don't mean what they say when they're upset," Rosie said. "I never really thought that was true. I always kind of figured they said *exactly* what they meant when they were upset, and it's the rest of the time they're careful about it. I don't think I want to hear what Dot might say right now." She unwound a curl to see if it had dried. Not all the way, and with the heat and humidity, it would fall right out if she took them down. She wound it back up and found a yellow kerchief to tie around her hair. "I wonder how long it'll take her to get over it. It's not going to be much fun living here if she doesn't."

"She will," Irene said with confidence. "It's only been a few days, Ro. It'll be okay." She shimmied her shoulders, like she was shaking the topic off. "What are you going to do today?"

Rosie made a face at herself, and at Rene, in the mirror. "Find one of those six-week typing courses, I guess. Look for work. Visit my folks." *Try to find the king demon,* but that didn't seem like what Irene wanted to hear, so Rosie kept it behind sealed lips.

Irene smiled brightly. "That's great. The college thing, Ro, have you been accepted anywhere?"

Rosie nodded, smiling as a nervous flutter danced in her belly. "The community college, at least. I'm waiting to see if I get into one of the four-year schools. I started applying the day Hitler shot himself, 'cause I knew the war couldn't last much longer and I reckoned I'd better get in before the boys came back."

"Well, even if the co-ed schools fill up, there's Marygrove," Irene said encouragingly. "You'll get in there. Good for you, Ro." She glanced at the clock. "I gotta get going to work. I don't want to lose that job. Not yet, anyway." She gave Rosie an apologetic look that Rosie brushed off.

"No point crying over spilt milk, right? You have a job and you should hold on to it as long as you can. Even if you do find an officer and settle right down and start having babies, having some money of your own is swell."

"That's right." Irene stopped on her way out the door to study Rosie. "While you're busy doing all those other things, Ro, you better make some time to talk to Rich, that's what I think."

Rosie nodded slowly, then more firmly. "You're right. I will."

Irene's pretty smile blossomed and she hurried off, the sound of her voice interacting with the other girls' sending a pang of envy through Rosie. Just a few days ago, it had been that easy for her, too, but a wall had gone up. Well, she'd have to chip it down somehow, nothing else for it. Buoyed by the thought, she got dressed in the coolest thing she owned, a sleeveless polka dot cotton print with a square neck and a yellow belt that matched her kerchief, and breezed past her housemates to catch the next tram and go see her folks.

✪ ✪ ✪

Mom and Pop's yard smelled like fresh-mown grass when Rosie arrived. Pop came out of the side shed, wiping his hands on a mostly clean rag as Rosie walked up the drive. "Looks good, Pop. What are you doing home on a Friday?"

He smiled. "Thanks, sweetheart. Took the week off to get things tidied up around here. How are you? Want to come in for some coffee?"

Rosie cupped a hand to her ear. "Was that an offer of lemonade I heard?"

Pop laughed. "Might could do, but it could mean you being hostess and making it yourself. The coffee's already on."

"Thanks to Mom, I bet. Come inside, Pop. I'm going to teach you how to make lemonade." Rosie hugged him and tucked her arm through his as they went indoors. "Where's Mom?"

"She volunteers at the church to make lunches for the Saturday social on Fridays."

"Oh, I forgot." Rosie ushered her father into the kitchen and found lemons. "First off, it's a waste to not grate the peel for zest, so let's do that. I think it softens the lemons up, too, so they're easier to juice."

Pops, amused, got the grater out. "You're really going to teach me to make lemonade?"

"Absolutely." Rosie walked him through it, juicing the lemons, then equal parts juice and sugar, with ice cubes from the freezer and water poured over them a cup at a time until it reached the perfect tartness. "Voila! Now you pour us each a nice tall glass and we sit around and sip lemonade like civilized people."

"Your mother will never believe I made this."

Rosie pointed at a cookbook on the corner of the kitchen counter. "Recipe's right in there, thanks to Mrs Meta Given. You could even pretend I didn't have a thing to do with it."

"She'll know I never would have thought of it on my own." Pop, smiling, poured them each a glass and they headed for the porch before Rosie balked. He glanced at her, surprised, then nodded, his expression clearing. "The living room, then. There's no breeze, but . . ."

"There's no gawkers, either." Rosie folded a leg under herself and sat in one of the chairs, taking a satisfied sip of lemonade. "It's good, Pop."

"Couldn't have done it without you. How are you, Ro?" His eyes went serious even if the question sounded gentle. Rosie thought he really wanted to know, and wished she could tell him everything.

She could tell him enough, though. She took another sip of lemonade, and, nodding, put the glass down. "I'm okay, Pop. I am. The thing with Goode, I'm not waking up with nightmares or anything." She took a breath. "Mom told you I got fired, though, right?"

Anger flashed in Pop's eyes. "For being a threat to the other girls. I've never heard such nonsense, Rosie."

"I know. I know. And I'm afraid the supe was right but I've got an appointment to talk to a lawyer anyway. Even if it smears my name all over town . . . well, it's pretty smeared anyway, and who knows, I might win and that might teach them they can't be bullies." Rosie turned her lemonade glass in its circle of condensation, quiet for a moment. "And I guess you know Rich is home."

"I do." Pop sounded unusually reserved. Rosie looked up to find him studying her. "You know you're not held to any promises you made, Ro. Rich left a long time ago, and you've grown up strong and independent in the years he's been gone."

An incredulous laugh escaped Rosie. She got up to join her father on the couch, hugging him. "You're the only person who's said anything like that, Poppy. Everybody else is asking when we're getting married. But Pop, I didn't tell you and Mom. I didn't tell anybody. I've been applying for colleges."

"Ro!" Delight filled Pop's voice. "Ro, have you? That's my girl. Take on the world, sweetheart. Do what your heart tells you to. Rich is a fine young man, and if you make it work with him, I'll be pleased, but don't put him before an education, if that's what you want. What will you study?"

"Gosh, I don't even know yet." Rosie pressed her hands over her nose and mouth, trying to hold back tears. "Really, Pop? Mom started telling me all over again I needed to move straight home when I got fired, and I can't even imagine what she'll think when I tell her things are rocky with me and Rich, or that I want to go to school."

"Your mother had a split lip and a VOTES FOR WOMEN sign the first time I saw her," Pop said with a smile. "She might want to keep you safe, Rosie, but in the end, she'll be proud of you. Have you been accepted anywhere yet?"

"One of the community colleges, but I'm hoping I'll get in to one of the four-year colleges. A co-ed one," Rosie said fiercely. "I'll take Marygrove if I have to, but I want to be in classes with the men, Pop. I want them to know I can do everything they're doing."

"Rich will know."

Rosie made a face. "He already does. He has to decide whether he likes it, though. And I have to . . ." Her eyes filled with tears and she rose to get her lemonade again, drinking it to calm herself. "Boy, I sure loved him, Pop. I was so scared when he went away. And now he's back and he grew up so tall and handsome, and part of me still loves him like crazy. But . . . love isn't always enough, is it, Pop? Sometimes it's not enough."

"And sometimes it is. Sometimes people love each other enough to work it out. You stay true to yourself, Rosie, and you see what comes of that."

"I'll try." Rosie sat again, looking into her lemonade. "How have things here been? With, you know. Me."

"We've been unusually popular," Pop said dryly. "Visits from people your mother hasn't seen since high school. Your mother has a real knack for turning them all upside-down. They come in looking for gossip, and before they've been here five minutes, they're promising Beth that they were only coming by to check on her. Five minutes after *that*, they're out the door not a word the wiser. I learned to keep my mouth shut and let her do the work."

Rosie glanced at the yard, then at Pop, suspiciously. "Did you really take the week off to tidy things up around here?"

Pop pulled his mouth long. "My boss might have encouraged me to take some time until the fuss died down. Paid leave, though, and it's not coming out of my vacation time, so I thought I might as well keep your mother company while she fielded the mobs. Turns out I didn't need to, but I'm enjoying it while I can."

"Good thing, too, or there wouldn't have been anybody home when I came by." Rosie finished her lemonade and stood with a sigh. "I guess I better get going, Pop. I'm going to try to get into one of those typing courses so I can maybe work around school. I hate to spend all my savings on school and leave myself with nothing when I come out."

Pop rose. "Your mother and I might be able to offer you a loan, sweetheart. Interest-free while you're in school, so you're left with something of your own at the end."

Escaped laughter rushed from Rosie's lips. "That's really nice of you, Pop. I'll think about that, okay?"

"All right. I'll tell your mother you came by. Try to visit again later in the week, Rosie. I know she'll want to see you."

"I want to see her too." Rosie gave him a hug and left, breathless with the morning heat as soon as she stepped out the door. A couple neighbors stopped and stared, so she gave them her best smile and kept her chin high as she headed for the tram.

TWENTY-TWO

There was a typing school downtown, with the next classes starting Monday. Rosie, marching up the stairs in a sweltering building, told herself the whole demon mess would be cleared up by then, and if it wasn't, she'd just have to find a way to work around it. The demon mess and the appointment with the lawyer, she reminded herself, making a face. Missing the first few days of typing class wouldn't go over well. Maybe she could find one starting in August.

Opening the door onto the office nearly made her change her mind about the whole thing anyways. All the windows were open, with fans blowing and every piece of paper weighted down with anything from pens to typewriters. Six rows of five typewriters each had listless young women banging away at keys. The whole room smelled sharp and sweet, like old sweat and perfume. An older woman, trying hard to be perky, rose and approached Rosie. "Good morning, miss. Are you interested in taking classes?"

Rosie put on her best smile and her brightest voice. "I sure am, ma'am. Where do I sign up?" Five minutes later and ten dollars poorer, she had a spot reserved in the upcoming class and had been penciled in for the one starting in August in case she couldn't make the July class.

Ten dollars equaled a whole month's rent. Whether in July or August, the class had better be worth it. She stopped at a pay phone and gave Pearl Daly a ring, but no one answered. Well, hopefully Rosie had told Harrison Vaughn the truth yesterday, and Pearl really *had* found a typing class. If not, Rosie would let her know about this one and, she thought with a wince, spot her the cash to pay for it. Still, at least it would help Pearl get her feet under herself, and Rosie figured she'd get paid back eventually.

She stood in the shade near the pay phone a few minutes to drink a soda and decide what to do next. Visit her folks, try to find a job, sign up for typing classes. Those were the things she'd told Irene she would do. That only left what she *hadn't* said she'd do for the day: try to find the demon king. Rosie made her way to the Ex Libris library on foot, sticking to the shade everywhere she could. Hank had police work to do, so the place sat abandoned. It had been fine coming in yesterday with a mission to fix the window, but now Rosie felt like a little kid sneaking somewhere she'd been told not to. She tiptoed around, poking at things for a few minutes before making herself shake the sensation off. Redeemers belonged in Ex Libris libraries. Redeemers belonged anywhere they wanted to be, she told herself firmly, and furthermore, so did girls like Jean, who might not have magic but wanted to help.

Too many of the books weren't in English. Rosie stopped prodding at them and went to balance on the beams, then practice on the vault, before moving through other exercises and practice fights that Hank had been teaching her. They seemed easier than before, like just one training session had settled them into her bones. It felt good, moving her body, even sweating in the increasing heat. Focusing on the physical workout cleared her mind the same way riveting did: repeating actions so smoothly and regularly that everything felt especially focused, like her whole purpose came down to each punch of steel or thump of leather, as she moved on to the punching bag. If only that clarity would offer an idea about how to find the demon king, she'd be in great shape.

"You're dropping your left." Hank came up behind her to correct her stance. Rosie exhaled, less surprised by his presence than she thought she should be, though she hadn't heard him come in. His hands were cool against her forearms, at least in comparison to the heat she'd generated by working out. "Feel that?" he murmured by her ear. "Feel where your shoulder is? Now extend your arm, not at speed. I want you to feel the right angle, so you know how it feels to *not* drop your shoulder. Speed will come." He kept his hand under her forearm, making sure her form stayed true as she threw a slow punch. A muscle on the outside of her shoulder moved differently when she did it right. Rosie nodded to say she felt the difference, and they went through the hit several more times with Hank guiding her. Then she threw one punch at full speed, knocking the bag several inches with the strength of the impact.

"There you go." Hank, pleased, dropped his hands, though he didn't move back. "Was it you who came in and fixed the window? Thanks."

"You're welcome." Rosie turned her head toward him, a smile pulling at her lips. "You snuck up on me, library man. Either you're not much of a demon, or I'm not much at sensing them. Is it lunchtime?"

Hank nodded. "I've got an hour. And I don't know which possibility makes me feel better, but I'm going to go with me not being much of a demon. I didn't surprise you, though. You didn't flinch."

"No." Rosie looked up at him, still smiling and without stepping back, so they stood intimately close. "I knew I didn't have anything to be afraid of."

"Don't you?"

Rosie's pulse leaped and a breath of laughter escaped her. Hank Vaughn couldn't have been more different from Rich Thompson if he'd tried. Blond and blue-eyed instead of black and green, slender build instead of broad, tinged with British reserve instead of American openness. And Hank only knew Rosie *now*, instead of having lingering memories of how she'd been to confuse with who she'd become. Hank didn't expect her to be the kind of girl happy to stay at home, because he'd met her as a working woman *and* a Redeemer.

Which didn't mean he knew her any better than Rich did. Just differently. Rosie wet her lips. Maybe she had something to be afraid of after all, but not Hank Vaughn's demon blood. Hank lowered his head a fraction of an inch. Rosie, flushed, stepped away with her heart beating wildly, and for some reason—a pretty obvious one, but she didn't want to think about it—remembered what she'd forgotten to tell Hank the evening before. "Oh my gosh, I didn't tell you. Irene says Helen Montgomery was having an affair with Superintendent Doherty at the factory. The one who fired me."

Hank lifted his head, all thought of flirtation clearly vanished. "Mrs Montgomery was having an affair with your *supe?*" Rosie remembered Jean's conviction that Harrison Vaughn had also had an affair with Helen Montgomery, and thought Hank's astonishment was at least as much from how far Mrs Montgomery had come down in the world as from anything else.

"That's what Irene said. I don't know what's at the middle of all this, Hank, me or the factory. Your dad doesn't own it, does he?"

"The Highfield factory? No. Dad's property is Birch Walk. Mother is friends with the family who owns the Highfield factory. They were at the party Monday night."

"But you didn't get any demon-sense off them." Rosie put both hands on the punching bag, leaning her forehead against its old leather. "Are you sure your empathy still works on demons? Maybe it was . . . I don't know. Being in Europe, with all the pressure of the war and all the fear and everything, maybe that heightened it? We know it still works on humans, but . . ."

"I hadn't thought of that." Hank's voice dropped to almost nothing. "I just never thought of that. Hah." Rosie had never heard a laugh that sounded less like one, but he made the sound again, just as sharp and bitter. "That could be. It makes more sense than some kind of conspiracy in Ex Libris, doesn't it? But man, I like the conspiracy idea better. Then it's them who're failing, not me. It's them who are broken, not . . ." He thumped a fist against his right thigh, and Rosie winced, looking away. "You tested me with humans," he said in a low voice. "I guess we need to find a demon to test me against."

"Well, the supe might know where to find one. Let's go talk to him."

"Yesterday you didn't think they'd let you on the premises."

Rosie gave him a bleak smile. "Then I guess we're going to have to remove him from them. Do you have to go back to work right now?"

"Are you sure about this?" Hank leaned over the Coupe's steering wheel, trying to make himself unnoticeable as they sat in a highway diner's parking lot. The big silver trailer's door stood open, people filtering in and occasionally leaving, sometimes with a bag of food but more often with a satisfied expression. A driver with a belly as big as his truck came out and climbed into the Victory Oil semi-trailer that Hank had parked beside. Hank swore as the truck pulled away, leaving them with no highway-side cover, and muttered, "Are you sure about this?" again.

"You've asked five times and the answer keeps being yes. Are *you* sure it's okay if you don't get back to the station this afternoon?" Rosie'd asked that about five times, too, and Hank's answer kept being yes too. She slumped in her seat, barely peeking over the dashboard. "The supe drives over here for lunch every day. It's only half a mile from the factory. Vera's always saying that if he would walk then at least he'd get some exercise to make up for all the lunch he eats, but he always drives."

Hank breathed, "Who's Vera," but obviously didn't expect an answer. "I'm not sure about this."

"Well, it's too late now, because that's his car." Rosie pointed at a Standard Six pulling off the highway into the parking lot. "I think you should be the one who, um. Waylays him."

"You mean kidnaps?"

Rosie nodded. "I've killed three people. If I get caught I'm in enough trouble without adding kidnapping to my crimes."

"Demons don't count," Hank muttered, "but if you're using that argument, I haven't killed anybody, so if you get caught, how much more trouble can you be in than what you already are, whereas I'll have kidnapping charges laid against an otherwise spotless record."

Rosie stared at him, then set her mouth. "Okay, true, but he's not going to get in a car with me."

"He knows you."

"Which is exactly why he won't get in a car with me! He knows I'm furious at him!"

"All right, all right." Hank climbed out of the car, glancing toward Doherty's Chevrolet. "You can drive, right?"

"Would I have suggested this if I couldn't?" Rosie got out the passenger side and stomped to Doherty's car as Hank went into the diner.

Doherty's door was unlocked, but there were no keys in the ignition. Rosie pulled down the sun visor, found nothing, and checked under the front seat: *voila*. An extra key. Smug at having found it, Rosie drove Doherty's car back to the factory, figuring if he turned out to be helpful, there was no point inconveniencing him, and if he turned out to be a demon, well, there'd be no explanation for anything, anyways. Besides, the factory was close enough that she could park Doherty's car and hurry back to the diner on foot before his lunch hour ended. She rolled down the back windows of Hank's car and threw herself on the floor there, panting like a well-dressed dog.

She'd barely caught her breath when a hand-cramping thrill of discomfort swept her. A moment or two later, the front doors opened and Doherty's obvious weight tilted the vehicle to the right. Rosie resisted the urge to sit up and gape at him, instead rubbing her hands to ease the cramps. Helen Montgomery's presence had been more of a tingle, not a sharp pain, but Rosie would bet anything that her ability to sense demons was improving. Even if it seemed impossible that flabby, grumpy Supervisor Doherty could be one. He had no panache. Rosie thought demons ought to have panache.

"I don't know what this city is coming to," Doherty snarled. "Stealing cars in broad daylight, women shooting men at work. I'm obliged for the lift, Mr Vaughn. Your family are fine people."

Hank tilted the car a little the other direction as he got in. "I'm sure you'd have just walked back, Mr Doherty, but with the heat as it is, I'm glad to offer you a ride. Would it have been better if it had been a man?"

"What? What nonsense are you talking?"

"You said women shooting men at work. Would John Goode's death have been better if a man had shot him?" Hank sounded deliberately placid, dull enough to make Rosie smile instead of sitting up to give Doherty a piece of her mind. The car pulled out, turning toward the factory, so as not to alarm Doherty where he could shout for help and perhaps still be heard.

"Of course not! Still a terrible shame. But it would make more sense, wouldn't you say? Nasty thought, women being killers. What's the world coming to?"

"I understand she was defending herself. That Goode had killed several women already."

"Then they should have had men around to protect them!"

Hank's voice went dry. "In the middle of a factory full of women who are working for the specific reason that the men have all gone off to war? If I'm not mistaken, Mr Doherty, you're probably the man they should have gone to for protection. Where were you Saturday morning?"

"At home, sleeping, like any God-fearing man should be!" The car turned left again and Doherty's bluster rose another notch. "Where are you going? This isn't the way to the factory. It's just straight down the highway."

"We're not going to the factory, Supe." Rosie finally sat up, shaking herself as she climbed onto the back seat. Doherty gave a startlingly shrill yelp, twisted to see Rosie, then threw a look of outraged accusation at Hank.

"What the hell is going on here? What are you doing with this criminal?"

"I'm not a criminal, Supe." Rosie turned her hands up, thinking of pain that had cramped them, and looked at Doherty. "I'm a Redeemer, and I'm betting you know what that means."

The fleshy superintendent paled, and the corner of Rosie's mouth turned up. "Hank, do you think we can find somewhere quiet to have a nice talk with Mr Doherty here? A long way away from other people? I think he's going to have some interesting things to tell us."

"I think I can find somewhere, sure, Miss Rosie," Hank said blandly. Rosie's smile widened as the car accelerated and Doherty looked wildly between them, and out the window, like he might be judging his odds if he threw himself out of the moving vehicle.

It seemed he didn't like what he came up with, because he blurted, "You can't do this! This is kidnapping! It's extortion! Blackmail! It's—"

"A friendly drive and a nice conversation," Hank said, still blandly.

"I'm in fear for my life!"

"Which one of you?" Rosie asked, honestly curious. "Jacob Doherty or the demon inside you? Or does Mr Doherty even exist anymore? I guess it doesn't matter. If he doesn't, then the thing inside him *should* fear for its life. How about up there, Hank? Down that power-line road?"

"It's as good a place as any. Better than some, I guess. Not much traffic. The earth's not going to be soft, but I have a shovel in the trunk."

"What are you going to do to me?" Doherty's voice shot high.

Rosie sighed as they pulled down the power line road and bumped along.

"I guess that depends on how cooperative you are. Hank makes deals sometimes, but I've had a really bad week and you're the son of a bitch who fired me." Rosie frowned at Hank in the rear-view mirror. "Wouldn't a demon of any rank, one who could do anything useful, have tried it by now? I mean, Goode tried to eat me and that ochim thing just about took me apar—"

"You got Hannah? No, of course you did, of course, I haven't seen her since the Sunday shift, since I fired—what did you do to her?"

"I Redeemed her," Rosie said bluntly. "She's dead. What are you?" Hank killed the engine as she asked, and the question echoed loudly in the silence.

"I'm nothing, I'm nobody, just a cog in the wheel. I was an artist once." Doherty's voice thinned, like he'd lost something. Like it wasn't *him* talking anymore, although Rosie guessed it never had been Doherty, not while she'd known him. "I was never good enough, even though I tried so hard," he whined. "It ate at me, like a black spot on my soul, until it finally got out and took everything that was left of me. I barely made it into my wife's body, and she tried to kill herself. Weak vessels, all I've ever been able to find are weak vessels, with no talent, no passion, no fire. So I looked for protection. That's all I do. What I'm told. I keep the wheels greased, that's all. Maybe sometime I'll please my protector well enough to be granted a chance at a stronger vessel, someone with ability. That hope has kept me going for seventy years."

Revulsion mixed with sympathy in Rosie's breast as Doherty spoke, but his last words wiped away any compassion she might have had for him. "You've been moving through people for seventy years? Taking over their lives? Killing them slowly? And that doesn't bother you?"

Doherty turned a flat expression on her. "Why should it? They're only human. I'm the embodiment of *art*."

"You're an embodiment of madness. You're not what people aspire to. You're what they struggle against. Jeez, you should have gone to art school or something, mister, and tried learning something instead of just whining about being a failure."

Doherty's eyes popped and Rosie rolled hers with exasperation. "I guess you're not real bright, are you? He obviously doesn't know anything, Hank. I'm going to just Redeem him. At least we'll have one less demon to worry about."

"No no no no no! I can tell you things! I can tell you what you want to know!" Doherty's gaze went shifty. "I can tell you about the hive."

Rosie glanced at Hank, whose head dropped in one small, sharp nod. Rosie shrugged and jerked her chin at Doherty. "Get out of the car and tell me about the hive."

"Don't let her touch me," Doherty begged Hank, but the blond man shrugged.

"She's the Redeemer, mate. I do what she says. Get out." He prodded Doherty, who all but fell from the car, already babbling.

"Goode was a punk, all right? He was trouble, and the hive doesn't tolerate that kind of nonsense, not usually, but the Enforcer, he wasn't in town, and it doesn't matter how much trouble somebody is, you want to stay in the hive, you toe the line, you don't go after each other, at least not in this town. You don't break ranks." His gaze flitted to Hank as Rosie got out of the car and Hank came around its front end. "You understand about not breaking ranks, right, kid? You were a soldier. You know how it is." His attention returned to Rosie. "Truth is, you did us all a favor, killing that kid, and I'm real sorry I had to fire you, but orders came from on hi— I mean, what could I do, the whole situation made the factory look bad, I couldn't just let it slide."

"Orders came from where," Rosie asked softly. Goode had been dangerous. The ochim—Hannah—had been maybe even more dangerous than that, if less of a wild card. Helen Montgomery had come at Rosie full-force, full of killing rage, but Doherty just seemed pathetic. To think she'd been afraid of him just a handful of days earlier, only to see his true blubbering colors now.

"It came down from the boss, I swear it did. I don't know if they cared, not really, but somebody did. I don't know who runs this city, Miss Ransom. I just do my job and keep my head down, like everybody else."

"He's lying." Hank finally spoke again, his voice soft. Rosie lifted her eyebrows and he gave a one-shouldered shrug. "Look at him. Sweating, making fists, trying to distract us. He's lying." He met Rosie's eyes and dropped his chin in another almost-invisible nod, and realization caught her.

He couldn't admit to his power, not in front of a demon, especially one they hadn't decided what to do with yet. If they cut a deal, Hank was as good as dead the minute word got out he could read emotions, and Rosie didn't believe for a minute that Doherty wouldn't sell Hank out if he got the chance. She stepped away from the supe, dropping her voice, but not quite enough, to speak to Hank. "Look, I think you're wrong. I think I should just Redeem him—"

Doherty's theatrical howl of fear almost derailed her, but Hank picked up the thread, shaking his head as he spoke. "We could Artifice him. He might turn out useful later, and we could always bring him back out."

"Do that," Doherty whimpered. "Do that, that's a good idea. Just don't Redeem me, I don't want to die—"

"No, if he doesn't know anything useful now, he's not going to learn anything trapped inside a drawing. I'm just going to—" Rosie lifted a hand toward Doherty, having no real idea of how to awaken the Redeeming magic when fear didn't have her in its grasp. She certainly didn't want to repeat the terrible scene with Pearl, but as she lifted her hand, Doherty gave an awful wailing scream and fell to his knees.

"The hive is holed up on the abandoned Pennicott factory." Hank went white, but Doherty kept babbling. "They've been there for years, keeping quiet, but there's more and more of us now, refugees from Europe, and pretty soon Detroit's going to be a demon town! We're going to take it over, the whole city, and once we're established here, the whole lake system will be ours! We're—"

Rosie whispered, "Oh my gosh, shut *up*," and spun around to knee Doherty in the head as hard as she could. His eyes crossed and he hit the ground almost before he stopped talking. Rosie stood above him, breathing hard, then looked up at Hank's stricken expression. It changed briefly as he focused on Doherty. When he met Rosie's eyes, he looked almost impressed. "I didn't teach you that."

"No, but you said hit hard parts with other hard parts and I figured my knee was tougher than my fist. What did he say, Hank? What scared you?"

"The Pennicott property." Hank swallowed. "My dad owns that."

TWENTY-THREE

They left Doherty in his own car at the factory, even though neither of them felt sure keeping him alive was smart. Rosie kept muttering, "He helped. I said I wouldn't kill him if he helped," like she might convince herself if she said it often enough, and Hank just shook his head every time she said it.

"I couldn't feel him," he finally said. "In the diner, in the car? I couldn't tell he was a demon, not until you said so. Then it hit me, the blankness in him. The emptiness. I couldn't even read him like he was human. I believed everything he projected, the offense, the anger, the fear."

"I think that was all real. They might eat the soul when they take over the body, but they bring their own corrupted soul in, don't they? There must be some emotion left in it." Rosie pressed her knuckles against her mouth, watching the street speed by. "Hank . . ."

"No." He snapped the word. "Not right now. I can't. I have to see—I have to see."

"Okay. All right. Just—" She took a breath, stopping herself, and shook her head. "Okay."

Hank nodded, not exactly thanking her, but she understood that he meant it. The humidity had burned off since lunch, leaving the air hazy with dust but no longer so thick to breathe. Rosie's lungs filled more easily, but it made her feel like she was preparing for a fight, and she didn't even know who with. Maybe Hank, maybe Harrison Vaughn, maybe a hive full of demons. "Should we stop at the library for weapons?"

A laugh escaped at the question's absurdity, and to her surprise, Hank cast a brief smile her way. He put on an old librarian's voice, querulous and rickety: "Yes, yes, Miss Ransom, you'll find the swords in the *S* section, after Steinbeck, and the battle-axes have been moved to *A*, after no one was able to find them under *B*. Now go along, child, I can't be bothered with your queries every other minute of my day."

"Mrs DeForest has never once said anything like that to me." Rosie smiled.

"Only because they don't actually keep weaponry in the public library," Hank assured her, then shook his head. "No, I don't think so. I'm not going to pick a fight right now. I just need to see . . ."

Rosie nodded. "If they're there." She took a breath, looking for something to say that wouldn't seem patronizing or like she was trying to give Hank something else to think about. "How big is the property?"

"About a block. It used to be Pennicott Manufacturing. They made stoves, but there was a fire about a decade ago."

"Oh! Oh, yeah. I remember that. Some of my friends' fathers worked there. I remember them being worried that it might not be rebuilt."

"Yeah. It was, obviously, but instead of rebuilding there, Dad——" Hank cleared his throat. "Dad moved the whole site down to the river. Easier to ship from there, and the waste could be dumped right in, instead of piping it somewhere. And he had big ambitions for expansion. There was money in kitchen appliances, but he wanted to start his own automotive line. There was room on the riverfront, land to be bought up for cheap. Cheaper than up here, and there weren't any families to move around. Dad doesn't like the kind of press that generates, even in the name of progress."

"I remember a couple of my friends' dads got jobs at other factories while they were rebuilding. But the equipment's probably all destroyed now."

"What didn't get wrecked in the fire was taken to the new factory, yeah." Hank glanced at her. "Why?"

"I used a riveting gun to shoot a demon a few nights ago," Rosie said. "I guess I was trying to imagine what might be there that I could use for a weapon."

"We're not getting out," Hank said firmly. "Doherty's probably going to call somebody, warn them that we might be coming to look. I don't want to risk getting caught."

"Doherty's not going to do anything," Rosie said with conviction. "He'd have to admit a Redeemer and a library man caught him if he did that, and they'll know he ratted them out. He wouldn't last a minute. So maybe we're not getting out *this* time, but we're going to have to sooner or later, aren't we? If there's a—a *hive* there . . ." She shuddered. "That word makes me squirm. It makes me think of bees and bugs crawling all over everything. It's worse than a nest, somehow."

"Nests have birds. Baby birds with open mouths, wanting to be fed. That sounds harmless. Swarms of bees don't. And demons aren't."

"Doherty didn't seem like much, for a demon. I kept expecting him to do something. Scream, or move fast, or . . ." Rosie sighed. "Or run his hands through fire without getting burned. I don't know."

"They're not all powerful, not any more than all humans are powerful. But when a lot of unkillable bees swarm . . ."

Rosie shivered. "Yeah. Do you think they could do it? Take over Detroit?"

"As far as I know, it's been almost two thousand years since demons actually took over a human city, since Rome. Most of them can't cooperate well enough. But if there's a daemon rex here . . . I don't know. Maybe."

"What happened in Rome?"

Hank's voice took on a strange note. "It burned, Rosie. Rome burned."

"Well what the heck good does that do, if they can't die?"

"Nero fiddled," Hank said. "Rome burned, and Nero fiddled, and the demons came to him. He caught them *in* the fiddle, in the fiddle itself. It was one of the greatest acts of magic humanity ever performed, and what do we remember? A tyrant who laughed while his city burned."

Rosie whispered, "Hank," in astonishment, and he performed a hard little smile. "Where's the fiddle now? It can't have been destroyed, can it? Or all the demons in it would be let loose."

"Safe, I think. I imagine. Ex Libris spirited it out of Europe at the start of the Great War, but only a handful of people have access to the records for locations of items like that. They can't move the Sistine Chapel or the Taj Mahal, but the smaller things they can and do, so no one can find them. It wasn't a fiddle," he added suddenly. "They hadn't been invented yet. It was a lyre."

"I don't even know what that is."

"It's little and pot-bellied. Like a cross between a fiddle and a squash."

Rosie laughed. "Delicious for dinner *and* an after-dinner concert. That's it up there, isn't it?" she said as Hank pulled over to a parking space on the sidewalk. "It doesn't look like anybody lives there."

"It wouldn't, if demons are hiding out there." Hank went silent. "I used to play around the building there. They'd let me help drive the lift trucks and guide the cranes. I haven't really been down to look at the site since it burned. I've driven past, but . . . " He shook his head, and Rosie found herself nodding in sympathy.

Tall fences, half beaten down with weather and time, surrounded the old factory site. What paint there had been had long since faded, visible only as peeling strips now, if at all. Wire and wood tangled together unpleasantly, and that was only the exterior, what was easily visible from the street. Hank got out of the car after all and, rather gentlemanly, came around to open Rosie's door after a few other vehicles had passed on the road. She smiled at him as they got out, and he took her hand as they ran across the road, Rosie keeping to his pace. "We can't be arrested for trespassing," he said, pushing aside a loose board. "Dad still owns the place. Come on."

Surprisingly tall grass grew around the fence, thick with a years-long lack of attention, and dry from the summer's heat. Rosie waded through a step or two ahead of Hank, testing the ground before she committed herself and beating down some of the worst snarls. Hank mumbled a thanks that acknowledged she'd eased the way for him, and she waved it off with a wiggle of her fingers.

Beyond the grass lay tarmac, melted and pungent under the sun. Rosie wrinkled her nose, testing that, too, with a toe, and Hank, at her side, smiled faintly. "You won't stick. Not too much, anyway. I used to play a game where I'd stand as still as I could for as long as I could, waiting to see if it would suck me down like a saber-toothed tiger. Like in the tar pits."

"I guess it never did."

"No, but I ruined a couple pair of shoes before Mother put a stop to that. Do you feel anything yet?"

"No. Do you?"

Hank shook his head. "Let's get closer."

"Okay, but I just want to be the one who says this isn't very much like staying away." The tarmac didn't quite pull Rosie's shoes off, but she felt it wanting to, and looked around to see if she could find any signs of where Hank, as a child, had wrecked his own shoes. Even if the marks had lasted this long, she doubted he would have been this far from the main building. Someone would have been paying attention to where the boss's son was.

"We couldn't exactly come in the front driveway," Hank pointed out. "If somebody's here, they'd notice that. Otherwise, believe me, I'd have been happy to drive up in the car. I don't run all that fast, and I hate the idea that something that could chase us might be in there. In Europe, I would have been able to tell from this far away."

"Well, I guess *I* can't tell from more than about fifteen feet, so let's hope we don't have to get that close to find out if there are monsters here." The factory itself still retained the general structure it had once held, but the external walls were scarred with smoke and fire marks that hadn't faded even after almost a decade. Once-solid concrete bricks crumbled both inward and outward, making a maze of hills and hiding places. Rosie scrambled up a pile of broken wall, trying to keep low, and looked beyond it into the building's wrecked interior.

In full daylight it seemed easy enough to navigate, but a thin layer of cloud cover would render it murky and nerve-wracking. Steel and concrete leaned and lay and lumped together everywhere, the remnants of old assembly lines now rusting heaps that smelled strongly of iron in the heat. Birds scattered at the broken-in ceilings as if offended that anyone chose to come near their roost. Rosie shivered, imagining how many rats and other rodents were likely to be hidden in the shadows.

"It looks all right." She turned back to offer Hank a hand, although he climbed up easily enough on his own, taking weight on his own hands to make up for where his leg might fail him. "Be careful of the glass."

He gave her a dirty look and she turned away, grinning at both of them. A few seconds later, he joined her in looking over the steeper inner wall, and pursed his lips. "I can lower you down. . . ."

"And jump down yourself? It makes more sense for me to lower you."

"I must outweigh you by—" Hank hesitated, a spark of panic in his eyes. "A lot," he said, rather than guess at her weight.

Rosie flexed a bicep just like Charles Atlas. "Probably, but I'm pretty tough. Come on, there's no point in getting this far and deciding I'm too fragile now." She lay down and shifted herself until she was relatively comfortable hanging over the wall, and waggled her fingers at Hank. "Go on, swing yourself over and then use my hand and arm to keep from falling."

"If I pull you off . . ."

"Then I'll land on top of you and have a nice soft landing. Come on, the concrete is digging into my ribs."

Hank, shaking his head, sat on the edge, turned over, and worked his way down, finding toeholds where he could. "It's not too bad."

"Good. We'll be able to climb back up again. Take my hand anyways, because if someth—*whoof!*" Hank took her hand just as old concrete crumbled beneath his foot and he jolted downward. Most of his weight yanked on Rosie's arm. Another grunt of pained effort escaped her as broken concrete dug deeper into her ribs and her shoulder socket stretched, but after a second or two, Hank found another foothold and some of the weight lessened. He looked up at her, whey-faced, and although her ribs hurt, Rosie widened her eyes in an expression meant to convey "See, I told you!" and "That was close!"

Hank grumbled, "Yeah, yeah," and edged farther down, until Rosie couldn't hold him anymore without risking her own perch. "It's okay," Hank muttered. "I'm almost there. There." His questing foot reached the ground and he stepped down.

Rosie sat up to rub her ribs, then took a deep breath and swung herself over the edge too, before the bruising decided it wanted her to stay in place. Hank guided her down, and she jumped the last few feet, landing in a crouch that twinged her ribs again. "Maybe we can go *out* the front door. . . ."

"Getting out should be easier. You can see where it's safe to climb, on the way up." He watched Rosie swing her arm and rub her shoulder until it didn't feel quite so stretched, then said, "Thanks," awkwardly. "You really are strong. I didn't think you could catch me."

"Never underestimate a riveter, library man."

The corner of Hank's mouth turned up. "I'll try not to again. Okay. I remember that there were some parts of the factory that weren't as badly damaged. If I were holing up here, that's where I'd go. You up for it?"

"Yeah. Just remember if we get a sense of them, we turn around and leave."

"I remember." Hank paused, looking around the wreckage. Old garbage had blown in and lay crowded into corners, rustling not, Rosie thought, with the wind, but with whatever lived and ate in them. Sunlight fell in shafts through holes in the walls and ceiling, even, in a few places, through unbroken windows so dirty they could hardly be distinguished except as slightly brighter squares in the walls. Dust, disturbed by their arrival, spun in the light as they walked through the factory. Once in a while Rosie heard a car outside, but mostly the burned building seemed entirely isolated from the rest of Detroit. She almost said, *What better place for demons?* out loud, but in the silence, even a whisper seemed like announcing their presence, and she kept quiet.

Hank stopped suddenly, just a few steps ahead of her. Rosie froze too, looking for what had stopped him, and then, realizing, trying to *feel* what had stopped him. Nothing at all, as far as she could tell, but he turned toward her with eyes just this side of scared spitless, and tipped his head back the direction they'd come. Rosie's own eyes widened in question and he nodded, hardly more than a shiver. She wouldn't have even seen it if she hadn't been expecting it. Heart in her throat, she turned and retraced their steps, glancing back often to make sure Hank stayed with her.

He did, but his spooked look didn't fade, even when they'd quietly scrambled up the same ledge they'd entered by, and he didn't speak until they'd scooted on their butts down the hill they'd climbed, and hurried in silence back to the car. Only inside it, with the doors closed and his hands on the wheel, with his gaze locked forward, did he say, "I can *still* feel them."

Rosie looked sharply toward the old factory. "I didn't feel anything. Are you—of course you're sure. What—what did it feel like?"

"Like you said." Hank sounded hoarse. "Like a hive. Squirming and writhing. I've never felt so many at once, so much emptiness. Purposeful emptiness. I don't know how to explain it. There must be dozens of them hiding in there, Rosie. Maybe more. Doherty was right. I don't know how I missed them. I've been by here a hundred times since I got home, and I never felt them."

"Get out of the driver's seat." Hank shot Rosie a startled look and she gestured at him. "Look at you. You're shaking. You're in no condition to drive, and I don't want to be sitting here talking about this. What if one of them goes by and senses *me*? Trade places with me. I'll drive us back to the library."

"Can you? That's a narrow fit, that alleyway."

"Would you be asking a man that question?" Rosie traded places with Hank, fired up the engine and pulled onto the street after a glance behind them told her the road was clear. A sleek Cadillac crossed the intersection ahead of them, and Rosie followed it with her gaze as she pulled up to the intersection a moment later. It turned at the Pennicott property driveway and a uniformed Negro man got out to open the gates. Hank took a sharp breath that Rosie echoed before gunning the Coupe and shooting across the intersection, leaving the Pennicott property behind.

Five blocks farther on, Rosie pulled over, shaking too much herself to trust driving if she didn't absolutely have to. "Hank, was that . . ."

"George," he whispered. "That was our driver, George. That was . . ."

Rosie worked her hands against the steering wheel and struggled to find the right words to say. "Look," she finally tried, quietly. "We know something's blocking your empathy. You've been past that old factory before, but you couldn't feel them until you knew they were there for sure. So something has to be blocking you, Hank. And I hate to say it, but . . ."

"But you think it's my father." Belief, worse than panic, settled into Hank's voice.

"That was his car, wasn't it? Your driver, and his car, and his property, and . . . wouldn't it make sense?" Rosie asked unhappily. "If anybody could do that, wouldn't it be your own family? And I'm sorry, I really am, but think about your dad, Hank." Her voice sounded small to her own ears. "Think how popular he is. How much people like him. If he's like you, a demon of—of empathy—"

"Music," Hank said clinically. "Demons who can affect emotion usually come from musicians of some sort. Music seems to have the most universal effect on our emotions. Not all of them develop that way, obviously, or there wouldn't be things like the ochim, but when they do appear, they're usually derived from musicians."

"The point is, if he can manipulate emotion, then doesn't that help to account for his popularity? Have you ever tried it?"

"Manipulating people's emotions for my own benefit?" Hank looked at Rosie coldly, then glanced away. "Not for my own benefit."

Rosie's eyes widened. "For somebody else's?" An unexpected smile split her face. "Did you help some friend get a girl, or something?"

Hank's voice softened, not in a good way. "No, Rosie. I more or less told you this already. How do you think I talked Detective Johnson into letting Pearl Daly go?"

"Oh. Oh! Oh, gosh, Hank. But darn it, that wasn't—that wasn't a wrong thing to do. It was a lot less awful than the mess I made trying to help her, if we're comparing monstrousness. Anyways, if it *is* your dad, doesn't it figure that you can't tell because he's a full demon and stronger than you? He could be masking this whole city. Could *have* been, at least, until you knew the truth for sure and got close enough to verify it. Your powers still work, Hank. Maybe you can't read him *because* he's your dad. Maybe—"

"If my father is a demon, Rosie, then what am I?" Hank's cool front broke like glass shattering, unrelenting pain in his features. "Did I get this power on the Front or was it always in me? He fought in the Great War, Rosie. That was more than twenty years ago. If a demon took him in

Europe, then I've never known Harrison Vaughn at all! He died before I was born and my father is a *demon*. My *blood* is a *demon's*. I am a monster, if that's true. I *am* a monster, and I should turn myself over to Ex Libris for execution."

"That's ridiculous. If they're that closed-minded, you shouldn't tell them anything at all, but if you *are* telling them something, what they should learn from it is that just because you've got magic doesn't mean you're automatically evil. I'm not. You're not. Maybe they've been killing all the people who could help them, all these centuries. Wouldn't that be rich?" Rosie folded her arms under her breasts and glowered at Hank. "Either way, you're not going to go tell them anything right now, because whether we like it or not, there's a demon hive and whatever *controls* a demon hive in Detroit right now, and you're the only person who can possibly help me stop it, so I'm not about to let you go get yourself killed. Now are you ready to do what we have to do, or do I need to bust your chops some more?"

Hank turned his face away, but muttered, "I'm ready," sullenly.

"Good." Rosie turned the car back on. "We're going over to Jean's and we're going to figure out a battle plan."

TWENTY-FOUR

Jean looked awful when she opened the door, with her skin all sallow and her hair dry and frizzy. She let them in, though, even if her eyes were swollen and red, and she made coffee while they told her about Doherty and the demon-infested factory. By the time Rosie had finished talking, some color had come back into Jean's cheeks, like the whole mess really did give her something else to think about. "So you want us three to go take on a demon hive? Hive," she added, almost under her breath, and shivered with enjoyment. "I like that. It's creepier than *nest*."

"The three of us can't," Hank said flatly. "Our only chance is to take out—"

"The demon king," Rosie said, when he couldn't. "Harrison Vaughn."

Hank shook his head, but he didn't contradict her. Jean poured everyone coffee and sat down with them. "Well, it shouldn't be too hard to draw him out, right? Hank just says, 'Hey, Dad, come here for a minute,' and Rosie does her magic. I want to see it this time. I was too scared last time to really see." Her voice held a vindictive note that Rosie wished Hank didn't have to hear, but he only shook his head again.

"If it is Dad, there's no way he's going to let himself be drawn into any situation where he's at all vulnerable. The demons know there's a Redeemer in Detroit. They probably even know it's Rosie. Dad didn't get to the top of the heap doing business by not playing it smart."

"He wasn't afraid of me yesterday," Rosie said suddenly. "He asked when I wanted to start boxing lessons. He wouldn't have done that if he thought I was going to hurt him."

"But he might have done it to arrange a time when he could get you alone and kill you. Did you agree to anything?" Hank sounded both grim and hopeful, as if she might be providing a necessary answer to a terrible situation.

"No. Your mom couldn't believe he was offering, and I guess we got off track. I'm supposed to call him, though. About a job, either for me or Pearl."

"You want Pearl to go work for my father when you think he's Detroit's daemon rex? Why don't you just put her out for the crows to pick over?"

"Well, if he is, at least it's an excuse to talk to him!"

"Hank doesn't need an excuse," Jean said again. "Harrison Vaughn is just dear old Dad. Maybe you could just find an artist and sneak into his room and imprison him while he's sleeping, Hank."

Rosie sat back, sloshing her coffee. "That's a really good idea."

"Yeah, and what happens to my mother if Dad wakes up during that?" Hank shook his head again. "I'd rather separate him. Talk to him."

"And say what? 'Excuse me, Dad, but are you an immortal soul-eating demon? Is it your fault Ruby and half a dozen other girls are dead? Did you turn your own mistress into a monster?'" Contempt dripped from Jean's questions.

Hank paled under the onslaught, but Rosie lifted her hands, silencing them both before he could retaliate. "Doherty said they don't step out of line, the demons. They do what they're told and work together or somebody called an 'Enforcer' comes after them. Is an Enforcer the same as the king, Hank? Is that how they work? Because Doherty said the Enforcer had been out of town, and your dad's been here, right? Maybe that means—"

He shook his head again before she finished. "Enforcers are just that. Muscle to keep the rank and file in line so the daemon rex doesn't have to bother with those kinds of details. Almost all the high-level demons have some kind of Enforcer, sometimes several. With a hive this size, I don't know why there wouldn't be one on hand to take care of problems like Goode."

Hairs stood up on Rosie's arms as she thought about the Lincoln Continental they'd seen at the factory. "What if . . . I mean, Enforcers must be pretty tough, right? Maybe kind of high-ranking themselves?" At Hank's nod, she went on. "What if there was somewhere else it was more useful to have your Enforcer? Somewhere they could be useful to you, but could still be called back when you needed them? We thought it was your dad at the factory, Hank, but I know at least one other person has been driven around in a car like that this week."

Hank's jaw went slack. "Senator Haas. You think a US *Senator* is Detroit's Enforcer?"

Rosie smiled weakly. "It's kind of hard to tell, isn't it? Since I killed Goode, who might have been the reason Haas was called back. When did he get in?"

"Friday afternoon. He had meetings with Dad and—" Hank broke off, shaking his head. "I've known him for years. I never . . ."

"Got the sense he was a demon? But we know your empathy's not working right, and probably the closer you are to your dad, the worse it works."

"I didn't get any demon-sense off the car, Rosie. If it was Haas, Dad was with him. Or . . . or maybe it was just too far away, with this damn blockage."

"Does it matter?" Jean demanded. "Whether you saw Haas today or not, does it change having to get to Harrison Vaughn?"

"It gives us one more face to our enemy, and somebody else to go through," Hank said. "We can only take them on one at a time. There's just not enough of us to risk two of them, much less a whole hive."

"But you've done what the library men want you to, haven't you?" Rosie asked. "You've found the nest. The hive. Can't you call in reinforcements now? We don't have to move now, do we?"

"Ruby's *funeral* is *tomorrow*," Jean half-wailed, half-snarled. "I want this done by then."

"Jean . . ."

Hank stopped with her name, looking unhappy, and for the second time, Rosie said what he didn't want to. "It was never likely we were going to get it all taken care of by then, Jean."

"Then what am I supposed to tell her parents? Her Nan? That I'm real sorry she's dead and someday all the people responsible will pay for it? What kind of comfort is that? How can I look them in the eye and say that?"

"You can't." Hank's voice deepened with implacable sympathy. "For all they know, Jean, the man responsible is already dead. Rosie killed him in self-defense late Friday night. That you and I and she know more about the whole situation is no reason to take what comfort Ruby's family can get from that away from them. I'm sorry we can't offer you the same comfort as quickly, or maybe ever. There aren't many total victories in this line of business, Jean. If you don't like that, if you can't handle it, then you need to get out now, while you still can."

Jean moved her hand violently, knocking her coffee cup aside. Steaming liquid sprayed across the table and floor, the cup breaking into thick shards when it bounced off the cupboard and landed sharply on the tile. Rosie's hand flew to her mouth, but Hank didn't so much as flinch. Jean stared at the mess, then leapt up and ran from the room, a bedroom door slamming a few seconds later.

For a moment neither Hank nor Rosie spoke. Then Rosie stood to pick up the broken pieces of coffee cup before finding a sponge and a mop to clean up the rest of the mess. Hank watched with disgust-tinged neutrality. "Why are you cleaning up her mess?"

Rosie, leaning on the mop, paused in disbelief to look over her shoulder at him. "How come you don't *know* this, mister empathic library man? I'm doing it because her best friend died and there's nothing she can do except get overwhelmed with feelings sometimes. Because I'm not a jerk, and I hope somebody would try helping me out if my whole life fell apart like that."

"Hasn't it?"

"No. Not like that. Not as bad as what she's going through." Rosie turned back to mopping, lifting the mop head to wring it out over the sink. "And even so, you *are* kind of a jerk, but you've been trying to help me anyways. So I'm cleaning up because she's having a hard-enough time without having to come back in here and see the stinky, sticky mess she made when she got reminded just how bad her heart is broken and how little she can do about it."

Hank turned his attention out the window. "You're a good person, aren't you, Rosie Ransom?"

Rosie shrugged. "I don't know. I try. Don't you?"

"Maybe not hard enough." Hank got up stiffly and came to stand beside Rosie, opening his hands. "What can I do?"

She handed him the dustpan full of cup shards. "Empty that and rinse the dishcloth before you wipe the cupboard doors down."

Hank did as he was told, the only sounds a clink of ceramic and the running tap water, while Rosie finished cleaning the floor and put the mop away. As she dried her hands, he said, "I keep it locked down as hard as I can."

"What?"

"You asked how come I didn't know why you were cleaning up. I keep the power locked down as hard as I can. Being bombarded by everybody's emotions is exhausting, and a whole lot of the time, people get really upset if you seem to notice they're in turmoil. Once in a while, somebody wants to talk but more often, they're trying to be stiff upper lip about it, and noticing something's wrong doesn't go over well. So if I'm out hunting, or if it's something like trying to get Detective Johnson to let Pearl Daly go, yeah, I've got it turned up, but if I'm just hanging out, like here? I keep it under wraps as much as possible."

"Hank." Rosie pressed her knuckles against her lips, watching him finish up his chores. "Maybe keeping it locked down is part of why you haven't been able to tell there are demons in Detroit. Maybe you're stunting yourself."

He smiled thinly. "I like the other idea better. The one where I'm being blocked. Because I don't think I could live, open to everybody's emotions all the time."

Rosie sighed. "I guess I can see that. Look, I'm going to go check on Jean-Marie. You think about whether we want to go for Senator Haas first, or whether we can figure out some way to just make sure he's not around your dad when we confront him."

"Yes, General." Hank waved a salute and went back to his coffee cup as Rosie left the kitchen to go knock on Jean's door. It stood a couple inches open, so although Jean didn't answer, Rosie pushed it open farther, saying, "Jeannie?" quietly.

"He's a real piece of work, your new beau." Jean sat in the corner on the far side of the bed, knees drawn up, arms wrapped around a pillow, and her voice muffled in it.

Rosie sighed, said, "He's not my beau," more for form's sake than anything else, and sat on the edge of the bed. Jean had a beautiful built-in wardrobe opposite the bed, oak with detailed flower molding. A vanity had been carved out of its center, and lipsticks and kerchiefs and jewelry lay on the surface and were hung on scattered hooks and knobs on its walls. From the colors, at least two of the lipsticks had been Ruby's, and Rosie recognized several of the kerchiefs as Ruby's too. It seemed like she would be right back, like she'd only stepped out for a minute, with all those things still in place, and Rosie's chest ached. "He's right, though. There isn't any point in telling her family all those things."

"You think I would've gotten so mad if I didn't know that?" Jean's voice remained muffled. "What'm I going to do, Rosie? What are we going to do?"

"We're going to clear the demons out of here as fast as we can. We're going to do everything we can do. And you're going to keep putting one foot in front of the other no matter how hard it is, because the only way out is through."

Jean laughed, sharp even through the pillow. "Aren't you supposed to tell me we can't do anything and everything happens for a reason? That God tests us but doesn't give us anything we can't handle?"

Rosie's reflection in the vanity mirror turned harder. "I used to think that was true, but I'm not sure anymore. I mean, when we were little, we never even dreamed that we could go work in factories like the men, right? And look at us. We can. So we *can* do something. Maybe whatever it is we're facing, we can always do *something*. And right now, we can fight. Maybe it's not enough, but it's something. And I guess if everything happens for a reason, then sometimes that reason is just life isn't fair and bad things can't always be stopped. And if God tests people like this, then he's just a son of a bitch. I don't think that's very comforting."

Jean lowered the pillow, just a movement in the edge of the mirror. "That's blasphemy."

"I guess it is. I think it's true, though." Rosie twisted on the bed to face Jean. "So do you still want to help?"

"You know I do."

"Yeah." Rosie got up and went to offer Jean her hands, pulling her to her feet. "I know running off to hide is the only way to get through it sometimes, too."

"As long as I don't do it when we're facing down demons." In the kitchen, the phone began to ring. Jean sighed from the bottom of her soul, and Rosie hugged her quickly.

"I'll get it. Are you home?"

"I'm sleeping."

Rosie nodded and hurried from the room, catching the phone on the fifth or sixth ring. Irene said, "Jean? Is Rosie there?" and Rosie said, "No, it's me," then shook herself. "I mean, this is Rosie, not Jean. Rene? Aren't you at work?" She looked for a kitchen clock and didn't find one. "What time is it?"

"Four thirty. The supe is trying to get hold of you and called me off the line." Irene sounded strained. "He wants to talk to you, Rosie. Will you talk to him?"

"Yeah, sure." Rosie shook her head as she spoke, though, wishing Irene could see her. "Rene, are you all right? You sound funny."

"Rich is here, Rosie. The supe called me off the line, and when I got to his office, Rich was here. He said the supe called him in to talk about what Rich had said yesterday and . . . that's not why, though, Rosie. That's not what the supe wanted. He . . . we're . . ."

"Rich? Rich is there? What did the supe wa . . ." Rosie's knuckles whitened around the phone as suspicion rose in her. "Put Doherty on the phone, Irene. I'll talk to him."

"I'm sorry, Ro." Irene's strained breathing went away from the phone to be replaced by Superintendent Doherty's smug "Miss Ransom."

"I'm going to Redeem you," Rosie whispered. "What do you want, Doherty?"

"Oh, you're not going to do anything to me, Miss Ransom. You're going to meet me at the Pennicott premises in an hour. I know an Enforcer who would like to meet you."

Surprise pulled a laugh from Rosie's throat. "Why would I do that?"

Doherty sighed happily. "Because your friends here just look so delicious, Miss Ransom. Especially the girl, a real beauty. I'd say I'd hate it if anything happened to her, but that just wouldn't be true." His voice darkened. "An hour, Redeemer. After that, I'm having your friends for dinner." He hung up, and Rosie let the handset fall from numb fingers. It cracked against the table and fell to the floor, a plastic corner chipped off.

"What is it?" Hank stood in the kitchen door, Jean half-hidden behind him, her fingers wrapped around his biceps hard enough that her knuckles were white.

"Doherty has Irene and *Rich*." Rosie said the second name incredulously. "He called Rich to—he said to talk to him about—Rich went in yesterday to plead my case," she said with a hard little laugh. "The supe called him in, said he wanted to talk about what Rich had said. He called him after lunch, Hank. We shouldn't have let him go."

Hank muttered, "Too late now. He's got them?"

"He's got them both, and he's taking them down to the factory. The old Pennicott factory, Hank. He says the Enforcer wants to see me."

Jean let go of Hank's arm, stepping around him. "Well, you can't go. It's a trap."

"I know it's a trap. Of course it's a trap. But what else can I do? If I don't, they're going to kill Rich and Irene."

"Stop for weapons." Hank's voice sounded thick. "If we leave right now, we can get to the library and pick up some primed Artifacts before we have to go to the factory."

"'Primed'?"

"Simple art," Hank said. "Line drawings, almost finished. If you can press one against a demon and draw the last line, it'll capture it, if the demon isn't too strong. Doherty, at least, if not the Enforcer. Him . . ."

"Him, I'm going to have to get my hands on." Rosie reached up to tighten the kerchief around her hair, as if that little thing made her ready for a fight. "Do you think your dad will be there?"

Hank gave a short, hard shake of his head. "It sounds like the Enforcer is trying to clean up the mess, maybe before Da—before the daemon rex hears about it, or knows how bad it is. Of course, if it's Haas . . ."

"If it's Haas. If it's your dad. If if if," Rosie said. "Let's just assume if, okay, Hank? Because that's pretty much as bad as it can get, right? If it's Haas, if it's your dad, then they know everything already. They know I'm a Redeemer, they know you're helping me, they kno—"

"They don't know about me." Jean met both their gazes, her eyes bright with greed. "They don't know about *me*, Rosie. They know about you and Hank, maybe they even know about Hank's empathy, but they don't know that I'm helping you. You gotta give me as many of those things as you've got, Hank. The architects?"

"Artifacts."

"Those, yeah." Eager color built in Jean's cheeks. "They'll be looking for you two, not me. I can take out some of the weaker ones, at the very least. I might even be able to get a knife or a—"

"Piece of rebar," Rosie said with a faint smile.

Jean nodded. "Rebar. A sword. A bullet, *something*, into some of them. Earn Rosie enough time to do her thing. I could help, Hank. I could be your ace in the hole."

Hank lifted his hands. "Into the car. We'll talk about it on the way."

The burned-out factory's gates stood open just enough to admit a car, like an invitation. Rosie and Hank parked on the street, though, figuring the gates could be closed and trap the vehicle inside, but that there were places they could squeeze out if they remained on foot. Besides, even open, the tilted, scraped-up bars managed to look less inviting than the broken section of fence Rosie and Hank had crawled through earlier. The factory beyond loomed forbiddingly, burn shadows multiplied and much deeper. It cut a rough skyline against the failing light, with no hint of activity or life inside. Rosie shifted her shoulders, feeling the totally unaccustomed weight of a sword strapped across her back, and wondered why her hands itched with the impulse to hold a weapon she hardly knew how to use.

Hank had a gun. Two, in fact, but when Rosie had asked for one, he'd asked if she had any experience with them. She hadn't, so he handed her a sword, pointing out it would be almost impossible to accidentally kill him with it as long as he stayed more than five feet away. Rosie hated his logic but couldn't argue with it. She murmured, "At least this time we're coming in the front gates," as if she could reassure herself somehow.

Hank chuckled. "Most of us."

"Is two enough for a 'most'?"

"It's going to have to be. We have about three minutes to get in there. Are you ready?"

Rosie nodded, lower lip caught in her teeth. "As ready as I can be. Are you going to be able to do this, Hank?"

"I'm not going to have any choice." His mouth thinned. "I can't feel many of them in there, Rosie. Not like this afternoon, when they felt like a pit, once I knew they were there. Either most of them have cleared out or I'm being blocked even more strongly than before."

"Why would they clear out?"

"The Enforcer might want to make sure he's the only one who looks good." Hank took a breath. "There's also a chance they're afraid."

Rosie brightened. "Really?"

"Redeemers are the monsters under the bed to the monsters under the bed," Hank murmured. "If you can defeat the Enforcer, that's going to cause a lot of chaos. Not enough to bring a hive down, but if the rex falls, then everything that's holding the hive together goes to pieces. They might turn on each other. Clearing them out, separating them early, before things get really bad, might leave enough pieces in place for a successor to step in."

"You mean they might be scared enough to lay in a contingency plan?" A smile pressed its way through Rosie's teeth. "I'd like that. I'd like to not be the only one scared spitless here."

"Are you?" Hank glanced at her. "You do a good job of hiding it."

"It wouldn't do much good for me to be sitting in a corner wailing, would it? It'd just invite them to come after us." She straightened her shoulders, feeling the sword's weight again, and nodded. "Let's go."

They passed through the gates and a door that stood mostly off its hinges, the metal twisted from heat. Rosie had never even held a sword before a few days earlier, but she reached up and checked it in its scabbard, making sure she would be able to pull it easily, and felt comforted. Dips and pits in the floor, worse for Hank than Rosie, were still more treacherous than they'd been in daylight, and they crept in, testing each step. They hesitated at every door, Hank stepping through to make sure the next room, fire-torn as it might be, was clear before Rosie followed him. They'd argued about that on the way over. Rosie figured she'd be safer going through first, since her touch could be deadly to a demon, but Hank figured a ranged attack could take her down and then they'd have no chance against the Enforcer.

He lifted his hand suddenly, stopping her creeping pace, and over the silence of her held breath she heard men's voices, taunting echoes in the darkness. Hank gestured with his chin, indicating a door in a mostly intact wall across what seemed like an impossibly vast stretch of junk-littered floor. "They're in there." His voice was hardly even a whisper, more just shaped words in what little moonlight filtered through filthy windows and open roofs.

"They're gonna ambush us," Rosie whispered back, with a nod at the empty space ahead of them. Hank shrugged one shoulder, as if to say *What can we do?* and Rosie pulled her sword free of its sheath. Hank's eyes went very blue, even in the faint light, and a smile crooked one corner of his mouth. He didn't move otherwise, though, just gazed down at her. Rosie's own smile of anticipation fell away into a heart-thudding awareness of his presence and the likelihood that they were both about to die. He lowered his head, just as he'd done earlier in the day at the library, and this time, Rosie began to lift her own.

A bone-ringing *clang* echoed from beyond the far wall. Rosie took a sharp breath, looking across the big room. Rich might be on the other side of that door. Rich and Irene both. Rosie breathed, "Let's go," but Hank had already moved, a gun she hadn't seen him draw held ready in his left hand.

The shadows stayed shadows, no monsters breaking free from them, until Rosie began to feel silly for creeping around with a sword in one hand. Other sounds, more than just voices, were audible from beyond the door: fists hitting flesh, grunts and curses, the sounds of men fighting. Rosie's heart beat harder, worry for Rich clouding her thoughts until she forgot to be cautious and broke into a run. Hank hissed, "Rosie!" after her, too late.

She didn't even see it, the thing flowing from the shadows, not until she'd stepped in it. Claws grabbed her ankle and oil surged up her leg, coating her in cool slippery nastiness. Terror flooded her, leaving her unable to even take a breath as the stuff pulled her to her knees. A face appeared in the slick surface, but she couldn't tell if it was her own or someone else's. She didn't exactly drop the sword, because her hand landed on its hilt when it clattered to the floor, but she couldn't pretend she'd set it down on purpose, either. A squeak of fear pushed out of her lungs, and without the magic, she knew she would be dead.

The power responded like it had at the factory, though, with Goode. It rose instinctively, spilling out of her to separate a demon's staining influence from the human soul it worked to devour. Pools of light shuddered to life under her hands, sizzling through the oil she knelt in. It seemed like everything burned this time, fire cleansing away corruption, because nothing else remained. A thin scream bubbled from the oil, and even in flames, it tried crawling up her arms, looking for a way into her. The fire didn't hurt her at all, although she could feel its heat licking the fine hairs on her arms. It burned only the demon, without rot rising in a mist and separating from the rest. It felt like it lasted forever and only a few seconds, all at the same time, and when the power winked out, Hank had only just reached Rosie's side. She stared up at him, wide-eyed with shock. "What was that?"

"A dying demon. It had used up the body it had and needed a new one. Too bad for it that it tried taking on yours."

"It was . . . there wasn't anything left," Rosie whispered. "No human soul left to save. Just the corruption to burn. How long does that *take?*"

"Depends on how tough the host is and how strong the demon is. Remember, I told you the really powerful ones can keep a body living for decades. And probably wouldn't chance a Redeemer even as a last-ditch hope for survival. Can you get up?" He curled his hand around her arm, encouraging her to her feet. He'd been doing that the whole time he'd been talking, Rosie realized. That, more than his efforts, got her up, her sword in hand, though she ended up staring at her shoes and dungarees, looking for signs of the oil that had just burned away. There were none.

"I thought they had . . . the ochim was a singer, you said. Or a composer. And the empathy comes from music too. I thought that was how they attacked, with . . ." Rosie started moving, mostly because Hank pulled her along, but then he answered and she stayed with him of her own volition, wanting to hear.

"With their muses? Again, the powerful ones can do that. Helen Montgomery just threw herself at you—"

"Screaming," Rosie pointed out.

"People seem to yell a lot when they're on the attack," Hank said, almost under his breath, before continuing in a more normal tone, since they didn't seem to have snuck in unnoticed after all. "Most of them are faster, stronger, and—" He flexed his right hand around his cane, like a cat putting claws out.

Rosie volunteered, "Pointier?" and he cast her a brief smile. "I was thinking *claw-ier*, but *pointier* probably works better. And pointier than humans. They're dangerous, but most of them can't attack *with* magic. They just *are* magic."

"Which makes them almost impossible to kill." Rosie stopped moving forward just long enough to press her eyelids together hard and recollect herself. "That's probably something I should have known before, Hank. The not-attacking-*with*-magic part."

"I'll put it in my notes for next time."

Rosie barked a quiet laugh and shrugged his hand off her arm. "Where'd you put your gun?"

"Away." Hank took it out again as they reached the door at the far side of the broken-down room. Rosie looked back at where they'd come and whispered, "Why was there only one of them waiting for us?"

Hank shook his head. "I don't know. I think the one left didn't have any choice."

"You mean the Enforcer told it to stay?"

"I mean I don't think it had enough body left to move out even if it wanted to. I've never seen one that far gone before. Another few days or weeks and it would have eaten even what was left of that body, and died."

"You keep telling me they can't die and then mentioning another way they do," Rosie muttered.

"I keep telling you humans can't kill them, which is different," Hank muttered back, and Rosie, instead of arguing about it, kicked open the door and swept in to meet their enemy.

TWENTY-FIVE

Harrison Vaughn wove around a boxing ring, fighting for his life. Superintendent Doherty danced around him, throwing punches not with Vaughn's expertise but the lazy confidence of a predator that knew it couldn't lose. Vaughn, under hot lights dangling from a raw-girdered ceiling, sweated profusely while Doherty kept his cool far more convincingly than he had just that afternoon. There were no other lights: the boxing ring stood in a pool of brightness, not unlike the one at the Vaughn estate, but the shadows crawling up to this one seemed far more sinister.

Rosie, instead of storming in, stopped short so close to the door that Hank ran into her. For a heartbeat they were both silent, captivated by the battle going on in front of them, before Hank swore and jolted past Rosie in a run.

Rosie snatched at the back of his shirt, missing by a fraction of an inch, and didn't go after him. Two Vaughn boys ought to be able to take care of Doherty by themselves. She heard that thought like it came from the distance, and had a look at it from that distance. Harrison Vaughn definitely wouldn't be in that ring if he was Detroit's daemon rex, probably wouldn't be in it if he was a demon at all. The sword, held in her loose fingers, felt heavier than before, as if righteousness had gone out of it and left it nothing more than a hunk of metal. Maybe it had been Haas all along, and demons like Goode had been left to run wild while he was in DC playing politics. Maybe *Doherty* was the Enforcer, after all.

Hank moved well when he wanted to, for a man with a bad leg. She could see the limp in his gait as he ran, but it hardly slowed him, and he vaulted into the sparring ring like the athlete he must have once been. He had something in his mouth, something short and blunt that he'd taken out while running, but Rosie couldn't see what it was. Doherty turned toward him, hissing with laughter, and Harrison Vaughn threw a punch that would have flattened any mortal man. It staggered Doherty, whose gaze snapped back to the older Vaughn with all laughter wiped away. Even Rosie, who had never seen a killing blow she hadn't herself dealt, could tell from the way Doherty raised his fist that Harrison wouldn't be getting up from the next hit. She shot into a run, far too late now, but hadn't made it more than a handful of steps when Hank jumped on Doherty's back and slapped a palm-sized piece of canvas against Doherty's forehead. Doherty screamed, and underneath it, Hank shouted incomprehensible words. The thing he'd held in his mouth fell. Harrison scrambled for it and came up with a pen and a befuddled expression. Hank, riding Doherty's back like a child playing horse, flailed for the pen. Harrison slapped it into Hank's palm and balled up a fist for another hit as Hank scrawled something on the canvas. Doherty's screams turned panic-stricken, pain-filled, and then silent.

He *shriveled*. Rosie skidded to a halt, staring in fascinated horror. She couldn't tell where it started, at his head or his feet or both, but Doherty collapsed in on himself, sucked upward toward the canvas smeared across his forehead. The disintegration looked like it should have sound, but Rosie couldn't hear anything over her own breathing, over the Vaughns' breathing, over the wind that moaned through open spaces at the top of the building. Still, it looked like joints should pop audibly, like bones should crack and skin tear with awful clarity. She couldn't tell how fast it happened, either: a blink of an eye and a drawn-out eternity all at once. Hank hung there in the air like he still clung to Doherty's back, even when Doherty seemed mostly gone. Then it ended with a noise like a small explosion, and Hank crashed to the boxing ring's floor. He coiled up, the bit of canvas crushed against his right knee as he clutched it with both hands. Rosie could hear his breathing now, strained with pain, and Harrison Vaughn dropped to the floor beside his son to gather him close.

A staccato clap echoed across the room, sending Rosie in a spin to see where it came from. Senator Haas's smooth politician's voice came out of the dark before he did, amusement thickening it. "What a show, Hank. What a performance. Very heroic, rushing in to save your father. We're all very impressed."

Hank, muffled against Harrison's leg, growled, "We?" and Valentine Vaughn emerged from the shadows.

✪ ✪ ✪

She had a little army with her. Senator Haas, whose oily good looks were greasier than ever, fell in one step behind her, and one step behind *him* came two others. One was a small, strong-jawed, red-headed woman whose eyes were so flat and calculating that despite her small size, Rosie tightened her grip on the sword and thought she would go for her first. The other, a man, looked just as threatening except that he was more expected and therefore less scary. Behind them was another pair of demons, both men, whose thick necks and dull gazes suggested they were there just for the fight. Finally, behind them came a third pair, the ones Rosie had come for in the first place.

Valentine Vaughn smiled, and at the same time, to the same degree, an uncanny likeness, so did Irene and Rich. She turned her head, taking in her adversaries—all two of them, Rosie thought, since Harrison Vaughn didn't seem likely to be much help, and given the way Hank held his own knee, it might just be Rosie herself against seven demons—and when her head turned, so did Rich and Irene's. Valentine waggled her fingers at Rosie in a coy greeting, with Irene and Rich echoing her. More than echoing, though. They moved in tandem, no visible hesitation between her actions and theirs.

Cold drained through Rosie, turning her knuckles white around the sword hilt. "What did you do to them?"

"Well." Valentine sighed enormously, as though about to relate a complex story that Rich and Irene were obliged to parrot. "I'm sure Hank told you about Redoubling, didn't he, dear? He should have. It takes so much effort, but it can be so very worth it." Her tone changed, flattening. "They're my safety net, Miss Ransom. Part of my essence is in them. You cannot kill me without killing them. You cannot kill them and kill me. If I feel in genuine danger, with the link already established, I can pour myself entirely into one or either of them, leaving this vessel behind. In a few minutes, they'll regain enough autonomy that they'll be able to act on their own, no longer echoing me, but influenced by my will, and then you'll have to go through them to reach me. They were almost embarrassingly easy," she said, undisturbed by Rich and Irene murmuring the words along with her. "So caught up in high emotion, in attraction, in guilt, oh, my, the guilt. It's always easier when there's guilt.

"Ah-ah-ah," she scolded as Rosie edged a step forward. "Remember: kill me and your friends die too, little Redeemer. Really, I insist you allow me to enjoy this. Watch her." She spoke to Haas and the others that time, her voice flattening again. The four of them spread out in a close half-circle, facing Rosie, while Valentine, flanked by Rich and Irene, sauntered to the boxing ring. Rich, especially, moved unnaturally, his every step mimicking Valentine's perfectly. His hips swayed as hers did, and his stride was no longer than hers. Irene's walk wasn't her own, but it didn't look so strange. Watching her step through the ring ropes in perfect synchronicity with Valentine only looked rehearsed, not alien. All three of them crouched together in front of Harrison and Hank, and all three of them reached for Hank's chin, the gesture tipping his head up, although only Valentine herself actually touched him. Hank recoiled.

"My poor darling," Valentine said with a sigh. "You tried so hard. I want you to know it wasn't your fault, Hank. My goodness, what a surprise it was to have you come home from war with so much power. If I'd suspected, really suspected, I'd have done something to press your talent into fruition when you were much younger and more malleable. As it was, I had to work, really *work*, a few times, to keep you from realizing. Do you have any idea how long it's been since I've had to work at anything?"

"No." Hank spat the word from a raw throat. "How long? How old are you? Were you ever really my mother?"

Absolute astonishment shifted Valentine's shoulders. "Of course I'm your mother, Harrison Alexander Vaughn! I've always been your mother! What a thing to say!" Her head tilted and her voice changed as she looked at the older Vaughn man. "I wasn't always his wife, mind you. I found her at almost the same time he did. Oh, she was splendid, just splendid. A nurse. A war nurse, no less. So empathetic. I'd been looking for a vessel like her for decades. Centuries! Really, though, Harry. I know I wasn't quite the woman you expected to marry, but you oughtn't have stepped out on me so much. Oh, truly, I'm very disappointed in Doherty. I did expect him to finish you off before the Redeemer got here." She transferred a fond smile to Hank. "Or until Hank did, I suppose. I didn't expect the heroics, darling. Save yourself some trouble, and don't bother with them again."

She rose and kicked Harrison Vaughn in the side of the head so smoothly and swiftly, as such a single motion, that Rosie didn't know it was happening until Vaughn toppled sideways. Rich and Irene echoed the action, an actual echo this time, just a bit slower than Valentine moved, like a line of chorus girls who had gotten their timing off. Hank flinched badly, as if he'd expected to take that kick himself, then twisted in distress, checking his father's fallen form. Apparently Vaughn wasn't dead, because Hank looked up at his mother with anger and confusion, but not rage and grief, contorting his features. "Why did you even marry him, then?"

Valentine's eyes widened. "Oh, he was very rich, sweetheart. Ambitious, intelligent, even handsome, but mostly rich. One war, oh my, that was dreadful, but anyone could see a second war was building. There was just so much opportunity, Hank. Not just making money—although I assure you, at my age, you learn to appreciate a solid nest egg—but all the chaos, the social upheaval? Goodness, who could resist? War is just a wonderful chance to make a power grab, trounce other demons, and blame it all on the humans."

"What?" Rosie's voice cracked on the single word.

Valentine swung to face her, Rich and Irene awkward marionettes in her wake. All three of them smiled brilliantly. "What did you expect, Miss Ransom? That my goal in life was to be one of thousands, eking out a pathetic existence beneath mortal attention? Ten years ago, I was hardly more than that, but in that blink of an eye, Detroit is mine and the rest of the American kings recognize me as a rival for the mid-west's dominion. Your silly war has opened avenues never before available. I wish it would go on forever, but I suppose all good things must come to an end. Imagine, though." She shivered delicately, with her doubles shuddering and twitching along. "Imagine if that odious Hitler had succeeded in destroying all that art. All those old demons released. All that rivalry reintroduced. How utterly appalling. Really, I vastly prefer your little heroes struggling to save the monuments of the world and leaving the playing field clear for the ambitious."

"You kept talking about how awful ambition was," Rosie said faintly. "All that stuff about staying at home with your soldier, like you'd done?"

"Well, for goodness' sakes, Miss Ransom, you could hardly expect me to encourage you to go out demon hunting, could you? You'll get yourself killed and be no use to me at all."

Rosie said, "What?" still faintly, but the four demons between herself and Valentine took their attention from her for the first time, staring instead at Mrs Vaughn. Senator Haas broke their silence, asking the same question Rosie had: "*What?*"

"Honestly," Valentine said to Rosie, "I thought I'd chosen better with him. He's useful in Washington, but for a creature who's supposed to show some initiative . . ." She shook her head disdainfully. Rich echoed the gesture, then shook his head harder, like he was trying to rid himself of the impulse to act as Valentine did. A few seconds later, he twitched his shoulders, settling into a stance very like, but not identical, to Valentine's, and smiled at Rosie. Valentine's smile, on his face. The expression fell away as he looked toward Haas, though, and spoke with Valentine's inflections, but no longer at the same time she did. "Of course I knew Miss Ransom was the Redeemer. That kind of awakening leaves a mark, and although I think poor Hank lost the ability to see it within an hour or two, *I* could still see it when I met her, and when was that? A day after? Two days? She'd done such a splendid job taking care of that odious little vampire that I thought the mouthy ochim should encounter her next. And that Montgomery woman."

Rich transferred his gaze to Harrison Vaughn, then pursed his lips with disappointment. "I should have mentioned she was dead before I kicked you," he said with a sniff. "I suppose I can wait until you wake up."

Rosie whispered, "Oh my God, Rich. Stop it," as, with a shudder of her own, Irene threw off Valentine's echo and turned a similarly disturbing smile toward her.

"I expect he'd like to, but he can't. I can almost hear him, screaming at the back of my mind." Her eyes rolled up and her head tilted, like she was listening, and her smile broadened. "It's lovely, really. Not quite music, but still, music to my ears. Now." Irene sashayed toward Rosie, crooking a finger like they were still confidantes. "I have a proposition for you, Redeemer. You can have these four. Haas and his darling team of useless Enforcers. In exchange, you forget all about little old me, and I promise I'll hardly ever bother you by sending useless demons your way for Redemption."

All four of Valentine's Enforcers exploded into action before Irene had finished speaking. Rosie thought they might just go after Valentine, in revenge for her offering them to Rosie. But the deadly-looking redhead went for Irene, and Rosie paled. Going after Irene *was* going after Valentine, at least as long as Hank's mother was Redoubled. The Enforcer moved faster than Rosie could, tackling Irene, and the two red-haired women went down in a tumbling heap. Rosie shrieked, flinging herself toward the fray, and hit the floor with a cry as one of the thick-necked fighters tackled her. Her sword bounced out of her hand, skidding across the floor and coming to rest dangerously near where Irene and the other redhead wrestled. Rosie felt the Enforcer's breath on her neck and smashed her head back, connecting with his nose. A crunch and a howl mingled just long enough for her to roll beneath his weight. She boxed his ears, bellowing with rage, and the demonic corruption separated from his soul so quickly that Rosie became dizzy with an influx of dark magic. The demon, or its body, at least, collapsed on top of her. She squirmed out from beneath it, trying not to scream, and scrambled for her lost sword.

A booted foot met her ribs, lifted her, and sent her rolling across the concrete floor. Rosie shoved to her hands and knees, breathing past the pain and almost feeling the muscle and bone reknit in her torso. Knives were flying by the time she got to her feet, the second bulky demon smart enough not to touch her. Rosie flung herself on the floor again, chasing

after the blades, and looked frantically for Hank. She could Redeem a soul
by killing or touching the host, but the library man had never said whether
she could do it without a killing blow, from a distance. Finding out she
couldn't, in the middle of a fight, seemed like a bad idea. A knife struck
her in the shoulder, driving her to the floor as white-hot pain filled her
back. She fumbled for the knife, trying to pull it free. Trying to convince
herself it would stop hurting, that it would heal, if she could get the blade
out. She would also have something to throw back at the monster, which
might be even more important than healing. Every motion sent more
waves of nauseating agony down her spine, and she cut her own fingers,
dragging the knife out of her shoulder. She rolled onto her back almost
blind with pain. A demon stood above her somewhere, and she couldn't see
well enough to find and kill it. A laugh wanted to escape, but even the idea
hurt. Rosie set her teeth together and shoved herself to sitting, then threw
the knife blindly in the direction it had come from.

"Jesus, Rosie!" Hank's shout echoed across the room half a second before
metal clanked against concrete. "Are you trying to kill me?"

"Sorry." The pain faded and her vision cleared enough that she saw
Hank on his feet beside the boxing ring, lifting one of his guns. Its report
thundered through the hard-walled room, as offensive as her throbbing
shoulder in its own way, but the thick-necked demon she'd been fighting
fell to the floor. Hank kicked the knife she'd thrown back toward her,
although it didn't come nearly far enough, and shouted, "Get up! Redeem
him before *he* gets up!"

Rosie lurched to her feet, snatched the knife up, and ran to shove it
into the demon's chest without letting herself think about the action. The
dance of light and power had barely begun when she turned away, but she
felt it rush to completion as she searched for her sword again.

Irene had it in one hand, and the red-haired demon woman in the
other. She held the redhead in the air, fingers clenched around the woman's
jaw. Even in the bad light, Rosie could see that the other demon's face
deforming from the pressure and strength of Irene's grip. Instead of
crushing the other woman's face, though, Irene shoved the sword through
her ribs and dropped her, letting her own weight gut her. Rosie swallowed

a sound of horror as Irene smiled Valentine's smile, shook the demon free of the sword, and looked around as if hoping for another victim.

Rosie looked too, and went cold to discover that in the few seconds she'd been watching Irene, Rich had seized Hank, knotting an arm around his throat. Hank's face was pale, not red: Rich hadn't begun choking him yet, but despite wrenching at Rich's arm and kicking at his knees, Hank obviously couldn't break free. Valentine Vaughn stood in the boxing ring, looking down at them with an expression of curiosity, as if, although her own Redoubled spirit moved Rich, she wasn't entirely sure what he would do with her son. Rich looked as incapable of making a decision, holding Hank immobilized. Rosie, chilled, wondered which of them, Rich or Valentine, wanted Hank dead, and which of them was stopping it from happening. Her hands ached, wanting a weapon or a Redemption, and she didn't even know where to start. Three of Valentine's Enforcers were dead. Irene kept smiling, holding the blood-wet sword, and Rich stood locked in paralysis. The fight hadn't even lasted two minutes, Rosie thought, and almost everyone was dead.

"Haas." Her voice sounded strange to her own ears. "Where did Haas go?"

He appeared as if she'd summoned him, dropping from above. Not on *her,* but on Valentine Vaughn, whose startled scream sounded as human as Rosie's own. Haas's weight bore her to the boxing ring mat, and Rich, shaken free of his paralysis, threw Hank away and leapt up to haul Haas off Valentine. Irene joined him, fluidly, and together they flung Haas halfway across the room, into the shadows. He twisted in the air and landed on three points, facing the fight, but skidded back a distance before catching enough traction to launch himself forward in a run.

Rich jumped the ring ropes to meet Haas's charge. Rosie broke into a run, hoping to catch him, and saw, in glimpses, the chaos unfolding in the boxing ring. Valentine leapt the ropes, bolting for the door that Rosie had been close to. Hank came to his feet, expression grim, and sighted with his pistol, plainly intending to shoot his own mother down. Rosie couldn't even catch enough breath for a scream of protest, but Irene stepped between Hank and his mother, her face a mask of terrified innocence. Rosie's stomach knotted, but Hank faltered. The fear drained from Irene's expression as she backhanded him hard enough to lift him from his feet. He landed in a lump on top of Harrison Vaughn, and Irene turned a toothy grin at Rosie.

Rosie slammed into Rich, tackling him at the knees, the way she'd seen football players do, and heard his head bounce off the concrete like a melon. Haas overshot, missing a killing blow and tumbling head over heels to spin and slide again before getting himself moving toward Rosie again. Rosie leapt to her feet, feeling frantically for weapons, *any* weapon that would keep the demon from getting his hands on her, then braced for an impact that never came.

Gunfire sounded a second time and Haas fell to the floor, surprise etched in his features. Rosie jerked a step forward, but *Jean* was there, coming out of the shadows like a demon herself, and pounced on Haas with a knife against his throat. She looked flushed with victory as she grinned up at Rosie. "He's still breathing. We don't want all of them dead, not if we want to hear what *Valentine Vaughn* is up to!" She almost shouted Mrs Vaughn's name. "Look at us, Rosie Ransom. Modern women who can't see past the ends of our own noses to think another woman might be the one getting her hands dirty! Boy, do we owe Hank an apology."

She put her hand in the air and Rosie pulled her to her feet, glancing her over quickly. She looked like she'd been in a fight, or several: bruises, scrapes, torn clothes, her hair awry, but her eyes were brighter than they'd been since Ruby's death. "There were only three of them that I found guarding the perimeter, but I took care of them, Rosie. I did it. I'm a demon hunter."

"Brava," Irene murmured from the boxing ring. "My goodness, what an intrepid little trio you are. I wondered where my scouts had gone, but I simply didn't imagine you had a third, Miss Ransom. That really was rather clever." She stepped over to Hank and his father, prodding their limp bodies with a toe. "Well, this is all rather inconvenient. I could keep your friends in thrall, but I'm afraid you'd Artifice them, and that would leave *me* weaker. So I'll give you a gift, Rosie. Redeem Haas and I'll let Miss Fandel and Mr Thompson go. Otherwise, I expect they might suddenly have the urge to kill themselves, and I'm sure you don't want that."

"Redeem him," Rosie echoed in surprise. Jean, at her elbow, hissed, "So he *does* know something useful!" and Rosie exhaled a breath of comprehension.

Irene smiled, sharp and unfriendly, then lifted the sword she still carried, examined its bloody length, and laid it gently against her own throat. "I've never done this before," she said with Valentine's cultured tones. "How many people can say they've experienced their own suicides? I think I could hold on just to the very moment of death, before fleeing back to my own body. Imagine using that pain and fear to influence someone. The opportunities are rife."

"Don't." Rosie's tongue felt thick in her mouth. "Don't. I'll Redeem him. Just let Rich and Irene go." Beside her, Jean made a terrible sound, the same sound Rosie fought from making herself. She cast a despairing glance at Jean, whose jaw worked and whose eyes bulged, but she gave a grief-stricken nod. They still wouldn't have Valentine if their friends died, and whatever knowledge Haas held didn't seem worth their lives.

"Redeem Haas," Irene purred, "and I'll let your friends go." Her head turned to examine the two Vaughn men fallen in the boxing ring. "I should have brought Harrison with me," she said in a voice filled with venom. "I owe him *years* of torment for this sham of a marriage." She returned her attention to Rosie, who had already knelt beside Haas. His eyes were open, face contorted with rage and his mouth working, but he hadn't yet recovered from the damage Jean's bullets had done.

There was blood, a lot of it, and pain, and fear, and a burning anger in Rosie's breast that might have allowed her to try Redeeming the soul, casting out the demon and saving the man, but even as she put her hands on his forehead and chest, she wondered if that would be cruel or kind. He might not live beyond the demon's departure, anyways. She had no way of knowing how badly injured he was. Even if he lived, Hank had shot him in the spine more than once. It seemed likely he would never move again, and who knew if that would be better or worse than dying now. Worst of all, though, was not knowing if expelling the demon might leave the man to die in pain, when now it seemed probable that only the monster would suffer.

The magic rose in her as she wondered, separating what remained of humanity from the stain of corruption. The demon held on, struggling to survive with far greater strength than any of the others had, and coming so close to succeeding that Haas overcame his injuries, yanking a hand upward to close it around Rosie's biceps. "You don't know. You don't know what it means, what she's done—"

Rosie inhaled so sharply it was almost a scream, then bent closer, whispering, "What? What do you mean, what—"

Haas *did* scream, a long thin wail of defeat that shivered into Rosie's bones and stayed, turning her cold from the marrow out. The demonic essence spun away, but the human soul lingered, bright color in search of guidance. Rosie stared at it helplessly, not knowing what to do or how to do it, then made a frantic scrabble with her hands, like she could catch the ephemeral thing and shove it back down into the laboring body beside her.

The light dissipated with her touch, leaving sparks that faded into her skin. Haas gave a rattling breath before falling still. A choked sound broke from Rosie's throat and she tried again, fumbling at nothing now, trying to bring it back and press life into a body it had left behind. Jean pulled her away from Haas's body. Rosie fell against her, hot tears burning her cheeks, but they both jerked their heads up as Irene's frightened voice, her *own* frightened voice, called, "Rosie?"

TWENTY-SIX

"I couldn't stop it. I couldn't stop her." Irene sat huddled in a ball, curled up in Rosie's arms and staring sightlessly at the Vaughn men. Jean had already unpiled them from one another. They were both bruised but breathing, and without a doctor, there wasn't anything else she could do for them. Rich hadn't woken up yet either, but after one futile effort to move him, Rosie and Jean had left him on the concrete floor to wake up on his own while Rosie tried to comfort Irene, who kept whispering, "I'm sorry I didn't believe you about the monsters, Rosie. I'm real sorry."

"It's okay. Nobody would." Rosie kissed her hair and rocked her, hating that she even wanted to ask, but she did: "Do you remember any of her thoughts? Her plans?"

"No." Irene shivered so hard she almost fell out of Rosie's arms. "It was like she was a—a balloon inside me, pushing me down. I couldn't get into the balloon. I can remember what she did, what I did, but not why." She looked at her hands, stained with the red-haired demon's blood, and started to cry.

"That's normal." Hank Vaughn spoke groggily, without moving from where he lay. "The few instances we have of recovering someone from a Redoubling, that's what they've reported. The balloon analogy is excellent." He drew a breath that sounded like it didn't so much fend pain off as acknowledge it, and worked carefully on sitting up. That brought his father's still form into his line of vision, and fear spasmed across his face. He moved too fast, or tried, and coiled on the floor again, trying to hold his head without touching it.

Jean said, "He's alive," and tension flowed out of Hank's spine, although he made no effort to sit up again. "We're all alive," Jean said after a moment. "Us cowboys. We made it. The Indians had a bad day."

". . . Valentine?"

"Well." Jean drew the word out, glancing at Rosie, then shrugged. "The chieftess got away."

"She let them go." Rosie hugged Irene closer to her. "She let Rich and Irene go after I Redeemed Haas."

"You should have—" Hank shook his head, the motion barely visible in the cradle of his arms. "I don't know. I don't know what you should have done."

"I would have tried to Redeem her, Hank. Not kill her. There was a second there with Haas where I thought . . ." Rosie gave up with a shrug. "Maybe it wouldn't have worked. I don't know. But I wasn't going to let her kill Rich and Irene, either, even if it meant letting her get away."

"I would have." Hank slowly pushed himself to sitting, his gaze bleak when it found Rosie's. "I was going to."

"I'm just as glad you didn't. Not just for them, but for you. I don't care if she's a demon. You shouldn't have to kill your own mother."

"She's not . . ."

Irene spoke. "But she is. It hurt her feelings when you said she wasn't." She gave a dry laugh and hid her face against Rosie's shoulder. "He's a monster, Ro."

"No. Even Valentine said so. Maybe if she'd gotten to him earlier, but no." Rosie shook her head, meeting Hank's eyes. "And even if he's got demon blood, it's what you do with yourself that counts, right?"

"Lucky me." Hank put his head in his hands. "My demonic parent didn't think I was worth guiding."

"She can hide things from you, Hank. Maybe you could hide things from her, too. Maybe keeping your empathy tamped down was how you protected yourself from her." Rosie let Irene go as Rich finally groaned and pushed to his hands and knees, halfway across the concrete floor. He saw Haas's body and gave a hoarse yell, jerking several feet away without really seeming to move his arms and legs, then came to his feet almost as jerkily, glancing around in confusion. The quick motions obviously made his head hurt: he lifted both hands to it, a wince racing across his features, and Rosie didn't think he asked anyone in particular when he said, "What the hell was that?"

Rosie and Irene both rose to climb through the ropes, and both hesitated, frowning at each other uncomfortably before Irene's shoulders caved and she fell back a step, eyes downcast. Rosie looked between Rich and Irene, though Rich didn't seem aware of the interplay, then slowly continued on, hopping down from the ring to go to Rich. "Are you all right?" She winced as deeply as he had, knowing he wasn't okay, but no other question seemed any good either.

His eyes were depthless in the shadows. "What the hell happened, Rosie? What did . . . what were they? What are you?"

"They were demons." Rosie's soft answer sounded wearily ridiculous to her own ears. "You were possessed by one, or by part of one, at least. By part of Valentine Vaughn. I'm a—I can kill them. The demons. They call it Redeeming. I'm a Redeemer."

"She . . . I was her. I was *her*. I couldn't even remember what it was like to be *me*. You knew about this? You didn't tell me?" Anger and disbelief warred in Rich's voice. "How could you not tell me?"

"It just happened. It started Friday night with Goode, and . . ." Rosie's shoulders lifted and fell. "What could I have said that you would have believed? Rich . . ." She reached out tentatively, but Rich's gaze pulled from her to Irene.

"Oh, my God, Irene. She was in you too." He left Rosie standing there with her hand extended, hurrying to the boxing ring even though the speed obviously made his head hurt more. He cleared the ropes and took Irene's face in his hands, murmuring to and examining her. Rosie couldn't hear him, and wasn't sure she wanted to. Irene unfolded her arms from around her ribs and stepped into Rich's embrace, hiding her face in his chest. He slipped an arm around her shoulders and the other hand into her hair, cradling her, and Jean, watching, folded her arms and bit a knuckle, gaze darting between the entwined pair and Rosie.

Rosie let her hand drop and her eyes close, trying to figure out if hurt or resignation or anger or all three slipped out on her sigh. When she looked up again, Hank knelt beside a wakening Harrison Vaughn, relief cragging age lines into his face. Jean still watched Rosie, sympathy etched deep in her gaze. Rosie turned her palms up and shrugged, not knowing what else to do, and came back to the boxing ring to help everyone out. They left in pairs, a small, shuffling band of broken spirits: Irene and Rich huddled together at the front, Hank, refusing any assistance with his father, limping in the middle, and Rosie, with Jean, taking up a strong rear position.

"It'll be all right," Jean said quietly, the first time words like that had passed her lips in a week.

"Yeah. Yeah, it's gonna be . . ." Rosie nodded, unable to quite say it herself. The six of them trooped through the building wreckage to the front door and came to slow, bemused stops to find the Cadillac no longer in the drive. Rosie gave a rueful little laugh. "Well, there's no reason for her to have walked out of here, is there, not when her driver was here."

"She's got a head start," Hank said dully. "We're never going to catch her."

"Rich, did Doherty drive you over in his car? Irene?" It took a moment for either of them to respond, Irene finally looking up with a nod that suggested she'd only barely heard the question. Rosie turned to Jean. "Can you drive them home? I'll drive Hank and Mr Vaughn home in their car, and . . ."

"And I'll come pick you up in mine after I've dropped Doherty's back off at the factory," Jean said.

"Don't let anybody see you."

A thin smile pulled Jean's mouth. "See, you're turning into a sneak after all, Rosie Ransom." She went with Rich and Irene, encouraging them to help her find Doherty's car while Hank looked like he would muster a protest, if only he could find the heart to.

Rosie shook her head. "Don't argue, library man. You two are both beat up pretty bad." And that didn't even touch on the emotional battering they'd taken. She got the keys off Hank and didn't say a word when both men crawled into the back of the car together.

The Cadillac sat in the Vaughns' driveway when they arrived. A knife of anticipation slid through Rosie's belly, but the driver, George, came out of the house as she parked, his forehead wrinkled with concern. "Mrs Vaughn flew through here, sir," he said to Harrison as they got out of the car. "Packed a bag and took the Jaguar. She said you'd know what it was all about."

Harrison nodded, though he didn't look like he knew what much of anything was about. Hank glanced back up the driveway. "She must have been moving like a bat out of hell for us to not cross paths with her."

Rosie said, "She probably went south," but nodded. "But yeah, she must've been. Look, you get your dad inside. I'll go make sandwiches or something."

"Bertha will take care of that."

Rosie looked at Hank blankly for a few seconds, then breathed a humorless laugh. "Right. I forgot you had people for that sort of thing. I'm amazed you knew how to make a peanut butter and jelly sandwich."

"Army teaches you all kinds of things." Hank accepted George's assistance getting Harrison Vaughn into the house, and though she knew she was understood to be welcome, Rosie sat on the expansive front steps instead of following them in. The whole awful mess at the abandoned factory had hardly taken an hour. The sun hadn't set yet, all gold and gleaming on the horizon. It seemed like it should be later, like they'd done a lot of dark things that should have taken place under the cover of night. Rosie shook her head and pulled her knees up to rest her cheek on them.

"Miss?" The maid, Bertha, came out. "Miss, there's food inside, if you'd like to come in."

"Thank you." Rosie got up and followed the woman in, suddenly remembering to say, "Hey, you make a good cup of coffee. I didn't get a chance to say that the other day."

Bertha gave her a startled look that turned into a quiet smile. "Mrs Vaughn says it's all in the beans, miss."

"I've met a lot of lousy coffee," Rosie disagreed. "Yours was good."

"Well, thank you, miss." Bertha led her into a ridiculously formal dining room where a plate of sandwiches and a pitcher of lemonade looked simple and out of place. Rosie glanced around for the Vaughns, then put her hand over her stomach as it rumbled, and sat down to eat.

Hank joined her a few minutes later. "Dad's resting. He says he doesn't remember what happened. He's lying, but I guess there's no point in pushing him about it."

"You're sure he's lying?" At Hank's nod, Rosie said, "So your empathy is working again."

He pulled his mouth in pained agreement. "Looks like it. Mom packed up every jewel in the house and lit out."

"The Jaguar should be easy enough to trace."

"Assuming she doesn't just dump it somewhere." Hank gave a reluctant laugh at Rosie's abrupt horror. "Well, wouldn't you?"

"I might *park* it somewhere *safe!*"

"Detroit girl," Hank said with a smile. They finished their sandwiches, and Rosie smiled as Bertha brought them milk and cookies, like they were six. "George can drive you home when we're done," Hank offered, but Rosie shook her head.

"Jean's dropping Rich and Irene off and coming to get me. I don't have any way to tell her not to. But we should save some of these cookies for her."

"I'll ask Bertha to make another couple sandwiches." Hank got up to do that, and came back not only with sandwiches, but with Jean, who looked tired and sweaty but also satisfied in the evening heat.

"Maybe we didn't get every demon in Detroit before the funeral," she said as she sat down to eat, "but I guess we got enough of them. I feel like Ruby can rest in peace now. And I'm not going to stop," she said to Hank, fiercely. "If you two are out there Redeeming and hunting demons, I'm going to be with you."

"At this point, Miss Diaz, I wouldn't dare argue with you." Hank hesitated. "I'd like to come to the funeral, if it's all right."

Jean gave him a steady look, then nodded. "I think that'd be fine. It's at one o'clock tomorrow."

Hank nodded. "I saw the notification in the paper. I'll be there."

"Thanks." Jean asked about Harrison, and Rosie let herself drift along without taking part in the conversation, wondering if anybody would ever find the bodies they'd left in the abandoned factory. All of them must have had people who'd loved them, once upon a time. It seemed like tipping Detective Johnson off might be the right thing to do, but then again, they'd dumped three bodies themselves in the past week. Drawing attention to more couldn't be smart.

"Where's the right side of the law in this?" she wondered quietly. The other two stopped talking to look at her curiously. "We have to stop the monsters, but is it right to let all those people who hosted the demons just . . . disappear? Shouldn't we call the cops, so at least they know to look for them?"

"Rosie . . ." Hank shook his head, but Jean shook hers harder, overriding Hank.

"Rosie's right. It's bad enough knowing Ruby's dead. Not knowing was just as bad in its way. It's stopped being about the demons now, hasn't it? It's about their families. If they've got people who love them, they need to know what's happened to them, if they can."

"And the ones we dumped?" Hank asked grimly.

Rosie shook her head. "We shouldn't have done that. I don't know what else we should have done, and it was all panicky and awful and I'm not gonna beat us up for doing it. But we shouldn't have, and next time— 'cause there's gonna be a next time—we need to have a plan for what to do instead."

"I think it's asking for trouble."

"It is. It is, library man. But it's still the right thing to do." Rosie lifted her chin. "I'll send a note to the police department to tell them to look at the Pennicott property. I won't write it. I'll cut out newsprint," she said with a wan smile. "Like spies do."

"That's going to direct attention right to us, Rosie," Hank warned. "To Valentine disappearing and Dad being a mess. Because it's his property. And if I'm caught up in it, you will be too, sooner or later."

"Then I guess we better get our stories straight."

"Not too straight." Hank sighed. "If we all say the exact same thing, we'll sound like we're lying. Rosie, we have to get my dad on board with this before we try. Without him agreeing, it'll never work."

"It's a heck of a conspiracy," Jean said. "A lot to keep quiet."

"Ex Libris has been doing it for centuries," Rosie argued.

"Millennia," Hank disagreed. "I'll talk to Dad, and talk to you tomorrow at the funeral, Rosie. Don't do anything until then. All right?"

"Okay. But we need to do this, Hank. It's just not right, otherwise." Rosie waited on Hank's nod, then looked at Jean. "We should probably get going. Try to get some sleep tonight."

"I feel like I might sleep well for the first time in a week," Jean said fiercely. "We'll see you tomorrow, Hank."

TWENTY-SEVEN

A note on Rosie's bedroom door, in Marge's handwriting, said Barb had mentioned a girl named Pearl Daly had called for Rosie a couple of times. Rosie took the note down and put it on her bedside table so she'd remember to call Pearl in the morning. Irene, hidden in her bed, didn't even lift her head as Rosie stripped filthy dungarees and her stained shirt off, looked at them in despair, and pitched them into the wastebasket. It'd probably be smartest to burn them, because the blood would never come out, and she'd need new Keds, too, but she couldn't do anything about any of that tonight. Overwhelmed by the thought of it all, she went to sleep quickly, without Irene ever having said a word.

She woke up earlier than expected, feeling like there were a million things to do. She had a casserole in the oven to bring over for Jean before anybody else got up, and had the oven off again before the day started getting *too* hot. Then she called her parents, who promised to be at the funeral, and went to get cleaned up as the rest of the girls started milling around the house.

A look in the mirror told her she should have cleaned up the night before, and that it was just as well nobody had taken a good look at her when she came in. Dirt and dried blood smeared her jawline and made a stiff mess of her hair. Well, Irene had a hairdryer and Rosie would just have to use it. She took a cool bath, scrubbing her skin until it turned bright red, and her hair until her scalp tingled with the effort. She got a dirty look from Dorothy when she emerged from the bathroom, but she didn't reckon she'd ever get back in Dot's good graces, so it didn't matter much. Irene was out of the bedroom and didn't come back while Rosie set her hair. Just when she'd gotten her hair done and a dress on, Irene called, "Rosie, phone," from the living room, and gave Rosie a nervous smile when she came out to take the phone.

"Hi, Rosie, it's Pearl, Pearl Daly? From—"

Rosie couldn't help smiling. "I know where you're from, Pearl. I'm sorry I wasn't around yesterday. Things got a little crazy."

"That's all right. I wondered if you wanted to go shopping this afternoon, though?"

"I can't." Rosie bit back an explanation as she glanced toward the living room clock. "Oh, gosh, it's only 9:30. I could meet you at Hudson's in half an hour and we could do a quick shop before I have to go, if you like."

"That would be swell! Are you sure?"

"I think it'd be good for me." It meant an awfully busy day, but it seemed like a nice, normal, ordinary girl thing to do, and Rosie thought she needed that as much as Pearl probably did.

An hour of shopping got Pearl a few smart new outfits at the department store, and as she came out of the dressing room to model the last one, Rosie said, "You'll look good working for Harrison Vaughn now."

Pearl's eyes widened in astonishment. "It's not a sure thing," Rosie said as sternly as she could. "You've got to take those typing classes, and work hard, but he said he had a place for a steady worker. And the rest of it is over, Pearl," she added more quietly. "There was a—a hive, here in Detroit, but its queen bee is gone and I think it's pretty well broken up. All the folks who were circling around us are . . ."

"Have buzzed off?" Pearl asked brightly, and Rosie laughed.

"Exactly. At least, I think so. So you're safe, okay? If you ever hear from Goode's . . . lady friend . . . in France, I'd like to know what she says, but I hope things will just be back to normal now."

"What's normal but something that's always changing, anyway?" Pearl smoothed her skirt before meeting Rosie's eyes. "All I know is my normal is a lot better thanks to you than it would have been, so I'll do anything I ever can to help you, Rosie Ransom. You can count on me."

To her own surprise, Rosie stepped forward to hug the other woman. "Me too. Give me a call any time, night or day."

Pearl looked at her critically. "Maybe day. You look like you need more sleep, young lady. Got to be bright-eyed and bushy-tailed to get a job these days, you know."

"I do know. Let's buy these, Pearl, because I really do have to get going early. A lot's happening today." The clothes cost fifty-eight dollars, and Pearl took the receipt to write an IOU on its reverse, signing it and handing it over to Rosie, who smiled. "When you're on your feet again, Pearl."

"I just don't want you to think I forgot."

"I don't." Rosie walked Pearl out to the tram and took one going the opposite direction, stopping at home to change into a dark purple dress and pick up the casserole before going over to Jean's house.

Jean's folks were already there, both dressed somberly, and Jean emerged from her room looking terrible, and knowing it, in black. She gestured at the dress, which fit perfectly but did her golden complexion no favors, and shook her head. "Ruby would hate seeing me in this."

Rosie got up to hug her. "What would she like seeing you in?"

"I don't know. Maybe that old green rag of mine. It was her favorite dress of mine."

"Let's see it." Rosie followed Jean back into her bedroom and Jean took the dress from the closet. Dark green and boxy, with a tiny floral print in taupe, it hardly qualified as a rag. Rosie nodded. "You should wear this, Jean-Marie. For you, for Ruby. It's exactly right."

Jean's eyes filled with tears. Rosie took the dress, put it aside, and hugged her tight until she managed to stop crying. "Okay, now," Rosie murmured. "Let's get you into this dress, and I'll fix your hair a bit, enough to put a hat on, and we'll be ready to go."

"I don't have a hat to match this dress."

"A black one will do. It's dark enough green, and if anybody says anything catty, I'll step on their toes with my heels."

Jean sniffled but smiled and, once dressed, looked at herself in the mirror, asking, "We did okay, right, Ro? We did okay."

"We did just fine, Jeannie. You can do this knowing that. We did just fine."

Jean nodded, and a few minutes later, they all got in the car to go to the church. Jean and her family went to sit with Ruby's Nan and parents, and Rosie, after offering her condolences, found her parents, and then, to her surprise and pleasure, Rich. He took her hand and sat with her through the service and the burial after, not, Rosie thought unhappily, that there was much left to bury. But it felt good to have Rich at her side. Not exactly like he'd never been gone, but good, like he belonged there. Like *she* belonged there. She saw Hank in the crowd, and gave him a grateful smile for having come. He nodded, giving her and Rich a thoughtful look, and didn't come over, even as the receiving line formed.

Rosie had already spoken with Ruby's folks, so stepped aside from the line. Rich came with her, keeping his voice low. "What really happened to her, Rosie?"

"Exactly what the papers said," Rosie said just as quietly. "But PFC Goode was a vampire."

Rich said, "Jesus," a little too loudly, but they were far enough from the main crowd to not draw attention. Rosie put her hand on his arm anyways, looking around. "Why don't we try to find some lemonade."

A brief smile creased his mouth, though it left his eyes not so much cool as sad. "You're so good at that. Being a good hostess. I always imagined how happy and comfortable our house would be, with you taking care of it. Of us. And me. But the lemonade is probably all at their house. Rosie, I just want a chance to talk to you."

Rosie's own smile felt pained. "There's a lot to talk about. I guess I imagined all that once, too."

"But it changed. Before this thing with Goode and Valentine Vaughn. It changed for you a long time before that, didn't it?"

"It changed a lot more when it turned out demons and monsters were real, but yeah. I'm sorry I didn't tell you when you were overseas. I didn't know how."

"No, I don't guess I would have either. What about the . . . the Redeeming? Would you have told me about that at all?"

"I don't know." Rosie folded her arms around herself, looking at yellowing grass across the cemetery. "I wanted to protect you from it."

Rich tried to smile. "I'm supposed to be the protector, Rosie."

"But I don't need one. I didn't in the first place, and now I'm stuck in this crazy thing that other people really do need protecting from. I wanted to keep you out of it. Safe."

"Didn't work, did it?"

Rosie ducked her head. "Not even a little bit."

Rich nodded. "But I guess I don't blame you for trying, even if I'm not sure what to think of my girl being the one trying to protect me."

"Am I?" Rosie met his eyes, caught between curiosity and concern. "Am I your girl?"

"I don't know, Rosie. Are you?" Rich studied her, then glanced across the graveyard himself. "Coming home, I just wanted to start life back where I left it. Settle down, find a job, get married, have some kids. Everything looks different now. And that's what you've been saying all along, but I didn't know *how* different it looked, Ro. Now I do. And now I don't . . ."

"Don't know if I'm the star you want to hitch your wagon to?" Rosie asked quietly.

Rich's mouth thinned. "Something like that, maybe. I hate the thought of giving it all up, Ro. We were good together, weren't we? But maybe we were just kids, too."

"We were, and we were. I don't know if we can start over, Rich. Not when we've got so much history. But maybe history doesn't mean picking up where we left off. Maybe we can just see what happens. No . . . no promises. No formalities. Maybe we can just see where it goes. Maybe we can just take some time and figure out if you're my guy, if I'm your girl. Maybe that's the smart thing to do."

"Yeah." Rich exhaled heavily, like the cares of the world rode on the breath. "I think that sounds good, Rosie."

"So do I." Rosie stood on her toes to kiss Rich's cheek. "So we'll start there. Now, look, it's about ninety-five degrees out here. Do you want to find some lemonade or not?"

Rich chuckled. "No, I'm going to head home. Promised the old man I'd do some work around the house before it got dark. I just wanted to talk to you, Ro. I didn't like leaving things hanging."

"You're a stand-up guy, Rich Thompson." Rosie kissed his cheek again and watched as he disappeared in the distance, heading for his car. She sighed, patted her hair, and looked at the receiving line, wondering if Jean needed any support.

Irene stood a few feet behind her, arms folded tightly around herself. "You were talking to Rich."

"Yeah." Rosie looked back as if she could still see him, then fanned herself with one hand. "I didn't know he was going to be here. It was good of him to come."

"I'm real sorry, Ro," Irene whispered. "Swear I'm not trying to steal your guy."

"Rene." Rosie reached out to try and take one of Irene's hands. "Look, if you can steal him, he's obviously not really my guy, right? Rich and me, we don't know where we're going. I mean, sure, it was kind of awful watching him go running right to you last night, but hon, how could I even blame him? Or you? You'd both just gone through the same thing, something I reckon nobody else can even imagine. I guess I might've headed your way too."

Irene unwound enough to let Rosie have her fingers, and Rosie squeezed them. "I'm not angry, okay? Maybe I don't know quite what I am, but I'm not gonna lose my best friend because of a fight over some boy. Even as decent a guy as Rich Thompson is." She squeezed Irene's hand again, then smiled up at the sky. "He sure is cute, though, isn't he?"

A surprised little laugh cut loose from Irene's throat. She clapped her hands over her mouth, brown eyes apologetic over her fingers before she parted them enough to whisper, "He sure is. Cuter than the pictures you have of him."

"He done growed up. I guess maybe we all did."

"I guess so." Irene hesitated. "I'm sorry I didn't believe you, too. About . . . all this."

"Aw, Rene. Why would you? Nobody in their right mind would. I just wish . . . I'm sorry you got caught up in it all the way you did. That wasn't supposed to happen."

"I didn't figure," Irene said dryly enough to make Rosie smile.

"No, I don't guess you did." She lifted her chin toward the receiving line. "They're almost done. Are you going to the McAnlys' after? I'm sure Jean-Marie is."

Irene shook her head. "I'm not sure she *is*. I overheard them talking. They're furious with her, Ro. They blame her for Ruby working at the factory, for not getting married and staying safe. They didn't say it in so many words, but they made it real clear she wasn't welcome."

Fury blazed through Rosie and fizzled into something close to tears. "Jean must be devastated. Well, to hell with them, then," she said as fiercely as she could. "Maybe we should get Jean and go back to our house, just so there's some noise and people around. Hank's here, or he was. He could come over too. And maybe I could catch Rich . . ." Rosie looked for him again, though she knew he was long gone.

"Well, let's not worry about making it a party," Irene said. "But maybe getting Jean before she breaks down entirely is a good idea. Did you drive?"

"Jean drove us. Oh, shoot, her parents. She drove her parents, too."

"Your folks can drive them home, and we'll go with Jean," Irene said. "I'll go get it all sorted out with the parents. You go get Jean. We'll meet at her car in ten minutes."

It took almost twenty to get Jean-Marie away from old school friends who didn't want to leave her, even though Jean kept edging toward Rosie and the car. Rosie finally said, "Why don't you all come over tomorrow?" with a quick look at Jean to make sure that was all right. "Maybe bring a dish or two by. I've been feeding Jean on Big Bob's all week, but a girl could use a home-cooked meal in times like this." With that plan in place, the girls were willing to let Jean go, and Rosie felt her weight sag on Rosie's arm as they headed for the car. "I'll drive," Rosie offered.

Jean managed a faint smile. "You just want to drive my Oldsmobile."

"There may be a grain of truth in that," Rosie allowed, and Jean gave her the keys. "We'll go to our house for a while," Rosie said as they met up with Irene. "Just so it's not going from all this bustle to total quiet all at once. But we can go over to your house and eat up that casserole after a bit. Tomorrow, those girls are going to bring more food than you can shake a stick at."

"Okay." Jean-Marie leaned her head against the car window, closing her eyes. Rosie caught Irene's eye in the rear-view mirror and Irene lifted a finger to her lips. Rosie nodded and they drove home silently, pulling into the driveway around dinnertime.

Dorothy was sitting on the front porch beside a big pile of boxes. She jumped to her feet when Rosie pulled into the drive and ran into the house, the screen door banging behind her. Rosie breathed, ". . . what?" but before she or Irene could get out of the car, all four of their housemates were on the porch, making a line across the top of the steps. Barb looked triumphant, her chin high and her eyes hard, and Dorothy had a similar expression, only more frightened. Wanda kept her gaze on the porch floor as Rosie got out of the car and walked forward, a knot of confusion and distress forming in her belly. "What on earth is going on?"

"We took a vote," Barb announced. "We don't want you here anymore, you murderess. We haven't slept a wink in the past week and we don't reckon we ever will again, with somebody like you under this roof. We packed up all your stuff, and we're not giving you your deposit back because of all the work that took."

A cold sweat broke on Rosie's skin, and though she believed them in her gut, she said, "Are you serious? Wanda? *Marge?*"

Wanda's gaze jerked up guiltily, then flinched back to the ground. Marge only shrugged, more indifferent than uncomfortable. Jean got out of the car behind Rosie and Irene, who stepped forward and said, "Some house vote, if you went behind our backs. What a nasty piece of work you are, Barbara Brandt. Where do you think she's supposed to go?"

"Not my problem," Barb said with a toss of her hair. "Back home to her folks, I guess. They can't throw her out, even if she's a freak. She's sure as heck never getting married now, not being a *known murderer.*"

The knot in Rosie's stomach twisted tighter, hurting so bad she almost laughed. She'd spent a whole week fighting demons, but she couldn't think of a thing to say or do in the face of ordinary girls being mean. Irene stalked up the stairs with such intent that even Barb stepped back and gave a shaky breath of relief when Irene just marched past her instead of doing something more physical. Three minutes later, Irene swept back out of the house again with a bag in one hand and a ten-dollar bill that she waved under Barb's nose in the other fist. "I took this right out of your kitty, because you're not stiffing Rosie for this month's rent on my watch, you nasty cow."

"Wh—what are you doing? Where are *you* going? You can't take my money!"

"The hell I can't," Irene snapped. "And if you think for a minute I'm gonna live with a bunch of mean or lily-livered girls who threw my best friend out without even having the nerve to talk to her about it, you've got another think coming. Good luck finding more housemates when I'm done telling everybody at the factory what cowardly witches you four are."

"Are you gonna run home to Rosie's folks, too?" Barb sneered. "Won't that be pretty, the two of you old maids living together forever?"

Jean, moving slow and ponderous as a tank, walked up the porch steps until she stood nose to nose with Barb. "They're not going to go home with their tails between their legs. They're better than that, and a whole lot better than you. *You* better start packing Rosie's stuff into my car."

Barb sneered again. "Who's gonna make me?"

Jean straightened and took a breath that filled her out until she looked big and dangerous. "Do you really want me to answer that question?"

Dorothy squeaked, "No!" and grabbed one of the boxes. "Come on, Barb. Come on, let's just *do* it, come *on*." Jean stood over all four of them as they moved boxes into her car, while Rosie watched with cold astonishment. She could hardly think, except to think it was a good thing Jean and Irene were with her. They seemed able to move and make plans, while all she could do was stand there in shock. Demons shouldn't be easier to deal with than Barb, for goodness' sake.

"Boy," she heard herself say. "Boy, I sure hope that you'll never need me someday."

Barb gave her a filthy look as she carried a box past. "What could *I* ever need *you* for?"

Rosie caught her breath, shaking off the cold that had seized her. "Honestly, Barb, I hope you never find out. Because if you do, you're going to regret this more than you can ever imagine. Not even because I'll refuse to help you." She started to smile. "Because I won't. I'll be there if you need me. And if you ever *do* need me, knowing that I'll be there is gonna stick in your craw for the rest of your life. Wow." She looked at Irene supervising Marge packing a box into the car, and at Jean, standing on the porch with her arms folded and an expression like a drill sergeant, and her smile broadened. "Wow. You know what? This is going to be terrific. This is exactly what I need. I don't have the factory job anymore, so this is a clean break from the whole life I used to live. I'm gonna be somebody else, doing new things, from here on out, and I can't wait to see what happens."

"Atta girl," Jean murmured as she came down the porch steps to open the Oldsmobile's front door. "Go on, get in . . . roomies."

Rosie, grinning, scrambled in to take the middle of the bench seat, with Jean climbing in the driver's side and Irene taking the passenger seat. They exchanged bright-eyed looks of excitement, and then Rosie leaned forward to thump her hands on the dashboard. "All right, girls. Let's go home."

Acknowledgements

. . . I've been sitting here trying to write this acknowledgements page and basically it just comes out to "WAAAAAAUGH LIFE WAS AWFUL I'M SORRY WAAAAAUGH."

There are a lot of people I should say thank you to, but because I haven't been keeping a running list I'm going to forget a bunch of them. Mary-Theresa Hussey, my editor-in-chief, of course, and copy editor Richard Shealy, although we had an unusually high number of disagreements about commas this time. Cover artist Lindsey Look, cover designer Tara O'Shea, and book designer The Barbarienne have conspired to make this a beautiful book, which I would be totally unable to do without them.

Michelle Sagara took the brunt of my war-room wailing over being behind schedule for *Redeemer* (and about a million other things), and the other Word Warriors—Ellen, Mika, Laura Anne, Sharpie, Robin, Pooks—helped get me through the interminable rough draft stages. Ladies, I hoped the war room would last six months when I started it back in 2009. Thank you all for keeping it going, and for being in there, getting the words done, year in and year out.

I am deeply, deeply grateful for Camille Lofters' friendship over the past few years, for Brian Showers' for the past decade and more, and for the Lady Writers Social Club (or whatever it is we call ourselves), consisting of Susan E Connolly, Ruth Frances Long and Sarah Rees Brennan. I have not been even a little bit as available or together or *anything* as I would have liked over the past couple years, which leaves me to suspect you really genuinely don't know how glad I am for all of your presences in my life. I love you all.

And, last as usual but never least, my thanks to my Dad, and to both my husband Ted and our son, who have all been there while I worked my way through a to-do list so long I thought I'd never see the end of it. This book isn't *quite* the end of it, but I can see it from here. I love you all, too.

Patron Acknowledgments

Over 400 readers have been exceptionally, unbelievably patient in waiting for this book to come to fruition. 'Thank you' is ridiculously inadequate, but it's all I've got. Thank you all *so much*.

A Warwick, Adrian Faulkner, Adrianne Middleton, Aetiyen, Aine, Alan Twigg, Albert Petterson, Aletia Meyers, Alice Ma, Alisha Kloc, Alison Gunnels, Allison Daugherty, Althea Clark, Amber Salem, Amelinda Webb, Amy Nesbitt, Amy Stromquist, Andrew Barton, Andrew Clark, Andrew Lin, Andy Rogers, Angela Beegle, Angela Korra'ti, Anne Burner, Ariane Tobin, Arvoitus, Ash K. Alexander, Axisor, Barb Eagle, Barb Moermond, Barbara Hasebe, Beanz, Becky Studley, Berni Phillips, Beth Cato, Beth Wodzinski, Beverly. Lee, Bill Harting, Blair, Brendan Hutt, Bretaigne Jones, Brian Nisbet, Brian Stanley, Bryant Durrell, CA Brandstatter, Caitriona Lawrence Magee, Cam Banks, Cam Mezé, Camille Lofters, Candace McIlroy, Carl Neely, Carl Rigney, Carol Connolly, Carol Guess, Carolina Pardo, Caroline Spott, Cat Wilson, Catherine Farnon, Catherine Fiorello, Catherine Sharp, CharlesDM, Charlotte Calvert, Charlotte Powell, Chris "Warcabbit" Hare, Chris Broggi, Chris Chen, Chris Hanrahan, Chris Heilman, Christer Boräng, Christie Lutsiak, Christina Le Galloudec, Christine Swendseid, Christopher Sarnowski, Christy Hopkins, Chrysoula Tzavelas, Chrystin McLelland, chx, Claire Foshee, Coby Haas, Colette Reap, Cori May, Cryolite, Crystal Reich, Curmudgeon of Phoenix Rising, Cynthia Teare, D Franklin, Danielle Ackley-McPhail, Danielle Ingber, Danielle Walther, Deanna Zinn, Debbie Matsuura, Debbie Ochsner, Deborah Alverson, Deborah Blake, Deborah Donoghue, Deirdre, Deirdre Murphy, Denise Moline, Diane

Dupey, Diane Nowell, Dina Willner, Donal Cunningham, Dorien Benaets, Dr K L Maund, drey, Edward Ellis, el edwards, Eleanor Blair, Elena Barrick, Eleri Hamilton, Eliel Mamousette, Elisabeth Bouynot, Elizabeth A. Mancz, Elizabeth B Handler, Elizabeth Cadorette, Elizabeth Poole, Elizabeth Turner, Ellen Million, Elli Ferguson, Emily Ervin, Emily Poole, Emma Bartholomew, Emma Harvey, Emma Pitt, Erica Who Likes To Stick Her Fingers In My Armpit, Erin James, Ernie Sawyer, Esha Bhatia, Evenstar Deane, Faith Hunter, Flash McDonnell, Gabe Krabbe, Garret Reece, Gavran, Gemma Tapscott, Genevieve Cogman, George Olive, Georgina Scott, Gerri Lynn, Gilles Massen, Gina Rinderle, Gretchen S., Gwen Frazer-Dennison, Hamish Laws, Harvey King, Haviva Avirom, Heather Fagan, Heather Joubert, Heather Knutsen, Heather Perry Baxter, HL Henrikson, Hollis Jade, Holly Payne, Holly Tidd, Idria Barone Knecht, Jackie Powers, Jacob Proffitt, Jaime Robertson, Jaime Wurth, James Brophy, James J Watkins, Jami Nord, Janet Barnard, Janne Tørklep, Jean Marie Diaz, Jean Tatro, Jean Valk, Jeff Adams, Jeff Linder, jeff lowrey, Jen Stein, Jen1701D, Jeni Young, Jenica Rogers, Jennifer Cabbage, Jennifer Dumont, Jennifer Flora Black, Jennifer van der Kolk, Jenny Barber, Jenny Schwartzberg, Jerel Heritage, Jessica Bay, Jessica Meade, Jill Smith, Jill Valuet, Joann Casper, Joann Zimmerman, Jodie Cooper, Joe Fernandez, Joerg Ritter, Johan Höglund, John Bogart, John Corrigan, Joliene McAnly, Jonathan Hixson, Joseph Alexander Hand, Joyce Ann McLaughlin, Judith Tarr, Judy Reiffers Weber, Julene Warwick, Julia Haynie, Juliana Veale, Julie Fore, Julie Kuhn, June Lundstrom, K. Gavenman, Kaitlin Thorsen, Karen Dubois, Karen Mahoney, Karl Kloeden, Kat Bonson, katastrophe, Kate Kirby, Kate Larking, Kate Malloy, Kate Sheehy, Katherine Beals, Katherine Ullman, Kathleen Hanrahan, Kathleen Tipton, Kathryn Duffy, Kathy Rogers, Katrina Lehto, Kayla Lowes, Kelli Nichols, Kerry aka "Trouble", Kiely Ohman, Kirt Dankmyer, Kristi Chadwick, Kristin Bledsoe, Kristina VanHeeswijk, Kristine Kearney, Krumpff, Kyna Foster, Larisa LaBrant, Laura Burchard, Laura Clay, Laura Wallace, LD Steele, Leah MacLean, LeAnn Haggard, Lee Bougourd, Leigh Ann Malloy, Lesley Mitchell, Lilly Ibelo, Limugurl, Liralen Li, Lisa Coker, Lisa Hornyak, Lisa Pegg, Lisa Soto, Lisa Stewart, Liz Oppelt, Lola McCrary, Lola Stockmaster, Lori Lum, Lorie York, Lorri Lynne Brown, Louise Inward, Louise Southwick, Luca Beltrami, Lyn Mercer, Lynette Miles, Madison W Fairbanks, Maggi Heffler, Marcia Carney, Maresa Welke, Margaret A. Menzies, Maria

Lima, Marie Brennan, Marilyn Fisher, Marion McDowell, Marithlizard, Marjorie Taylor, Mark Sutter, Marsha Simmons, Mary Agner, mary anne walker, Mary Flores, Mary Hargrove, Maura McHugh, Max Kaehn, Megan Pokorny, Megan Rogers, Melanie C. Duncan, Melissa Glasser, Melissa Siah, Melissa Tabon, Michael Bentley, Michael Bernardi, Michael Bowman, Michael Carroll, Michael Feldhusen, Michael Nichols, Michele Schenck, Michelle Carlson, Michelle Curtis, Michelle Ossiander, Michelle Titanich, Mikaela Lind, Moira Bhu, Moritz Am-Ende, Morwenna Gaskain, My Darling Blue Haired Angie, Nancy Shuert, Nancy Weston, Neal Levin, Niamh O'Brien, nick eden, Nicolai Buch-Andersen, ompiled, Orjan Westin, Pam Blome, Pam East, Pam Hatler, Pamela Dyer-Bennet, Pamela M Roberts, Pat Knuth, Pat Reitz, Patricia O'Neill, Patricia Pooks Burroughs, Patrick Malone, Patty Lindsell, Paul Bulmer, Paul Knappenberger, Paul-Gabriel Wiener, Paula Foscarini-Craggs, Peter Griffith, Phil Sevetson, Philip Obermarck, Rachel Blackman, Rachel Chiapparine, Rachel Coleman, Rachel Gollub, Rachel Maloney, Rachel Narow, Rachel Reither, Rachel V., Rachel Vance, Rachel Voorhies, Rachel Zuffa, Rebecca & Stephen Jones, ReBecca Richardson, Rebecca Sims, Regis M. Donovan, Robert Lai, Robin D. Owens, Robynne Smith, Rosanne Girton, Ruth Stuart, S.L. Gray, Sam Dailey, Sandra Jakl, Sara Harville, Sarah Brooks, Sarah Brown, Sarah Foscarini Wilkes, Sarah Goslee, Sarah Troedson, Sarah Wishnevsky, Scott Drummond, Scott Philo, Sean Collins, Sean Mulhern, Shannon Scollard, Sharis Ingram, Sharon Sayegh, Sharrow, Shawn Capistrano, Shawn Tumey, Shel Kennon, Shell Coleman, Sherry Menton, Shevaun Frazier, Simone, Simran Khalsa, Siobhain McShane-Loy, Skye Christakos, Sonia Murphy, Stephanie Claypoole, Stephanie Dawson, Stephen Bradley, Stephen Hood, Stephen T, Stuart Chaplin, Sumi Funayama, Susan Crites, Susan E. Shelly, Susannah Cowtan, Suzanne McLeod, T.E. Stacy, Taiyo, Tal S, Tammy DeGray, Tania Clucas, Tantris Hernandez, Tanya Koenig, Tara 'Whatever Floats Your Boat' Lynch, Tara Fremont, Tara Teich, Tarja Rainio, Tasha Turner, Teresa Nichols, terrio, Thirzah Brown, Tiana Hanson, Tiff Arnold, Tiff Reynolds, Tina Bounds, Tobias Buckell, Tom & Rosie Murphy, Trip Space-Parasite, Valentine Lewis, Van der Jonckheyd, Vickie Turrell, Victoria Hench, Victoria Michaels, Walt Boyes, Wanda, Weird Andy in Atlanta, Yi-Mei Chng

About the Author

According to her friends, CE Murphy makes such amazing fudge that it should be mentioned first in any biography. It's true that she makes extraordinarily good fudge, but she's somewhat surprised that it features so highly in biographical relevance.

Other people said she began her writing career when she ran away from home at age five to write copy for the circus that had come to town. Some claimed she's a crowdsourcing pioneer, which she rather liked the sound of, but nobody actually got around to pointing out she's written a best-selling urban fantasy series (The Walker Papers), or that she dabbles in writing graphic novels (Take A Chance) and periodically dips her toes into writing short stories (the Old Races collections).

Still, it's clear to her that she should let her friends write all of her biographies, because they're much more interesting that way.

More prosaically, she was born and raised in Alaska, and now lives with her family in her ancestral homeland of Ireland, which is a magical place where it rains a lot but nothing one could seriously regard as winter ever actually arrives.

CE Murphy can be found online at mizkit.com, @ce_murphy, fb.com/cemurphywriter, and at her newsletter, tinyletter.com/ce_murphy/.